BLINDSIGHT

How far will people go to obtain donors for eye operations? Murder is beyond comprehension. But seeing is believing. . . .

"GRABS THE READER . . . MAINTAINS SUSPENSE WITH SURPRISING STORY TWISTS."
—*Pittsburgh Press*

"RIVETING." —*Nashville Banner*

VITAL SIGNS

Dr. Cook explores the frightening possibilities of experimental fertilization—the passion to create life, and the power to destroy it. . . .

"CONSTANT SUSPENSE . . . BELIEVABLE AND CHILLING." —*Houston Chronicle*

"VINTAGE COOK . . . NONSTOP ACTION."
—*Kirkus Reviews*

HARMFUL INTENT

The explosive story of a doctor accused of malpractice— a fugitive on the run who pierces the heart of a shocking medical conspiracy . . .

"A REAL GRABBER." —*Los Angeles Times*

"TRULY EXCITING." —The Associated Press

O9-ABF-846

continued . . .

MUTATION

On the forefront of genetic research, a brilliant doctor tries to create the son of his dreams—and invents a living nightmare. . . .

"HOLDS YOU PAGE AFTER PAGE."

—Larry King, *USA Today*

"*REALLY* FRIGHTENING."

—*Booklist*

MORTAL FEAR

A major scientific breakthrough becomes the ultimate experiment in terror when middle-aged patients begin to die—of old age. . . .

"A CHILLING ODYSSEY INTO THE ORIGINS OF LIFE—AND DEATH."

—*USA Weekend*

"COOK'S BEST BOOK SINCE *COMA*."

—*People*

OUTBREAK

Murder and mystery reach epidemic proportions when a devastating plague sweeps the country. . . .

"HIS MOST HARROWING MEDICAL HORROR STORY."

—*The New York Times*

"THE ULTIMATE NIGHTMARE . . . SPINE-TINGLING INTRIGUE AND FEVER-PITCHED ACTION."

—*The Associated Press*

continued ...

ABDUCTION

ROBIN COOK

BERKLEY BOOKS, NEW YORK

ABDUCTION

A Berkley Book / published by arrangement with
the author

PRINTING HISTORY
Berkley edition / November 2000

The Penguin Putnam Inc. World Wide Web site address is
http://www.penguinputnam.com

ISBN: 0-425-17736-X

BERKLEY®
Berkley Books are published by The Berkley Publishing Group,
a division of Penguin Putnam Inc.,
375 Hudson Street, New York, New York 10014.
BERKLEY and the "B" design
are trademarks belonging to Penguin Putnam Inc.

PRINTED IN THE UNITED STATES OF AMERICA

10 9 8 7 6 5 4 3 2 1

For Cameron.
Welcome to life, "LITTLE LITTLE"

CHAPTER ONE

An odd vibration roused Perry Bergman from a restless sleep, and he was instantly filled with a strange foreboding. The unpleasant murmur put him in mind of fingernails scraping down a blackboard. He shuddered and threw off his thin blanket. As he stood up, the vibration continued. With his bare feet on the steel deck, it now reminded him of a dentist's drill. Just beneath it he could detect the normal hum of the ship's generators and the whir of its air conditioning fans.

"What the hell?" he said aloud, even though there was no one within earshot to provide an answer. He'd helicoptered out to the ship, the *Benthic Explorer,* the previous evening after a long flight from Los Angeles to New York to Ponta Delgada on the Azorean island of San Miguel. Between the time zone changes and a long briefing about the technical problems his crew was experiencing, he was understandably exhausted. He didn't like being awakened after only four hours of sleep, especially by such a jarring vibration.

Snatching the ship's phone from its cradle he punched in the number for the bridge. While he waited for the connection to go through he peered out the porthole of his V.I.P. compartment on his tiptoes. At five foot seven Perry didn't think of himself as short, just not tall. Outside, the sun had barely cleared the horizon. The ship cast a long shadow across the Atlantic. Perry was looking west over a misty, calm sea whose surface resembled a vast expanse of beaten pewter. The water undulated sinuously with low, widely separated swells. The serenity of the scene belied the goings-on below the surface. The *Benthic Explorer* was being held in a fixed position by computer driven commands to her propellers as well as to her bow and stern thrusters over a portion of the volcanically and seismically active Mid-Atlantic Ridge, a twelve-thousand-mile-long, jagged range of mountains that bisects the ocean. With the constant extrusion of enormous quantities of lava, submarine explosions of steam, and frequent miniearthquakes, the submerged cordillera was the antithesis of the ocean surface's summer tranquillity.

"Bridge," a bored voice responded in Perry's ear.

"Where's Captain Jameson?" Perry snapped.

"In his bunk as far as I know," the voice said casually.

"What the hell is that vibration?" Perry demanded.

"Beats me, but it's not coming from the ship's power plant if that's what you're asking. Otherwise I would have heard from the engine room. It's probably just the drilling rig. Want me to call the drilling van?"

Perry didn't answer; he just slammed the phone down. He couldn't believe whoever was on the bridge wasn't moved to investigate the vibration on his own. Didn't he care? It irked Perry to no end that his ship was being operated so unprofessionally, but he decided to deal with that issue later. Instead he tried to focus on getting into his jeans and heavy wool turtleneck. He didn't need someone to tell him the vibration might be coming from the drilling rig. That was pretty obvious. After all, it was difficulty with the drilling operation that had brought Perry here from Los Angeles.

Perry knew that he had gambled the future of Benthic Marine on the current project: drilling into a magma chamber within a seamount west of the Azores. It was a project that was not under contract, meaning the company was spending instead of being paid, and the cash hemorrhage was horrendous. Perry's motivation for the undertaking rested on his belief that the feat would capture the public's imagination, focus interest on undersea exploration, and rocket Benthic Marine to the forefront of oceanographic research. Unfortunately, the endeavor was not going as planned.

Once he was dressed, Perry glanced in the mirror over the sink in the cubbyhole bathroom. A few years ago he wouldn't have taken the time. But things had changed. Now that he was in his forties, he found that the tousled look that used to work for him made him look old, or at best, tired. His hair was thinning and he required glasses to read, but he still had a winning smile. Perry was proud of his straight, white teeth, especially since they emphasized the tan he worked hard to maintain. Satisfied by his reflection, he dashed out of his compartment and ran down the passageway. As he passed the doors to the captain's and first mate's quarters, Perry was tempted to pound on them to vent his irritation. He knew the metal surfaces would reverberate like kettledrums, yanking the sleeping occupants from their slumbers. As the founder, president, and largest shareholder of Benthic Marine, he expected people to be more on their toes while he was on board. Could he be the only one concerned enough to investigate this vibration?

Emerging onto the deck, Perry tried to locate the source of the strange hum, which was now merged with the sound of the operating drill rig. The *Benthic Explorer* was a four-hundred-fifty-foot vessel with a twenty-story drilling derrick amidship that bridged a central bay. In addition to the drilling rig, the ship boasted a saturation diving complex, a deep-sea submersible, and several remote-controlled mobile camera sleds, each mounted with an impressive array of still cameras and television camcorders. Combining this equipment with an extensive lab, the *Benthic Explorer* gave its parent company, Benthic Marine, the ability to carry out a wide range of oceanographic studies and operations.

Perry saw the door to the drilling van open. A giant of a man appeared. He yawned and stretched before hoisting the straps of his coveralls over his shoulders and donning his yellow hard hat, which had SHIFT SUPERVISOR written in block letters over the visor. Still stiff with sleep, he headed in the direction of the rotary table. He was obviously in no hurry despite the vibration coursing through the ship.

Quickening his pace Perry caught up to the man just as two other deckhands joined him.

"It's been doing this for about twenty minutes, chief," one of the roustabouts yelled over the noise of the drilling rig. All three men ignored Perry.

The shift foreman grunted as he pulled on a pair of heavy work gloves and blithely walked out across the narrow metal grate spanning the central well. His sangfroid impressed Perry. The catwalk seemed flimsy and there was only a low, thin handrail to block the fifty-foot drop to the ocean surface below. Reaching the rotary table, the supervisor leaned out and placed both gloved hands about the rotating shaft. He didn't try to grip it tightly but rather let it rotate across his palms. He cocked his head to the side while he tried to interpret the tremor transmitted up the pipe. It took only a moment.

"Stop the rig!" the giant shouted.

One of the roustabouts dashed back to the exterior control panel. Within a moment the rotary table came to a clanking halt and the grating vibration ceased. The supervisor walked back and stepped onto the deck.

"Chrissake! The bit's busted again," he said with an expression of disgust. "This is fast becoming a god-damned joke."

"The joke is that we've only drilled for two or three feet in the last four or five days," the remaining roustabout said.

"Shut up!" the giant intoned. "Get the hell over there and raise the drill string to the well head!"

The second roustabout joined the first. Almost immediately there was a new sound of powerful machinery as the winches were engaged to do the foreman's bidding. The ship shuddered.

"How can you be sure the bit's broken?" Perry yelled over the new noise.

The foreman looked down at him. "Experience," he yelled then turned and strode off toward the ship's stern.

Perry had to run to catch up. Each of the foreman's strides was double his. Perry tried to ask another question but the foreman either didn't hear or was ignoring him. They reached the companionway and the foreman started up, taking the stairs three at a time. Two decks above he entered a passageway and then stopped outside a compartment door. The name on the door was MARK DAVIDSON, OPERATIONS COMMANDER. The foreman knocked loudly. At first the only response was a fit of coughing but then a voice called out to come in.

Perry pressed into the small compartment behind the foreman.

"Bad news, chief," the foreman said. "I'm afraid the drill bit's busted again."

"What the hell time is it?" Mark asked. He ran his fingers through his messy hair. He was sitting on the side of his bunk dressed in skivvies. His facial features had a puffy look, and his voice was thick with sleep. Without waiting for a reply he reached for a pack of cigarettes. The air in the room was imbued with stale smoke.

"It's around oh-six-hundred," the foreman said.

"Jesus," Mark said. His eyes then focused on Perry. Surprise registered. He blinked. "Perry? What are you doing up?"

"There's no way I could have slept through that vibration," Perry said.

"What vibration?" Mark asked. He looked back at the foreman, who was staring at Perry.

"Are you Perry Bergman?" the foreman asked.

"Last time I checked," Perry said. Sensing the foreman's unease gave him a modicum of satisfaction.

"Sorry," the foreman said.

"Forget it," Perry said magnanimously.

"Was the drill train rattling?" Mark asked.

The foreman nodded. "Just like the last four times, maybe a little worse."

"We only have one more diamond-studded tungsten carbide bit left," Mark lamented.

"You don't have to tell me," the foreman said.

"What's the depth?" Mark asked.

"Not much change from yesterday," the foreman said.

"We've got out thirteen hundred thirty-three feet of pipe. Since the bottom is just shy of a thousand feet and there's no sediment, we're down into the rock about three hundred and forty feet, give or take a few inches."

"This is what I was explaining to you last night," Mark said to Perry. "We were doing fine until four days ago. Since then we've gone nowhere, maybe two or three feet tops, despite using up four drill bits."

"So you think you've hit up against a hard layer?" Perry said, thinking he had to say something.

Mark laughed sarcastically. "Hard ain't the word. We're using diamond-studded bits with the straightest flutes made! Worse yet is we got another hundred feet of the same stuff, whatever it is, before we get to the magma chamber, at least according to our ground-penetrating radar. At this rate we'll be here for ten years."

"Did the lab analyze the rock caught in the last broken bit?" the foreman asked.

"Yeah, they did," Mark said. "It's a type of rock they'd never seen before. At least according to Tad Messenger. It's composed of a type of crystalline olivine that he thinks might have a microscopic matrix of diamond. I wish we could get a bigger sample. One of the biggest problems of drilling in open sea is not getting a return of circulated drilling fluids. It's like drilling in the dark."

"Could we get a corer down there?" Perry asked.

"A lot of good that would do if we can't make any headway with a diamond-studded bit."

"How about piggybacking it with the diamond bit. If we could get a real sample of this stuff we're trying to drill through, maybe we could figure out a reasonable game plan. We got too much invested in this operation to give up without a real fight."

Mark looked at the foreman, who shrugged. Then he looked back at Perry. "Hey, you're the boss."

"At least for now," Perry said. He wasn't joking. He wondered how long he was going to be the boss if the project came to naught.

"All right," Mark said. He put his cigarette down on the edge of an overflowing ashtray. "Pull the drill bit up to the well head."

"The boys are already doing that," the foreman said.

"Get the last diamond drill bit from supply," Mark said. He reached for his phone. "I'll have Larry Nelson get the saturation dive system up and running and the submersible in the water. We'll replace the bit and see if we can get a better sample of what it is we're drilling into."

"Aye, aye," the foreman said. He turned and left while Mark lifted his phone to his ear to call the diving commander.

Perry started to leave himself when Mark held up his hand to motion for him to stay. After finishing his call to Larry Nelson, Mark looked up at Perry.

"There's something I didn't bring up last night at the briefing," he said. "But I think you ought to know about it."

Perry swallowed. His mouth had gone dry. He didn't like Mark's tone of voice. It sounded like more bad news.

"This might be nothing," Mark continued, "but when we used the ground-penetrating radar to study this layer we're trying to drill through like I mentioned before, there was an unexpected incidental finding. I got the data here on my desk. Do you want to see it?"

"Just tell me," Perry said. "I can look at the data later."

"The radar suggested that the contents of the magma chamber might not be what we thought from the original seismic studies. It might not be liquid."

"You're joking!" This new information added to Perry's misgivings. It was by accident the previous summer that the *Benthic Explorer* had discovered the seamount they were presently drilling. What was so amazing about the find was that as part of the Mid-Atlantic Ridge, the area had been extensively studied by Geosat, the U.S. Navy's gravity measuring satellite used to create contour maps of the ocean bottom. Yet somehow this particular undersea mountain had evaded Geosat's radar.

Although the *Benthic Explorer* crew had been eager to get home they'd paused long enough to make several passes over the mysterious mount. With the ship's sophisticated sonar they did a cursory study of the guyot's internal structure. To everyone's surprise the results were as unexpected as the mountain's presence. The seamount appeared to be a particularly thin-skinned, quiescent volcano whose liquid core was a mere four hundred feet beneath the ocean floor. Even more astounding was that the substance within the magma chamber had sound propagation characteristics identical to those of the Mohorovičić discontinuity, or Moho, the mysterious boundary between the earth's crust and the earth's mantle. Since no one had ever been able to get magma from the Moho, although both Americans and Russians had tried during the Cold War, Perry decided to go back and drill into the mountain in hopes that Benthic Marine might be the first organization to sample the molten material. He reasoned that the material's analysis would shed light on the structure and perhaps even the origin of the earth. But now his *Benthic Explorer*'s operations commander was telling him that the original seismic data might be wrong!

"The magma chamber may be empty," Mark said.

"Empty?" Perry blurted.

"Well, not empty," Mark corrected himself. "Filled with some kind of compressed gas, or maybe steam. I know extrapolating data at this depth is pushing ground-penetrating radar technology beyond its limits. In fact a lot of people would say the results I'm talking about are just artifact, sorta off the graph so to speak. But the fact that the radar data doesn't jibe with the seismic worries me just the same. I mean, I'd just hate to make this huge effort only to get nothing but a bunch of super-heated steam. Nobody's going to be happy with that, least of all your investors."

Perry chewed the inside of his cheek while he mulled over Mark's concern. He began to wish he'd never heard about Sea Mount Olympus, which was the name the crew had given the flat-topped, underwater mountain that they were trying to poke a hole into.

"Have you mentioned this to Dr. Newell?" Perry asked. Dr. Suzanne Newell was the senior oceanographer on the *Benthic Explorer.* "Has she seen this radar data you're talking about?"

"Nobody's seen it," Mark said. "I just happened to notice the shadow on my computer screen yesterday when I was preparing for your arrival. I was thinking about bringing it up at your briefing last night but decided to wait to talk to you in private. In case you haven't noticed, there's a bit of a morale problem out here with certain members of the crew. A lot of people have begun to think that drilling into this guyot's a bit like tilting at windmills. People are starting to talk about calling it quits and getting home to their families before the summer's over. I didn't want to add fuel to the fire."

Perry felt weak-kneed. He pulled Mark's chair out from his desk and sat down heavily. He rubbed his eyes. He was tired, hungry, and discouraged. He could kick himself for betting so much of his company's future based on so little reliable data, but the discovery had seemed so fortuitous. He'd felt compelled to act.

"Hey, I don't like to be the bearer of bad news," Mark said. "We'll do what you suggested. We'll try to get a better idea of the rock we're drilling. Let's not get overly discouraged."

"It's kind of hard not to," Perry said, "considering how much it is costing Benthic Marine to keep the ship out here. Maybe we should just cut our losses."

"Why don't you get yourself something to eat?" Mark suggested. "No sense making any snap decisions on an empty stomach. In fact, I'll join you if you can wait for me to shower. Hell! Before you know it we'll have some more information about this crap we've hit up against. Maybe then it will be clear what we ought to do."

"How long will it take to change the bit?" Perry asked.

"The submersible can be in the water in an hour," Mark said. "They'll take the bit and the tools down to the well head. Getting the divers down there takes longer because they have to be compressed before we lower the bell. That'll take a couple of hours, more if they get any compression pains. Changing the bit is not hard. The whole operation should take three or four hours, maybe less."

Perry got to his feet with effort. "Give me a call in my compartment when you're ready to eat." He reached for the door.

"Hey, wait a sec!" Mark said with sudden enthusiasm. "I got an idea that might give you a boost. Why don't you go down with the submersible? It's reputed to be beautiful down there on the guyot at least according to Suzanne. Even the submersible pilot, Donald Fuller, the ex–naval line officer, who's usually a tight-lipped, straight-arrow kind of guy, says the scenery is outstanding."

"What can be so great about a flat-topped, submerged mountain?" Perry asked.

"I haven't gone down myself," Mark admitted. "But it has something to do with the geology of the area. You know, being part of the Mid-Atlantic Ridge and all. But ask Newell or Fuller! I tell you, they're going to be ecstatic about being asked to go back down. With the halogen lights on the submersible and the clarity of the deep sea water, they said the visibility is between two and three hundred feet."

Perry nodded. Taking a dive wasn't a bad idea since it would undoubtedly take his mind off the current situation and make him feel like he was doing something. Besides, he'd only been in the submersible once, off Santa Catalina Island when Benthic Marine took delivery of the sub, and that had been a memorable experience. At least he'd get a chance to see this mountain that was causing him so much aggravation.

"Who should I tell that I'll be part of the crew?" Perry asked.

"I'll take care of it," Mark said. He stood up and pulled off his T-shirt. "I'll just let Larry Nelson know."

CHAPTER TWO

Richard Adams pulled a pair of baggy long johns from his ship's locker and kicked the door closed. Once he had the underwear on he donned his black knit watch stander's hat. Thus attired he left his compartment and banged on Louis Mazzola's and Michael Donaghue's doors. Both responded with a slurry of expletives. The curses had lost their sting since they constituted such a large percentage of these crew members' vocabularies. Richard, Louis, and Michael, professional divers, were the hard drinking, hard living sort who regularly risked their lives by welding underwater if that were required, or blowing things up like reefs, or changing bits during submarine drilling operations. They were underwater hard-laborers and proud of it.

The three had trained together in the U.S. Navy, becoming fast friends as well as accomplished members of the Navy's UDT force. All had aspired to become Navy Seals, but that turned out not to be in the cards. Their predilection for beer and fistfights far exceeded that of their fellows. That the three had grown up with alcoholic, brutish, abusive, bigoted, blue-collar, wife-beating fathers was an explanation for their behavior, but not an excuse. Far from being embarrassed by their patriarchal examples, the three looked upon their harsh childhoods as a natural progression to true manhood. None of them ever gave even a passing thought to the old adage: Like father like son.

Manliness was a critical virtue for all three men. They were ruthless in punishing anyone they perceived as being less manly than they who had the nerve to enter a bar in which they were drinking. Their judgment fell heavily on "shyster" lawyers and fat-assed Army personnel. They also condemned anyone they deemed a dork, a nerd, or a queer. Homosexuality bothered them the most, and as far as they were concerned, the military's "don't ask don't tell" policy was ridiculous and a personal affront.

Although the Navy tended to be lenient with divers and tolerated behavior it wouldn't brook with other personnel, Richard Adams and his buddies pushed the envelope too far. One hot August afternoon the men retreated to their favorite hole-in-the-wall diver's bar on San Diego's Point Loma. It had been an exhausting day of difficult diving. After numerous rounds of boiler-makers and an equal number of arguments about the current baseball season, they were shocked and dismayed to see a couple of Army guys jauntily walk in. According to the divers at their court-martial, these men proceeded to "love it up" in one of the back booths.

The fact that the soldiers were officers only made the divers' outrage all the more impassioned. They never asked themselves why a couple of Army officers might be in San Diego, a known Navy and Marine town. Richard, their perennial ringleader, was the first to approach the booth. He asked—sarcastically—if he could join the orgy. The Army men, mistaking Richard's meaning—which was for them to get the hell out—laughed, denied any orgy of any sort, and offered to buy him and his friends a round of celebratory drinks. The result was a one-sided brawl that put both Army officers into Balboa Naval Hospital. It also put Richard and his friends into the brig and eventually out of the Navy. The Army men happened to have been members of JAG, the Army's Judge Advocate General corps.

"Come on, you assholes!" Richard yelled when the others still hadn't appeared. He glanced at his diving watch. He knew Nelson would be pissed. His orders on the phone had been to get to the diving command center ASAP.

The first to appear was Louis Mazzola. He was almost a head shorter than Richard, who stood six feet. Richard thought of Louis as a bowling ball kind of guy. He had meaty features, an omnipresent five o' clock shadow, and short dark hair that lay flat on his round head. He appeared to have no neck; his trapezius angled out from his skull without any indentation.

"What's the hurry?" Louis whined.

"We're going on a dive!" Richard said.

"So what else is new?" Louis complained.

Michael's door opened. He was somewhere between Richard's rawboned silhouette and Louis's stockiness. Like his friends he was well muscled and in obviously good shape. He was also equivalently slovenly, dressed in the same baggy long johns. But in contrast to the others he had on a Red Sox baseball cap with the visor angled off sideways. Michael hailed from Chelsea, Massachusetts, and was an avid Sox and Bruins fan.

Michael opened his mouth to complain about being awakened, but Richard ignored him and set out for the main deck. Louis did likewise. Michael shrugged and then followed. As they descended the main companionway, Louis called ahead to Richard: "Hey, Adams, you got the cards?"

"Of course I got the cards," Richard shot back over his shoulder. "Have you got your checkbook?"

"Screw you," Louis said. "You haven't beat me in the last four dives."

"It's been a plan, man," Richard returned. "I've been setting you up."

"Screw the cards," Michael said. "Have you got your porno mags, Mazzola?"

"You think I'd go on a dive without them?" Louis questioned. "Hell! I'd rather forget my fins."

"I hope you checked to make sure you've got the mags with the chicks and not the dudes," Michael teased.

Louis stopped abruptly. Michael bumped into him.

"What the hell are you saying?" Louis growled.

"I'm just checking to make sure you brought the right ones," Michael said with a wry smile. "I might want to borrow them, and I don't want to find myself looking at any shlongs."

Louis's hand shot out and he grabbed a handful of Michael's long johns top. Michael responded by grabbing Louis's forearm with his left hand and balling his right hand into a fist. Before it could go further, Richard intervened.

"Come on, you dorks!" Richard yelled, inserting himself between his two friends. With an upward blow he knocked Louis's arm aside. There was a tearing sound, and Louis's hand came away with a torn swatch of Michael's undershirt clutched in his fingers. Like a bull seeing red, Louis tried to push past Richard. When that didn't work he tried to grab Michael's top over Richard's shoulder. Michael howled with laughter and ducked away.

"Mazzola, you meathead!" Richard yelled. "He's just trying to pull your chain. Chill out, for chrissake!"

"Bastard!" Louis hissed. He threw the swatch of torn fabric he'd yanked out of Michael's undershirt at his tormentor. Michael laughed again.

"Come on!" Richard said with disgust as he continued down the passageway. Michael reached down and picked up the piece of fabric. When he pretended to stick it back onto his chest, Louis laughed in spite of himself. Then they ran to catch up to Richard.

When the divers emerged onto the deck they could see that the derrick was raising the pipe.

"They must have broken the bit again," Michael said. Both Richard and Louis nodded. "At least we know what we'll be doing."

They entered the diving van and draped themselves over three folding chairs near the door. This was where Larry Nelson, the man who ran all the diving operations, had his desk. Behind him, on the right-hand side of the van and extending all the way down to the far end, was the diving console. Here were all the readouts, gauges, and controls for operating the diving system. On the left side of the van's dash were the controls and monitors for the camera sleds. Also on the left side was a window that looked out on the central well of the ship. It was down this central well that the diving bell was lowered.

The diving system on the *Benthic Explorer* was a saturation system, meaning the divers were expected to absorb the maximum amount of inert gas during any given

dive. That meant that the decompression time required
to rid themselves of the inert gas would be the same no
matter how long they stayed at pressure. The system was
composed of three cylindrical deck decompression
chambers (DDC), each twelve feet wide and twenty feet
long. The DDCs were hooked together like enormous
sausages with double pressure hatches separating them.
Within each were four bunks, several fold-down tables,
a toilet, a sink, and a shower.

Each DDC also had an entrance port on the side and
a pressure hatch on the top where the diving bell, or
personal transfer capsule (PTC), could mate. Compression and decompression of the divers took place in the
DDC. Once they had reached the equivalent pressure of
the depth where they were to work, they climbed up into
the PTC, which was then detached and lowered into the
water. When the PTC reached the appropriate depth the
divers opened the hatch through which they'd entered
the bell and swam to the designated workstation. While
in the water the divers were tethered with an umbilical
cord containing hoses for their breathing gas, for hot
water to heat their neoprene dry suits, for sensing wires,
and for communication cables. Since the divers on the
Benthic Explorer used full face masks, communication
was possible, although difficult, due to voice distortion
in the helium-oxygen mixture they breathed. The sensing wires carried information about each diver's heart
rate, breathing rate, and breathing-gas oxygen pressure.
All three levels were monitored continuously on a real-
time basis.

Larry looked up from his desk and regarded his second team of divers with disdain. He couldn't believe how
slovenly, brazen, and unprofessional they invariably appeared. He noted Michael's jaunty baseball cap and ripped

shirt, but he didn't say anything. Similar to the Navy, he tolerated behavior in the divers that he would not tolerate with other members of his team. Three other divers who were equally aggravating and obstreperous were still in one of the DDCs, decompressing from the last dive on the well head. When diving to almost a thousand feet, decompression time is measured in days not hours.

"I'm sorry to have awakened you clowns from your beauty sleep," Larry said. "It took you long enough to get down here."

"I had to floss my teeth," Richard said.

"And I had to do my nails," Louis said. He flapped his hand in a swishy, loose wrist fashion.

Michael rolled his eyes with mock disgust.

"Hey, don't start!" Louis growled while eyeing Michael. He poked one of his meaty fingers in his friend's face. Michael batted it away.

"All right, listen up, you animals!" Larry yelled. "Try to control yourselves. This is going to be a nine-hundred-and-eighty-foot dive to inspect and change the drill bit."

"Oh, something new, eh, chief?" Richard said in a high, squeaky voice. "This is the fifth time this dive's been done and the third time for us. Let's get on with it."

"Shut up and listen," Larry commanded. "There's something new involved. You're going to be piggy-backing a corer on the diamond bit so that we can see if we can get a decent sample of whatever the hell we're trying to drill into."

"Sounds good," Richard said.

"We're going to speed up compression time," Larry said. "There's some brass aboard who's in a hurry for results. We're going to see if we can get you down to depth in a couple of hours. Now I want to hear immediately if there's any joint pain. I don't want anybody playing macho diver. Understand?"

All three divers nodded.

"We'll lock in chow as soon as it comes up from the galley," Larry continued. "But I want you guys in your bunks for the compression, and that means no screwing around and no fights."

"We're going to play cards," Louis said.

"If you play cards do it from your bunks," Larry said. "And I repeat: no fights. If there are any, the cards are coming out. Do I make myself clear?"

Larry eyed each man in turn, who averted his gaze. No one contested the terms of the arrangement.

"I'm going to take this rare silence as acquiescence," Larry said. "Now, Adams, you'll be red diver. Donaghue, you'll be green diver. Mazzola, you'll be bell diver."

Richard and Michael cheered and then leaned across to one another and high-fived. Louis blew out disgustedly through pursed lips. The bell diver's job during the dive was to remain inside the PTC to play out the tethers for the red and green divers and watch the gauges; he did not enter the water except in an emergency. Although this position was safer, it was looked down upon by divers. The designations of red and green diver were used to avoid any confusion in communications with topside that might occur if given or surnames were used. On the *Benthic Explorer* red diver was recognized to be the on-site leader.

Larry reached down on his desk and picked up a clipboard. He handed it over to Richard. "Here's the pre-dive checklist, red diver. Now get your asses in DDC1. I want to start compression in fifteen minutes."

Richard took the clipboard and led the way out of the van. Once outside, Louis began a long lament about being bell diver, complaining that he'd been bell diver on the last dive.

"I guess the chief thinks you're the best at it," Richard said while giving Donaghue a wink. He knew he was goading Louis. But he couldn't help it. He felt relieved that he'd not been selected, since it was his turn.

As the group passed the occupied DDC3 each man took the time to glance through the tiny viewing port and give a thumbs-up sign to the three occupants, who still had several more days of decompression ahead of them. Divers might fight with each other at times, but they also shared a close camaraderie. They respected each other because of the inherent risks. The isolation and danger of being on a saturation dive was ironically similar in certain respects with being in a satellite circling the globe. If a problem occurred it could be hairy, and it was difficult to get you back home.

At DDC1 Richard was first through the narrow round entrance port on the cylinder's side. It required him to grasp a horizontal metal bar, lift his legs, and enter feet first by wiggling through the aperture.

The interior was utilitarian, with the bunks at one end and emergency breathing apparatuses hanging from the walls. All the diving gear, including the neoprene suits, weight belts, gloves, and hoods, and other paraphernalia, was in a pile between the bunks. The diving masks were up in the diving bell with all the hoses and communication lines. At the other end of the DDC was the exposed shower, toilet, and sink. Saturation diving was a communal affair of the first order. There was no privacy whatsoever.

Louis and Michael entered right after Richard. Louis climbed directly up inside the diving bell while Michael started sorting through the material on the floor. As

Richard called out the names of individual pieces of equipment, either Louis or Michael would yell out whether it was present or not, and Richard would check it off on his list. Anything not present was immediately handed through the open port by one of the watch standers.

When the four pages of checklist were completed, Richard gave a thumbs-up to the dive supervisor via the camcorder mounted on the ceiling.

"Okay, red diver," the supervisor said over the intercom, "close and dog the entrance hatch and prepare to start compression."

Richard did as he was told. Almost immediately there was the hiss of the compressed gas, and the needle on the analog pressure gauge began to rise. The divers happily took to their bunks. Richard pulled the worn deck of playing cards from his long johns pocket.

CHAPTER THREE

Perry emerged from the interior of the ship and stepped out onto the grate that formed the deck of the fantail. He was dressed in a maroon jogging suit over sweats—Mark's suggestion. He told Perry it was what he'd worn the last time he'd been in the submersible. The quarters were tight, so the more comfortable the clothes, the better, and layers were good because it could be cool. The outside water temperature was only around forty degrees, and it was foolish to expend too much battery power on heat.

At first Perry found walking on the metal grate disconcerting since he could see down into the ocean surface some fifty feet below. The water had a cold, gray-green look. Perry shivered despite the pleasant ambient temperature, and he wondered if he should go on the dive after all. The strange foreboding that he'd awakened with returned, raising the hackles on the back of his neck. Although he wasn't claustrophobic per se, he'd never been comfortable when he found himself in a tight space like the interior of the submersible. In fact one of Perry's most horrid memories as a child was having been caught hiding under the covers by his older brother. His brother pounced on him instead of pulling the covers back and, for a time that seemed like an eternity, wouldn't let him out. Occasionally Perry still had nightmares that he was back in that cloth prison with the desperate sensation he was about to smother.

Perry stopped and stared at the little submarine, which was sitting on chocks at the very stern of the ship. Angled over it was a large derrick capable of swinging the vessel out over the water and lowering it to the surface. Workers were swarming around the craft like bees hovering around a hive. Perry knew enough to recognize they were participating in the predive check before launch.

Perry was relieved that the vessel looked considerably larger than it had when it was in the water, a fact that appeased his recently awakened claustrophobia. The submersible was not as tiny as many were. It was fifty feet long with a twelve-foot beam, and bulbous in shape, like a bloated, HY-140 steel sausage with a fiberglass superstructure. There were four view ports made of eight-inch-thick, conical sections of Plexiglas: two forward and one to either side. Hydraulic manipulator arms, folded up under the bow, made it look like an enormous crustacean. The hull was painted scarlet with white lettering along the sides of the sail. Its name was *Oceanus*, after the Greek god of the outer sea.

"Handsome little devil, isn't she?" a voice said.

Perry turned. Mark had come up behind him.

"Maybe it'd be better if I didn't go on the dive after all," Perry said, trying to sound casual.

"And why is that?" Mark asked.

"I don't want to be a bother," Perry said. "I came out

here to be a help, not a hindrance. I'm sure the pilot would prefer not to have the equivalent of a tourist tagging along."

"Poppycock!" Mark said without hesitation. "Both Donald and Suzanne are thrilled you're coming. I spoke with them not twenty minutes ago, and they said as much. In fact that's Donald on that scaffolding, supervising the connection to the launching crane. I understand you've never met him."

Perry followed Mark's pointing finger. Donald Fuller was an African American with a shaved head, a neat pencil-line mustache, and an impressively muscled frame. He was dressed in crisply ironed dark blue coveralls with epaulets and a shiny name tag. Even from a distance Perry could appreciate the man's martial bearing, especially when he heard his deep, baritone voice and his clipped, no-nonsense manner as he called out commands. During the current operation there was no doubt who was in charge.

"Come on," Mark urged before Perry could respond. "Let me introduce you."

Reluctantly, Perry allowed himself to be led over to the submersible. It was painfully obvious that he would not be able to get out of diving on the *Oceanus* without a significant loss of face. He'd have to admit to his fears, and he hardly thought that would be appropriate. Besides, he had enjoyed his first ride on the sub even though that had been done in only a hundred feet of water just outside of the harbor on Santa Catalina, a far cry from the middle of the Atlantic Ocean.

Once Donald was satisfied with the submersible's connection to the hoisting cable, he swung down from the scaffolding and began walking around the boat. Although the topside dive team had responsibility for the exterior predive check, Donald wanted to make his own visual check on all the penetrations through the pressure hull. Mark and Perry caught up to him at the bow. Mark introduced Perry as the president of Benthic Marine.

Donald responded by clicking his heels and saluting. Before Perry knew what he was doing, he saluted back. Only Perry didn't really know how to salute; he'd never executed the gesture in his life. He felt as pathetic as he probably looked.

"Honored to meet you, sir," Donald said. He was standing ramrod straight with his lips pressed together and his nares flared. To Perry he appeared like a warrior about to do battle.

"Pleased to meet you," Perry said. He gestured toward the *Oceanus*. "I don't want to interrupt you."

"No problem, sir," Donald snapped back.

"I also don't have to go on this dive," Perry said. "I don't want to be in the way. In fact . . ."

"You won't be in the way, sir," Donald said.

"I know this is an operational dive," Perry persisted. "I wouldn't want to take your attention away from your job."

"When I am piloting the *Oceanus,* no one takes my attention away from my job, sir!"

"I appreciate that," Perry said. "But I won't be at all offended if you feel I should stay topside. I mean, I'll understand."

"I'm looking forward to showing you the capability of this craft, sir."

"Well, thank you," Perry said, recognizing the futility of trying to excuse himself graciously.

"My pleasure, sir," Donald snapped.

"You don't have to call me sir," Perry said.

"Yes, sir!" Donald responded. Then his mouth formed

into a thin smile when he realized what he'd said. "I mean, yes, Mr. Bergman."

"Call me Perry."

"Yes, sir," Donald said. Then he allowed himself a second smile when he realized he'd slipped again in so many seconds. "It's hard for me to change my ways."

"I can see that," Perry said. "I guess it's not a wild guess that you got your experience for this type of work in the armed forces."

"That's affirmative," Donald said. "Twenty-five years in the submarine service."

"Were you an officer?" Perry asked.

"Indeed. I retired as a commander."

Perry's eyes wandered to the submersible. Now that he'd reconciled himself to the upcoming dive, he wanted reassurance. "How's the *Oceanus* been performing?"

"Flawlessly," Donald answered.

"So it's a good little ship?" Perry asked. He patted the cold steel pressure hull.

"The best," Donald said. "Better than anything I've ever piloted, and I've been in quite a few."

"Are you just being patriotic?" Perry asked.

"Not at all," Donald said. "First of all, it can go deeper than any other manned craft I've piloted. As I'm sure you know, it's got a certified operating depth of twenty thousand feet and a crush depth not until thirty-five thousand. But even that's deceiving. With the built-in safety margin, we could probably dive to the bottom of the Mariana Trench without a hitch."

Perry swallowed. Hearing the term *crush depth* brought back the shiver he'd experienced a few minutes before.

"Why don't you give Perry a quick rundown on the

rest of the *Oceanus*'s statistics," Mark said. "Just to refresh his memory."

"Sure," Donald said. "But stand by for a second." He cupped his hands around his mouth and yelled out to one of the workmen completing the predive check: "Have the TV camcorders been checked out on the inside?"

"That's an affirmative!" the worker responded.

Donald directed his attention back to Perry. "The craft's sixty-eight tons with room for two pilots, two observers, and six other passengers. We have lockout capability for divers, and we can be mated to the DDCs if the need arises. We've got life support for a maximum of two hundred sixteen hours. Power comes from silver zinc batteries. Propulsion is from a varivec propeller, but maneuverability is also enhanced with vertical and horizontal thrusters directed by twin joysticks with top-mounted thumb balls. There's short-range, narrow-beam, and side-scan sonar, ground-penetrating radar, proton magnetometer, and thermistors. Recording equipment includes silicon-intensified target video camcorders. Communications are with FM surface radio and UQC underwater telephone. Navigation is inertial."

Donald paused while he let his eyes roam around the submersible. "I think that covers the basics. Any questions?"

"Not for the moment," Perry said quickly. He was afraid Donald might ask him a question. The only thing Perry retained out of the entire monologue was the thirty-five-thousand-foot crush depth figure.

"Ready to launch the *Oceanus*!" a voice crackled over a loudspeaker.

Donald herded Perry and Mark away from the sub. The hoisting wire became taut. With a creak the submersible lifted from the deck. It was kept from swinging by multiple launching lines attached at key points along the hull. A high-pitched squeak heralded the movement of the davit as it swung the boat out off the stern of the ship and started lowering it toward the water.

"Ah, here comes the good doctor," Mark said.

Perry turned briefly to look behind him. A figure was emerging through the main door into the ship's interior. Perry did a rapid doubletake. He'd only seen Suzanne Newell once before and that was when she'd presented the original seismic studies on Sea Mount Olympus. But that had been in L.A., where there was no dearth of beautiful people. Out in the middle of the ocean on the utilitarian *Benthic Explorer* with its nearly hundred percent frowzy male crew, she stood out like a lily in a patch of weeds. In her late twenties, she was vibrant and athletic looking. Dressed in coveralls similar to those worn by Donald, she gave off a stunning gender message which was the absolute antithesis of Donald's. A dark blue baseball cap, with a gold braid embroidered on the visor and BENTHIC EXPLORER sewn across the crown, was perched on top of her head. Out of the back of the hat just above the adjustment band protruded a ponytail of thick, shiny chestnut hair.

Suzanne saw the group and waved, then headed in their direction. As she approached, Perry's mouth slowly dropped open, a response that was not lost on Mark. "Not bad, huh?" Mark said.

"She's rather attractive," Perry admitted.

"Yeah, well, wait a few days," Mark said. "She gets better the longer we're out here. Quite a shape for a geophysical oceanographer, wouldn't you say?"

"I haven't met too many geophysical oceanographers," Perry said. Suddenly he thought that maybe the dive wouldn't be so bad after all.

"Too bad she isn't a medical doctor," Mark said under his breath. "I wouldn't mind her doing a hernia check on me."

"If you'll permit me, I'll continue getting the *Oceanus* ready for the dive," Donald said.

"Of course," Mark said. "The new bit and the corer will be up shortly, and I'll have them loaded directly into the tray."

"Aye, aye, sir!" Donald said with a salute. He walked back to the edge of the fantail and looked down at the descending submersible.

"He's a bit stiff," Mark said, "but one hell of a reliable worker."

Perry wasn't listening. He couldn't take his eyes off Suzanne. She had an unmistakable spring to her step; her smile was friendly and welcoming. With her left hand she was pressing two large books against her chest.

"Mr. Perry Bergman!" Suzanne exclaimed, reaching out with her right hand. "I was delighted to hear you'd come out to the ship and am thrilled that you're going to dive with us. How are you? You must be recovering from a long flight."

"I'm just fine, thank you," Perry said while shaking hands with the oceanographer. Then he unconsciously reached up to make sure his hair was appropriately arranged over the thinning spot on the top of his head. He noted that Suzanne's teeth were as white as his own.

"After our meeting in Los Angeles I never got to tell you how pleased I was that you decided to bring *Benthic Explorer* back to Sea Mount Olympus."

"I'm glad," Perry said, forcing a smile. He was bewitched by Suzanne's eyes. He couldn't tell if they were blue or green. "I only wish the drilling were proceeding more successfully."

"I'm sorry about that," Suzanne said. "But I have to admit, from my personal, selfish perspective I'm a happy camper. The seamount is a fascinating environment, as you're about to see, and the drilling problems are getting me down there. So you won't hear any complaints from me."

"I'm glad it's making somebody happy," Perry said. "What's so fascinating about this particular seamount?"

"It's the geology," Suzanne said. "Do you know what basaltic dikes are?"

"I can't say that I do," Perry admitted. "Other than I suppose they're made out of basalt." He laughed self-consciously and decided that her eyes were a light blue tinted green by the surrounding ocean. He also realized that he liked the sparing way she used makeup. She seemed to be sporting only the slightest bit of lipstick. Cosmetics were a sore subject for Perry and his wife. She worked as a makeup artist for a movie studio and wore a significant amount herself, to Perry's chagrin. Now their eleven- and thirteen-year-old daughters were following their mother's example. The issue had become a full-blown feud that Perry had little chance of winning.

Suzanne's smile broadened. "Basalt dikes are indeed made of basalt. They are formed when molten basalt is forced up through fissures in the earth's crust. What makes some of them so intriguing is that they're geometric enough to look manmade. Wait till you see them."

"Sorry to interrupt," Donald said. "The *Oceanus* is ready to dive and we should be on board. Even in a calm sea it's dangerous to have her moored too long next to the ship."

"Yes, sir!" Suzanne said smartly. She saluted crisply

but with a lingering, mildly mocking smile. Donald was not amused. He knew she was teasing him.

Suzanne gestured for Perry to precede her down the companionway that led to a combination dive platform and launching dock. Perry started but hesitated as another involuntary shudder rippled down his spine. Despite his efforts to reassure himself about the safety of the submersible and despite his anticipation of Suzanne's pleasant company, the foreboding he'd experienced earlier came back like a cold draft through an underground crypt which is what he thought the interior of the *Oceanus* was going to feel like. A voice in the back of his mind was telling him he was crazy to lock himself up inside a boat in the middle of the Atlantic Ocean that was already sunk.

"Just a second!" Perry said. "How long is this dive going to take?"

"It can be as short as a couple of hours," Donald said, "or as long as you'd like. We usually stay down as long as the divers are in the water."

"Why do you ask?" Suzanne asked.

"Because . . ." Perry sought for an explanation. "Because I have to call back to the office."

"On Sunday?" Suzanne questioned. "Who's at the office on Sunday?"

Perry felt himself blush anew. Between the night flights from New York to the Azores he'd gotten his days mixed up. He laughed hollowly and tapped the side of his head. "I forgot it was Sunday. It must be early Alzheimer's."

"Let's move out!" Donald announced before descending to the dive platform below.

Perry followed, one step at a time, feeling like a ridiculous coward. Then, despite his better judgment, he inched across the swaying gangplank. It was shocking how much motion was involved in what appeared to be a calm sea.

The gangplank lead directly to the top of the *Oceanus*'s sail. The deck of the submersible was already awash since the vessel was close to being neutrally buoyant. With some difficulty Perry got himself through the hatch. As he worked his way down into the sub he had to press tight against the steel ladder's icy cold rungs.

The interior was as tight a space as Mark had warned. Perry began to doubt the claims that there was room for ten people. They'd have to be packed like sardines. Contributing to the cramped atmosphere, the walls of the front of the sub were lined with gauges, LCD readouts, and toggle switches. There wasn't a square inch without a dial or knob. The four viewing ports seemed tiny within the profusion of electronic equipment. The only positive was that the air smelled clean. In the background Perry could make out the hum of a ventilation fan.

Donald directed Perry to a low-slung chair directly behind his on the port side. In front of the pilot's seat were several large CRT monitors whose computers could construct virtual images of the seafloor to help in navigation. Donald was using the FM radio to talk with Larry Nelson in the dive control van as he continued the predive check of the equipment and electrical systems.

Perry heard the hatch close above with a thud followed by a distinctive click. A few moments later Suzanne dropped down from the sail with a good deal more agility than Perry had exhibited. She'd even managed to do it with the two large books in hand. She proceeded to hand them to Perry.

"I brought these for you," she said. "The thick one is on oceanic marine life and the other is on marine geology. I thought it might be fun for you to look up some of the things we'll be seeing. We don't want you to get bored."

"That was thoughtful," Perry commented. Little did Suzanne realize, he was far too anxious to be bored. He felt the way he did when he was about to take off in an airplane: There was always the chance that the next few minutes would be his last.

Suzanne sat down in the starboard pilot's seat. Soon she began flipping toggle switches and calling out the results to Donald. It was apparent the two worked as a team. Once Suzanne joined in the predive check, haunting pinging sounds began reverberating through the confined space. It was a unique sound that Perry associated with old World War II submarine movies.

Perry shivered again. He closed his eyes for a moment and tried not to think about his childhood trauma of being pinned under the covers by his brother. But the ploy didn't work. He looked out the view port to his left and struggled to comprehend why he felt he was making the worst decision in his life by taking this short, routine dive. He knew it wasn't a rational feeling since he recognized he was with professionals for whom this dive was commonplace. He knew the submersible was reliable and that he'd recently paid for an overhaul.

All at once Perry started. A masked face had materialized literally before his eyes. An involuntary, pitiful squeak escaped from Perry's lips before he realized he was looking into the face of one of the submersible's handlers who'd entered the water with scuba equipment. A moment later Perry saw other divers. In a slow-motion underwater ballet the divers quickly detached the handling lines. There was a knock on the outside of the hull. The *Oceanus* was on its own.

"All-clear signal received," Donald said into the radio mike. He was talking to the launch team supervisor on the fantail. "Request permission to power away from the ship."

"Permission granted," a disembodied voice responded.

Perry felt a new linear motion add to the passive roll, yaw, and pitch of the sub. He pressed his nose against the view port and saw the *Benthic Explorer* move out of his field of vision. With his face still pressed against the Plexiglas he looked down into the oceanic depths where he was about to descend. The sunlight did strange visual tricks as it refracted off the undulating water surface above, making him imagine he was staring into the maw of infinity.

With another shiver Perry acknowledged he was as vulnerable as an infant. A combination of vanity and stupidity had drawn him into this alien environment in which he had no control of his destiny. Although he was not religious, he found himself praying that the little underwater cruise would be short, sweet, and safe.

CHAPTER FOUR

"No contact," Suzanne said in response to Donald's question whether the sonar echo sounder showed any unexpected obstacles beneath the *Oceanus*. Even though they were bobbing around in open ocean, part of the predive check was to make sure no other submarine craft had surreptitiously moved under them.

Donald took the VHF radio mike and established contact with Larry Nelson in the diving van. "We're clear of the ship. Oxygen is on, scrubbers are on, hatch is closed, underwater phone is on, grounds are normal, and the echo sounder is clear. Request permission to dive."

"Is your tracking beacon activated?" Larry's voice questioned over the radio.

"That's affirmative," Donald said.

"You have permission to dive," Larry said with a small amount of static. "Depth to the well head is nine hundred ninety-four feet. Have a nice dive."

"Roger!" Donald said.

Donald was about to hang up the mike when Larry

added, "The DDC is nearing depth so the bell will be starting down ASAP. I'd estimate the divers will be at the site in half an hour."

"We'll be waiting," Donald said. "Over and out." He hung up the mike. Then to his fellow submariners he added, "Dive! Dive! Vent the main ballast tanks!"

Suzanne leaned forward and threw a switch. "Venting the ballast tanks," she repeated so there was no chance for misunderstanding. Donald made an entry on his clipboard.

There was a sound like a shower in a neighboring room as the cold Atlantic water rushed into the *Oceanus*'s ballast tanks. Within moments the craft's buoyancy plummeted, and once negative she silently slipped beneath the surface.

For the next few minutes both Donald and Suzanne were totally occupied, making sure all systems were still operating normally. Their conversation was restricted to operational jargon. In a rapid fashion they went through most of the predive checklist for the second time while the submersible's descent accelerated to a terminal velocity of a hundred feet per minute.

Perry occupied his time by looking out the view port. The color went from its initial greenish blue to rapidly advancing indigo. In five minutes all he could see was a blue glow when he looked upward. Downward it was dark purple fading into blackness. In stark contrast, the interior of the *Oceanus* was bathed in a cool electronic luminosity from the myriad monitors and readout devices.

"I believe we're a little front heavy," Suzanne said once all the electronic equipment had been checked.

"I agree," Donald said. "Go ahead and compensate for Mr. Bergman!"

Suzanne threw another switch. A whirring noise could be heard.

Perry leaned forward between the two pilots. "What do you mean, 'compensate' *for me*?" His voice sounded funny even to himself. He swallowed to relieve a dry throat.

"We have a variable ballast system," Suzanne explained. "It's filled with oil, and I'm pumping some of it aft to make up for your weight forward of the center of gravity."

"Oh!" Perry said simply. He leaned back. As an engineer he understood the physics. He was also relieved they weren't referring to his timidity, which his self-consciousness had irrationally suggested.

Suzanne turned the variable ballast pump off when she was satisfied with the boat's trim. Then she turned around to face Perry. She was eager to make his dive to the seamount as positive as possible. Once they were back on ship, she hoped to present him with a case for conducting purely exploratory dives on the guyot. At the moment, the only time she got down there was to change the drill bit. She'd had no luck persuading Mark Davidson of the value of research-inspired dives.

Adding to Suzanne's anxiety was the widespread rumor that the drilling operation would be scrapped because of technical problems. Sea Mount Olympus would be abandoned before she could get a closer look. That was the last thing she wanted, and not only because of her professional interests. Just before leaving on the current project, she had what she hoped was the final breakup of an unhealthy, volatile relationship with an aspiring actor. At the moment returning to L.A. was the last thing she wanted to do. Perry Bergman's sudden appearance on-site was serendipitous. She could take her case right to the top.

"Comfortable?" Suzanne asked.

"I've never been more comfortable in my life," Perry averred.

Suzanne smiled despite the obvious sarcasm in Perry's response. The situation was not looking good. The Benthic Marine president was still tense as evidenced by his gripping the arms of his seat as if he were about to leap out of it. The books that she'd made the effort to bring were lying unopened on the floor grate.

For a moment Suzanne studied the taut president whose eyes looked everywhere but into hers. What she could not tell was whether Perry's anxiety was from apprehension of being in the submersible or just a reflection of his basic personality. Even on her first meeting with the man six months ago, she had found him a mildly eccentric, vain, and nervous guy. He was obviously not her type in addition to being short enough for her to look directly in the eye in her tennis shoes. Yet despite having little in common with him especially since he was an engineer-cum-entrepreneur and she a scientist, she trusted that he'd be receptive to her arguments. After all, he'd already responded positively to her request to bring the *Benthic Explorer* back to Sea Mount Olympus even if it was only to drill into the supposed magma chamber.

Sea Mount Olympus had been Suzanne's main preoccupation for almost a year, since she'd stumbled on its existence by switching on the side-scan sonar on the *Benthic Explorer* out of boredom when the ship was heading back to port. Initially, her curiosity only involved her inability to explain why such a massive, apparently extinct volcano had not been detected by Geosat.

But now, after making four dives in the submersible, she was equally fascinated by the geological formations on its flat crown, especially since she'd only been afforded the opportunity to explore in the immediate vicinity of the well head. But then the most intriguing fact emerged when she took it on herself to date the rock that had been brought up with the broken drill bit.

To Suzanne the results were startling and a lot more intriguing than the rock's apparent hardness. From the seamount's position near the Mid-Atlantic Ridge, she expected the rock sample's age to register in the seven-hundred-thousand-year range. Instead it had tested to be around four billion years old!

Knowing that the oldest rocks ever found on earth's surface or on the ocean floor were significantly less ancient than this figure, Suzanne had thought that either the dating instrument was out of whack, or she'd made some stupid procedural error. Unwilling to risk ridicule, she decided to keep the results to herself.

With painstaking care she spent hours recalibrating the equipment, and then running additional samples over and over. To her disbelief, the results were all within three or four hundred million years of each other. Still believing there had to be a dating instrument malfunction involved, Suzanne had Tad Messenger, the head lab tech, recalibrate it. When she ran the sample again, the result was within a few million years of the previous one. Still in doubt, Suzanne reconciled herself to waiting until she got back to L.A. so she could use the university lab's equipment. Meanwhile the results were hidden away in her ship's locker. She tried to reserve judgment, but her interest in Sea Mount Olympus soared.

"We have hot coffee in a Thermos aft if you'd like some," Suzanne said. "I'd be happy to get it for you."

"I think I'd be happier if you stay at the controls," Perry said.

"Donald, how about turning on the outside lights for a moment," Suzanne suggested.

"We're only passing through five hundred feet," Donald said. "There's nothing to see."

"It's Mr. Bergman's first open ocean dive," Suzanne said. "He should see the plankton."

"Call me Perry," Perry said. "I mean, why be formal while we're packed in here together like so many sardines in a can?"

Suzanne acknowledged Perry's offer of informality with a smile. She was only sorry he so clearly was not enjoying the trip.

"Donald, as a favor to me, turn on the lights," Suzanne said.

Donald complied without further comment. He reached forward and snapped on the external halogen lamps on the port side. Perry turned his head and glanced out.

"Looks like snow," he said.

"It's trillions of individual plankton organisms," Suzanne explained. "Since we're still in an epipelagic zone, it's probably mostly phytoplankton, or plant plankton that can carry on photosynthesis. Along with the blue-green algae, those are the guys who are at the bottom of the entire oceanic food chain."

"I'm glad," Perry said.

Donald switched the lights off. "No sense in using up valuable battery power with that type of reaction," he explained to Suzanne sotto voce.

In the ensuing darkness, Perry witnessed twinkling bursts of muted neon green and yellow sparkles. He asked Suzanne what it was.

"That's bioluminescence," Suzanne said.

"Is it the plankton?" Perry asked.

"It could be," Suzanne said. "If so, it would probably be dinoflagellates. Of course, it could also be tiny crustaceans or even fish. I've put a yellow bookmark in the marine life book marking the bioluminescence section."

Perry nodded but made no attempt to pick up the text.

Nice try, Suzanne thought glumly. Her optimism about ensuring Perry's enjoyment sagged appreciably.

"*Oceanus,* this is *Benthic Explorer,*" Larry's voice sounded in the acoustic phone speaker. "Suggest a course two hundred and seventy degrees at fifty amps for two minutes."

"Roger," Donald said. He quickly made the course adjustment with the joysticks and changed the power output to the propeller to the suggested fifty amps. He then noted the changes on his clipboard.

"Larry has plotted our position by tracking our pinger and relating it to the bottom hydrophones," Suzanne explained. "By powering forward while descending we'll reach bottom directly at the well head. It's like we're gliding to the target."

"What will we do until the divers arrive?" Perry asked. "Just sit and twiddle our thumbs?"

"Hardly," Suzanne said. She forced another smile along with a shallow laugh. "We'll unload the drill bit from the tray along with the tools we're carrying. Then we'll back off. At that point we'll have about twenty to thirty minutes to explore around the site. That's the part I think you are going to truly enjoy."

"I can't wait," Perry said with the kind of sarcasm Suzanne was beginning to dread. "But I don't want you doing anything out of the ordinary on my behalf. I mean, don't try to impress me. I'm already impressed enough."

Suddenly the monotonous pinging of the sonar changed. The sub was nearing the bottom, and the forward short-range sonar had a solid contact. The tiny screen showed the well head and the pipe snaking down from above. Donald jettisoned several of the descent weights and the craft's gliding plunge slowed. He then began a careful adjustment of the variable ballast system to achieve neutral buoyancy.

While Donald was busy pumping oil, Suzanne reached behind her and turned on a small CD player. It was part of her master plan. All at once the sound of Igor Stravinsky's *Rite of Spring* filled the sub's interior. Taking the music as a cue, Donald leaned forward and switched on the outside lights.

Perry's eyes widened as he glanced out the view port. The planktonic snow had all but disappeared, and the clarity of the icy water was more than he imagined. He was able to see for several hundred feet, and what he saw left him flabbergasted. He'd expected a flat, featureless plain similar to what the bottom looked like on his dive off Santa Catalina Island. At most he thought he might see a few sea cucumbers. Instead he was gazing at a misty tableau the likes of which he'd never imagined: huge, dark gray, columnar forms with flat tops dotted the landscape, jutting up in a stepwise fashion like the frozen pistons of an enormous engine. The haunting shapes extended out as far as Perry could see. A few long-tailed, big-eyed fish lazily darted in and around them. On some of the rock ledges sea fans and sea whips waved sinuously in the current.

"Good God!" Perry exclaimed. He was mesmerized, especially with the dramatic music in the background.

"Rather exceptional, eh?" Suzanne said. She was encouraged. Perry's reaction to the scenery was his first auspicious response.

"It looks like some ancient temple area," Perry exclaimed.

"Like Atlantis," Suzanne suggested. She was intent on milking the situation for all it was worth.

"Yeah!" Perry blurted. "Like Atlantis! Jeez! Can you imagine bringing tourists down here and telling them that it was Atlantis? What a freaking gold mine this could be."

Suzanne cleared her throat. Bringing tourists down to her precious seamount was the last thing she wanted to see happen, but she appreciated Perry's enthusiasm. At least he was engaged.

"Current is less than an eighth of a knot," Donald said. "Coming up on the well head. Prepare to off-load the drill bit."

Suzanne swung around to attend to her duties as co-pilot. She powered up the servos for the manipulator arms. Meanwhile Donald set the *Oceanus* down expertly on the rock floor. While Suzanne prepared to lift the drill bit and tools from the submersible's tray, Donald used the UQC phone.

"On the bottom," Donald said. "Off-loading the payload."

"Roger," Larry said in reply over the speaker. "I guessed as much when I heard Suzanne's music. Is that the only freaking CD she has?"

"It's the best one for the scenery down here," Suzanne interjected.

"If we make any more dives I'll loan you some New Age CDs," Larry answered. "I can't stand that classical stuff."

"Am I looking at basaltic dikes out here?" Perry questioned.

"That's my guess," Suzanne said. "Have you ever heard of the Giant's Causeway?"

"Can't say that I have," Perry said.

"It's a natural rock formation on the northern coast of Ireland," Suzanne said. "It looks something like what you're seeing here."

"How big is the top of this seamount?" Perry questioned.

"I'd estimate about four football fields," Suzanne said. "But, unfortunately, that's nothing but a guess. The problem is we haven't had enough bottom time to explore the whole thing."

"Well, I think we ought to," Perry said.

Right on! Suzanne said to herself. She had to resist the temptation to yell out to ask if Larry and Mark had heard Perry's comment over the UQC.

"Does the whole top of the mountain look just the same as it does here?" Perry asked.

"No, not entirely," Suzanne said. "On the limited amount we've seen there are some areas of more typical undersea lava formations. On the last dive, though, we caught a glimpse of what might be a transverse fault, but we were called back before we could check it out. The mount remains largely unexplored."

"Where was the fault in relation to the well head?" Perry asked.

"Due west from here," Suzanne said. "Just about in the direction you're looking right now. Can you see a particularly high row of columns?"

"I think so," Perry said. He pushed his face against the Plexiglas to try to look slightly behind the sub. There was a row of columns at the edge of his visibility. "Would finding a transverse fault be significant?" he asked.

"It would be astounding," Suzanne responded. "They occur up and down the Mid-Atlantic Ridge system, but finding one at such a distance from the ridge, and through the middle of what we assume is an old volcano, would be quite unique."

"Let's go take a look," Perry suggested. "This place is fascinating."

Suzanne grinned in triumph. She glanced at Donald. Even he couldn't suppress a smile. He'd been sympathetic to Suzanne's plan but had not been optimistic.

It took Suzanne only a few minutes to unload everything that Mark had stowed in the submersible's tray. Once the material was lined up next to the well head, she folded the manipulating arms into their retracted position.

"So much for that job," Suzanne said. She turned off the power to the servo links.

"*Oceanus* to surface control," Donald said into the UQC mike. "The payload has been off-loaded. What's the status of the divers?"

"Compression is nearing depth," Larry's voice reported over the speaker. "The bell should be starting its descent shortly. ETA on the bottom, thirty minutes give or take five."

"Roger!" Donald said. "Keep us informed. We are going to move due west to investigate a scarp we caught sight of on the last dive."

"Ten-four," Larry said. "We'll let you know when the bell is lifted off the DDC. We'll also let you know when it is passing through five hundred feet so you can take up an appropriate position."

"Roger!" Donald repeated. He hung up the UQC mike. With his hands resting gently on the joysticks he jacked up the power to the propulsion system to fifty amps. He expertly guided the submersible away from the well head, careful to avoid the vertical run of pipe. A few moments later the *Oceanus* was slowly flying over the strange topography of the guyot's top.

"What I believe we're looking at here is a pristine section of the mantle's crust," Suzanne said. "But how and why the lava cooled to form these polygonal shapes is beyond me. It's almost like they're gigantic crystals."

"I like the idea of it being Atlantis," Perry said. His face remained glued to the view port.

"We're coming up to the place where we glimpsed that fault," Donald said.

"It should be just over that ridge of columns coming up," Suzanne said for Perry's benefit.

Donald cut back on the power. The submersible slowed as they cleared the ridge.

"Wow!" Perry commented. "It certainly drops off quickly."

"Well, it's not a transverse fault," Suzanne said as she got a full view of the formation. "In fact, if it were a fault at all it would have to be a graben. The other side is just as steep."

"What the hell is a graben?" Perry asked.

"It's when a fault block falls in relation to the rock on either side," Suzanne explained. "But something like that doesn't happen on the top of a seamount."

"It looks like a huge rectangular hole to me," Perry said. "What would you say? About a hundred and fifty feet long and fifty wide?"

"I'd say that's about right," Suzanne said.

"It's incredible!" Perry commented. "It's like some giant took a knife and cut out a chunk of rock just the way you'd take a plug out of a watermelon."

Donald powered the *Oceanus* out over the hole, and they all looked down.

"I can't see the bottom," Perry said.

"Neither can I," Suzanne said.

"Neither can our sonar," Donald said. He pointed to the echo sounder monitor. It wasn't getting a return signal. It was as if the *Oceanus* were poised over a bottomless pit.

"My word!" Suzanne said. She was dumbfounded.

Donald gave the monitor a tap, but there was still no readout.

"That's very strange," Suzanne said. "Do you think it's malfunctioning?"

"I can't tell," Donald reported. He tried changing the adjustments.

"Wait a sec," Perry voiced tensely. "Are you two pulling my leg?"

"Try the side-scan sonar," Suzanne suggested, ignoring Perry for the moment.

"It's just as weird," Donald said. "The signal is aberrant unless we want to accept the pit's only six or seven feet deep. That's what the side-scan monitor is suggesting."

"Clearly the hole is a lot deeper than six or seven feet," Suzanne said.

"Obviously," Donald agreed.

"Hey, come on, you guys," Perry said. "You're starting to scare me."

Suzanne turned briefly to face Perry. "We're not trying to scare you," she said. "We're just mystified by our instruments."

"My guess is there's one hell of a thermocline just within the rim of this formation," Donald said. "The sonar has to be bouncing off something."

"Would you mind translating that?" Perry said.

"Sound waves bounce off sharp temperature gradi-ents," Suzanne said. "We think that's what we have here."

"In order to get a depth readout we have to descend ten or fifteen feet into the pit," Donald said. "I'll do that by decreasing our buoyancy, but first I want to change our orientation."

With short bursts Donald used the starboard front thruster to turn the submersible until it became parallel with the long axis of the hole. Then he manipulated the variable ballast system to make the sub negatively buoy-ant. Gradually the submersible started down.

"Maybe this isn't such a good idea," Perry said. He was nervously looking back and forth between the side-scan sonar monitor and his view port.

The UQC speaker cracked to life: "Surface control to *Oceanus*. The bell is lifting off the DDC as I'm speak-ing. The divers will be passing through five hundred feet in about ten minutes."

"Roger, surface control," Donald said into the mike. "We're about one hundred feet west of the well head. We're going to check out an apparent marked thermo-cline in a rock formation. Communications might be in-terrupted momentarily, but we'll be on station for the divers."

"Ten-four," Larry's voice said.

"Look at the luster of the walls," Suzanne remarked as the submersible sank below the tip of the huge hole. "They're perfectly smooth. It almost looks like obsid-ian!"

"Let's head back to the well head," Perry suggested.

"Could this be an opening into an extinct volcano?"

Donald asked. A slight smile flitted across his otherwise rigid face.

"That's a thought," Suzanne said with a laugh. "Although I have to say I've never heard of a perfectly rectilinear caldera." She laughed again. "Our dropping down in here like this reminds me of Jules Verne's *Journey to the Center of the Earth*."

"How so?" Donald asked.

"Have you read it?"

"I don't read novels," Donald said.

"That's right, I forgot," Suzanne said. "Anyway, in the story the protagonists entered a kind of pristine netherworld via an extinct volcano."

Donald shook his head. His eyes stayed glued to the thermistor readout. "What a waste of time reading such rubbish," he said. "That's why I don't read novels. Not with all the technical journals I can't get to."

Suzanne started to respond but changed her mind. She'd never been able to make a dent in Donald's rigid opinions about fiction in particular and art in general.

"I don't mean to be a pest," Perry said, "but I—"

Perry never got out the last part of his sentence. All at once the submersible's descent accelerated markedly and Donald cried out, "Christ almighty!"

Perry gripped the sides of his seat with white-knuckle intensity. The rapid increase in downward motion scared him, but not as much as Donald's uncharacteristic outburst. If the imperturbable Donald Fuller was upset, the situation must be critical.

"Jettisoning weights!" Donald called out. The descent immediately slowed, then stopped. Donald released more weight and the sub began to rise. Then he used the portside thruster to maintain orientation with the long axis of the pit. The last thing he wanted was to hit up against the walls.

"What the hell happened?" Perry demanded when he could find his voice.

"We lost buoyancy," Suzanne reported.

"We suddenly got heavier or the water got lighter," Donald said as he scanned the instrumentation.

"What does that mean?" Perry demanded.

"Since we obviously didn't get heavier, the water indeed got lighter," Donald said. He pointed to the temperature gauge. "We passed through the temperature gradient we suspected, and it was a lot more than we bargained for—in the opposite direction. The outside temperature rose almost a hundred degrees Fahrenheit!"

"Let's get the hell out of here!" Perry cried.

"We're on our way," Donald said tersely. He snapped the UQC mike from its housing and tried to raise the *Benthic Explorer.* When he had no luck, he returned the mike to its cradle. "Sound waves don't come in here and they don't go out either."

"What is this, some sort of sonar black hole?" Perry asked irritably.

"The echo sounder is giving us a reading now," Suzanne said. "But it can't be true! It says this pit is over thirty thousand feet deep!"

"Now why would that be malfunctioning?" Donald asked himself. He gave the instrument an even harder rap with his knuckles. The digital readout stayed at 30,418.

"Let's forget the echo sounder," Perry said. "Can't we get out of here faster?" The *Oceanus* was rising, but very slowly.

"I've never had trouble with this echo sounder before," Donald said.

"Maybe this pit could have been some kind of magma pipe," Suzanne said. "It's obviously deep, even though we don't know how deep, and the water is hot. That suggests contact with lava." She bent forward to look out the view port.

"Could we at least turn off the music?" Perry said. It was reaching a crescendo that only added to his anxiety.

"Well, I'll be damned!" Suzanne exclaimed. "Look at the walls at this level! The basalt is oriented transversely. I've never heard of a transverse dike. And look! It has a greenish cast to it. Maybe it's gabbro, not basalt."

"I'm afraid I'm going to have to pull rank here," Perry snapped with uncamouflaged exasperation. He'd had it with being ignored. "I want to be taken up to the surface, *pronto*!"

Suzanne swung around to respond but only managed to open her mouth. Before she could form any words a powerful, low-frequency vibration shook the submersible. She had to grab the side of her seat to keep from falling. The sudden quake sent loose objects flying to the floor. A coffee mug hit and shattered; the shards skittered across the floor along with pens that had fallen. At the same time, there was a low-pitched rumbling that sounded like distant thunder.

The rattling lasted for almost a minute. No one spoke although an involuntary squeak escaped from Perry's lips as the blood drained from his face.

"What on earth was that?" Donald demanded. He rapidly scanned the instruments.

"I'm not sure," Suzanne said, "but if I had to guess, I'd say it was an earthquake. There's a lot of them up and down the Mid-Atlantic Ridge."

"An earthquake!" Perry blurted.

"Maybe this old volcano is awakening," Suzanne said. "Wouldn't that be a trip if we got to witness it!"

"Uh-oh!" Donald said. "Something is wrong!"

"What's the problem?" Suzanne asked. Like Donald her eyes made a quick circuit of the dials, gauges, and screens in her direct line of sight. These were the important instruments for operating the submersible. Nothing seemed amiss.

"The echo sounder!" Donald said with uncharacteristic urgency.

Suzanne's eyes darted down to the digital readout located close to the floor between the two pilot seats. It was decreasing at an alarming rate.

"What's happening?" she asked. "Do you think lava is rising in the shaft?"

"No!" Donald cried. "It's us. We're sinking, and I've jettisoned all the descent weights. We've lost our buoyancy!"

"But the pressure gauge!" Suzanne yelled. "It's not rising. How can we be sinking?"

"It mustn't be working," Donald said frantically. "There's no doubt we're sinking. Just look out the damn view port!"

Suzanne's eyes darted to the window. It was true. They were sinking. The smooth rock face was moving rapidly upward.

"I'm blowing the ballast tanks," Donald barked. "At this depth there won't be much effect, but there's no choice."

The sound of compressed air being released drowned out Stravinsky's *Rite of Spring* but only for twenty seconds. At such a pressure the compressed air tanks were quickly exhausted. The descent was not affected.

"Do something!" Perry yelled when he could find his voice.

"I can't," Donald yelled. "There's no response to the controls. There's nothing left to try."

CHAPTER FIVE

Mark Davidson was dying for a cigarette. His addiction was absolute, although he found giving them up was easy since he did it once a week. His craving was maximum when he was relaxing, working, or anxious, and at the moment, he was very anxious indeed. For him, deep diving operations were always a walk on the wild side; from experience he knew how quickly things could go horribly wrong.

He looked up at the large institutional clock on the wall of the diving van, with its monstrous sweep second hand. Its intimidating presence made the passage of time hard to disregard. It had now been twelve minutes since there had been any contact with the *Oceanus*. Although Donald had specifically warned that there might be a short communication break, this seemed longer than reasonable, especially since the submersible had not responded to Larry Nelson's last message. That was when Larry had tried to tell them that the divers were passing through five hundred feet.

Mark's eyes darted down to the pack of Marlboros he'd casually tossed onto the diving van's countertop. It was an agony not to reach over, take one out, and light up. Unfortunately, there was a newly instituted prohibition about smoking in the ship's common areas, and Captain Jameson was a stickler about rules and regulations.

With some difficulty Mark pulled his eyes away from the cigarettes and scanned the van's interior. Everyone else present seemed calm, which only made Mark feel more tense. Larry Nelson was sitting perfectly still at the diving operations monitoring station along with the sonar operator, Peter Rosenthal. Just beyond them were the two watch standers, who were in front of the diving system's operating console. Although their eyes were constantly scanning the pressure gauges of the two pressurized DDCs and the diving bell, the rest of their bodies were motionless.

Across from the watch standers was the winch operator. He was perched on a high stool in front of the window looking out on the central well. His hand rested on the gear shift for the winch. Outside, the cable attached to the shackle on top of the diving bell was being played out at the maximum permitted velocity. From a neighboring drum came a second, passive cable that contained the compressed gas line, hot water hose, and communications wires.

At the far end of the van was Captain Jameson, absently sucking on a toothpick. In front of him were the controls that formed an extension of the bridge. Even though the ship's propellers and thrusters were being controlled by computer to keep it stationary over the well head, Captain Jameson could override the system if the need arose during diving operations.

"God damn it!" Mark spat. He slammed a pencil he'd been unconsciously torturing to the countertop and stood up. "What's the divers' depth?"

"Passing through six hundred ten feet, sir," the winch operator reported.

"Try the *Oceanus* again!" Mark barked to Larry. He started to pace back and forth. He had a bad feeling in the pit of his stomach, and it was getting worse. He began to lambaste himself for encouraging Perry Bergman to go on the dive. Being personally aware of Dr. Newell's interest in the seamount and her desire to make purely exploratory dives, he worried that she might try to impress the president to get her way. That might mean she'd pressure Donald to do things he might not normally do, and Mark was aware that Dr. Newell was the only person on the ship who potentially had that kind of influence over the normally strictly-by-the-book ex–naval line officer.

Mark shuddered. It would be a disaster of the first order if the submersible got wedged in a fissure or a crevice where it may have descended to examine a particular geological feature up close. That had almost happened to the submersible *Alvin,* out of Woods Hole, and the near tragedy had been on the Mid-Atlantic Ridge, not that far away from their present location.

"Still no response," Larry said after several unsuccessful tries to raise the *Oceanus* on the UQC.

"Any sign of the submersible on side-scan sonar?" Mark demanded from the sonar operator.

"That's a negative," Peter said. "And bottom hydrophones have no contact with their tracking beacon. The thermocline they found must be impressive. It's like they dropped down into the ocean floor."

Mark stopped his pacing and looked back at the

clock. "How long has it been since that tremor?" he asked.

"That was more than a tremor," Larry said. "Tad Messenger measured it four point four on the Richter scale."

"I'm not surprised—it knocked over that pile of pipe on the deck," Mark said. "And as much as we felt it up here, it would have been a hell of a lot worse on the bottom. How long ago was it?"

Larry looked down at his log. "It's been almost four minutes. You don't think that has anything to do with our not hearing from the *Oceanus,* do you?"

Mark was reluctant to answer. He was not superstitious, yet he hated to voice his worries, as if articulating them made them that much more possible. But he was concerned that the 4.4 earthquake may have caused a rock slide that trapped the *Oceanus*. Such a catastrophe surely wasn't out of the question if Donald had indeed descended into a narrow depression at Suzanne's insistence.

"Let me talk to the divers," Mark said. He walked over to Larry and took the mike. While he pondered what he wanted to say, he glanced up at the monitor where he could see the tops of the heads and the foreshortened bodies of the three men.

"Shit, man!" Michael moaned. "You just kicked me in the balls!" His voice came out as a series of squeaks and squeals that would have been mostly unintelligible to normal humans. The distortion was a function of the helium he was breathing in place of nitrogen.

At the equivalent pressure of 980 feet of seawater, nitrogen acted as an anesthetic. Replacing the nitrogen with helium solved the problem but caused marked changes in voice. The divers were used to it. Although they sounded like Walt Disney's Donald Duck, they could understand each other perfectly.

"Then get your balls out of my way," Richard said. "I'm having trouble getting these freaking fins on."

All three divers were wedged up inside the diving bell, whose pressure hull was a sphere a mere eight feet in diameter. Crammed in with them were all their diving equipment, many hundreds of feet of looped hose, and all the necessary instrumentation.

"Get out of the way, he says," Michael jeered. "What do you want me to do, step outside?"

A speaker crackled to life. It was mounted at the very apex of the sphere next to a tiny camcorder fitted with a fish-eye lens. Although the divers knew they were being constantly observed, they were totally indifferent to the surveillance.

"Let me have your attention, men!" Mark commanded. In contrast to the divers', his voice sounded relatively normal. "This is the operations commander."

"Holy crap!" Richard complained as he eyed the swim fin that was giving him the problem. "No wonder I can't get this freaking thing on. It ain't mine. It's yours, Donaghue." Without warning Richard clobbered Michael over the head with the flipper. Michael was troubled by the blow only because it knocked off his prized Red Sox cap. The cap tumbled down into the trunk, coming to a rest on the sealed hatch.

"Hey, nobody move!" Michael said. "Mazzola, get my hat for me! I don't want it to get wet." Michael was already fully outfitted for the dive in his neoprene dry suit complete with the buoyancy control vest and weights. The ability to bend over, as would be required to retrieve the hat, was out of the question.

"Gentlemen!" Mark's voice was louder and more insistent.

"Screw you," Louis said. "I might be bell diver, but I'm not your slave."

"Hey, listen up, you animals!" Larry's voice yelled from the tiny speaker. The sound reverberated around the cramped sphere at a level just shy of pain. "Mr. Davidson wants a word with you, so shut up!"

Richard shoved the flipper and its mate into Michael's hands, then looked up at the camera. "All right already," he said. "We're listening."

"Stand by for a moment," Larry's voice said. "We didn't realize the helium unscrambler wasn't on line."

"So let me have my fins," Richard said to Michael in the interim.

"You mean the ones I have on aren't mine?"

"Duh!" Richard voiced mockingly. "Since you're holding yours in your hands they can't be on your feet, birdbrain!"

Michael squatted awkwardly, clutching his fins under his arm, and stripped those from his feet. Richard snatched them away disdainfully. Then the two divers clumsily bumped into each other as they struggled to slip on their respective flippers at the same time.

"Okay, men," Larry's voice said. "We're on line with the scrambler so stop screwing around and listen up! Here's Mr. Davidson."

The diver's didn't bother to look up. They slouched against the sides of the PTC and assumed bored expressions.

"We haven't been able to raise the *Oceanus* on the UQC or track it on sonar," Mark's voice said. "We're anxious for you to make visual contact. If you don't see them when you arrive at the well head, let us know and we'll give you further instructions. Understand?"

"That's affirmative," Richard said. "Now can we get back to getting ready to dive?"

"That's affirmative," Mark said.

Richard and Michael stirred, and by giving each other an iota of leeway they managed to get their flippers on their feet. Michael even tried to reach his hat while Richard proceeded to don his buoyancy vest and weight belt, but it was beyond his grasp, as he'd feared.

Five minutes later the winch operator's voice told them they were passing through nine hundred feet. With that announcement the descent slowed appreciably. While Richard and Michael tried to stay out of the way, Louis readied the hoses. As the bell diver it fell to him to handle the lines.

"Powering the exterior lights," Larry announced.

Richard and Michael twisted themselves enough to glance out the two tiny view ports opposite each other. Louis was too busy to look out either of the two remaining windows.

"I see bottom," Richard said.

"Me, too," Michael said.

With a single main hoisting cable the diving bell was rotating slowly, although its rotation was restricted by the life-support lines. The bell would rotate in one direction for several revolutions and then turn and go the other way. As the bell settled down to the 980-foot mark and stopped, the rotation slowed to a stop as well, but not before each diver had been afforded a 360-degree view.

Since the bell was suspended fourteen feet above the rock face at one of the higher sections of the seamount's summit, the divers could see a relatively wide area bounded by the illumination of the exterior halogen lights. Their view was somewhat restricted only to the west, where it was blocked by a ridge of rock. To Richard and Michael the ridge appeared like a series of connected columns whose crest was slightly higher than their line of sight. But even that formation was at the periphery of the sphere of light.

"Do you see the sub?" Richard asked Michael.

"Nope," Michael said. "But I can see the bits and the tools by the well head. They're all stacked up nice and neat."

Richard leaned away from the view port and tilted his face up toward the camcorder.

"That's a negative on the *Oceanus*," he said. "But she's been here."

"That means there will be a change in the dive plan," Larry's voice answered. "Mr. Davidson wants red and green divers to proceed due west. Can you make out a scarp in that direction?"

"What the hell is a scarp?" Richard asked.

"It's a wall or cliff," Mark's voice cut in.

"Yeah, I guess," Richard said. He looked back out at the columnar ridge.

"Mr. Davidson wants you to proceed over the ridge," Larry said. "How high is the ridge in relation to the bell?"

"About even," Richard said.

"All right, swim over the ridge and see if you can make visual contact with the submersible. Mr. Davidson thinks there might be a crevice. And watch the temperature. Apparently there's quite a gradient in the area."

"Got it," Richard said.

"Remember," Larry added, "you're limited to a one-fifty deep excursion dive. Don't rise more than ten feet above the bell. We don't want any bends to muck things up. Understood?"

"Got it," Richard repeated. Larry's admonitions were the standard for a saturation dive.

"Bell diver," Larry said, "the breathing mixture is to stay at one and a half percent oxygen and ninety-eight and a half percent helium. Do you copy?"

"I copy," Louis said.

"One last thing," Larry said. "Red and green diver, I don't want any of you macho bums taking any chances, so be careful!"

"Check!" Richard said. He gave a thumbs-up sign for the camcorder's benefit while making a scornful face at Michael and saying: "Telling us to be careful down here is like telling your kid to be careful before sending him out to play in the middle of the interstate."

Michael nodded but he wasn't listening. This part of the dive was serious. He was all business while attaching his umbilical and other paraphernalia. When he was ready Louis handed him his full face mask cradled in a bright orange fiberglass helmet. Michael held it under his arm to wait for Richard. Despite his extensive experience he always got butterflies just before entering the water.

Richard quickly followed suit with his equipment. Then he took two underwater lights, tested both, and handed one to Michael. When he was ready he nodded to Michael, and they both put on their helmets at the same time.

The first thing they checked after Louis opened the manifold was the gas flow. Next was the hot water, a necessary adjunct since the outside water temperature was only thirty-six degrees; it was difficult for a diver to work if he was cold. Finally they tested the communications and their sensor lines. When all was in order, Louis informed topside and asked for permission for the divers to enter the water.

"Permission granted," Larry's voice responded. "Open the hatch!"

With some difficulty and a lot of grunts Louis squeezed his bulky frame down into the trunk of the bell.

"My hat!" Michael yelled, although his voice was muffled by the sound of his escaping breathing gas.

Louis grasped the baseball hat and handed it up to Michael. Michael gingerly hung it on one of the many protuberances in the bell. He treated it as his most valuable possession. What he didn't admit was that he considered it his lucky charm.

Louis undogged the pressure hatch and, with some difficulty, raised it. He secured it against the wall. Below, the luminous aquamarine seawater rose menacingly up through the trunk. All three divers breathed a silent sigh of relief when it predictably stopped just shy of the lip of the hatch. They all knew it would, but they also knew that if it did not there was no place to go.

Richard gave Michael a thumbs-up sign. Michael returned the gesture. Richard then carefully climbed down through the trunk. Once he was free he dropped out the bottom of the bell.

For Richard, getting out of the cramped bell was a relief he likened to being born. The sudden freedom was exhilarating. The only part of him that could sense the coolness of the water was his gloved hands. He scanned the area while adjusting his buoyancy. It took him only a moment to see the dark shape cruising just at the periphery of light. It wasn't the submersible. It was a shark with luminous eyes. The length of the huge fish was more than twice the diameter of the diving bell.

"We got company," Richard said calmly. "Toss down my rebar just in case and have Michael bring his." Of all the fancy antishark paraphernalia on the market, Richard preferred a simple, three-and-a-half-foot metal rod. It had been his experience that sharks avoided the rod like the plague if it was just pointed in their direction. During a feeding frenzy he wasn't as confident it would work, but in that situation, nothing worked one hundred percent.

Seconds later the rebar came down and clanked mutely against the rock. A moment later Michael's legs appeared as he struggled out of the trunk. Once he was free the two divers made eye contact. Richard gestured in the direction of the shark, which now wandered into the light.

"Ah, it's only a Greenland shark," Richard said to Louis, who made sure Michael had heard it as well. Now Richard was even less concerned. It was a big shark, but not dangerous. He knew that another name for the monster was sleeper shark because of its sluggish habits.

After Michael made his adjustments Richard pointed toward the ridge. Michael nodded and the two started off. Both held their lights in their left hands and the rebars in their right. As accomplished swimmers they covered the distance in a short time without rushing. At a pressure of almost thirty atmospheres the sheer work of breathing the viscous, compressed gas sapped their energy.

Inside the diving bell Louis was frantically playing out both sets of tethers. He didn't want to restrict the divers or give them too much slack lest they get tangled up. Until the divers got down to work the bell

diver was a busy man. The job required concentration
and quick reflexes. At the same time Louis was handling the lines, he had to keep his eye on the pressure
gauges and the digital oxygen percentage readout. On
top of that he was in constant communication with each
diver and with diving control up in the diving van. To
keep his hands free, a headset kept a tiny speaker in
his ear and a microphone positioned over his mouth.

Out in the water the two divers swam to the top of
the ridge and paused. At that distance from the diving
bell the amount of illumination fell off sharply. Richard
motioned to his flashlight and both turned them on.

Behind them, the diving bell glowed eerily like an
orbiter nesting in a rocky, alien landscape. A stream of
bubbles issued from the bell and dribbled toward the
far-off surface. Ahead, the divers faced darkness fading to indelible blackness with only a faint hint of a
glow when they looked up toward the surface almost a
thousand feet above. In the back of their minds they ·
knew the huge shark was somewhere just beyond their
vision. Shining their lights forward provided meager
cones of light that penetrated the icy darkness only forty
to fifty feet ahead.

"There's a drop-off beyond the ridge," Richard reported. "This must be the scarp."

Louis relayed the information up to the dive station.
Although the dive control could listen to the divers and
talk to them, Larry preferred to use the bell diver as an
intermediary. The combination of the helium voice distortion and the noise of the divers' breathing gas flow
made comprehension by those up in the diving van extremely difficult even with the helium unscrambler on-
line. It was much more efficient to use the bell diver
since he was more accustomed to the speech distortions.

"Red diver," Louis called out. "Control wants to know if you see any sign of the *Oceanus*."

"That's negative," Richard said.

"How about a crevice or a hole?" Louis relayed.

"Not at the moment," Richard reported, "but we're about to start down this rock wall."

Richard and Michael swam over the edge and down the face of the cliff.

"The rock is as smooth as glass," Richard commented. Michael nodded. He'd run his hand along it briefly.

"You're coming up on your last one hundred feet of hose," Louis said. He quickly took the last loops down from their storage hooks, already cursing under his breath. Soon he'd be coiling it all up again. Divers rarely wandered this far from the diving bell, and it was just his luck to be assigned as the bell diver when they did.

Richard stopped his descent. He grabbed Michael to stop him as well. Richard pointed to his wrist thermometer. Michael looked at his and did a double take.

"The water temperature just changed," Richard reported. "It just went up almost one hundred degrees. Shut off our hot water!"

"Red diver, are you shitting me?" Louis asked.

"Michael's reads the same," Richard said. "It's like we've climbed into a hot tub."

Richard had been shining his light down as they descended, searching for the base of the scarp. Now he shined it around. At the very periphery of illumination he could just make out a wall opposite the one they were descending.

"Hey! Apparently we are in some kind of huge

crevice," he said. "I can just barely see the other side. It must be about fifty feet wide."

Michael tapped Richard on the shoulder and pointed off to their left. "There's an end to it as well," he said.

"Michael's right," Richard said when he'd looked. Then he swung around and pointed the light in the opposite direction. "I guess it's like a box canyon 'cause I can't see a fourth side, at least not from where we are."

"Hey," Michael said. "We're sinking!"

Richard looked at the wall behind him. It was true they were sinking—more quickly than he would have thought possible. There was little sensation of resistance against the water.

Richard and Michael gave a few powerful kicks upward. To their astonishment there was little effect. They were still sinking. With a mixture of confusion and alarm, both responded by reflex and inflated their buoyancy vests. When that seemed to have little effect, they released their weight belts. Still significantly negatively buoyant, they jettisoned their rebars. Finally with some continued kicking their descent slowed and stopped.

Richard pointed upward and the two started swimming. Despite the heavy work of breathing they were swimming hard. The strange sinking episode had unnerved them, and to make matters worse, they were beginning to feel the heat through their suits.

The two were even with the top of the cliff when a sudden sustained vibration swept up from the depths like a shock wave. For a few seconds both men were mildly disoriented. They had trouble breathing and swimming at the same time. The shaking was similar to what they had experienced in the diving bell on the descent, only much worse. They realized this was an underwater earthquake, and both of them intuitively sensed they were at or near the epicenter.

For Louis, the quake was even more violent. At the moment of impact he'd been frantically hauling in the tethers, which had gone suddenly slack. He'd been forced to let go of the lines to keep himself from being impaled on one of the many wall-mounted protrusions.

Richard recovered enough to take a breath although doing so was painful. The pressure wave had bruised his chest. As an experienced diver, his first response was to check on his buddy, and he frantically searched by spinning around. For a heart-stopping second he could not find Michael. Then he looked down. Michael appeared to be clawing his way up through the water. Richard reached down to lend a hand. When he did, he realized that they were both sinking—and sinking fast.

With no other way to decrease his weight Richard joined Michael in an attempt to swim upward. In desperation they even discarded their lights to free their hands. But they made no progress. If anything, they seemed to be going down. Then they plummeted, caroming off the rock wall as they were inexorably sucked into the abyss.

Inside the bell Louis had recovered his balance enough to grab the tethers, which were still slack. Quickly he pulled in a loop, but before he could get it over the rack, there was a sudden tug in the opposite direction. At first he tried to hold the lines from going out, but it was impossible. Had he held on, they would have pulled him from the bell.

Louis cursed as he frantically got out of the way of the hoses, which were now being yanked out of the bell at a furious rate. It was as if Richard and Michael were lures that had been taken by a gigantic fish.

"Bell diver, are you all right?" Larry's voice asked.

"Yeah, I'm all right!" Louis yelled. "But something crazy is going on! The hoses are going out at a hundred miles an hour!"

"We can see that on the monitor," Larry said urgently. "Can't you stop it?"

"How?" Louis pleaded through tears. He glanced at the remaining hose. There wasn't much left. He froze. He had no idea what to expect. The last loops whipped out of the bell and for a brief moment the lines went taut. Then to Louis's utter horror they were torn from their housings and disappeared down into the trunk and out into the unforgiving sea.

"Oh, my god!" Louis cried as he struggled to turn off the gas supply manifold.

"What's happening down there?" Larry demanded.

"I don't know," Louis cried. Then to add to his terror the vibration and rumbling started again. Frantically he reached out to grab whatever he could as the diving bell shook as though it were a salt shaker in the hand of a giant. He screamed, and as if in answer to a prayer, the shaking lessened to a mere trembling. At the same time he became aware of a sizzling sound and a red glow that penetrated through the view ports.

Letting go of the death grip he'd had on the high-pressure piping, Louis twisted to glance out one of the view ports. What he saw made him freeze anew. Over the nearby ridge, which the divers had so recently scaled, came a surreal cascade of glowing, red hot lava. The leading edge sputtered and popped and smoked as it turned the icy water into steam.

When Louis recovered enough to find his voice, he threw his head back to look up into the camcorder lens.

"Get me out of here!" he shrieked. "I'm in the middle of a goddamn erupting volcano!"

The van's interior had become quiet. A sense of shock hung over the room. The only noise came from the deck-mounted motors driving the winches that were hauling up the diving bell and the life-support lines. Moments before, utter pandemonium had prevailed as it became apparent they'd lost two divers in some kind of pyroclastic catastrophe. The only consolation was that the third diver was okay, and he was on his way up.

Mark took a long, nervous drag on his Marlboro. Oblivious to the new rules, he'd reached for his cigarettes by reflex at the first rumblings of trouble, and now that the extent of the tragedy had rapidly unfolded, he was chain-smoking out of pure anxiety. Not only had he managed to lose a hundred-million-dollar submersible with two trained operators plus two experienced saturation divers; he'd also lost the president of Benthic Marine. If only he hadn't encouraged Perry Bergman to make the dive. For that he was solely responsible.

"What the hell are we going to do?" Larry asked in stunned bewilderment. Even he was smoking although he was supposed to have given it up six months before. As the diving supervisor he, too, felt responsible for the disastrous outcome.

Mark sighed heavily. He felt weak. He'd never had a single loss of life on his watch in his entire career, and that included hairy diving operations in some dicey locations like in the Persian Gulf during Desert Storm. Now he'd lost five people. It was too much to think about.

"The bell is passing through five hundred feet," the winch operator called out to no one in particular.

"What about the drilling operation?" Larry wondered aloud.

Mark took another long drag on his cigarette and almost burned his fingers. Angrily he stubbed it out, then lit another.

"Get ready to launch the camera sled," Mark said. "We got to look at what's going on down there."

"Mazzola was pretty clear," Larry quavered. "As we were pulling him up he said the whole top of the seamount as far as he could see was molten lava, bubbling up from behind the ridge. And we're recording almost continuous tremors. Hell, we're sitting on a live volcano. Are you sure you want the sled down in that kind of an inferno?"

"I want to see it," Mark said slowly, "and I want to record it. I'm sure there's going to be one hell of an inquiry about this whole mess. And I want to look at the area where the canyon or hole was that the *Oceanus* disappeared into. I've got to be sure there's no chance . . ." Mark did not finish his sentence. He knew in his gut it was hopeless; Donald Fuller had dropped the submersible down into a volcanic vent just prior to its erupting.

"Fair enough," Larry conceded. "I'll have the crew get the sled ready to go. But what about the drilling? I hope you're not thinking of sending down another dive team if and when this volcano quiets down."

"Hell no!" Mark said with emotion. "I've lost interest in drilling into this freaking mountain, especially now that Perry Bergman is no longer with us. It was his foolhearty obsession, not mine. If the camera sled confirms that the vent hole or whatever it was is filled with fresh lava, and we can't find any trace of the *Oceanus,* we're getting the hell out of here."

"That sounds good to me!" Larry said. He stood up. "I'll get the sled ready and in the water ASAP."

"Thanks," Mark said. He leaned forward and buried his head in his hands. He'd never felt worse in his life.

CHAPTER SIX

Suzanne was the first to recover enough from the terror of the precipitous descent to find her voice. Hesitantly she said, "I think we've stopped! Thank God!"

For a time that had seemed an eternity to its three terrified occupants, the submersible had fallen like a stone down the mysterious shaft. It was as if they had been sucked down an enormous drain in the bottom of the ocean. During the plummet the *Oceanus* had been totally unresponsive to the controls no matter which Donald Fuller manipulated.

Although initially the plunge had been straight down, the boat had eventually begun to spiral and even carom off the walls. One of the first such collisions destroyed the outside halogen lights. Another stripped off the starboard manipulator with a grinding crunch.

Perry had been the only one to scream during the ordeal. But even he fell silent once the helplessness of their situation had sunk in. He could only watch helplessly as the digital depth recorder whirred into the thousands. The numbers had flashed by so quickly, they'd become a blur. And when twenty thousand feet approached, all he'd been able to think about was the chilling statistic he'd heard earlier: the *crush depth*!

"In fact, I don't think we're moving at all," Suzanne added. She was whispering. "What could have happened? Could we be on the bottom? I didn't feel an impact."

No one moved a muscle, as if doing so might disturb the sudden but welcome tranquillity. They were breathing shallowly in short gasps, and beads of perspiration dotted their foreheads. All three were still holding on to their seats for fear the plunge would recommence.

"It feels like we stopped, but look at the depth gauge," Donald managed. His voice was raspy from dryness.

All eyes returned to the readout that only moments earlier had inexorably held their gaze. It was moving again, slowly at first but then rapidly gathering speed. The difference was that it was moving in the opposite direction.

"But I don't feel any movement," Suzanne said. She exhaled deeply and tried to relax her muscles. The others did likewise.

"Nor do I," Donald admitted. "But look at the gauge! It's going crazy."

The readout device had returned to its previous furious whirring.

Suzanne leaned forward slowly as if she thought the submersible was precariously balanced and her movement might tip it over an edge. She peered out the view port, but all she could see was her own image. With the outside lights sheared off from collisions with the rock, the window was as opaque as a mirror, reflecting the interior light.

"What's happening now?" Perry croaked.

"Your guess is as good as ours," Suzanne answered. She took a deep breath. She was beginning to recover.

"The depth gauge says we're rising," Donald said. He glanced at the other instruments, including the sonar monitors. Their erratic signals suggested there was a lot of interference in the water, particularly affecting the short-range sonar. The side-scan was a bit better, with less electronic noise, but it was difficult to interpret. The hazy image hinted that the sub was sitting stationary on a vast, perfectly flat plain. Donald's eyes went back to the depth gauge. He was mystified; in contrast to what the sonar was suggesting, it was still rising, and faster than it had been moments before. Quickly he reopened the ballast tanks, but there was no effect. Then he put the dive planes down and added more power to the propulsion system. There was no response to the controls. But they continued to rise nonetheless.

"We're accelerating," Suzanne warned. "Rising like this we'll be on the surface in just a couple of minutes!"

"I can't wait," Perry said with obvious relief.

"I hope we're not coming up under the *Benthic Explorer*," Suzanne said. "That would be a major problem."

Everyone's eyes were riveted to the depth gauge. It passed through one thousand feet and showed no sign of slowing. Five hundred feet shot by. As it passed one hundred feet Donald said urgently: "Hold on! We're going to broach badly."

"What does 'broach' mean?" Perry yelled. He heard the desperation in Donald's voice, and it sent a new chill through him.

"It means we're going to leap out of the water!" Suzanne shouted. Then she repeated Donald's warning. "Hold on!"

As the frantic whirring of the depth gauge reached a crescendo, Perry, Donald, and Suzanne once again grabbed their seats and held tight. Holding their breath they braced themselves for the impact. The depth gauge reached zero and stopped.

Immediately following that final click of the gauge, a loud sucking noise emanated from somewhere outside the craft. After that, comparative silence reigned within the sub. Now the only sound was a combination of the ventilation fan and an augmented but still muffled electronic whir of the propulsion system.

Almost a minute passed without the slightest sensation of movement.

Finally Perry breathed out. "Well," he said. "What happened?"

"We can't be airborne for this long," Suzanne admitted.

Everyone relaxed their death grips and looked out their respective view ports. It was still as dark as pitch.

"What the hell?" Donald questioned. He looked back at his instruments. The sonar monitors were now filled with meaningless electronic noise. He turned them off. He also dialed down the power to the propulsion system, and its whirring stopped. He looked at Suzanne.

"Don't ask me," Suzanne said when their eyes met. "I haven't the slightest idea what's going on."

"How come it's dark outside if we're on the surface?" Perry asked.

"This doesn't make any sense," Donald said. He looked back at his instruments. Reaching forward, he put power back to the propulsion system. The whirring noise reappeared but there was no motion. The craft stood absolutely still.

"Somebody tell me what's going on," Perry demanded. The euphoria he'd felt a few moments earlier had dissipated. They obviously were not on the surface.

"We don't know what is happening," Suzanne admitted.

"There's no resistance to the propeller," Donald reported. He turned the propulsion system off. The whirring died away for a second time. Now the only sound was the ventilation fan. "I think we are in air."

"How can we be in air?" Suzanne said. "It's totally dark and there is no wave action."

"But it's the only explanation for the sonar not working and the lack of resistance to the propeller," Donald said. "And look. The outside temperature has risen to seventy degrees. We've got to be in air."

"If this is the next life, I'm not ready for it," Perry said.

"You mean we're out of the water entirely?" Suzanne still had trouble believing it.

"I know it sounds crazy," Donald admitted. "But it's the only way I can explain everything, including the fact that the underwater phone doesn't work." Donald next tried the radio and had no luck with that either.

"If we're sitting on dry land," Suzanne said, "how come we haven't tipped over? I mean, this hull is a cylinder. If we were on dry land, we'd surely roll over on our side."

"You're right!" Donald admitted. "That I can't explain."

Suzanne opened an emergency locker between the two pilot seats and pulled out a flashlight. Turning it on, she directed it out her view port. Pressed up against it on the outside was cream-colored, coarse-grained muck.

"At least we know why we didn't tip over," Suzanne said. "We're sitting in a layer of globigerina ooze."

"Explain!" Perry said. He'd leaned forward to see for himself.

"Globigerina ooze is the most common sediment on the ocean floor," Suzanne said. "It's composed mainly of the carcasses of a type of plankton called foraminifera."

"How can we be sitting in ocean sediment and be in air?" Perry asked.

"That's the question," Donald agreed. "We can't, at least not in any way that I know of."

"It's also impossible for globigerina ooze to be this close to the Mid-Atlantic Ridge," Suzanne said. "That sediment is found in the middle of the abyssal plains. Nothing makes sense."

"This is absurd!" Donald snapped. "And I don't like it at all. Wherever we are, we're stuck!"

"Could we be completely buried in the ooze?" Perry asked hesitantly. If he was right, he did not want to hear the answer.

"No! Not a chance," Donald said. "If that were the case there would be more resistance to the propeller, not less."

For a few minutes no one spoke.

"Is there any chance we could be inside the seamount?" Perry asked, finally breaking the silence.

Donald and Suzanne turned to face him.

"How could we be inside a mountain?" Donald asked angrily.

"Hey, I'm only making a suggestion," Perry said. "Mark told me this morning he had some radar data that suggested the mountain might contain gas, not molten lava."

"He never mentioned that to me," Suzanne said.

"He didn't mention it to anyone," Perry said. "He wasn't sure of the data since it was coming from a shallow study of the hard layer we were trying to drill through. It was an extrapolation, and he only mentioned it to me in passing."

"What kind of gas?" Suzanne asked while her mind tried to imagine how a submerged volcano could become void of water. Geophysically speaking it seemed impossible, although she knew that on land some volcanoes did collapse in on themselves to form calderas.

"He had no idea," Perry said. "I guess he thought the most promising candidate was steam held in by the extra-hard layer that was giving us so much trouble."

"Well, it can't be steam," Donald said. "Not at a temperature of almost seventy degrees."

"What about natural gas?" Perry suggested.

"I can't imagine," Suzanne said. "This close to the Mid-Atlantic Ridge, it's a geologically young area. There can't be anything like petroleum or natural gas around here."

"Then maybe it is air," Perry said.

"How could it get here?" Suzanne asked.

"You tell me," Perry said. "You're the geophysical oceanographer. Not me."

"If it is air, there is not a natural explanation that I know of," Suzanne said. "It's as simple as that."

The three people stared at each other for a beat.

"I guess we'll have to crack the hatch and see," Suzanne said.

"Open the hatch?" Donald questioned. "What if the gas is not breathable or it's even toxic?"

"Seems to me we have little choice," Suzanne said. "We have no communications. We're a fish out of water. We've got ten days of life support but what happens after that?"

"Let's not ask that question," Perry said nervously. "I say we crack the hatch."

"All right!" Donald said with resignation. "As captain I'll do it." He stood up from his pilot's seat and took a giant step over the central console. Perry leaned out of the way so that Donald could pass.

Donald climbed up inside the sail. He paused while Suzanne and Perry positioned themselves just underneath him.

"Why don't you just undog it but not open it," Suzanne offered. "Then see if you smell anything."

"Good idea," Donald said. He took Suzanne's suggestion, grabbing the central wheel and turning it. The sealing bolts retracted into the hatch's body.

"Well?" Suzanne called up after a few moments. "Smell anything?"

"Just some dampness," Donald said. "I guess I'll go for it."

Donald cracked the hatch for a brief moment and sniffed.

"What do you think?" Suzanne asked.

"Seems okay," Donald said with relief. He opened the hatch about an inch and smelled the damp air that flowed in. When he was satisfied it was as safe as he could determine, he pushed the hatch all the way up and poked his head out the top. The air had the salty dampness of a beach at low tide.

Donald slowly rotated his head through 360 degrees, straining his eyes in the darkness. He saw absolutely nothing but intuitively he knew that it was a big space. He was staring into a silent, alien blackness as frightening as it was vast.

Poking his head back inside the submersible, he asked for the flashlight.

Suzanne got it for him, and as she handed it up she asked what he'd seen.

"A whole lot of nothing," he replied.

Reemerging from the hatch, Donald shined the flashlight in the distance. The mud stretched away in all directions as far as the light could penetrate. A few isolated mirrorlike puddles of water reflected back at him.

"Hello!" Donald called after cupping his hands around his mouth. He waited. A slight echo seemed to come from the direction of the *Oceanus*'s bow. Donald yelled again; a distinct echo came back in what he estimated to be around three or four seconds.

Donald climbed back down into the submersible after lowering the hatch. The others looked at him expectantly.

"This is the damnedest thing I've ever seen," he said. "We're in some kind of cavern that apparently was recently filled with water."

"But now it's filled with air," Suzanne said.

"It's definitely air," Donald said. "Beyond that, I don't know what to think. Maybe Mr. Bergman is right. Maybe we've somehow been pulled inside the seamount."

"The name is Perry, for chrissake," Perry said. "Give me the light! I'm going to take a look." He took the flashlight from Donald and clumsily climbed the ladder up through the sub's sail. He had to hook one elbow around the top rung and jam the flashlight into his pocket to raise the heavy, wedged-shaped hatch.

"My god!" Perry exclaimed after he had imitated Donald's actions, including testing for echoes. He climbed back down but left the hatch ajar. He handed the flashlight to Suzanne, who took her turn.

When Suzanne returned the three looked at each other

and shook their heads. None of them had an explanation although each hoped one of the others might.

"I suppose it goes without saying," Donald began, breaking an uncomfortable silence, "we're in a difficult situation to say the least. We cannot expect any help from the *Benthic Explorer.* With the series of earthquakes, they'll naturally assume we suffered some kind of disaster. They might send down one of the camera sleds, but it's not going to find us in here, wherever the hell we are. In short, we're on our own with no communication and little food and water. So . . ." Donald paused as if thinking.

"So, what do you suggest?" Suzanne asked.

"I suggest we go out and reconnoiter," Donald said.

"What if this cavern, or whatever it is, floods again?" Perry questioned.

"It seems to me we have to take the chance," Donald said. "I'll be willing to go on my own. It's up to you if you want to join me."

"I'll go," Suzanne said. "It's better than just sitting here and doing nothing."

"I'm not staying here by myself," Perry announced.

"Okay," Donald said. "We have two more flashlights. Let's take them but only use one to conserve the batteries."

"I'll get them," Suzanne said.

Donald was the first one out. He used the ladder rungs mounted on the side of the sail and the hull to climb down. The rungs were there to provide access to the submersible when it was in its chocks on the afterdeck of the *Benthic Explorer.*

Standing on the final rung, Donald shined the light down at the ground. Gauging how deep the *Oceanus* had sunk, he estimated the mud was twenty to twenty-four inches deep.

"Is something the matter?" Suzanne asked. She was the second one out and could see that Donald was hesitating.

"I'm trying to guess how deep the muck is," he said. Still holding on to a rung, he lowered his right foot. It disappeared into the ooze. It wasn't until the mud reached the lower edge of his kneecap that he felt solid ground.

"This is not going to be pleasant," he reported. "The mud is knee-deep."

"Let's hope that's our only problem," Suzanne said.

A few minutes later the three were standing in the mud. Save for a slight glow emanating from the open submersible hatch, the only light came from Donald's flashlight. It cast a meager cone of light in the utter blackness. Suzanne and Perry carried flashlights, too, but as Donald had suggested, they were not turned on. There was no sound in the vast dark space. To conserve the submersible's batteries, Donald had turned off most everything in the sub, even the ventilation fan. He'd left on one light to serve as a beacon to help them find the sub again if they wandered too far afield.

"This is intimidating," Suzanne said with a shudder.

"I think I'd use a stronger word," Perry said. "What's our game plan?"

"That's open to discussion," Donald said. "My suggestion is we head in the direction the *Oceanus* is pointing. That seems to be the closest wall, at least according to my echo." He looked at his compass. "It's pretty much due west."

"Seems like a reasonable plan to me," Suzanne said.

"Let's go," Perry said.

The group set out with Donald in the lead followed

by Suzanne. Perry brought up the rear. It was difficult walking in the deep mud and the smell was mildly offensive.

There was no talk. Each was acutely aware of the precariousness of the situation, especially the farther they got from the submersible. After ten minutes Perry insisted they pause. They had not come to any wall, and his courage had waned.

"Walking in this muck is not easy," Perry said, avoiding the real issue. "And it also stinks."

"How far do you think we've gone?" Suzanne asked. Like the others she was out of breath from exertion.

Donald turned and looked back at the submersible, which was no more than a smudge of light in the inky blackness. "Not that far," he said. "Maybe a hundred yards."

"I would have said a mile, the way my legs feel," Suzanne remarked.

"How much farther to this supposed wall?" Perry asked.

Donald yelled again in the direction they were going. The echo came back in a couple of seconds. "I'd guess somewhere in the neighborhood of three hundred yards."

Sudden movement and a series of slapping sounds in the darkness to their immediate left made them all jump. Donald whipped the light around and shined it in the direction of the noise. A stranded fish made a few more agonal flip-flops against the wet mud.

"Oh, my gosh, that scared the bejesus out of me," Suzanne admitted. Her hand was pressed against her chest. Her heart was racing.

"You and me both," Perry confessed.

"We're all understandably on edge," Donald said. "If

you two want to go back, I'll continue the reconnoiter myself."

"No, I'll stick it out," Suzanne said.

"Me, too," Perry said. The idea of returning to the submersible by himself was worse than forging ahead through the mire.

"Then, let's move out," Donald said. He started off again and the others fell in behind him.

The group slogged ahead in silence. Each step into the unknown blackness ratcheted up their fears and anxiety. The submersible behind them was being swallowed up in the darkness. After another ten minutes they were all as tense as a piano wire about to snap, and that was when the alarm sounded.

The short burst of sound crashed out of the stillness like cannon fire. At first the group froze in their tracks, frantically attempting to determine from which direction the alarm had come. But with the multiple echoes it was impossible to tell. In the next instant they were all slogging their way back toward the submersible.

It was flight in full panic; a mad dash for supposed safety. Unfortunately, the mud did not cooperate. All three tripped almost immediately and fell headfirst into the odious ooze. Regaining their feet, they tried to run again, with the same result.

Without a word to establish consensus, they resigned themselves to a slower gait. After a few minutes, their lack of significant headway made the futility of their flight apparent. Since there had been no surge of water refilling the cavern, all three stopped within steps of each other, their chests heaving.

The multiple echoes from the horrendous alarm died out and in their wake the preternatural stillness returned.

Once again it settled back over the inky darkness like the smothering blanket in Perry's nightmare.

Suzanne raised her hands. The muck, which she knew was a combination of planktonic carcasses and feces of innumerable worms, dripped from her fingers. She wanted desperately to wipe her eyes, but she didn't dare. Donald, who was slightly ahead, turned to face Suzanne and Perry. Mud was streaked across the glass of his flashlight, reducing its effect so that he was lost in shadow to the others. They could just make out the whites of his eyes.

"What in God's name was that alarm?" Suzanne managed. She spit some grainy debris from her mouth. She didn't want to think of what it might have been.

"I was afraid it meant the water was returning," Perry admitted.

"Regardless of what its actual meaning is," Donald said, "for us it has an overarching significance."

"What are you talking about?" Perry questioned.

"I know what he means," Suzanne said. "He means that this is no natural geological formation."

"Exactly!" Donald said. "It's got to be a remnant of the Cold War. And since I had top-secret clearance in the United States submarine service, I can tell you it's not our installation. It has to be Russian!"

"You mean like some kind of secret base?" Perry asked. He glanced around the black void, now more awestruck than frightened.

"That's the only thing I can imagine," Donald said. "Some kind of nuclear submarine facility."

"I suppose it's possible," Suzanne said. "And if it is, our future is suddenly significantly brighter."

"Maybe yes, maybe no," Donald said. "First, it's going to make a difference only if somebody is still manning the facility. If there is, then our next worry has to be how much they want to keep it a secret."

"I hadn't thought of that," Suzanne admitted.

"But the Cold War is over," Perry said. "Surely we don't have to worry about that old cloak-and-dagger stuff."

"There are people in the Russian military who feel differently," Donald said. "I know because I have met them."

"So what do you think we should do at this point?" Suzanne asked.

"I think that question has just been answered for us," Donald said. He raised his free hand and pointed over the shoulders of the others. "Look over there, in the direction we were going before the alarm sounded!"

Suzanne and Perry spun around. About a quarter of a mile away a single door was slowly opening inward into the blackness. Bright artificial light spilled from the room beyond into the dark cavern, forming a line of reflection that extended to their feet. The trio was too far away to see any interior details, but they could tell the light was intense.

"So much for the question whether the facility is manned or not," Donald said. "Obviously, we are not alone. Now the question becomes how happy they are to see us."

"Do you think we should walk over there?" Perry asked.

"We don't have much choice," Donald said. "We'll have to go at some point."

"Why didn't they just come in here and meet us in person?" Suzanne asked.

"A good question," Donald said. "Maybe it has something to do with the welcome they are planning for us."

"I'm getting scared again," Suzanne said. "This is very bizarre."

"I've never stopped being scared," Perry admitted.

"Let's go meet our captors," Donald said. "And let's hope they don't consider us spies—and that they are familiar with the terms of the Geneva Convention."

Straightening himself, Donald started forward, seemingly oblivious to the mud sucking at his feet. He passed his two companions, who had to admire his courage and leadership.

Perry and Suzanne hesitated for a moment before falling in behind the retired naval commander. Neither spoke as they resignedly trudged in his footsteps toward the beckoning door. They had no idea whether it would provide deliverance or further trials, but as Donald had said, they did not have any choice.

CHAPTER SEVEN

It was slow going. At one point, Perry slipped and fell back into the mire. He was covered with the ooze.

"The first thing I'm going to do is demand a shower," Perry sputtered trying to lighten the mood. He was not successful. No one responded.

As they approached the open door, they hoped that their misgivings would be allayed. But no welcoming figures appeared at the threshold, and the light spilling out into the darkness was so bright they were unable to see inside. It was even difficult to look at the opening without shielding their eyes.

When they got close enough, they could appreciate that the door was almost two feet thick with a ring of huge throw bolts countersunk into its periphery. It looked like a door to a vault. The edges of the massive portal were angled in. It was obviously constructed to withstand the enormous pressure of seawater flooding the cavern.

At about twenty-five feet from the wall Suzanne and

Perry stopped. They were reluctant to proceed without a clearer idea of what they were getting into. They studied the door for clues. From what they could tell, it appeared as if the walls, floor, and ceiling within were constructed of stainless steel that gleamed like mirrors.

Donald had continued ahead on his own, and although he did not step over the threshold, he leaned in. With his forearm acting as a shield against the reflected light, he surveyed the room.

"Well?" Suzanne called. "What do you see?"

"It's a large, square room made out of metal," Donald yelled back over his shoulder. "There's a couple of huge shiny balls in it but nothing else. There also doesn't appear to be any door except this entrance. And I can't tell where the light is coming from."

"Any sign of people?" Perry asked.

"That's a negative," Donald said. "Hey, I think the balls are made of glass. And they must be four to five feet in diameter. Come and take a look!"

Perry glanced at Suzanne. He shrugged. "Why put off the inevitable?"

Suzanne was gripping her arms. She shuddered. "I was hoping by the time we got over here I'd have a better feeling about all this, but I don't. This can't be a submarine base. We're talking about an engineering feat that would make building the Great Pyramid seem like a walk in the park."

"Then what do you think it is?" Perry questioned.

Suzanne turned to look back toward the submersible. The light from the open door was illuminating it despite the distance. Beyond it was blackness. "I truly have no clue."

When Donald saw that Suzanne and Perry were looking back at the submersible, he went ahead and stepped over the threshold into the room. Immediately he put his hands out to balance himself to keep from falling. A combination of the wet mud on his shoes and the polished metal made the floor as slippery as ice.

Once he had his equilibrium Donald again scanned the room. Now that his eyes had partially adjusted he could see much better, including hundreds of reflections of himself in all directions. The walls, floor, and ceiling were seamless. The only apparent door was the one he'd entered through. He specifically searched for a source of the dazzling light but mysteriously could not find any. When his line of sight took in the huge glass balls, he did a double take. He was now able to appreciate that the glass was not entirely opaque. They were clear enough to just make out what was inside.

"Suzanne, Perry!" Donald yelled. "There are a couple of people in here after all. But they're sealed inside glass spheres. Get in here!"

A moment later Suzanne and Perry appeared at the door.

"Careful about the floor!" Donald warned. "It's as slick as ice."

Sliding their feet in short movements as if skating without skates, Suzanne and Perry staggered over to Donald's side, eager for a better look at the glass spheres.

"My word!" Suzanne exclaimed. "They're floating around in some kind of fluid."

"Do you recognize them?" Donald asked.

"Should I?" Suzanne responded.

"I think I do," Donald said. "I think it's two of our divers."

Suzanne stared at Donald in disbelief. Then, to get a better look, she cupped her hands around her eyes and leaned against one of the spheres, the surface so opalescent it reflected the room's bright illumination.

"I think you're right," Suzanne said. "I can just make out the *Benthic Explorer* logo on the neoprene suit and the side of the helmet."

Perry mimicked Suzanne by shielding his eyes with his hands and pressing them against the same sphere Suzanne was gazing into. Donald did likewise from another angle.

"He's breathing!" Perry said. "He must be alive."

"There's something like an umbilical cord coming from some kind of device pressed up against his abdomen," Suzanne said. "Can anybody see where it goes?"

"It goes under him," Donald said. "To the base of the container."

Suzanne moved away enough to allow her to bend down. The sphere had a flat area on which it sat. She did not see any penetrations, and if there were any they would have come directly through the floor.

"This is as astounding as the cavern," Suzanne said while regaining her feet. She reached out and touched the sphere with the tip of her index finger. The material looked like glass but she was not sure what it was.

The others straightened up.

"How on earth did they get here?" Perry asked.

"A lot of questions," Donald said, "and very few answers."

"Are you still thinking this is some kind of military installation?" Suzanne asked Donald.

"What else could it be?" Donald demanded defensively.

"If these divers are alive in these spheres, I can't even guess what the technology is," Suzanne said. "They look like a couple of giant embryos. Not that I can explain the cavern either. Even this room is a step beyond."

"Beyond what?" Donald asked.

"The door!" Perry cried.

All eyes shot to the entrance. The massive door was silently closing.

Frantically the three tried to rush back to it to keep it from sealing them in, but the slippery floor hindered their progress. By the time they arrived the door was almost closed. Collectively they leaned against it to force it back open, but with its mass and the slick floor it was a useless endeavor. With a resounding thud the door closed. Then they heard the muffled mechanical sound of the numerous throw bolts sliding into place.

With renewed sense of terror the three moved away from the door.

"Somebody is controlling all this," Suzanne said gravely. Her worried eyes swept around the seamless room. "And now we are trapped."

"It's got to be Russians," Donald said.

"Enough about the Russians!" Suzanne shouted. "You were in the military too long. You see everything in terms of yesterday's hostilities. This isn't about Russians."

"How do you know?" Donald yelled back. "And don't you dare denigrate my service to my country."

"Oh, please!" Suzanne intoned. "I'm not disparaging your naval service. But look around, Donald! This isn't anything earthly. Look at the light, for goodness' sake." Suzanne held out her hand. "There's no light source, but the illumination is totally even. And there's no shadow."

Perry held out his hands and tried to form shadows, but it was impossible. Donald watched but did not try it himself.

"It's a uniform photon flux that must be penetrating these walls somehow," Suzanne said. "And if I had to guess I'd say there was a significant ultraviolet component."

"How can you tell?" Perry said.

"I can't," Suzanne admitted. "Not for sure since the human eye doesn't pick up ultraviolet, but to my mind there's a definite distortion of the blue of our coveralls and the maroon of your jogging suit."

Perry looked down at his clothing. To him the color was the same as it always had been.

"The spheres!" Donald yelled.

All eyes shifted to the glass balls. Their opalescence had suddenly and dramatically increased so that they were glowing. A moment later there was a cracking sound, and beginning at both apices the spheres opened like enormous flowers losing their petals. With a gush of fluid the divers spilled out onto the floor.

Donald was the first to overcome his shock. As quickly as he could, he rushed to Richard's side. Realizing the unconscious diver was trying to breathe, Donald pulled off the man's helmet and tossed it aside. Richard coughed violently.

Perry rushed to Michael. While he removed Michael's helmet he could hear Richard's coughing. Michael, however, was not even breathing. Calling upon his CPR training, Perry knew what to do. First he hauled Michael from the debris of the collapsed sphere, pulling his still attached umbilical with him. After a quick check to make sure the diver's mouth was clear, he pinched his nostrils closed, took a breath, and gave Michael a lungful of air. Turning his head to the side, Perry took another breath. He was about to repeat the cycle when he noticed that Michael's eyes were open.

"What the hell are you doing, man!" Michael questioned. He pushed Perry's face away, which was inches from his own.

"I was doing mouth-to-mouth," Perry said. He got to his feet. "I didn't think you were breathing."

"I'm breathing!" Michael insisted. He made a face of disgust and wiped his mouth with the back of his hand. "Believe me, I'm breathing."

Richard's coughing jag came to an abrupt end, and he blinked away the tears it had brought on. His first concern was Michael. When he saw that his buddy was alive and well, he glanced around the room before looking up at the others.

"What's going on?" he asked. "What happened?"

"That's the million-dollar question," Perry answered.

"Where the hell are we?" Richard asked. His eyes took a second quick dash around the room. A perplexed expression clouded his face.

"An equally interesting question," Perry said.

"Were you looking for us on your dive?" Donald asked Richard.

For a moment Richard merely looked confused. Then Donald's question helped restore his memory. "Oh, my god!" he cried. "We were on a nearly thousand-foot sat dive! We didn't decompress!" Richard struggled to his feet. His legs were wobbly, especially on the slippery floor. "Michael, we've got to get into the DDC!"

"Take it easy!" Donald said. He grabbed Richard around the upper arm to calm him and keep him from falling. "There's no DDC here. Besides, you're all right. Obviously you don't have the bends."

Richard's confusion deepened. He extended his legs and his arms to check his joints. Blinking repeatedly, he looked around the room again, and while doing so no-

ticed the umbilical connecting him to the base of the
collapsed sphere. "What the hell is this?" he demanded.
He grasped the composite group of hoses and wires and
immediately let go. His lips curled in revulsion. "Jeez,
it feels soft, like I'm holding someone's intestines."

"It has to be some kind of life support," Suzanne
said, speaking up for the first time since the divers had
emerged from their shells. "Considering the shape you're
in without decompressing, I guess it had something to
do with that as well."

Richard gingerly touched the device attached to his
stomach. It was the size and shape of the head of a toilet plunger. As soon as he touched it, it detached. Catching it in his hand, he looked at its business end. To his
horror a series of wormlike appendages protruded from
it, their wriggling heads soaked in blood—his blood.

"Ah!" Richard cried. He dropped the device, which
quickly retracted into the base of the flattened sphere like
a disappearing vacuum cleaner cord. In a panic Richard
unzipped the front of his neoprene suit down to his pubis.
When he looked at his stomach he cried out again. There
were six puncture wounds in a circular pattern around his
navel.

After watching Richard, Michael struggled to his feet
and hesitantly looked down at his own stomach. He was
dismayed to see a similar apparatus. With an expression
mirroring Richard's, he reluctantly touched it with his
index finger. To his relief it immediately detached and
retracted. Opening his dive suit he found the same peculiar pattern of oozing stab wounds around his um-
bilicus.

"Holy crap!" Michael voiced. "It looks like we were
stabbed a bunch of times with an ice pick." He shivered. "I can't stand blood."

Richard zipped his suit back up and then tried to take a few steps on shaky legs. He reached out and supported himself against the wall. "Man, I feel like I've been drugged."

"I feel like I was run over with a goddamn truck," Michael said.

"Where's Mazzola?" Richard asked.

"We wouldn't have any idea," Donald said. "What happened during your dive?"

Richard scratched the back of his head. At first all he could remember was getting into the DDC for the compression, but then, with Michael's participation, they both were able to remember sketchy details of the descent in the bell and entering the water.

"Is that it?" Donald asked. "Nothing after you left the bell?"

Richard nodded. Michael did the same.

"How come you guys all look like you've been in a pigpen?" Richard asked. He didn't wait for an answer. Instead, he looked more closely at the walls. "What is this, some kind of hospital or something?"

"It's no hospital," Donald said. "We can't tell you much else other than how we got here, but that includes how we got dirty."

"That's a start," Richard said. "Fire away!"

Donald explained while the two divers slouched against the wall. It was a hard story to swallow, and their eyes narrowed in disbelief.

"Oh, come on!" Richard scoffed. "What is this? Some kind of a put-on?" He regarded the trio with suspicion. This had to be a prank. Michael nodded in agreement.

"This is no put-on," Donald assured him.

"Just look around this room," Suzanne said.

"Listen!" Donald said, trying to be patient. "Can't either of you remember anything about how you got here? Didn't you see anybody?"

Richard shook his head. With his foot he pushed around the deflated segments of the sphere. The material was now limp instead of rigid and brittle. "Are you serious about us being inside this stuff? You said it looked like glass. It sure doesn't now."

"It did just a short time ago," Suzanne assured him.

"What we think is that this is a Russian submarine base," Donald continued.

"Correction!" Suzanne interrupted. "That's what you think."

"Russians?" Richard echoed. "No shit!" He visibly straightened up. He looked around the room with renewed interest, as did Michael. Both put their hands against the highly polished walls. Richard rapped on the glossy surface with his knuckle. "What is this stuff anyway, titanium?"

Suzanne started to answer but was interrupted by a hissing noise. Everyone looked back to the locations where the spheres had stood. A vapor billowed out of the exposed holes. Quickly an acrid smell pervaded the sealed chamber, and everyone's eyes began to tear.

"We're being gassed!" Suzanne cried before she was overcome by violent coughs.

The group shrank back in terror, pressing themselves against the cold metal walls in a vain attempt to get away from the gas. But before long everyone was coughing and squeezing their eyes shut against the burning sensation.

"Get on the floor!" Donald cried.

Everyone except Perry flattened themselves on the floor while trying ineffectually to cover their mouths and noses with their hands. Perry stumbled back to the door to the cavern and began pounding on it, while screaming for it to be opened.

The door did not budge, but Perry had the presence of mind to notice something despite his panic and physical torment. He was not blacking out nor was he even feeling the slightest bit dizzy. The gas seemed not to have the lethal effect he most feared.

With strength of will Perry held his coughing in check and managed to crack his eyes for an instant despite the discomfort. The room was thick with the foglike vapor. Perry couldn't see far, but he noticed that his arms were suddenly bare.

Curious as to what could have happened to the sleeves of his jogging suit, Perry squinted. He saw that his sleeves had fallen into tatters. They were hanging in shreds as if he'd dipped his arms into acid.

Aware that his whole body now felt cool, Perry patted his hands along his chest. His jogging suit—indeed, all his clothes—were suffering the same fate as his sleeves. The fabric of the clothing itself was progressively losing its structural integrity.

Perry had had nightmares in the past when he was under stress that he was naked in public. Suddenly it was coming to pass as he felt his clothes peel from his body in strips. He clutched at them and felt them disintegrate in his hands.

"It's our clothes!" Perry shouted to the others. "The gas is dissolving our clothes!"

At first fear kept everyone else from responding. Perry yelled his message again and stumbled forward in the fog, almost tripping over Donald. "The gas is dissolving our clothes," he repeated. "And I don't feel any mental effect whatsoever."

Donald pushed himself up to a sitting position. His

coveralls experienced the same fate as Perry's jogging suit. Quickly he patted himself to verify that he was indeed becoming naked. But he couldn't open his eyes; the gas stung too much. Even without the visual confirmation, he was convinced. He called out to the others: "Perry's right!"

Suzanne, like Perry, was able to get her eyes open intermittently. She saw that it was true about her clothes. Her coveralls literally fell apart. She also noticed that there was no effect on her mental state despite the discomfort she felt in her throat and chest. Relieved, she got to her feet.

Richard and Michael pushed themselves up into sitting positions. With the drugged feeling they were still experiencing, they could not tell if the gas was affecting their consciousness, but both were coughing heavily. For them, the respiratory effect was more difficult than it was for the others.

"My dive suit's fine," Richard managed between coughs. But then he made the mistake of running his hand over his shoulder. When he did, the neoprene completely depolymerized. At his touch it fell into tiny spheres.

Through blinks, Michael had glimpsed the fate of Richard's suit. He glanced intermittently at his own suit, reluctant to touch it or even move, but Richard reached out and gave his shoulder a sharp slap. The effect was instantaneous. One minute the dive suit looked normal, the next it was running off Michael like so many drops of water.

Suddenly, an alarm sounded and a red light on the wall opposite the door to the cavern began to flash— moments before, that same wall had appeared seamless.

Through the caustic vapor, the five began to discern the outline of an open doorway below the light.

The alarm ceased after a few minutes but the light continued to blink. Then they noticed the sound of a high-pitched whistle. Air was being forced through a narrow vent.

Perry advanced slowly toward the flashing light. When he reached the wall, he saw that the outline of the door was more distinct. He felt around its edges. When he did he could feel a steady current of air pushing in. That explained the whistling. He tested with his foot to make sure the floor was level across the threshold. Then he stepped through.

Perry was immediately relieved. The curtain of fast-moving air kept the acrid gas from the hallway he'd entered. The walls, floor, and ceiling were constructed of the same polished metal as the gas-filled room, but the level of illumination was significantly less. Twenty feet ahead Perry could see that the corridor opened up into another chamber.

Perry poked his head back through the air curtain.

"There's another room," he shouted. "And it's clear. Quick!"

The other four struggled to their feet and moved toward the blinking light. Suzanne had to guide Donald; he couldn't stand to open his eyes. In a minute, the entire party made it into the new room.

The gas wore off swiftly. They were so relieved that they weren't troubled by the complete disintegration of their clothes. All five were stark naked, but other concerns were more pressing. Ahead the second room beckoned.

"Let's move," Donald said. He gestured for Perry to precede them since he was already in the lead.

Perry flattened himself against the wall and motioned for Donald to pass. "I think you should be first. You're still the captain of the ship."

Donald nodded and pushed past. Perry fell in behind him followed by Suzanne. The two divers brought up the rear.

"It's pretty obvious what's going on now," Donald said.

"I'm glad it's obvious to you," Perry said.

"What do you mean?" Suzanne asked.

"We're being prepared for interrogation," Donald said. "It's a recognized technique to strip away a person's sense of identity as a way to break down resistance. Our clothes are certainly part of our identity."

"I don't have any resistance," Perry said. "I'll tell whoever it is whatever they want to know."

"Donald, does that mean you know what that gas was?" Suzanne asked.

"That's a negative," Donald said.

Donald halted at the second room's threshold and peered in. It was considerably smaller than the first chamber although it, too, was lined with the same mysterious, metallic material. From where he was standing, he could make out a glass-doored exit as well as a white hall begin with what appeared to be framed pictures on the walls. Within the chamber he noticed that the floor sloped toward the center, where there was a grate, and the ceiling peaked to a central point with a second grate.

"Well?" Suzanne questioned. From where she was she couldn't see what lay ahead.

"It looks encouraging," Donald said. "There's a relatively normal looking corridor beyond a glass door."

"Then let's move," Richard called impatiently from behind Suzanne.

With both hands on the doorjamb for support, Donald moved first one foot onto the sloped floor and then brought the other to it. As he'd anticipated he began to slide once he let go. He slid for about three feet with his hands flailing to keep from falling. At that point the floor angled out to be almost level. He turned and warned the others.

Everyone was careful except Michael. Having grown up in Chelsea, Massachusetts, where he'd played hockey since age five, he wasn't concerned about the slick floor. But its angle took him by surprise. His feet went out from under him on his first step, and he careened into the others like a bowling ball. In a flash the entire group was a pile of entwined naked limbs.

"For chrissake!" Donald snapped. He extricated himself and helped Suzanne to her feet. The others struggled up by themselves. Michael was hardly remorseful. Now that his eyes were open, he was much more interested in appreciating Suzanne's body. Richard swore and cuffed Michael on the top of his head. Michael shoved Richard in return, effectively sending them both to the ground again.

"Knock it off!" Donald shouted. Being careful not to fall, he separated the two divers. Richard and Michael obeyed, but continued to glare at each other.

"My god!" Suzanne voiced. "Look!" She pointed back at the doorway they'd just come through. Everyone gaped in astonishment. The doorway was silently sealing over, as if the metal wall were fusing together. Within moments the opening was gone without a trace. The wall was seamless.

"If I'd not seen that with my own eyes, I'd never believe it," Perry said. "It's supernatural, like a movie special effect."

"I can't begin to understand the technology," Suzanne said. "I think it lets the Russians off the hook."

A deep gurgling sound then issued from the central grate. All eyes turned in its direction.

"Oh no!" Suzanne said. "What's coming now?"

Before anyone could respond, a clear fluid that looked like water bubbled up through the central floor grate. The group shrank back, then scrambled toward the glass door. The angle and slippery surface of the floor forced them to their hands and knees. The first to the door began to bang on the glass, desperate for a way to open it. Behind them the inrushing water had become a geyser; the water level was rising rapidly.

Within minutes they were waist-deep in water. Moments later they were all treading water watching with horror as the ceiling approached. Even if they could keep treading indefinitely, there soon would be no room to breathe. Rapidly the group was forced together while struggling for the last remnants of air in the very peak of the ceiling. As the strongest swimmers, Richard and Michael were at the center directly below the grate and, in a desperate attempt to find more air, they stuck their fingers through the holes and tried to pull the grate from its housing.

But their efforts were fruitless. The grate would not budge, and the water level continued to rise until the room was filled to the ceiling. No sooner had everyone gone under, than the room began to drain, and at an extraordinary rate. Within seconds there was headroom again; within minutes Donald and Richard, the tallest of the five, felt their feet brush the floor.

Soon there was a loud, rude sucking noise as the last of the water disappeared down the drain, and the group was left in a wet, naked heap in the central basin of the concave floor. For some time no one moved. A combination of utter terror, panic-driven exertion, and having inadvertently swallowed sizable gulps of the fluid left them physically and emotionally exhausted.

Donald finally pushed himself up to a sitting position. He felt light-headed. He had an odd feeling that more time had passed than he could account for. It occurred to him that they might have been drugged by the water that had filled the room. He closed his eyes for a moment and rubbed his temples. When he reopened his eyes he looked at the others. They all appeared to be sleeping. He looked toward the glass door when his gaze shot back to Suzanne.

"Good Lord!" Donald muttered. He couldn't believe his eyes. Suzanne was bald! Donald ran a hand over the top of his head, but he'd kept it shaved for several years. He felt for his mustache. It was gone! Raising his forearm he saw that, too, was totally devoid of hair. He glanced down at his chest; there wasn't a hair there.

Donald shook Perry, then nudged Suzanne. When both of them were awake enough to understand what he was saying, he filled them in.

"Oh, no!" Perry cried. He sat bolt upright. Using both hands he reached up and gingerly touched his scalp. There was no hair, only smooth skin. He pulled his hands away as if he'd touched something hot. He was horrified.

Suzanne was more curious than dismayed. Something had rendered them completely hairless. How had it happened—and why?

"What's happening?" Richard asked. His words were slurred. He sat up, then had to steady himself. "Ooo . . . I feel like I tied one on."

"I'm a bit dizzy myself," Perry admitted. "Maybe

there was something in the water. I know I swallowed some."

"I think we were drugged," Donald said.

"We all swallowed a lot of the water," Richard said. "It's hard not to in that kind of ordeal. That was worse than submarine escape training."

"I think I know what is going on," Suzanne said.

"Yeah, me, too," Perry said. "We're being tortured and humiliated."

"All techniques of interrogation," Donald added.

"I don't think it has anything to do with interrogation," Suzanne said. "The strange intense light, the acrid gas, and now the depilation suggests something else."

"What's depilation?" Richard asked.

"It's what happened to your head," Perry said.

Richard blinked. He stared at Perry, then touched the top of his head. "My god, I'm bald." He looked over at Michael, who was still slumbering. Then he reached over and gave him a shove. "Hey, you hairless wonder. Wake up!"

Michael had trouble opening his eyes.

"I think we're being decontaminated," Suzanne said. "I think that's what all this is about: getting rid of microorganisms like bacteria and viruses. We've effectively been sterilized."

No one spoke. Perry nodded as he considered what Suzanne had said. He thought it was possible.

"I still think all this is to prepare us for interrogation," Donald said. "Sterilizing us doesn't make sense to me. I don't know if it is Russians who are behind this or not, but somebody wants something from us."

"Maybe we're going to know pretty soon," Perry said. He nodded toward the glass door, which was now ajar. "I think the next stage is ready."

Donald unstably struggled to his feet. "There was definitely some kind of drug in the water," he said. He waited until a fresh episode of dizziness passed, then headed toward the open door. Where the slippery floor angled up he had to go on all fours. Once he reached the doorway, he stood up and looked down a white, fifty-foot corridor.

"I feel drugged but I also feel strangely hungry," Suzanne said.

"I was just thinking the same thing," Perry admitted.

"Listen, you guys," Donald called. "Things are looking up. There're living quarters down at the end of this hallway. Let's mobilize!"

Suzanne and Perry got their feet under them and stood up, battling the same fleeting dizziness Donald had experienced.

"I guess living quarters means beds," Suzanne said. "And that sounds good to me. Besides, I want out of this room in case that water comes back."

"My feelings exactly," Perry said.

Richard and Michael had fallen back asleep. Suzanne gave them both a poke but neither stirred. Perry lent a hand.

"Whatever was in that water affected them more than us," Suzanne said as she shook Richard to get him to open his eyes.

"They felt drugged from being in the spheres, even before the dousing," Perry said. He pulled Michael, who groaned to be let alone, up to a sitting position.

"Let's move it!" Donald called. "I don't want this door to close before you're all out of here."

Despite their groggy state, the warning about the door penetrated Richard and Michael's stupor, and they got to their feet. As they moved their mental state rapidly improved. By the time the group joined Donald, the divers were even talking.

"This isn't half bad," Richard said as he inspected the corridor with lidded eyes. Instead of mirrorlike metal, the walls and ceiling were a high-gloss white laminate. Framed, three-dimensional pictures lined the walls. The floor was covered with a tight-weave white carpet.

"These pictures are something else," Michael commented. "They're so realistic. It looks like I can see into them for twenty miles."

"They're holographs," Suzanne said. "But I've never seen a holograph with such vivid, natural color. They are startling, especially in this otherwise white environment."

"They all look like scenes from ancient Greece," Perry said. "Whoever our tormentors are, at least they're civilized."

"Let's go, men!" Donald called. He was standing impatiently just over the next threshold. "We've got some tactical decisions to make."

"Tactical decisions," Perry mimicked in a whisper to Suzanne. "Doesn't he ever relax this military posturing?"

"Not often," Suzanne admitted.

The group walked the length of the hallway and paused, taken aback by the scene in front of them. After the series of stark, industrial chambers, they were unprepared for the room's sumptuousness. The decor was futuristic, with lots of mirrors and white marble, yet it had a calm, cool, inviting ambiance. A dozen, canopied, couchlike beds with white cashmere blankets lined both walls. Five of the beds were invitingly turned down with folded clean clothes lying atop each pillow. In the background, soft instrumental music completed the mood.

Down the center of the room stretched a large, low

table with chaiselike, deeply cushioned chairs. The table was laid for a meal with covered servers and pitchers of iced drinks. The dishes were white, the tablecloth was white, and the flatware was gold.

"If this is heaven, I'm not ready," Perry said when he had recovered enough to speak.

"I don't think chow smells this good in heaven," Richard said. "And I just realized I'm more hungry than tired." He started forward with Michael at his heels.

"Hold up!" Donald said. "I'm not sure we should eat anything. The food's probably drugged or even worse."

"You really think so?" Richard said with obvious disappointment. He wavered, looking back and forth between Donald and the laden table.

"And those mirrors," Donald said, pointing to the huge sheets that formed the far end of the room. "I'd assume they are two-way, which would mean we're being watched."

"Who the hell cares, if they treat us like this," Michael said. "My vote is we eat."

Suzanne's eyes fell on the folded garments on each bed. She had not noticed them sooner because they were white like most everything else and blended perfectly with the white linen. She went over to the nearest bed. She lifted the garments and shook them out. There were two simple pieces: a long-sleeved tunic that opened at the front and a pair of boxer shorts. Both were made of a silky white satin, and both were curiously seamless.

"My word! Pajamas!" Suzanne commented. "Now this is downright thoughtful." Without a moment's hesitation, Suzanne pulled on the shorts. The tunic was generously proportioned and came to knee length, covering the boxers. It tied with a gold braided rope. Along the sides were several pockets.

Suzanne's dressing reawakened everyone's self-consciousness. The four men grabbed clothing sets from the beds and donned them.

Michael eyed himself in the mirrors at the end of the room. "Not much to these things," he said. "But they're comfortable."

Richard laughed at him. "You look like a faggot."

"As if you don't, asshole," Michael shot back hotly.

"That's enough!" Donald barked. "There's to be no fighting among ourselves. Save it for whoever it is we'll be facing. Which brings me to the issue of setting up watches to stand guard."

"What the hell are you talking about?" Richard asked. "This isn't some kind of military exercise. I'm going to eat and then I'm racking out. I'm not standing any watch."

"We're all tired," Donald said. "But there is a door to consider that we don't have any control over."

All eyes swung around to gaze at the door at the end of the room opposite the mirrors. It was white like everything else and was without a knob, latch, or hinges.

"We have to stay vigilant," Donald added. "I don't want these Russians or whoever these people are sneaking in here and doing whatever they want to us."

"Judging by the pains they have taken with these accommodations, I don't think your paranoia is justified," Suzanne said. "And I thought we decided we're not dealing with Russians here."

"Well, you people argue about all that," Richard said. He walked over to the table and lifted the cover of one of the chafing dishes. The savory aroma filled the room.

"What is it?" Michael asked. He leaned over to look.

"I don't have a clue," Richard said. He lifted the spoon. The steaming food was cream colored and had a pasty consistency, like hot cereal's. "It looks like Cream of Wheat, and it smells mighty good." He brought the spoon to his mouth and tasted it. "Well, I'll be damned! How'd they know? It tastes like my favorite food: steak."

Michael took a taste. "Steak? What, are you crazy? It tastes like sweet potatoes."

"Get outta here!" Richard complained. "You and your sweet potatoes." He sat down on one of the chaises and helped himself to a sizable ladle of the food. "You're always talking about sweet potatoes."

Michael sat opposite and took a portion for himself. "Hey, I'm sorry," he said sarcastically. "I happen to like sweet potatoes."

Suzanne and Perry stepped to the table, their curiosity piqued by this exchange. They were experiencing almost irresistible hunger. Suzanne was the next to try the food.

"That's incredible," she remarked. "It tastes like mango."

"That's hard to believe," Perry said. "Because to me it tastes exactly like fresh corn right off the cob."

Suzanne took another taste. "To me it's mango, without a doubt. Maybe there's some way it tricks our brains to interpret the taste according to our own predilections."

Even Donald was intrigued. He came over to the table and tried a minute amount. He shook his head in disbelief. "It tastes like biscuits to me: fresh buttermilk biscuits." He took one of the chairs. "I guess I'm as hungry as everybody else."

Everyone helped themselves to varying amounts of the curious food. They found it difficult to resist going back for seconds. They also discovered that the iced drink had a similar variable effect. It tasted different to each person, according to his or her preference.

As soon as the group's ravenous hunger had been slaked, the exhaustion and sleepiness that they'd experienced earlier returned, and with a vengeance. Fighting against sagging eyelids they pushed back from the table and sought their separate beds. No sooner had they drawn up the covers than everyone but Donald fell into a deep, hibernating sleep. Donald struggled vainly in hopes of maintaining a vigil, but it was impossible. Within minutes he, too, was slumbering.

The moment Donald's eyes closed, tiny red lights appeared on the canopy of each bed. At the same time, a glow emanated from the canopy and enveloped the sleeping individual below in a violet halo.

CHAPTER EIGHT

The tiny red lights above the beds in the living quarters switched momentarily to green and the violet glow faded. A moment later the green lights blinked off.

Perry was the first to wake up. It was not a gradual transition but rather a sudden change from deep sleep to full consciousness. For a few seconds he stared at the canopy above him, attempting to put the strange structure in context and orient himself. But he couldn't. He'd awakened to nothing like what he expected: namely, the blank ceiling of the supposed V.I.P. suite on the *Benthic Explorer*.

Perry was confused, but as soon as he turned his head, it all came back to him. It hadn't been a dream. The *Oceanus*'s horrifying plunge to unfathomable depths had been a reality.

There was a simple, black clothes tree standing within reach of his bed. A set of white satin drawers and tunic similar to those he'd put on were hanging on it. Perry realized he felt quite naked under the coverlet. He lifted the edge of the cashmere blanket and looked at himself. Not only was he naked, he detected the same peculiar ring of puncture wounds around his navel as he'd seen on Richard and Michael when they'd emerged from the spheres.

Perry let out a low-pitched cry, then leaped from the bed to examine his wounds more carefully. He spread the soft skin of his abdomen. The puncture wounds were not deep and they weren't painful, much to Perry's relief. Most important of all, they seemed healed.

As Perry absorbed this discovery, he had another shock. His legs and groin were hairy again! He inspected his forearm and discovered that the hair had returned there, too. He put a hand to his scalp, and smiled.

Perry grabbed the clothes from the ebony rack and pulled them on as he transversed the length of the room.

His reflection in the mirror practically made him swoon. His scalp was covered with a full head of hair. It was only about an inch long, but it was as thick and dark as it had been when he was in junior high school. He felt like he'd discovered the fountain of youth.

Perry heard the others stirring. He turned in time to see Donald and Suzanne slipping back into their clothes. Richard and Michael were sitting on the edges of their beds, gawking at the surroundings. Their clothes were neatly piled in their laps.

"Just as I thought," Donald said to no one in particular. "I knew those bastards would be in here screwing around with us when we were sleeping. That's why I wanted to set up watches."

"It isn't all bad," Perry said as he sauntered over. "We've got hair! Can you imagine? Mine is thicker than it was when I lost it."

"I noticed my hair," Suzanne said with less enthusiasm.

"Aren't you thrilled?" Perry said.

"I preferred the length I had yesterday," Suzanne said. "Or actually the length I had three days ago."

"What do you mean, three days ago?" Perry questioned.

"Yesterday was July twenty-first," Suzanne said. "Right?"

"I guess," Perry said. He wasn't sure thanks to the overnight flight to the Azores.

"Well, my watch, which someone took off my wrist but was nice enough to leave behind, says it's now the twenty-fourth."

Suzanne's watch had been the only one to last through the gassing. Its gold bracelet band remained undissolved.

"Maybe whoever removed it advanced the date," Perry suggested. The idea of being asleep for three days was disturbing, to say the least.

"It's possible," Suzanne said. "But I doubt it. I mean, to grow as much hair as we have, it would have taken more than three days. Maybe we've been asleep for a month and three days."

Perry shivered. "A month?" he gulped. "I can't imagine. Besides, the hair growth we've had has to have come from some kind of amazing treatment. My hair's back to the way it was when I was fourteen. I'll tell you something: as a businessman, I'd kill to find out the secret. Can you imagine? What a product."

"They didn't do me any favors," Donald said. "I didn't want hair on my head."

"Did you notice the puncture wounds on your stomachs?" Suzanne asked Perry and Donald.

They both nodded.

"I think that means we were on life support of some kind," Suzanne said. "Maybe the same kind our divers had been on in those spheres."

"That was my thought," Perry said. "I suppose they had to keep us on something if we were out so long."

"Hey, are you guys okay?" Suzanne called over to Richard and Michael, who were finishing dressing.

"I'm all right," Richard said. "Except for the fact that I was wishing this was all a bad dream."

"Drugging us is in violation of the Geneva Convention," Donald growled. "We're civilians! Who knows what these puncture wounds mean. They could have given us anything—AIDS, or truth drugs."

"Actually, I feel really good," Perry admitted. He flexed his arms and stretched his legs. It was as if his body as well as his hair had been rejuvenated.

"Me, too," Michael said. He touched his toes and then ran in place for several strides. "I feel as if I could swim for twenty miles."

"I got my hair back but now my beard's gone," Richard said. "Explain that!"

The other men reflexively stroked their chins. It was true. They had no stubble.

"This is getting more and more interesting," Perry said.

"I'd say it's getting more and more surreal," Suzanne said. She looked closely at Perry's cheeks. Previously he'd had a definite five o'clock shadow. Now his complexion was perfectly clear.

"Hang on, guys!" Richard exclaimed. He pointed at the door on the wall opposite the mirrors. "Looks like we're being let out of the cage."

All eyes turned to see the door silently open. Beyond was another long white corridor with framed holographs.

The light coming from the other end of it was bright and natural.

"That looks like daylight," Suzanne said.

"It can't be daylight," Donald said. "Unless we got moved somehow."

Perry felt a chill go down his spine. Intuitively he knew that everything that had happened so far was a preamble of what was going to happen in the next few minutes. The problem was he had no idea what it was going to be.

Richard walked to the doorway to get a better look. He shielded his eyes against the brightness reflecting off the glossy white walls.

"Can you see anything?" Suzanne asked.

"Not much," Richard admitted. "It opens up at the end and there's a wall opposite. It must be open to the sky. Let's go!"

"Hold up a minute," Suzanne said. Then she looked at Donald. "What do you say? Should we go? Obviously our hosts expect us to."

"I think we should go but as a group," Donald said. "We should stick together as much as we can, but maybe we should pick one person to speak for us if we encounter our captors."

"Fine," Suzanne said. "I nominate Perry."

"Me?" Perry squeaked. He cleared his throat. "Why me? Donald's still the captain."

"True," Suzanne said. "But you are the president of Benthic Marine. Whoever is holding us might appreciate the fact that you speak with some authority, especially about the drilling operation."

"You think the reason we're down here is because of the drilling?"

"It has crossed my mind," Suzanne said.

"Still, Donald's been in the military," Perry whined. "I haven't. What if this *is* a Russian military base?"

"I think it is safe to say it is not a Russian base," Suzanne replied.

"It's not completely out of the question," Donald said. "But I think Perry is a good choice regardless. It will give me a better chance to assess the situation, especially if things get hostile."

"Richard and Michael!" Suzanne called. "Do either of you have an opinion about who speaks for us?"

"I think the prez should be the one," Michael said.

Richard merely nodded. He was impatient to go.

"Then it's decided," Suzanne said. She gestured for Perry to lead them down the corridor.

"Okay!" Perry said with more alacrity than he felt. He tightened the golden braid around his tunic, squared his shoulders, and headed toward the corridor. Richard gave him a supercilious glance as he passed and then fell in behind him. The others followed in single file.

Perry slowed as he approached the end of the hallway. He was even more certain the light streaming in was sunlight since he could feel its radiant warmth. He gauged the space ahead to be an open sky enclosure approximately twenty-feet square.

About six feet away Perry stopped and Richard bumped up against him.

"What's the matter?" Suzanne asked. She pushed past Richard.

Perry didn't answer since he didn't know exactly why he'd stopped. Slowly he leaned forward so that he could see progressively more of the opposite wall. He was looking for the top, but he couldn't yet see it. After a step forward he tried again. This time he could see the top of the wall which he estimated to be about fifteen feet high. Above that he could see feet, ankles, bare calves, and the hems of outfits like the one he had on.

Perry straightened up and turned to the others. "There are people on top of the opposite wall," he whispered. "They're dressed the way we are."

"Really?" Suzanne questioned. She leaned forward to try to see for herself, but she was too far back.

"I can't be positive," Perry said. "But I think they're wearing these same flimsy satin clothes we are." He and everyone else had assumed the flimsy, weird, lingerie-like outfits were prisoners' garb.

"Come on!" Richard said, even more impatient now. "This I gotta see. Let's go!"

"Why would they be dressed like ancient Greeks?" Suzanne asked Donald.

Donald shrugged. "You've got me. Let's just move out and see for ourselves."

Perry led the way. With his hand over his eyes to shield against the glare of a square of bright sky, he looked up. What he saw astounded him to the point that he stopped dead in his tracks and his mouth gaped in wonderment. Suzanne bumped into him and the rest of the group nudged against her all equally dumbfounded.

They were standing in a penlike enclosure. Fifteen feet above was a glass-enclosed loggia ringed by a marble balustrade and supported by fluted columns whose capitals were encrusted with gilded sea creatures. Fronting the enclosure the entire loggia was packed with people pressed against the glass and staring down in unmoving, silent, intense curiosity. As Perry had surmised from his limited earlier view, they were all dressed in the same identical, loose-fitting satin tunics and shorts.

Perry had had no specific mental image of what the people were going to look like, but what he was confronted with hadn't even been part of his imagination which leaned toward expecting fiercer-looking captors. Before he'd caught the glimpse of the satin outfits he'd anticipated uniforms, and he'd expected stern if not openly hostile expressions. Instead he found himself staring at the most beautiful collection of people he'd ever seen, whose faces reflected an almost divine serenity. Although the ages varied from tiny children to vigorous elders, the vast majority were in their early to midtwenties. Everyone radiated good health with lithe bodies, sparkling eyes, lustrous hair, and teeth so white they made Perry think of his own as being yellow by comparison.

"I don't believe this!" Richard gushed as he took in the spectacle.

"Who are these people?" Suzanne asked, her voice an awed whisper.

"I've never seen such a gorgeous group of people," Perry managed. "Every one of them. There's not even an average-looking one in the bunch."

"I feel like we're rats in a huge experiment," Donald said under his breath. "Look at them gawk at us! And remember, appearances can be deceptive! Keep in mind these people have been toying with us for their own amusement. All this show might be some kind of trap."

"But they're stunningly beautiful," Suzanne commented as she slowly turned to take in more, "particularly the children and even the aged. How could this be a trap? I can tell you one thing for sure, seeing these people certainly puts to bed for certain the idea of this being a secret Russian submarine base."

"Well, they're not American either," Perry said. "There's not one overweight person in the entire crowd."

"This must be heaven," Michael said in a dazed whisper.

"I think it is more like a zoo," Donald spat. "The difference is that here we're the animals."

"Try to think of something positive," Suzanne suggested. "I have to say I'm relieved."

"Well, there is one thing," Donald commented. "At least I don't see any weapons."

"You're right!" Perry said. "That's definitely encouraging."

"Of course they don't need any weapons, with us imprisoned down here and them up there," Donald added.

"I suppose that's true," Perry said. "What do you think, Suzanne?"

"I can't think," Suzanne said. "This whole experience continues to be too surreal. Are we looking at a patch of sky up there?"

"It certainly looks like it," Perry said.

"Do you think there is a chance we could have been transported eastward when the *Oceanus* fell down the shaft?" Suzanne asked. "I mean, could we be on one of the Azores Islands?"

"The only way we're going to find out is if they decide to tell us," Donald said.

"Who cares where we are," Michael said. "Check out the women! What bodies! Can they be real or are we just imagining this?"

"That's an interesting thought," Suzanne said. "Last night—or whenever it was that we ate—the food tasted as we wished. Could that be happening now with our vision? I mean, it's another sense. Maybe we're seeing what we want to see."

"That's too far out for me to even contemplate," Perry

said. "I've never been a big believer in the supernatural."

"Hey, who the hell cares," Richard said. "Look at that chick with the long brown hair. What a figure! Hey, she's looking at me."

Richard smiled broadly, raised his hand, and waved enthusiastically. The woman smiled back and held up her hand, pressing her palm against the glass.

"Hey!" Richard crooned. "She likes me!" Richard blew kisses, which made the woman smile more broadly.

Encouraged by Richard's success, Michael made eye contact with a woman with shiny, jet black hair. She acknowledged him by putting her palm against the glass just as Richard's acquaintance had done. Michael went crazy jumping up and down and waving frantically with both hands. The woman responded by laughing heartily, although there was no sound because of the glass.

Suzanne lowered her gaze and got Donald's attention. "I don't see any suggestion of hostility," she said. "They all look so peaceful."

"It's probably just a ruse," Donald said. "A way of putting us off guard."

Perry reluctantly took his eyes off the beautiful people to consult with Suzanne and Donald. Richard and Michael continued their antics for the benefit of the two women. They were both trying to improvise a sign language.

"What are we going to do?" Perry asked.

"I personally don't like standing here making a spectacle of myself," Donald said. "I suggest we go back to the living quarters and wait to see what happens. Obviously the ball's in their court. Let them come to us in our office, so to speak."

"But who are these people?" Suzanne questioned. "This is bizarre, like a science fiction movie."

Perry was about to respond but the words stuck in his throat. He pointed over Suzanne and Donald's shoulders. One of the enclosure's walls was mysteriously opening. Behind it was a staircase leading up to the loggia.

"Well," Suzanne exclaimed. "Like you said, Donald, the ball is in their court, and I think we're being invited to a face-to-face meeting."

"What should we do?" Perry questioned nervously.

"I think we should go up," Donald said. "But let's go slowly and stay together. And, Perry, you do the talking like we decided."

Richard and Michael had not seen the silent appearance of the stairway thanks to their communication gestures which had competitively progressed to pure silliness. Above, the crowd was responding gleefully to their antics which only encouraged them to new heights. But when they caught sight of the stairs, they bolted for them. They were both eager to make more intimate contact with their newfound female friends.

"Hold it!" Donald barked. He'd stepped sideways to block the divers' mad dash. "Fall in! We're going as a group and Mr. Bergman is doing the talking."

"I gotta meet this brunette," Richard said eagerly.

"I got a date with the raven-haired honey," Michael added out of breath.

Both divers tried to step around Donald, but he reached out and grasped their upper arms in a viselike grip. They both started to protest but changed their minds when they saw Donald's face. The ex–naval officer's nostrils were flared and his mouth pressed into a grim line of determination.

"I suppose it can wait a few minutes," Richard managed.

"Yeah, sure," Michael said. "There'll be time."

Donald let go of the divers' arms, then gestured for Perry to lead the way.

Perry had a good deal more self-assurance as he started up the stairs than he'd had earlier in the corridor. Confronting a mixed group of handsome individuals in matching lingerie seemed less intimidating than what his imagination had previously conjured up. Yet the uniqueness of the circumstances undermined his confidence as he progressed. He found himself wondering if Michael could be right about the whole scene being a collective hallucination and thereby be an elaborate trap as Donald suggested. But then Perry's normally optimistic nature had trouble thinking up a rationale for a trap, especially since whoever these people were, they didn't have to spring any trap since they were already completely in charge of the situation.

The beautiful people, as Perry called them to himself in his confused musings, had initially surged forward to crowd around the head of the stairs like a group of teenagers anticipating the appearance of a rock star. But as Perry and the others neared the top they shrank back. Even this confused Perry since they retreated as if in fear or at least in attentive respect like people would do around a trained but potentially ferocious animal.

Perry mounted the top step and stopped. Ten feet away the throng of beautiful people were arranged in a semicircle. No one moved. No one spoke. No one smiled.

Perry had assumed their captors would be the first to speak. He hadn't planned to go first but eventually decided to break the ensuing uncomfortable silence with a tentative, "Hi."

His greeting brought on a few giggles from the beautiful people but not much else. Perry turned to glance back at his colleagues for suggestions. Suzanne shrugged. Donald had nothing to volunteer. He still seemed far more mistrustful than Perry felt.

Perry turned back to the crowd. "Does anyone speak any English?" he called out in desperation. "Any English at all or maybe some Spanish?" Perry could speak a little.

A couple stepped forward. Both appeared to be in their midtwenties, and like everyone else, they were shockingly handsome. They had archetypally perfect features which reminded Perry of images he'd seen on ancient cameos. The man had blond hair of medium length. His eyes were an intense sky blue. The woman had fiery red hair with a prominent widow's peak. Her green eyes were as bright as emeralds. Both had rosily radiant, flawless skin. Back in L.A., there would be no question: these two were movie star material.

"Hello, friends, how are you?" the man said with a perfect American accent. "Please don't be afraid. You'll not be harmed. My name is Arak and this is Sufa." The man gestured toward the woman next to him.

"I'd like to say hi, too," Sufa said. "What would each of you like to be called?"

Perry was stunned to hear such regular English come out of their mouths. It was oddly reassuring to hear something so familiar, given the alien quality of everything they'd encountered since the *Oceanus* sunk.

"Who are you people?" Perry managed.

"We are inhabitants of Interterra," Arak said. His resonant baritone was not dissimilar to Donald's.

"And where the hell is Interterra?" Perry demanded. Without meaning to, his voice had a harsh edge. It had suddenly occurred to him that perhaps this whole setup was some kind of elaborate joke, rather than the kind of trap Donald feared.

"Please!" Arak said solicitously. "I know you are confused and exhausted, and you certainly have a right to be after what you've been through. We are well aware how taxing the decontamination sequence can be, so please try to relax. There's a lot of excitement in store for you."

"Are you expatriate Americans?" Perry asked.

Both Arak and Sufa slapped their hands over their mouths in a vain effort to contain their laughter. All the beautiful people close enough to hear Perry's question did the same.

"Please excuse our laughter," Arak said. "We don't mean to be rude. No, we are not Americans. We Interterrans happen to be quite accomplished in your languages. English in all its varieties happens to be Sufa's and my specialty."

Suzanne leaned next to Perry's ear and whispered: "Ask them again where Interterra is."

Perry complied.

"Interterra is beneath the oceans," Arak said in response. "It resides in a gap between what you people call the earth's crust and the earth's mantle. It's an area your seismic scientists call the Mohorovičić discontinuity."

"This is an underground world?" Suzanne blurted. She looked up at what appeared to be a patch of sky filled with sunlight. She was stupefied.

"Undersea is more correct," Sufa interjected. "But please . . . we know you will have many questions. They will all be answered in due time. For now we graciously beg for your forbearance."

"What's forbearance?" Richard asked.

"It means patience," Sufa said. She smiled graciously.

"But we do need to know how we should address each of you," Arak said.

"I'm Perry, president of Benthic Marine," Perry said while patting his chest. He then identified the others by their full names.

Arak stepped forward and presented himself directly to Suzanne. He was a good head taller than she. He held his right arm outstretched with his palm facing her. He gestured toward it with his other hand. "Perhaps you will do me the honor of an Interterran greeting," he said. "Press your palm against mine."

Suzanne hesitated and furtively glanced at Perry and Donald before complying. Her hand was a good deal smaller than Arak's.

"Welcome, Dr. Newell," Arak said once their hands had met. "We are particularly pleased that you have come to visit us." He bowed and took his hand away.

"Well, thank you," Suzanne said. She was confused yet flattered that she'd been singled out for an individual welcome.

Arak backed away. "Now, my honored guests," he said. "You will be taken to your quarters, which I'm sure you will find agreeable."

"Wait a sec, Arak!" Richard called. He raised himself up on his tiptoes. "There's a gorgeous brunette somewhere around here who's dying to meet me."

"And there's a raven-haired beauty that I want to meet," Michael said.

The two divers had been scanning the crowd for the women since they'd come up the stairs. To their chagrin they'd not been able to spot either one.

"There will be plenty of time for socializing," Arak

said, "but for now it is important to get you to your rooms since you've yet to eat and properly wash. There will be a gala celebration for your arrival later, which we hope you will all attend. So, please follow me."

"This will only take a couple of minutes," Richard said. He started forward, intending to walk around Arak and Sufa and mingle in the crowd. But Donald grabbed him as hard as he had when they were downstairs.

"Knock it off, sailor!" Donald snarled under his breath. "We stay together! Remember!"

Richard glared back for a moment, fighting the urge to tell Donald to drop dead. He was so close to connecting with that beautiful woman, it was hard to deny himself. Self-restraint had never been his strong point. But once the intensity of Donald's gaze gave him pause, he relented.

"I guess some chow's not a bad idea," he said to save face.

"You'd better stay in line, bro," Donald snapped. "Otherwise you and I are going to be banging heads."

"Just for the record," Richard said. "I ain't afraid of you."

CHAPTER NINE

Suzanne put one foot ahead of the other as she followed Arak and Sufa but she felt disconnected, as if her feet were not solidly on the ground. It wasn't dizziness that she was feeling, but it was close. She'd heard the psychiatric term *depersonalization* and wondered if she was suffering some variation of it. Everything she was experiencing felt so surreal. It was as if she were in a dream, although her senses seemed very tangibly engaged. She could see, smell, and hear just like normal. But nothing else was making sense. How could they be under the ocean!

As a geophysical oceanographer Suzanne was well aware that the Mohorovičić discontinuity was the name given to a specific layer within the earth that marked an abrupt change in the velocity of sound or seismic waves. It was located approximately two and a half to seven miles beneath the ocean floor and about twenty-four miles beneath the continents. She also knew that its eponymous name came from the Serbian seismologist who'd discovered it. But despite having a name, no one had any idea what the layer represented. As far as she knew, neither she nor any other geologist or seismologist had ever considered the possibility it was an enormous, air-filled cavern. The idea was too preposterous to have been seriously entertained.

"Please give our secondary humans the courtesy they deserve," Arak called out to his fellow Interterrans as he moved forward into their midst. "Back up and give us room!" He motioned for the people to give way, and they silently complied.

"Please!" Arak said gently to Suzanne and the others as he gestured toward an open lane leading out from under the roof of the loggia. He moved ahead and waved for them to follow. "As soon as we depart the foreign arrival hall, it will only be a short journey to your accommodations."

As if watching herself in a movie Suzanne walked between the crowds of Interterreans. She sensed that Perry was directly behind her and imagined that Donald and the divers were close as well. The situation was no longer scary. The beautiful people were full of smiles and gave furtive, almost shy gestures of greeting. Suzanne found herself unable to keep from smiling in response.

Can this truly be happening? she kept asking herself as she followed Arak. *Is this a dream?* Everything was certainly surreal enough, yet there was no doubt she could feel the cool marble on her bare feet and the caress of a gentle breeze on her cheeks. Never had she felt such subtle sensory details in a dream no matter how realistic it had been.

Sufa turned to Suzanne. "You'll notice that you people are true celebrities. Second-generation humans are very, very popular. You are all so refreshingly stimulating. I better warn you that you will be in great demand."

"What do you mean, 'second-generation humans'?" Suzanne questioned.

"Now, Sufa," Arak chided gently. "Remember what we decided! These guests are going to be introduced more slowly to our world than we've done with others in the past."

"I remember," Sufa replied. Then to Suzanne she added: "We'll be discussing everything in due time, and all your questions will be answered. I promise you."

The group soon emerged onto a spacious verandah that opened up into a stupendously colossal underground cavern so immense, it gave the impression of being outdoors. The illumination was like daylight although there was no sun. The domed ceiling was a pale blue like the color of the sky on a hazy summer day. A few thin clouds floated lazily with the breeze.

The verandah was at the side of a building located on the outer edge of a city. Stretching out from the balustrade was a bucolic vista of rolling hills, lush vegetation, and lakes with a few towns in the near distance. The buildings were constructed of black basalt, highly polished and fashioned into a mixture of curves, domes, towers, and classically columned porticos. In the far distance a series of conical mountains rose up from wide bases to fan out against the dome above to form gargantuan supporting columns.

"If you'll all wait for just a moment," Arak said. He then spoke softly into a tiny microphone on an instrument attached to his wrist.

The five "second-generation humans" were spellbound by the unexpected beauty and breathtaking dimensions of the subterranean paradise. It was beyond anything that their imaginations could have possibly conjured. Even the divers were speechless.

"We're waiting for a hovercraft," Sufa explained.

"Is this Atlantis?" Perry asked, his mouth agape.

"No!" Sufa said, mildly offended. "This is not Atlantis. This city is Saranta. Atlantis is due east from here. But you can't see it. It's behind those columns that support the surface protuberances you people call the Azores."

"So Atlantis does exist?" Perry said.

"Well, of course," Sufa said. "But personally I don't find it nearly as agreeable as Saranta. It's a young, up-start city with rather brazen people if you ask me. But you'll have to judge for yourselves."

"Ah, here we go," Arak exclaimed as a domed, saucer-like craft silently materialized at the base of the steps. It arrived so quietly, only those who happened to be looking in the proper direction saw its arrival.

"Sorry it took so long," Arak said. "There must be a particularly high demand at the moment for some reason. But please, after you." He gestured down the steps toward an open entrance port that had miraculously appeared on the side of the saucer.

The group descended the steps and boarded the craft, which was hovering motionlessly several feet off the ground. It was about thirty feet in diameter with a clear, domed top similar to the kind of purported UFOs seen on the covers of tabloids at grocery checkout lines. Inside was a circular banquette cushioned in white with a black, round central table. There were no controls.

Arak was the last to board, and as soon as he did, the entrance port disappeared as silently and as myste-riously as it had appeared.

"Ah, it's always the way," Arak complained after glancing around at the interior. "Just when we're trying to impress you we get one of the old hovercrafts. This one is on its last legs."

"Stop complaining," Sufa said. "This vehicle is perfectly serviceable."

Suzanne glanced at Donald, who raised his eyebrows ever so slightly. Suzanne looked around the hovercraft. She was so full of questions she didn't know where to begin.

Arak placed his hand, palm down, in the center of the black table and leaned forward. "Visitors' palace," he said. He then leaned back and smiled. A moment later the scenery outside began to move.

Suzanne reflexively reached out to grasp the edge of the table to steady herself, but it wasn't necessary. There was no sensation of motion nor was there any sound. It was as if the craft were staying still and the city moving as they rose some hundred feet before accelerating horizontally.

"You'll be instructed how to call and use these air taxis very soon," Arak said. "You'll have plenty of time to explore."

Several heads nodded. The *Benthic Explorer* team was overwhelmed by everything they were seeing. They seemed to be cruising through the center of a bustling metropolis with countless people going about their business and thousands of other air taxis zipping in every direction.

For Suzanne, this world seemed full of strange contradictions. The city and the advanced technology seemed so futuristic yet the trees and vegetation had a hauntingly prehistoric aspect. The flora reminded her of what had flourished during the Carboniferous period three hundred million years ago.

Soon the shiny black basalt multistoried buildings gave

way to a less dense, apparently residential area with grass, trees, and pools of water. The crowds of people disappeared as did the swarms of air taxis. Now there were only individual people or small groups walking in the parks. Many were accompanied by curious-looking pets that Suzanne thought were a chimeric combination of dog, cat, and monkey.

The scenery began to slow as they approached a magnificent walled palace compound. It was dominated by a large, central, domed structure supported by fluted black Doric columns. Sprinkled around the enclosure were numerous other smaller buildings oval in shape and constructed of the familiar polished black basalt. Walkways snaked through crystal pools, expanses of lawn, and patches of luxurious ferns.

The air taxi stopped its horizontal movement and rapidly descended. A moment later the port opened as silently and as mysteriously as it had before.

"Dr. Newell," Sufa said. "This will be your cottage. If you wouldn't mind, please disembark. I will accompany you to be sure you are comfortable." She gestured toward the exit.

A flustered Suzanne glanced from Sufa to Donald. She had not expected to be separated from the group, and she was well aware Donald felt they should remain together.

"What about the others?" Suzanne asked. She tried to read Donald's expression, but couldn't tell what he wanted her to do.

"Arak will see to their accommodation," Sufa said. "Each will have his own bungalow."

"We were hoping to stay together," Suzanne said.

"But you will," Arak said. "This palace and its grounds are just for you visitors. You'll take your meals together and if you want to double up in the lodges for your sleeping arrangements, that is up to you."

Suzanne's and Donald's eyes met. Donald shrugged. Assuming that left the decision up to her, she climbed out of the hovercraft. Sufa followed. A moment later the saucer silently moved across the lawn to stop at a neighboring cottage.

"Come on!" Sufa encouraged. She'd started up the walkway but had turned back when she was aware that Suzanne wasn't behind her.

Suzanne took her eyes off the hovercraft and hurried to catch up with her host.

"You will be meeting up with your friends for a meal shortly," Sufa said. "I just want to be certain your accommodations are acceptable. Besides, I thought you'd like to take a quick refreshing swim before eating. That was my first wish when I emerged from the decon experience."

"You experienced what we went through?" Suzanne questioned.

"I did," Sufa said. "But it was a long, long time ago. Several lifetimes, actually."

"Excuse me?" Suzanne said. She assumed she'd not heard correctly. The phrase *several lifetimes* didn't make any sense.

"Come!" Sufa said. "We have to get you settled. The questions must wait." She took Suzanne's arm. Together they climbed the few steps from the walkway and entered the cottage.

Suzanne stopped just beyond the door, awestruck by the decor. In sharp contrast to the black exterior, the interior was almost exclusively white: white marble, white cashmere, and multiple mirrored surfaces. It reminded Suzanne of the living quarters where she had so recently slept but on a much more lavish scale. An added feature was an azure pool that stretched from inside the room to the outdoors. The pool was fed by a waterfall that cascaded out of the wall.

"The room doesn't please you?" Sufa questioned with concern. She'd been watching Suzanne's face and mistook her wonderment for dissatisfaction.

"Whether I like it or not is hardly the question," Suzanne said. "It's unbelievable."

"But we want you to be comfortable," Sufa said.

"What about the others?" Suzanne asked. "Are their quarters anything like this?"

"They are identical," Sufa said. "All the visitors' cottages are the same. But if there is something else you might need, please tell me. I'm sure we can provide it."

Suzanne's eyes moved to the enormous circular bed, which was on a raised marble dais at the center of her quarters. A large canopy was draped above it. From its circumference hung gathered bundles of sheer white fabric.

"Perhaps you could tell me what you feel is lacking," Sufa said.

"Nothing is lacking," Suzanne said. "The room is breathtaking."

"Then you do like it," Sufa said with relief.

"It's stunning," Suzanne said. She reached out and touched the marble wall. Its surface was polished to a mirrorlike perfection, and it felt warm as if heated by inner radiation.

Sufa stepped over to a cabinet that lined the wall to the right. She gestured down its length. "Inside here you have media consoles, extra clothing, reading material in your language, a large refrigerator with a selection of refreshments, personal toilet articles that you'll recognize, and just about anything else you might need."

"How do I open it?" Suzanne asked.

"Just use a voice command," Sufa said simply. She pointed at one of two doors on the wall opposite the cabinetry. "Personal facilities are through there."

Suzanne walked over to stand next to Sufa and faced the cabinet. "What exactly do I say?"

"Whatever it is you're looking for," Sufa explained. "Followed by an exclamatory word like 'please' or 'now'."

"Food, please!" Suzanne said self-consciously.

No sooner had she uttered the words when one of the cabinet doors opened to reveal a sizable refrigerator well stocked with containers of liquid refreshment and solid food of varying consistency and color.

Sufa bent over and glanced inside. She shuffled through some of the contents. "I might have known," she said, standing back up. "I'm afraid you have just the standard selection, even though I requested some specialty items. But it doesn't matter. A worker clone will get you anything you might desire."

"What do you mean, 'worker clone'?" Suzanne asked. The term sounded ominous.

"Worker clones are the workers," Sufa said. "They do all the manual work in Interterra."

"Have I seen a worker clone?" Suzanne asked.

"Not yet," Sufa said. "They prefer not to be seen until they are called. They favor their own company and their own facilities."

Suzanne nodded as if she understood, but it was not in the way Sufa surmised. Suzanne nodded because she knew that in most situations of bigotry, the dominant group always attributed attitudes to the oppressed which made the oppressors feel better about the oppression.

"Are these worker clones true clones?" Suzanne asked.

"Absolutely," Sufa said. "They've been cloned for ages. Their primary origin was from primitive hominids, something akin to what you people call Neanderthals."

"What do you mean, we people?" Suzanne said. "What makes us different from you besides the fact that you are all so gorgeous?"

"Please . . ." Sufa begged.

"I know, I know," Suzanne repeated with frustration. "I'm not supposed to ask any questions, but your answers to even simple questions always demand some explanation."

Sufa laughed. "It's confusing you, I'm sure," she said. "But we're just asking you to be patient. As we've intimated, we've learned from experience that it is best to go slowly with the introduction to our world."

"Which means you have had visitors like us in the past," Suzanne said.

"For sure," Suzanne said. "We've had many over the last ten thousand years or so."

Suzanne's mouth slowly dropped open. "Did you say ten thousand years?"

"I did," Sufa said. "Prior to that we had no interest in your culture."

"Are you suggesting—"

"Please," Sufa interrupted. She took a deep breath. "No more questions unless they are about your accommodations. I have to insist."

"All right," Suzanne said. "Let's get back to the worker clones. How do I call one?"

"A voice command," Sufa said. "It's the same for most everything in Interterra."

"I just say 'worker clone'?" Suzanne asked.

" 'Worker clone' or just 'worker,' " Sufa said. "Then, of course, it has to be followed by an exclamatory word that you feel comfortable with. But the phrase has to be said as a true exclamation."

"I could do it right now?" Suzanne asked.

"Of course," Sufa said.

"Worker, please," Suzanne said. She maintained eye contact with Sufa. Nothing happened.

"That wasn't enough of an exclamation," Sufa explained. "Try it again."

"Worker, please!" Suzanne cried.

"Much better," Sufa said. "But it doesn't have to be so loud. It's not the volume that counts. It's the intended meaning. Humanoids have to know without equivocation that you want them to appear. Their default mode is not to come, so as to be less bothersome."

"Did you mean to use the term *humanoid*?" Suzanne asked.

"Of course," Sufa said. "Worker clones look very humanlike although they are a fusion of android elements, engineered biomechanical parts, and hominid sections. They are half-machine, half-living organisms who conveniently take care of themselves and even reproduce."

Suzanne stared at Sufa with an expression that was a combination of dismay and disbelief. Sufa interpreted it as fear.

"Now, don't worry," Sufa said. "They are very easy to deal with and are inordinately helpful. In fact, they are truly wonderful creatures as you will undoubtedly discover. Their only minor drawback is that, like their particular hominid forebears, they are unable to speak— but they will understand you perfectly."

Suzanne continued to stare. Before she could ask another question, one of the doors opposite the cabinets opened and in walked a statuesque woman. Suzanne realized she'd been expecting a grotesque automaton, but the woman before her was hauntingly beautiful with classical features and blond hair, alabaster skin, and dark, penetrating eyes. She was wearing black satin coveralls with long sleeves.

"Here is a fine example of a female worker clone," Sufa said. "You'll notice she is wearing a hoop earring. They all wear them for some reason I've never understood, although I believe it has something to do with pride or lineage. You'll also notice that she is rather comely, as are the male versions. But most importantly, you'll find her amenable to your wishes. Whatever you want, just tell her and she will try to do it, short of injuring herself."

Suzanne stared into the woman's eyes; they were like dark pools. Her facial features were as sculptured and attractive as Sufa's yet they bore no expression.

"Does she have a name?" Suzanne questioned.

"Heavens no," Sufa said with a chuckle. "That certainly would complicate things. We wouldn't want to personalize our relationship with workers. That's part of the reason they have never been engineered to speak."

"But she will do what I ask?"

"Absolutely," Sufa said. "Anything at all. She can pick up your clothes, wash them, draw your bath, restock your refrigerator, give you a massage, even change the temperature of the water in your pool. Whatever you want or need."

"At the moment I think it would be best if she left," Suzanne said. She shuddered imperceptibly. The idea of someone being half alive and half machine was disquieting.

"Go, please!" Sufa said. The woman turned and left

as quietly as she'd appeared. Sufa looked back at Suzanne. "Of course, next time you call for a worker clone it will most likely be a different one. Whoever is available comes."

Suzanne nodded as if she understood, but she didn't. "Where do they come from?"

"Underground," Sufa said.

"Like in caves?" Suzanne asked.

"I suppose," Sufa said vaguely. "I've never been down there nor do I know anyone else who has. But, enough about worker clones! We have to get you over to the dining hall for your meal. Would you like to swim or bathe? It's entirely up to you, but there isn't an over-abundance of time."

Suzanne swallowed. Her throat was dry. Given everything she'd been presented with, she found it difficult to make even a simple decision. She looked over at the pool. Its color, now more aquamarine than azure, was as inviting as its gently flickering surface.

"Maybe a swim would be a good idea," Suzanne said.

"Excellent," Sufa answered. "There are fresh clothes in the cabinet. And shoes, too, I might add."

Suzanne nodded.

"I'll wait for you outside," Sufa said. "I have a feeling it would be good for you to be alone for a few minutes to catch your breath."

"I think you are right," Suzanne said.

CHAPTER TEN

The dining room was situated in a building similar in size and shape to the cottages but without a bed. It was also open to the exterior but faced the dramatic central pavilion rather than the expansive lawns and fern thickets. Its long central table was like the one in the decon area's living quarters. The deeply cushioned chaises looked the same, too.

The group had arrived from their separate lodgings at about the same time, in distinctly different moods about their circumstances. Richard and Michael pointedly refused to acknowledge any misgivings. They were completely exhilarated, like two children let loose in the theme park of their dreams and intent on taking advantage of every available perquisite. Perry was also excited about the possibilities inherent in this new world, but he remained outwardly cooler than the giddy divers. Suzanne was still more confused than excited. She continued to toy with the notion that they were experiencing a kind of collective hallucination according to their own predilections. In contrast to everyone else, Donald was sullen, convinced as he was that the whole construct was an elaborate, purposeful delusion toward some nefarious end.

The conversation centered on the saucer ride and the marvels of their accommodations. Richard and Michael were the most animated, particularly after they learned that Suzanne's worker clone had been female. Richard hinted at the desires that might be sated by such a pliant creature.

Suzanne was appalled, and let him know in no uncertain terms. "Try to act like you're from a civilized race!"

The food was similar to the fare they had had in the decon quarters, with the same curious variation in perceived taste although it was presented in elaborate, self-serve courses. It was brought out by two extremely handsome men in black satin, long-sleeved overalls that zipped up the front. Each was wearing a hoop earring.

Suddenly Donald threw his gold fork with some force onto his gold platter. The clatter was surprisingly loud in the marbled room as it reverberated off the stone walls. Richard was caught in midsentence, describing the plunge he took in his pool, with his mouth stuffed with what he insisted was a dollop of hot fudge sundae. Suzanne jumped from fright and dropped her own fork with somewhat less of a clatter, emphasizing to herself how tense she was. Michael choked on what he was experiencing as sweet potato pie.

"How can you people eat under these circumstances!" Donald shouted.

"What circumstances?" Richard asked, his mouth still brimming with food. His eyes darted rapidly around the room, fearful that the place had been invaded.

Donald leaned toward Richard. "What *circumstances*?" he repeated with accentuated derision while shaking his head in scornful wonderment. "The thing I've never been able to understand about saturation divers is whether they have to be stupid in order to be willing to do it, or whether it's the pressure and inert gas that destroys the handful of brain cells they may have had when they started."

"What the hell are you talking about?" Michael asked, taking immediate offense.

"I'll tell you what I'm talking about," Donald snapped. "Look around you! Where the hell are we? What are we doing here? Who are these people dressed up like they're going to a college toga party?"

For a few minutes there was silence. Everyone avoided Donald's glare. They had been scrupulously avoiding such questions.

"I know where we are," Richard said finally. "We're in Interterra."

"Oh, jeez," Donald exclaimed, throwing up his hands in frustration. "We're in Interterra," he repeated. "That explains everything. Well, let me tell you, it tells us nothing. It doesn't tell us where we are or what we're doing here or who these people are. And they now have us conveniently isolated in separate living quarters."

"They said they would tell us all we want to know," Suzanne said. "They asked us to be patient."

"Patient!" Donald mocked. "I'll tell you what we're doing here. . . . We're prisoners!"

"So what!" Richard said.

Silence reigned again. Michael put down his fork, chastened by Donald's outburst. Richard resumed enjoying his dessert, brazenly staring Donald down. Suzanne and Perry just watched, as did the mute worker clones.

Richard took another large bite of his dessert. With

his mouth still full, he said, "If we're prisoners, I want to see how these people treat their friends. I mean, just look at this place. It's fantastic. If you don't want to eat, Fuller, don't! Me, I like this stuff, so screw you!"

Donald leaped to his feet with the intention of lunging across the table at Richard. Perry intervened before punches could be thrown.

"All right, you two," Perry yelled. "Stop baiting each other! Let's not fight amongst ourselves. Besides, you're both right. We don't know squat about the what, where, and why we're here, yet we're being treated well. Maybe even too well."

Perry let go of Donald's arm when he felt the man relax and glanced over at the immobile worker clones, wondering if this mild outburst bothered them. But it didn't. Their faces were as immobile and blank as they had been throughout the meal.

Donald followed Perry's line of sight while straightening his tunic. "You see what I mean," he growled. "They even have jailors keeping tabs on us while we eat."

"I don't think that's the case," Suzanne said. Then in a louder voice, she added, "Workers, go, please!"

Without any acknowledgment of Suzanne's command the two worker clones disappeared through one of the three doors leading from the dining lodge.

"So much for the watchful eyes of the attendants," Suzanne said.

"Ah, that doesn't mean a thing," Donald said. His eyes roamed the chamber. "There's probably hidden mikes and camcorders all over this room."

"Hey," Michael said. "Looking at this dish and fork, I've been wondering. Is this stuff real gold or what?"

Suzanne picked up her own fork to gauge its weight.

"I was thinking about that earlier," she said. "Surprisingly enough, I believe it is."

"No shit!" Michael said. He picked up the plate and hefted the two items. "We got a small fortune here."

"We're being treated okay for the moment," Donald said, returning to the main topic.

"You think it is going to change?" Perry asked.

"It could change in a second," Donald said with a snap of his fingers. "As soon as they've gotten whatever it is they want, who knows what will happen. We're completely vulnerable."

"It could change, but I don't think it will," Suzanne said.

"How can you be so sure?" Donald demanded.

"I can't be sure," Suzanne admitted. "But it stands to reason. Look around. These people, whoever they are, are so advanced. They don't need anything from us. In fact I think we stand to learn extraordinary things from them."

"I know we've been avoiding this issue," Perry said. "But when you say they are so advanced, are you suggesting that these people are aliens?"

Perry's question brought on another period of silence. No one knew quite what to think much less say.

"You mean like people from another planet?" Michael said finally.

"I don't know what I'm suggesting," Suzanne said. "But we all experienced the astounding ride in the saucer. It must represent some kind of maglev technology that none of us has ever heard of. And we're supposed to be under the ocean, which I still have trouble accepting. But I have to tell all of you. The Mohorovičić discontinuity definitely exists, and no one ever has been able to explain it."

Richard waved a dismissive hand. "These people are no aliens. Christ, did you see those girls! Hell, I've seen a lot of movies about aliens, and they sure didn't look like these people."

"They could be altering their appearance to our liking," Suzanne said.

"Yeah," Michael said. "That's what I thought at first. We're dreaming they look so good."

"That's why I don't give a goddamn," Richard said. "It's what's in my mind that counts. If I think they're gorgeous, they're gorgeous."

"The real issue is their motives," Donald said. "It was no accident that brought us here. It's even more apparent that we were literally sucked down that shaft. They want something from us or we'd already be dead."

"I think you are right that we were specifically brought here," Suzanne said. "Sufa admitted several things to me. First, she confirmed that what we'd gone through was a decontamination."

"But why were we decontaminated?" Perry asked.

"She didn't say," Suzanne said. "But she admitted that they have had visitors like us in the past."

"Now that is interesting," Donald said. "Did she say what happened to them?"

"No, she didn't," Suzanne said.

"Well, you guys can worry yourselves sick," Richard commented. Then he put his head back and yelled. "Worker clones, come!"

Instantly two humanoids appeared, one male and one female. Richard took one look at the female and glanced at Michael conspiratorially. "Pay dirt!" he whispered with unbridled excitement.

"Richard," Suzanne called. "I want you to promise

that you will not do anything that will embarrass us or put us in jeopardy as a group."

"What are you, my mother?" he asked. Then he glanced up at the female worker clone and said: "How about some more of that dessert, honey?"

"Me, too," Michael said. He clanked his golden fork on his golden dish.

Donald started to rise but Perry restrained him again. "No fighting," Perry said. "It's no use."

Richard smiled provocatively at Donald, relishing the man's frustration and anger.

A soft chime interrupted the muted background music and echoed about the room. A moment later Arak energetically swept into view. He was attired in the standard fashion with a small addition. Around his neck was a plain blue velvet ribbon that perfectly matched the particular blue hue of his eyes. It was tied in a simple bow.

"Hello, my friends," he called exuberantly. "I trust that your meal was to your liking."

"It was great," Richard answered. "But what is it made out of? I mean, it doesn't look anything like what it tastes like."

"It's mostly planktonic proteins and vegetable carbohydrates," Arak said. He rubbed his hands enthusiastically. "Now then! What about the celebration I mentioned to you earlier? You have no idea how many people here in Saranta are extremely pleased about your arrival to our city. We've had to turn people away. You see, we're not a city that gets many visitors from your world: certainly not like Atlantis to the east or Barsama to the west. Everyone is anxious to meet you. So that brings us to the pivotal question: are you willing to come over to the pavilion or are you too tired from the decon?"

"Where's the pavilion?" Michael asked.

"Right there," Arak said, pointing out the open end of the dining hall. "The celebration is to be held in the pavilion here on the visitors' palace grounds. It's very convenient. In fact it's only a little more than a hundred yards, so we can walk. What do you all say?"

"Count me in," Richard said. "I never pass up a party."

"Likewise," Michael said.

"Splendid!" Arak said. "What about the rest of you?"

There was an awkward silence. Perry eventually cleared his throat. "Arak, to be truthful, we're a little nervous."

"I'd use a stronger word," Donald said. "Frankly, before we do anything, we'd like to have some idea who you people are and why we are here. We know our presence is not an accident. To put it bluntly, we know we were abducted."

"I empathize with your concerns and your curiosity," Arak said. He spread his hands palms up in a conciliatory gesture. "But, please, for tonight allow my experience to prevail. I've dealt with visitors to our world before, not terribly many, it is true, and not in as large a group, but still enough to know what is best. Tomorrow I will answer all your questions."

"Why wait?" Donald demanded. "Why not tell us now?"

"You don't realize how stressful the decon procedure was," Arak said.

"Can you at least tell us how long the procedure lasted?" Suzanne asked.

"A little more than one of your months," Arak said.

"We were asleep for over a month?" Michael questioned in disbelief.

"Essentially, yes," Arak said. "And it's stressful on the brain as well as the body. Tomorrow you will have to deal with more startling information. We've learned that it is easier to absorb when our visitors are rested. Even one night makes a big difference. So please, tonight relax, either here together or alone in your lodges or, best of all, with us at our celebration of your arrival."

Perry searched Arak's face. The man's blue eyes held his gaze and exuded a sincerity he could not deny. "Okay," he said. "At this point I don't think I can sleep anyway. So, I'll come, but tomorrow I'm going to hold you to your word."

"Fair enough," Arak said. He looked at Suzanne. "And Dr. Newell, what is your pleasure?"

"I'll come," Suzanne said.

"Marvelous," Arak said. "And you, Mr. Fuller? What is your decision?"

"No," Donald said. "Under the circumstances I would find celebrating rather difficult."

"Very well," Arak said, rubbing his hands again in obvious delight. "This is wonderful indeed. I'm glad most of you are willing to come. There would have been a lot of disappointed people if I had returned alone. Mr. Fuller, I understand your feelings and respect them. Please enjoy your rest. The worker clones will do your bidding."

Donald nodded morosely.

"Now, let's get on our way," Arak said to the others. He motioned toward the open end of the dining hall.

"Will there be eats at this party?" Richard asked.

"Absolutely," Arak said. "The finest Saranta can muster."

"Then I'll skip seconds on my dessert," Richard said. He tossed his spoon onto the table, stood up, stretched, and belched loudly.

Suzanne glared at him. "Richard, have some respect

for the rest of us even if you don't have it for your-self."

"But I do," Richard said with a sly smile. "I restrained myself from farting in this mixed company."

Arak laughed. "Richard, you are going to be a big hit. You're delightfully primitive."

"Are you yanking my chain?" Richard asked.

"Not at all," Arak said. "You'll be in great demand, I assure you. Come on! Let's show you off!" With a wave, Arak started toward the open end of the room.

"All right!" Richard said, giving Michael an enthu-siastic thumbs-up sign. Michael returned it with equal exuberance.

"Let's party!" Michael cried. The two divers eagerly followed Arak.

Suzanne looked at Perry, who shrugged and said, "This is crazy, going to a celebration under these cir-cumstances, but we might as well take it all in stride."

Then she glanced at Donald. "Are you sure you don't want to come?"

"Yeah, I'm sure," Donald said gloomily. "But if you two want to fraternize, be my guests."

"I'm going because I might learn some more," Suzanne said. "Not to fraternize, as you put it."

"Come on!" Perry called from the far end of the room.

"We'll see you later," Suzanne said. She hurried after Perry and the others, who were already on their way across the lawn.

Donald mulled over what Arak had said. All he knew for sure was that he didn't trust him. From Donald's point of view the man was too ingratiating. All this fan-tastic hospitality had to be some kind of trap. Yet Don-ald had no idea for what purpose other than to get them off their guard.

Donald turned and looked out the end of the room. The group was halfway to the columned pavilion and silhouetted against its illuminated exterior. Redirecting his eyes, Donald stared at the two worker clones, who were standing motionless to the side against the wall. They appeared so human it was hard for Donald to believe they were part machine as Arak had said. Maybe it was just another lie, Donald thought.

"Worker, I want some more drink," Donald said.

The female worker clone immediately picked up the pitcher on the sideboard and stepped over to the table. Her shoulder-length hair was sorrel colored. She had pale, translucent skin. Leaning over she began to fill Donald's cup.

Donald suddenly grabbed her wrist without warning. Her skin felt cold beneath his fingers. She did not jump or even appreciably respond. Instead she kept on pouring.

Donald tightened his grip to get a reaction, but it was to no avail. The woman finished filling the glass then righted the pitcher despite Donald's grasp. Donald was taken aback. The woman was shockingly strong.

Tilting his head back Donald looked up into the woman's frozen face. She did not try to detach herself from his grasp but rather blankly returned his stare. Donald let go of the woman's arm.

"What is your name?" he asked.

She did not respond verbally or in any other fashion. Other than rhythmical breathing there was no other movement. She didn't even blink.

"Worker clone, speak!" Donald ordered.

Silence persisted. Donald looked over at the male worker clone, but there was no response from him either.

"How come you people work and the others don't?" Donald asked.

There was no response from either clone.

"All right," Donald said. "Workers, leave!"

Instantly the two workers went to the door from which they'd come and disappeared. Donald got up and opened the door. Beyond it, a stairway descended into darkness.

Closing the door, Donald walked over to the open end of the room. He looked out at the scene. The light, which had been so bright earlier, had faded, as if the nonexistent sun had nearly set. Donald could just make out Arak and the others approaching the pavilion. He shook his head. He wondered again if he was dreaming. Everything seemed so bizarre yet disturbingly real. He felt his arms and his face. He felt normal to his touch.

Donald took a deep breath. Intuitively he knew that he was facing the most demanding mission of his career. He hoped that his training wouldn't fail him, particularly his training regarding being a prisoner of war.

CHAPTER ELEVEN

In their own scatological vernacular, Richard and Michael were "scared shitless," but their unspoken credo was to deny it. Just like their reaction to the perils of saturation diving they responded with a distorted macho bravado designed to conceal their true feelings.

"Do you think those girls we saw earlier will be here at the party?" Richard asked Michael. They had lagged a few steps behind the others en route to the celebration in the pavilion.

"We can always hope," Michael responded.

They walked in silence for a few steps. They could hear Arak talking with Suzanne and Perry, but they didn't care to listen.

"Do you really think we were asleep for over a month?" Michael asked.

Richard stopped short. "You're not going soft on me, are you?"

"No!" Michael insisted. "I was just asking." Sleep had never been the solace for Michael that it was for others. As a child he used to be plagued with night-mares. After he'd gone to sleep, his father would come home drunk and beat up his mother. When he woke up, he tried to intervene, but the result was always the same: he, too, was beaten. Unfortunately, the process of sleep got inextricably associated with these episodes, so for Michael the idea of being asleep for a month was a source of enormous anxiety.

"Hello!" Richard said while giving Michael a series of slaps on the face. "Anybody home?"

Michael deflected Richard's irritating jabs. "Cut it out!"

"Remember, we're not worrying about all this horse-shit," Richard said. "There's something screwy going on here sure as shooting, but who cares. We're going to enjoy ourselves, not like that jerk, Fuller. God! Just lis-tening to him talk makes me glad we were tossed out of the freakin' Navy. Otherwise we'd be taking orders from guys like him."

"Of course we're going to enjoy ourselves," Michael insisted. "But I was just thinking, like, you know, it's a long time to be zonked."

"Well, don't think!" Richard said. "You'll get your-self all screwed up."

"All right!" Michael said.

Suzanne called out for them to catch up; she and the others were waiting.

"And to top it all off, we got to deal with old mother hen," Richard added.

The two divers caught up to the rest of the group, who'd stopped at the base of the steps leading up to the pavilion entrance.

"Is everything okay?" Suzanne asked them.

"Peachy," Richard said, forcing a smile.

"Arak just told us something you two might find interesting," Suzanne said. "I assume you've noticed how it is getting dark as if the sun had set."

"We noticed," Richard said testily.

"They have night and day down here," Suzanne said. "And we learned the light comes from bioluminescence."

The two divers tilted their heads back to look straight up.

"I see stars," Michael said.

"Those are relatively small pinpoints of blue-white bioluminescence," Arak said. "It was our intent to re-create the world as we knew it, which certainly included the circadian cycle. The difference from your world is that our days and nights are longer, and they are the same length year-round. Of course our years are longer as well."

"So you lived in the external world before you moved down here," Suzanne said.

"Absolutely," Arak answered.

"When did you make the move?" Suzanne asked.

Arak held up his hands defensively. He laughed. "We are getting ahead of ourselves. I'm not supposed to be encouraging you to ask questions this evening. Remember, that's to be tomorrow."

"Just one more," Perry pleaded. "It's an easy one, I'm sure. Where do you get all your energy down here?"

Arak sighed with exasperation.

"It's the last question, I promise," Perry said. "At least for tonight."

"And you are a man of your word?" Arak questioned.

"For sure," Perry said.

"Our energy comes from two main sources," Arak said. "First is geothermal by tapping the earth's core. But that creates the problem of getting rid of excess heat, which we do in two ways. One by allowing magma to well up along what you people call the mid-oceanic ridge, and two by cooling with circulated seawater. The seawater heat exchange requires a large volume, which does provide us an opportunity to filter out plankton. The downside is that the process creates oceanic currents, but you people have learned to live with them, particularly the one you call the Gulf Stream.

"The second source of energy is from fusion. We split water into oxygen, which we breath, and hydrogen, which we fuse. But this is the kind of discussion we'll be having tomorrow. Tonight I want you to experience and enjoy, mostly enjoy."

"And we aim to do just that," Richard said. "But tell me, is this going to be a wet or dry party?"

"I'm afraid that is a term I'm not familiar with," Arak said.

"It refers generally to alcohol," Richard said. "Do you people have any on hand?"

"But of course," Arak said. "Wine, beer, and a particularly pure spirit we call crystal. The wine and the beer are similar to what you are used to. But the crystal is different, and I advise you to go easy until you are accustomed to it."

"No need to worry, bro," Richard said. "Michael and I are professionals."

"Let's party!" Michael said enthusiastically.

Perry and Suzanne had to be nudged forward. Both had been bowled over by Arak's explanations, particularly Suzanne. All at once she had answers to two of the mysteries of oceanography, namely, why magma wells up at the mid-oceanic ridges and why there are oceanic currents, particularly the Gulf Stream. The answers to both questions had completely eluded scientists.

The group climbed the stairs with Arak in the lead. As they passed between two of the massive columns supporting the domed roof, Suzanne caught sight of Richard's overeager expression. Worried what his conduct might be under the influence, she leaned toward him and whispered, "Remember to behave yourself."

Richard glanced at her. His expression was one of scornful disbelief.

"I'm serious, Richard," Suzanne added. "We have no idea what we are up against, and we don't want to put ourselves in any more jeopardy than we already are. If you have to drink, do it sparingly."

"Drop dead!" Richard said. He quickened his pace and caught up to Arak just as two oversized bronze doors swung open.

The first thing that greeted the visitors was the murmur of thousands of excited voices as they reverberated around the pavilion's vast, white marbled interior. The level they'd entered formed a ballustraded balcony that ran around the circular hall. Together the group moved to the top of a grand staircase and looked down.

"Talk about a party!" Richard cried. "My god! There must be a thousand people here."

"We could have had ten thousand if we'd had the room," Arak told them.

In the center of the huge domed ballroom was a round pool illuminated in such a way as to make it appear like an enormous aquamarine cabochon jewel. Surrounding the pool was a foot-high, ten-foot-wide lip. Numerous stairways connected the balcony to the level below.

The floor of the pavilion was packed with people. Everyone was dressed in the same simple white satin outfits except for an occasional worker clone in their usual black. The worker clones were carrying large trays loaded with golden goblets and food. Each guest sported a velvet ribbon tied around his or her neck just like the one Arak had on. Only the color varied, not the size, the shape, or the way it was tied. And as before, everyone was strikingly beautiful or handsome.

Word that the visitors had arrived spread like wildfire through the crowd. Conversations stopped and faces tilted up. It was a dramatic sight to look down on so many silently expectant people.

Arak raised his hands over his head with his palms toward the audience. "Greetings to everyone! I am pleased to announce that all our visitors, save one, have graciously deigned to come to our celebration of their arrival to Saranta."

A general cheer erupted from the audience as everyone lifted their arms, mirroring Arak's gesture.

"Come!" Arak said. He motioned for the group to follow him as he started down the broad flight of stairs.

Richard and Michael scampered forward eagerly, followed by a more hesitant Suzanne and Perry.

"This is too much!" Richard whispered in excitement. "Look at the women! It looks like a Victoria's Secret slumber party."

"Every one of them could be a centerfold," Michael responded.

"It's hard to keep this all in perspective," Suzanne whispered to Perry. "I feel like we're in a 1950's Cecil B. DeMille movie spectacular."

"I know what you mean," Perry answered. "It also gives me an idea what it's like to be a rock star. These people are really happy to see us. And look how young everybody is. Most of these people appear as if they're in their early twenties."

"True, but there's a significant number of children," Suzanne said. "I can see a few that can't be any more than three or four."

"Not very many senior citizens," Perry commented.

At the base of the stairs the people shrank back as the group descended, but as soon as they reached the floor, the crowd surged forward with their hands held up, palms forward.

Suzanne and Perry instinctively retreated a few steps back despite the obvious warmth of the crowd. In contrast Richard and Michael allowed themselves to be engulfed. The two divers soon realized that the crowd wanted physical contact with their hands, and the divers happily reached out to touch the palms that sought theirs. It was a greeting similar to the one Arak had employed when he'd first welcomed Suzanne earlier.

"I love you all," Richard cried out, to the pleasure of the Interterrans in his immediate vicinity, but he selectively chose the palms of young, beautiful women as he worked his way through the crowd. In his enthusiasm he even grabbed a few and kissed them—which brought the festivity to a sudden, screeching halt.

Richard eyed the women he'd kissed and wondered for a fleeting moment if he should retreat up the stairs. The stunned women proceeded to touch their lips, then examine their fingers as if they expected to see blood. Clearly kissing was not part of the Interterrans' normal salutational repertoire. Richard glanced guiltily at Michael, who was equally tense at the precipitous change in the mood of the crowd. "I couldn't help myself," Richard explained.

Three women he'd kissed looked at each other and burst out laughing. Then all three launched themselves simultaneously at Richard to return the gesture. The crowd cheered with delight and pressed in around the two divers even more. After several fumbled attempts at kissing, the three women graciously moved away to make room for others.

A sly smile spread across Richard's face. "Looks like we're going to be teaching these chicks a thing or two," he said beaming. He felt encouraged enough to be even more demonstrative. Michael, seeing Richard's successes, quickly followed suit. But soon their activities were interrupted by a worker clone who had responded to a suggestion of Arak's to give their guests something to drink. The clones arrived and pressed golden goblets into their hands.

Even Suzanne and Perry's reserve began to erode in the face of the infectious conviviality. They were surrounded by friendly, beautiful people eager to press palms with them. Some of the welcomes were the very young children Suzanne had seen when they'd first arrived. Suzanne asked one of them her age after being impressed by her flawless English and apparent intelligence.

"How old are *you*?" the child asked without answering Suzanne's question.

Suzanne was about to respond when a man who could have played a Greek god in the Cecil B. DeMille movie she'd imagined asked her if she lived with a mate. Before Suzanne could answer this curious question an older man, no less attractive, asked her if she knew her parents.

"Just a moment here," Arak said, coming between Suzanne and her admirers. "As you all know, we have specifically told our guests that their questions must wait until tomorrow. It is only fair that ours wait as well.

Tonight is to celebrate this wonderful event for Saranta and to enjoy."

"Hey, Arak!" Richard yelled from the center of a group of fans. He was holding up his golden goblet. "Is this the crystal liquor you were talking about?"

"It is indeed," Arak called out.

"It's fantastic!" Richard yelled back. "I really dig it."

"I'm glad," Arak said.

"One other thing," Richard yelled. "Don't you guys have any music? I mean, what's a party without music?"

"Right on," Michael yelled.

"Workers, music!" Arak shouted over the din. Within moments background music miraculously could be heard over the babble. It was as soothing as the music in the decon living quarters.

Michael let out a contemptuous laugh.

"I'm not talking about elevator music," Richard shouted back at Arak. "I mean something with some base and a beat. Something we can dance to."

Arak barked another order to the worker clones and soon the music changed.

Richard and Michael exchanged bewildered glances. The music had more base and a beat, but with its strange syncopation it was not like any music they had ever heard.

"What the hell is this?" Michael asked. He cocked his head to the side to listen better.

"Beats me," Richard said. He closed his eyes and moved his head in an undulating fashion. At the same time he took a few unsteady steps and swiveled his hips. His movements brought some giggles from the girls he'd amassed around him.

"You like that, huh?" Richard questioned.

The women nodded.

Richard brought his goblet to his lips and tossed off the entire drink, to the surprise of the people around him. Putting the vessel on the floor he grabbed the hand of the nearest woman and charged toward the raised platform surrounding the pool in the center of the arena. With lots of laughter the crowd gave way and shouted encouragement to the couple. Reaching his goal, Richard leaped up and dragged the woman with him. He turned to face her and was momentarily taken aback by her beauty. Having seen so many beautiful people he'd already had begun to take it for granted, but he was particularly struck by this one's looks.

"You're gorgeous!" he whispered, his words slightly slurred.

"Thank you," she said. "You're attractive as well."

"You think so?" Richard asked.

"You're very entertaining," the woman said.

"I'm glad," Richard said. He then had to take a lateral step to regain his balance. For a second the image of the woman went out of focus. He was feeling lightheaded.

"Are you all right?" the woman asked.

"Yeah, I'm fine," Richard assured her. He could feel the ends of his fingers tingling. "That crystal stuff packs a wallop."

"It's my favorite," the woman said.

"Then it's mine, too," Richard said. "Hey, do you want to learn to dance?"

"What does that mean exactly?" the woman asked.

"Like I was doing before," Richard said. "Only we do it together."

Richard closed his eyes and repeated his earlier gyrations. It only lasted for a second since he had to open his eyes to catch his balance a second time. The crowd responded with cheers and applause. They shouted for more.

Richard faced out into the audience and did an exaggerated bow. There were more cheers. Turning back to the woman, Richard began to strut, twist, and shake as best as he could to the music. The woman watched him with great interest and amusement but had trouble imitating him. The only thing she was able to do with any degree of accomplishment was raise her hands in the air and move them as Richard was doing.

"Let me show you," Richard said. He reached out and grasped the woman about the hips and tried to get her to shake rhythmically. She couldn't get the idea but found her awkward attempts hilarious. So did the crowd.

Suzanne and Perry watched with understandable misgivings. Suzanne told Perry she was worried that Richard was drunk, and Perry agreed. But they couldn't help but notice how much the crowd was enjoying his antics.

"Your friend is very amusing," a voice said behind Perry. He turned to face a darling young woman whom he guessed to be around eighteen. She had lively light blue eyes that reminded him of Suzanne's and an infectious smile. She reached out with her palm. Perry pressed his against hers self-consciously; he could feel his face flush. The woman was disarmingly attractive and several inches taller than he.

"My name is Luna," the woman said in a voice that made Perry's knees feel weak.

"I'm Perry."

"I know," Luna said. "You are very appealing. I see you have whiter teeth than Richard."

Perry blushed even more. He nodded. "Thank you," he managed to say.

Luna's eyes drifted out toward the center of the arena. "Can you dance like Richard?"

Perry glanced back at the diver, who was now doing an interpretation of break dancing. At that moment he was on his back spinning around with his legs thrust up in the air.

"I can, I suppose," Perry said noncommittally. "Maybe not quite as well as Richard. He's a bit more extroverted than I. But to tell you the truth, I haven't tried dancing for a few years."

"I think Richard is as good as an entertainment clone," Luna said. She seemed to be mesmerized by Richard, who was now moon walking to the enjoyment of the crowd.

"That's a compliment I bet Richard has never gotten before," Perry said.

Forever the follower, Michael took the hand of one of the women surrounding him and joined Richard on the pool's raised border. No sooner had he started to dance than a dozen other women stepped up on the platform to join in.

There was now a bevy of beautiful women surrounding Richard and Michael, trying to move their arms and swivel their hips in imitation of the two tipsy divers. But it was not easy. Even the divers were having trouble coordinating their movements to the peculiar beat of the music.

Several of the more adventuresome young Interterran men climbed onto the platform to attempt the strange dance. Richard was not amused. Without interrupting his gyrations, he worked his way over to each of the men in turn. With sudden, exaggerated movements of his hips, he knocked each in turn off the platform. The crowd and even the men themselves loved it, thinking it was all part of the exercise.

After a half hour of uninterrupted dancing, the limits of endurance were reached. Forever the leader, Richard swept his arms out and grabbed as many women as he could before collapsing in giggles to the floor. Michael aped Richard's maneuver, adding to the pile to create a tangle of legs, arms, and lightly clad, perspiring torsos. The recumbent divers didn't mind keeping up with the palm pressing, and the women were happy to return the favor with kisses. At Arak's suggestion, worker clones rushed up with more drinks.

"This place is a dream come true," Michael cried after taking a swig from his freshly filled goblet.

"Poor Mazzola," Richard said. "Good old bell diver misses all the fun."

"What do you think this crystal liquor is made from?" Michael asked. He peered into his glass. The fluid was completely transparent.

"Who cares?" Richard squealed as he reached out and gave an exuberant one-armed hug to one of the women pressed up against his chest. In the process he spilled his drink on his chest to the merriment of all who noticed.

"Michael, I have something for you," a blue-eyed, dark brunette said.

"What, gorgeous?" Michael asked. He was on his back, gazing up at the inverted image of the woman who was standing next to the raised platform. She smiled and held up a small jar.

"I want you to try some caldorphin," she said as she unscrewed the jar's top. She extended the jar toward Michael, who used his free hand to scoop out a glob of the creamy contents. "That's a bit more than you need," she said, "but it's okay."

"Sorry," Michael said. "What do I do with it?" He brought it to his nose and sniffed. It was odorless.

"Rub it on your hand," she said. "I'll do the same and then we touch palms."

"Hey, Richie," Michael said as he rolled over and sat up. "Here's something new." Richard didn't respond. He was busy getting another refill of crystal.

Michael rubbed the cream on his palm and then looked up at the attractive woman who'd given it to him. She had a dreamy look about her, her eyes were half closed. Slowly she raised her hand, and Michael pressed his palm against hers.

The reaction for Michael was swift and overpowering. His eyes shot open, then closed in utter pleasure. For a few minutes of rapturous ecstasy he couldn't move. When he was finally able to, he snatched the jar away from the woman. He reached over and yanked on Richard's arm.

"Richie!" Michael yelled. "You got to try this stuff."

Richard tried to detach himself from Michael's grasp, but Michael hung on. "Hey, can't you see I'm occupied," Richard said. He was trying to kiss two women at the same time.

"Richie, you got to try this stuff," Michael repeated. He held out the jar.

"What the hell is it?" Richard said. He pushed himself up on one elbow.

"It's hand cream," Michael said.

"You're interrupting me to try some hand cream?" Richard couldn't believe it. "What's the matter with you?"

"Try it," Michael said. "It's like no hand cream you've ever tried. It's better than coke. I tell you it's dynamite!"

Sighing, Richard reached out and took a small amount of the cream and rubbed it on his hands. He looked up at Michael. "So, now what's supposed to happen?"

"Press your palm against one of the girl's," Michael said.

Richard beckoned one of the two he'd just been kissing, but she motioned for him to wait. She took a bit of the cream for herself, rubbed it into her palm, and then pressed hers against Richard's. The result was the same as it had been for Michael. It took Richard a full minute to pull out of the blissful delirium that enveloped him.

"Oh, my god" Richard cried. "That was like an orgasm. Gimme some more!"

Michael snatched the jar away from his groping hand.

"Find your own," he said.

Richard made another lunge for the jar, but Michael batted his hand away.

Perry was in the middle of explaining to Luna what it meant to be the president of Benthic Marine when he felt someone tap him on the shoulder. It was Suzanne. She looked concerned.

"Richard and Michael are starting to quarrel," Suzanne said. "I'm worried. Arak is seeing to it that their glasses are never empty, and they're already very drunk."

"Uh-oh!" Perry said. "That could spell trouble." He glanced in the divers' direction and saw them pushing and shoving each other.

"I think we'd better walk out there and try to control them," Suzanne said.

"I guess you're right," Perry said. He hated to leave Luna.

"Let them have their fun," a voice said behind Suzanne. "Everyone is enjoying them. They're quite lively." She turned to find the same man who'd asked her if she lived with a mate.

"We're afraid their behavior could become disruptive," Suzanne said. "We don't want to take advantage of your hospitality."

"Let Arak worry about their behavior," the man said. "As you can see, he is encouraging their drinking."

"I noticed that," Suzanne said. "It's not a good idea."

"Leave it up to Arak," the man said. "It's his job to take care of them, not yours. Besides, I'd like to talk with you in private for a moment."

"You would?" Suzanne responded. She was nonplused by the request. She glanced back at the divers and was relieved to see they'd stopped their squabbling and had settled back down into their bevy of reclining women. Suzanne looked at Perry, wondering if he'd heard the man's request. He had. Perry smiled mischievously and gave Suzanne an encouraging nudge.

"Why not?" Perry whispered leaning toward her. "We're supposed to be enjoying ourselves, and the diver emergency has passed for the time being."

"It will be just for a moment," the man said.

"What do you mean, 'in private'?" Suzanne asked. She took in the stranger's chiseled features and liquid eyes and felt her heart skip a beat. She'd never seen a man quite so classically handsome, much less spoken with one.

"Well, not really in private," the man said with a disarming smile. "I thought we could just withdraw a few steps or perhaps climb the stairs to the balcony. I only wish to be able to speak to you alone for a moment."

"Well, I suppose," Suzanne said. She looked back at Perry.

"I'll be right here," Perry said, "with Luna."

Suzanne let herself be led up the stairs.

"My name is Garona," the man said as they climbed.

"Mine is Suzanne Newell," Suzanne responded.

"That I know," Garona said. "Dr. Suzanne Newell, to be precise."

They reached the top of the stairs and leaned against the balustrade. Below, it was apparent the gala was a great success: laughter and lively conversation drifted up from the throng. Most people were milling around the central pool area where the divers and their harem were the focus of attention. The crowd was orderly, gracious, and respectful. Those closest to the dancing were constantly giving way so that those on the periphery could move up to get a close-up view.

"Thank you for giving me this moment," Garona said. "It's unfair for me to monopolize your time."

"It's quite all right," Suzanne said. "It's a relief of sorts to step back and get this overview."

"I had to talk with you to tell you I find you irresistible," Garona said.

Suzanne peered into Garona's handsome face. She expected to see at least a faint vestige of a sly smile. Instead he was regarding her with a warm, smiling intensity that suggested utter sincerity.

"Run that by me again," Suzanne said.

"I find you absolutely irresistible," Garona repeated.

"You do?" Suzanne asked. She chuckled nervously.

"Truly," Garona said.

Suzanne's eyes wandered back to the crowd to give her a chance to process this unexpected encounter. She hesitated before turning back to him. "You're very flattering, Garona," she said. "At least I think you are. So I'm sorry if I seem skeptical, but with all these absolutely gorgeous and flawless females, I find it a bit hard to believe you'd be interested in me. I mean, I know my limitations. In the irresistible arena, I'm no competition for any of these women here."

Garona's smile never faltered. "Perhaps it is hard for you to believe," he said. "But nonetheless it is true."

"Well, than I am sincerely flattered," Suzanne said. "But perhaps you could tell me why you find me so irresistible."

"It's hard to put into words," Garona said.

"At least give it a try," Suzanne said.

"I suppose I'd have to say it involves your freshness or your innocence. Or perhaps it's your alluring primitiveness."

"Primitiveness?" Suzanne echoed. "That's how Arak characterized Richard."

"Well, he definitely has it, too," Garona said.

"And that's supposed to be a compliment?" Suzanne asked.

"Here in Interterra it is," Garona said.

"What exactly is Interterra?" Suzanne asked. "And how long has it been in existence?"

Garona smiled patronizingly and shook his head. "I've been warned against answering any questions other than purely personal ones about myself."

Suzanne rolled her eyes. "Sorry," she said with a touch of sarcasm. "I guess it just slipped out."

"It's quite all right."

"So, I have to think up some personal questions?"

"If you'd like," Garona said.

"Well . . ." Suzanne said as she tried to think of one. "Have you always lived down here?"

Garona roared with laughter, loudly enough to attract the attention of two men on the floor below. They looked up, waved when they recognized Garona, and began making their way toward the stairs.

"I'm sorry I laughed," he said, "but your question underlines how wonderfully innocent you are. It's so refreshing. I'd love to get better acquainted. When you have had enough of the festivities and you want to leave, let me know. I'd love to take you to your room. We can spend some intimate time together pressing palms, just you and I. What do you say?"

Suzanne's mouth slowly dropped open as the true meaning of Garona's proposal dawned on her. She laughed mockingly. "Garona, I don't believe this," she said. "Only a short time ago I thought I was going to die. Now I'm in a fantasyland with a great-looking guy making a pass at me and wanting to come to my room. How am I supposed to respond?"

"Just say yes," Garona said.

"I'm afraid I'm a little too stunned to reply so smoothly."

"I can appreciate that," Garona said. "But I can comfort you and make you relax."

Suzanne shook her head. "I don't think you understand. I'm having trouble just thinking straight."

"You excite me," Garona said. "You enthrall me. I want to be with you."

"I have to give you high marks for persistence," Suzanne said.

"We will talk more later," Garona said. "Here come two of my friends."

Suzanne turned to see the two men who'd been roused by Garona's outburst of laughter mount the top step of the main stairway and approach. She couldn't help but notice that both were as attractive as Garona. They walked arm in arm, like two lovers.

"Greetings, Tarla and Reesta," Garona said. "Have you met our honored guest, Dr. Suzanne Newell?"

"Not yet," the two men said in unison. "We were hoping to have the honor." They both bowed elegantly.

Suzanne forced a smile. This was all so enchantingly odd. She felt it all had to be a dream.

Richard knew he was drunk, but he'd certainly been drunker in the past. His inebriation didn't seem to deter any of the women who were still flocking around him. He was aware the faces of the women changed as he danced, meaning there was a rotation of sorts, but it didn't matter since they were all so beautiful.

Without meaning to, he bumped up against Michael hard enough to knock both of them off balance. They collapsed to the floor, too limp to hurt themselves. When they realized what had happened, they laughed so hard, they brought tears to their eyes.

"What a party!" Michael cried when he'd recovered enough to speak. He wiped his eyes with the back of his hand.

"Nobody's going to believe us when we get home," Richard said. "Especially when we tell them that every single chick is available. I mean, it's like a turkey shoot. It's unreal."

"The men down here just don't care," Michael said. "Hey, look at that girl over there."

"Which one?" Richard asked. He rolled over and tried to follow Michael's line of sight through the milling crowd. His eyes finally came to rest on a statuesque red-head walking arm in arm with a young boy.

"Wow," he said.

"I saw her first," said Michael.

"Yeah, but I'm going to get her first."

"No way."

"Screw you," Richard said as he scrambled to his feet.

Michael reached out and grabbed one of Richard's legs and tripped him. He fell head first and skidded off the edge of the platform, striking his forehead on the floor. He wasn't hurt, but he was angry, especially when Michael tried to run past him toward the girl.

Richard managed to put a foot out in time to trip Michael. As he tried to get up, Richard threw himself on top of him. Then he grabbed the front of his tunic and punched him in the nose.

The sudden violence caused the party-goers to shrink back in alarm. A collective gasp was uttered as Michael's nose began to bleed.

Michael bucked Richard off his body and got his legs under him. Richard tried to do the same, but Michael caught him on the side of the head with a blow that sent him sprawling back to the floor.

"Come on, you bastard," Michael taunted. "Get up and fight." Blood trickled down the front of his chin and dripped onto the floor. He swayed on his feet.

Richard got to his hands and knees. He looked up at Michael. "You're a dead man," he growled.

"Come on, you twerp!" Michael responded.

Richard pushed himself up to a standing position, but he, too, was unsteady on his feet.

Arak, who'd been at some distance from the divers when their melee started, pushed through the stunned and silent crowd. He stepped between the two drunken divers.

"Please," he said. "Whatever is the problem we can resolve it."

"Outta my way," Richard spat. He shoved Arak to

the side and launched a roundhouse blow to Michael's head. Michael ducked but lost his balance in the process and fell to the floor. Richard lost his balance when the blow failed to connect.

"Worker clones, restrain the guests!" Arak yelled.

Richard and Michael both managed to get themselves upright and throw several more ineffectual punches before two large male worker clones intervened. Each grabbed a diver in a bear hug. Richard and Michael continued trying to hit each other until they were moved a body length apart. At that moment Perry pushed through the crowd.

"Have you idiots forgotten where you are?" Perry shouted. "For chrissake, no fighting! What's the matter with you two?"

"He started it," Richard said.

"He started it," Michael said.

"No, he did."

"No, it was him."

Before Perry could respond to this juvenile tit-for-tat, the divers suddenly broke out laughing. Every time they tried to look at each other they laughed harder. Soon everyone but Perry and the worker clones were laughing as well. At Arak's command the worker clones let go of the divers, who immediately exchanged high fives.

"What was the fighting about?" Arak asked Perry.

"Too much of your crystal," Perry said.

"Perhaps we should switch them to a less potent drink," Arak said.

"Either that or cut them off completely," Perry said.

"But I don't want to ruin the party," Arak said. "Everyone is enjoying them immensely."

"It's your party," Perry said.

Richard and Michael started back toward the platform.

"I tell you what," Richard whispered to Michael. "We'll make it fair. I'll shoot you for the redhead."

"Okay," Michael said.

"You call," Richard said. "Odds or evens."

"Evens," Michael said.

On the count of three, they both threw out a single finger. Michael smiled with satisfaction. "Justice!" he exclaimed.

"Crap!" Richard said.

"Now where the hell is she?" Michael questioned. The two divers scanned the crowd.

"There she is," Richard said. He pointed. "And she's still with the little squirt."

"I'll be back in a flash," Michael said. He made a beeline for the woman whom he noticed was watching his approach with great interest.

"Hi, baby," Michael said, avoiding making eye contact with the preteen beside her. "My name is Michael."

"My name is Mura. Are you hurt?"

"Hell, no," Michael said. "A little tap on the nose doesn't hurt old Michael. No way."

"We are not accustomed to seeing blood," Mura said.

"Listen!" Michael said, "How would you like to come over and rub palms with me? We got our own little party going on over by the pool."

"I'd love to touch palms with you," Mura said. "But first, may I introduce Sart?"

"Yeah, hi, Sart," Michael said offhandedly. "You've got a great looking mother here, but why don't you go off and play with some friends."

Both Mura and Sart giggled. Michael wasn't amused.

"Pretty funny, huh?" he questioned irritably.

"Unexpected is a better word," Mura managed.

Michael reached out and took Mura's arm. "Come on, honey." To the youngster he said, "See you later, Sart."

With Mura in tow, Michael strutted with a few unplanned wobbles back to Richard and the rest of the group. Richard had singled out two women who were particularly demonstrative in their affection for him. He introduced them as Meeta and Palenque. One was blond and the other brunette, and both were incredibly voluptuous.

"Richie, meet Mura," Michael said proudly.

Richard pretended not to notice the striking redhead. Instead he pointed over Michael's shoulder and asked about the preteen. Michael looked behind and was irritated to see the boy had tagged along.

"Beat it, kid," Michael snapped.

Mura ignored Michael and encouraged Sart to step forward. She introduced him to Richard.

"Hey, nice to meet you, Sart," Richard said. "You, too, Mura. Why don't you two take a load off and sit down?"

"We'd enjoy that," Mura said.

"Indeed," Sart added.

Michael rolled his eyes in frustrated irritation as Richard managed to preempt his triumph. For a moment he considered cold-cocking Richard on the spot.

"Hey, you, too, Mikey," Richard goaded. "Come on, buddy, take a seat and relax! It'll do you good. After all, we're all one big, happy family."

That comment brought giggles from all the Interterrans within earshot, only adding to Michael's embarrassment. He swallowed his pride and sat down.

"Listen, Mikey," Richard continued. "My little blond

bombshell, Meeta, just told me something interesting. Everybody loves to swim in Interterra."

"No kidding," Michael said, lightening up. "Did you mention that we were professionals?"

"Of course," Richard said. "But I'm not convinced they quite got what I was talking about. Seems that the idea of work is not something they can relate to."

"If you swim for work, does that mean you like to swim?" Meeta asked.

"Sure we like to swim," Michael said.

"Well, why don't we all take a dip?" Meeta suggested.

"Why not," Mura agreed. "You people need to cool down."

"I think it is a wonderful idea," Sart said.

Richard looked at the inviting aquamarine pool. "Are you talking about swimming right now?" he asked.

"What time could be better?" Palenque said. "We're all so warm and sweaty."

"But our clothes," Richard said. "We'll be sopping."

"We don't wear clothes when we swim," Meeta said.

Richard looked at Michael. "This place just keeps getting better and better," he said.

"Well?" Meeta questioned. "What do the professional swimmers say?"

Richard swallowed. He was afraid to say anything lest he wake up.

"I say we go for it," Michael cried.

"Wonderful!" Meeta said. She leaped to her feet and helped Palenque to hers. Sart got up and gave Mura a hand. In the blink of an eye the Interterrans unabashedly threw off their tunics and stepped out of their shorts. In their naked nubile splendor, they all dove cleanly into the water and swam out toward the center of the pool with strong, practiced strokes.

Richard and Michael were momentarily too stunned
to follow. Instead they glanced around at the people in
the immediate vicinity. To their added surprise, no one
had taken much notice other than Perry. Then Richard
and Michael's eyes met.

"What the hell are we waiting for?" Richard asked
as he smiled drunkenly.

In a rush, the two divers clumsily struggled to get
out of their clothes. At the same time, they made a dash
for the pool. Michael had trouble with his shorts and
ended up tripping. Richard was more successful and was
soon racing toward the shallow area at the center of the
pool.

On his arrival Richard was literally set upon by Meeta
and Palenque who playfully and repeatedly dunked him.
Richard took the harassment from the naked beauties
gleefully but was soon out of breath. By the time Michael
arrived and engaged in similar activities with Mura, since
Sart and Palenque had swum to the far end of the pool,
Richard was content to languish in a place where he and
Meeta could sit with their heads above the surface.

"Richard, Richard, Richard," Meeta cried happily as
she repeatedly pressed her palm against his and stroked
his head. "You are the most primitively attractive visitor
we've ever had in Saranta. Maybe in all of Interterra for
at least several thousand years."

"I thought only my mother appreciated me," Richard
said jokingly.

"You knew your mother?" Meeta questioned. "How
quaint."

"Of course I knew my mother," Richard said. "Don't
you know yours?"

"No," Meeta said with a laugh. "No one in Interterra

knows his mother. But let's not get into that. Instead, why don't you take me to your room?"

"Now there's an idea," Richard said. "But what about your friend Palenque? What will we say to her?"

"Anything you like," Meeta said unconcernedly. "But it's easiest to just ask her. I'm sure she'll want to come. And Karena. I know she wants to come, too."

Richard tried to act nonchalant, but he was afraid his surprise at this unexpected good fortune was all too apparent. At the same time with this auspicious turn of events, he wished he hadn't drunk quite so much.

It was a boisterous group that set out from the pavilion to the dining hall. Suzanne, Perry, and the divers were singing old Beatles songs at the top of their lungs to the delight of their companions who, surprisingly, knew the words. Suzanne was walking with Garona, Perry with Luna, Richard with Meeta, Palenque, and Karena, and Michael with Mura and Sart.

Although Suzanne and Perry had resisted drinking very much, what they had drunk had gone to their heads. They were not nearly as drunk as Richard and Michael, but both recognized they were tipsy. They were also enjoying themselves immensely.

Arak had bid them farewell as the gala wound down and promised to meet with them in the morning. He had wished them a pleasant rest and had thanked them for coming to the celebration.

"Hey," Richard called out when they'd finished a rendition of "Come Together." "Don't you guys know any songs of your own?"

"Of course," Meeta said. Immediately the Interterrans burst into song, and although the words were in

English, the beat was as irregular as the music at the gala had been.

"Cut!" Richard cried out. "That sounds too weird. Let's go back to the Beatles."

"Richard, let's be fair," Suzanne said.

"It's all right," Meeta said. "We'd rather sing your songs."

"Michael? What the hell are you doing with the glasses?" Richard asked when he saw that his partner was carrying several empty goblets.

"I asked Arak," Michael said. "He told me I could take them. They're gold. I bet I have enough money here for a down payment on a new pickup truck."

Richard leaned over and snatched one of the goblets.

"Hey, gimme that back," Michael demanded.

Richard laughed. "Go out for a pass. I'll hit you long!"

Michael handed the rest of the goblets to Mura. Then he staggered ahead for the pass. Richard tossed the goblet like a football, and it spiraled into Michael's hands. Everyone clapped. Michael took a bow, lost his balance, and fell. Everyone giggled and clapped harder.

"We have pets that play that game," Mura said.

"I saw some pets when we were flying in," Suzanne said. "They looked like composite creatures."

"They are," Mura said.

"Do you have sports games down here?" Richard asked.

Michael came back and collected the rest of his goblets.

"No, we don't have sports," Meeta said. "Unless you mean mind games, things like that."

"Hell, no!" Richard said. "I mean like hockey or football."

"No," Meeta said. "We don't have physical competition."

"Why not?" Richard asked.

"It's not necessary," Meeta said. "And it is unhealthy."

Richard glanced at Michael. "No wonder the men are all such wimps," he said. Michael nodded.

"How about 'Lucy in the Sky with Diamonds,'" Suzanne suggested. "It seems so apropos."

A few moments later, still singing the refrain, the group stumbled into the dining hall. It was dark, but the Interterrans somehow brought up the illumination. Perry was about to ask how it was done when he noticed Donald. The former naval officer had been sitting silently in the dark. His face was as grim as it had been when they'd left for the celebration.

"My gosh," Richard said. "Mr. Straight Arrow is right where we left him."

Michael proudly deposited his cache of golden goblets on the table with fanfare.

Richard lurched over to a position across the table from Donald. He dragged the three women with him like trophies. "Well, Admiral Fuller," he said in a mocking tone while comically saluting. "I guess you can tell by our present company and booty that you really missed out."

"I'm sure I did," Donald said sarcastically.

"You can't imagine how great it was, smart ass," Richard said.

"You're drunk, sailor," Donald said scornfully. "Luckily, some of us have enough self-control to keep our wits about us."

"Yeah, well, let me tell you what's wrong with you," Richard said, pointing a wavering finger at Donald's face. "You still think you are in the goddamned Navy. Well, let me tell you something. You ain't."

"You're not only stupid," Donald hissed. "You're disgusting."

Something snapped in Richard's brain. He shoved the women away and launched himself across the marble table, catching Donald by surprise. Despite his inebriation, he was able to straddle the man and land a few ineffectual punches on the side of his head.

Donald responded by enveloping Richard in a bear hug. Locked in a violent embrace, both men rolled off the chaise Donald had been sitting on. Neither man could do much damage to the other, but pummeled each other with short punches nonetheless. They did succeed in crashing into the table which caused Michael's goblet collection to fall to the floor with a great clatter.

The Interterrans shrank back in dismay, while Suzanne and Perry intervened. It wasn't easy, but they finally managed to separate the two men. This time it was Richard's turn to have a bloody nose.

"You bastard," Richard sputtered as he touched his nose and looked at the blood.

"You're lucky your friends are here," Donald told him. "I might have killed you."

"That's enough," Perry said. "No more baiting and no more fighting. This is ridiculous. You're both acting like children."

"Idiot!" Donald added. He shook off Perry's restraining arms and straightened his satin tunic.

"Jerk!" Richard retorted. He moved away from Suzanne and turned to his three women friends. "Come on, girls!" he said. "Let's go to my room, where I won't have to look at this guy's ugly mug."

Richard took a few unsteady steps toward the women,

but they shrank back. Then, without another word, they
fled out the open end of the room into the night. Richard
hurried after them but stopped at the edge of the lawn.
The women were already halfway back to the pavilion.

"Hey!" Richard yelled through cupped hands. "Come
back! Meeta . . ."

"I think it's time you went to bed," Suzanne called
after him. "You've caused enough trouble for one night."

Richard turned back into the room, disappointed and
angry. He slammed his open palm down on the table-
top hard enough to make everyone in the room jump.
"Shit!" he shouted to no one in particular.

As Perry pushed open the door of his cottage with a
trembling hand he did his best to hide and let Luna enter
before him. It had been a long time since he'd been
alone with a woman like this. He had no idea whether
his anxiety was from marital guilt or from recognizing
Luna's inappropriate youth. On top of that he was tipsy
with drink, but even more intoxicating than the crystal
was the fact that an absolutely gorgeous young woman
found him attractive.

As Perry struggled to conceal his nervousness he was
sensitive enough to notice that Luna was agitated herself.

"Can I get you something?" Perry asked. "I'm supposed to have food and drink available." He watched as
the girl went over to the pool and bent down to test its
temperature.

"No, thank you," Luna said. She began to wander
aimlessly around the room.

"You seem upset," Perry said. For lack of anything
better to do, he went over and sat on the bed.

"I am," Luna admitted. "I've never seen a person act the way Richard did."

"He's not our best ambassador," Perry said.

"Are there many people like him where you are from?" Luna asked.

"Unfortunately, his type is not uncommon," Perry said. "Usually there's a history of abuse that gets handed down from generation to generation."

Luna shook her head. "Where does the stimulus for the abuse come from?"

Perry scratched the top of his head. He'd not meant to get into a sociological discussion nor did he feel capable at the moment. At the same time he felt he had to say something. Luna was looking at him intently. "Well, let's see," he said. "I haven't really thought about this too much, but there's a lot of discontentment in our society from heightened expectation and a sense of entitlement. Few people are ever really satisfied."

"I don't understand," Luna said.

"Let me give you an example," Perry said. "If somebody gets a Ford Explorer the next thing they see is an ad for a Lincoln Navigator, which makes the Explorer seem unappealing."

"I don't know what those are," Luna said.

"It's just stuff," Perry said. "And we're conditioned through relentless advertising to feel it's never the right stuff."

"I don't understand that kind of covetousness," Luna said. "We don't have anything like that here in Interterra."

"Well, then it's hard to explain," Perry said. "But anyway there's a lot of discontentment that especially comes to a head in poor families which have even less stuff than everyone else, and within families people tend to take it out on each other."

"It's sad," Luna said. "And frightening."

"It can be," Perry agreed. "But we're kinda conditioned not to think about it since it all drives our economy."

"It seems strange to have a society that encourages violence," Luna said. "Violence is shocking for us since we have none in Interterra."

"None?" Perry asked.

"No, never," Luna said. "I've never seen a person hit another. It makes me feel weak."

"Then why don't you sit down?" Perry said. He patted the bed next to him, feeling self-consciously transparent. Nonetheless Luna came to the bed and sat down beside him.

"You don't feel dizzy, do you?" Perry asked, struggling to make conversation now that she was so close. "I mean, you're not going to faint or anything?"

"No, I'll be all right."

Perry looked into Luna's pale blue eyes. For a moment he couldn't speak. When he could he said, "You know, you are very young."

"Young? What does that have to do with anything?"

"Well . . ." Perry said, searching for words. He wasn't sure himself whether he was referring to her reaction to Richard's behavior or his reaction to her. "When you're young you haven't had as much experience as when you are older. Maybe you haven't had time to see violence."

"Listen, there's no violence here," Luna said. "It's been selected against. Besides, I'm not as young as you probably imagine. How old do you think I am?"

"I don't know," Perry stammered. "About twenty."

"Now you seem to be upset."

"I guess I am a little," Perry admitted. "You could be my daughter."

Luna smiled. "I can assure you I'm over twenty. Does that make you feel better?"

"Some," Perry admitted. "Actually, I don't know why I feel so nervous. Everything is so nice here, but it's still quite unnerving."

"I understand," Luna said. She smiled again and raised her palms toward his.

Self-consciously Perry put his against hers. "What is this with our hands?" he asked.

"It's just the way we show love and respect. You don't like it?"

"When it comes to showing love I'm partial to kissing," Perry said.

"Like Richard was doing this evening?"

"A bit more intimately than Richard's technique," Perry said.

"Show me," Luna said.

Perry took a breath, leaned over, and lightly kissed Luna on the lips. When he pulled back, Luna responded by touching her lips gently with the very tips of her fingers as if amazed by the sensation.

"Do you dislike it?" Perry asked.

Luna shook her head. "No, but my fingers and palms are more sensitive than my lips. But show me more."

Perry swallowed nervously. "Are you serious?"

"I'm sure," Luna said. She moved closer to him and looked at him with those dreamy eyes. "I find you very alluring, Mr. President of Benthic Marine."

Perry wrapped his arms around her and pulled her down onto the white cashmere coverlet.

Michael was in seventh heaven. Mura was the woman of his dreams. It couldn't get better than this. He didn't even mind Sart's continued presence. The boy was in the pool, leaving him to enjoy Mura by himself.

Just when Michael was about to pass out from sheer delight, his rapture was interrupted by a knock at his door. He tried to ignore it, but finally staggered to the door, stark naked. He felt even drunker on his feet. "Who the hell is it?" he demanded.

"It's me, your buddy Richard."

Michael opened the door. "What's the problem?"

"No problem," Richard said. He tried to look around Michael. "I just thought maybe you might need some help, if you know what I mean."

It took Michael's drugged brain a few seconds to catch Richard's drift. He glanced back at Mura on the circular bed, then back to Richard.

"Are you kidding?" Michael asked.

"No," Richard said. He smiled crookedly.

"Mura," Michael called out. "Do you mind if Richard comes in and joins us?"

"Only if he promises to behave," Mura called back.

Michael looked back at Richard with an exaggerated expression of surprise. "You heard the lady," he said with a sly smile. He opened the door wider and let Richard into the room. As the two men approached the bed Mura held up both hands.

"Come on, you two primitives!" she said. "I'd love to press palms with you both."

The two divers exchanged a glance of appreciative disbelief before Michael climbed back onto the bed, and Richard struggled out of his satin garments. As Richard settled next to Mura, he said, "You people are pretty free with love."

"It's true," Mura said. "We have lots of love. It's our wealth."

A short time later the two drunken divers were swooning with pleasure in Mura's arms. It wasn't sex per se, since in their drugged state neither was capable of consummation, but nonetheless they couldn't have been more content.

Sart had observed Richard's arrival from the far end of the pool. He was both attracted and repelled by Richard. Mainly, he was curious. After tiring of swimming he got out of the water, dried himself off, then walked over to the blissful threesome. Mura smiled up at him. She had her arms around both divers, who had fallen fast asleep.

Mura motioned for Sart to sit down on the bed. She'd been gently stroking both divers' backs but was happy to let Sart take over with Richard. That freed her to concentrate on Michael.

Sart initially just stroked Richard's back as Mura had been doing, but tiring of this, he began to improvise. First he rubbed Richard's exposed arm and shoulder. Richard's skin felt intriguingly strange to Sart. It wasn't as firm as Interterran skin and had many curious, tiny imperfections. Sart transferred his attentions to Richard's head, where he'd noticed a small, poorly defined, bluish red discoloration within the hairline above his ear. As Sart bent over to examine this flat blemish more closely, touching it gently with the tip of his finger, Richard's eyes popped open.

Sart smiled at him dreamily and went back to his tender stroking.

"What the hell?" Richard cried. He knocked Sart's hand to the side. With drunken clumsiness he leaped from the bed.

Sart stood up as well. He wondered if the mark above Richard's ear was inordinately sensitive. Maybe he should not have touched it.

Richard's sudden movement was enough to awaken Michael. Sleepy and dazed, he sat up despite Mura's restraining arm. He saw Richard swaying by the bedside and glaring at Sart, who looked somewhat guilty.

"What's the matter, Richie?" Michael asked with a slurred, gravelly voice.

Richard didn't answer. Instead he wiped his hand over his head while continuing to glower at Sart.

"What happened, Sart?" Mura asked.

"I touched Richard's blemish," Sart explained. "The one above his ear. I'm sorry."

"Michael, come here!" Richard snapped. He waved Michael away from the bed while walking unsteadily in the direction of the pool.

Michael got to his feet feeling giddy from the short snooze. He followed Richard. The two men staggered out of earshot. Michael could tell that Richard was major-league perturbed.

"What's going on?" Michael asked in a whisper.

Richard wiped his mouth with the back of his hand. He was still glaring back at Sart.

"I think I figured out why all these guys don't care if we make it with their women," Richard whispered back.

"Why?" Michael asked.

"I think they're all a bunch of queers."

"Really?" Michael looked back at Sart. The possibility had crossed his mind at the gala when he'd seen so many men walking around arm in arm, but then he'd forgotten about it in the general excitement.

"Yeah, and I'll tell you something else," Richard said.

"That little nerdy squirt over there has been rubbing my back and head. The whole time I thought it was the girl."

Michael laughed despite Richard's evident rancor.

"It's not funny," Richard snapped.

"I bet Mazzola would think it was funny," Michael said.

"If you tell Mazzola, I'll kill you," Richard hissed.

"You and ten other people," Michael scoffed. "But, in the meantime, what do you want to do?"

"I think we should show this little twerp what we think of his kind," Richard said. "The guy had his hands all over me, for chrissake. I'm not about to let that pass without a reaction. I don't think we should let any of these people get the wrong idea of our persuasion."

"All right," Michael said. "I'm with you. What do you have in mind?"

"First, get rid of the girl!" Richard said.

"Oh, no! Do we have to?" Michael questioned.

"Absolutely," Richard said impatiently. "And ditch the long face. You can tell her to come back tomorrow. It's important to teach this guy a lesson, and we don't want an audience. She'd yell bloody murder and the next thing you'd know we would be dealing with a couple of those worker clones."

"Okay," Michael said. He took a breath to fortify himself and walked back to the bed.

"Is Richard all right?" Mura inquired.

"He's fine," Michael said. "But he's tired. In fact, we're both tired. Maybe exhausted is a better word. Plus we're drunk, as I'm sure you've noticed."

"It hasn't bothered me," Mura said. "I've been enjoying myself."

"I'm glad," Michael said. "But now we're wondering if we could put off any more palm pressing until tomorrow. What I mean is, maybe you should leave."

"Certainly," Mura said without hesitation. She immediately slid off the bed and began dressing. Sart did the same.

"I don't want you to get the wrong impression," Michael said. "I'd like to see you tomorrow."

"I understand you are tired," Mura said graciously. "Don't worry. You are our guests, and I will return tomorrow if it is your wish."

Sart cinched his braided rope around his waist and looked back at Richard, who'd not moved from where he was standing halfway to the pool's edge.

"Sart," Michael said, following the boy's line of sight. "Why don't you hang around? Richard wants to apologize for scaring you when he leaped off the bed."

Sart looked at Mura. Mura shrugged. "It's up to you, my friend."

Sart looked back at Michael, who smiled and winked at him.

"If the guests wish me to stay, I will stay," Sart said. He stepped back to the bed with a bit of swagger and sat down.

"That's wonderful," Michael said.

Mura finished dressing and went first to Michael and then to Richard to press her palm against each of theirs one last time. She told them both that they had given her great pleasure to be with them, and said she was eager to see them the following day. Before closing the door behind herself she bid them good night.

After the sound of the door closing drifted away, there was a brief, uncomfortable silence. Richard and Michael eyed Sart while Sart looked back and forth between the two men. Sart began to fidget. He stood up.

"Perhaps I should call for more drink," Sart said, to make conversation.

Richard forced a smile and shook his head. Then he approached Sart with a gait that suggested he didn't quite know where his feet were.

"How about more food?" Sart said.

Richard shook his head again. He was within an arm's distance of the boy. Sart took a step back.

"Me and my buddy here have something important we want to say to you," Richard told him.

"This is true," Michael said. He walked equally as unsteadily around the end of the bed to join Richard, effectively boxing Sart in a corner between the bed and the wall.

"To put it bluntly, so there is no misunderstanding," Richard continued, "we can't stand queers like you."

"In fact they make us a little crazy," Michael said.

Sart's eyes darted from one drunken, sneering face to the other.

"Perhaps it would be best if I go," Sart said nervously.

"Not before we're absolutely certain you know what we're talking about," Richard said.

"I don't know what you mean by 'queer,'" Sart admitted.

"Homo, gay, fag, fairy," Richard said derisively. "The term doesn't matter. The point is we don't like guys who like men. And we have a sneaking suspicion you fall into that category."

"Of course I like men," Sart said. "I like all people."

Richard looked at Michael then back at Sart. "We don't like bisexuals either."

Sart made a dash for the door, but he didn't make it.

Richard grabbed one arm while Michael grabbed a handful of hair.

Richard quickly got Sart's other arm as well and with a triumphant laugh pinned both behind the boy. Sart struggled, but it was no use, especially with Michael still clutching a shock of his hair. Once the boy was immobilized, Michael punched him in the stomach, doubling him over.

Both divers let go of the boy and then laughed while they watched him take a few staggering steps. Sart was desperately trying to catch his breath. His face was purple.

"Okay, pansy," Richard slurred. "Here's one for putting your filthy paws on me."

Richard lifted Sart's face with his left hand and hit him with his right. It was not a jab but rather a wild, roundhouse uppercut behind which he put his entire weight. This second blow caught the boy full in the face, crushing his nose, sending him hurling backward off his feet, and inadvertently smashing his head against the sharp corner of the marble nightstand. Unfortunately the cold stone penetrated several inches into the back of the youngster's skull.

Richard was initially unaware of the fatal consequences of his powerful punch. He was too preoccupied by the intense pain of his bruised knuckles. Wincing, he cradled his throbbing hand with his other and cursed loudly.

Michael watched in horror as Sart's flaccid body came to a rest. Bits of brain tissue oozed from the ugly wound. Suddenly sober, Michael bent down over the stricken boy, who was making gurgling sounds.

"Richard!" Michael called out in a loud whisper. "We got a problem!"

Richard refused to respond. He was still in pain, pacing the room and shaking his hand in the air with his fingers widely spread.

Michael stood up. "Richard! Christ! The guy's dead."

"Dead?" Richard echoed. The finality of the word shattered Richard's self-absorption.

"Well, almost. His head's caved in. He hit the goddamned table."

Richard staggered back to where Michael was standing and looked down at Sart's motionless form. "Holy shit!" he said.

"What the hell are we going to do?" Michael demanded. "Why'd you hit him so freakin' hard?"

"I didn't mean to, okay!" Richard shouted.

"Well, what are we going to do?" Michael repeated.

"I don't know," Richard said.

At that moment Sart's battered body let out a final sigh and the gurgling stopped.

"That's it," Michael said with a shudder. "He's dead! We got to do something and fast."

"Maybe we should get outta here," Richard said.

"We can't get out of here," Michael complained. "Where are we going to go? Hell, we don't even know where we are."

"All right, let me think," Richard said. "Shit, I didn't mean to hurt him."

"Oh, sure," Michael said sarcastically.

"Well, not that much," Richard said.

"What if someone comes in here?" Michael questioned.

"You're right," Richard said. "We've got to hide the body."

"Where?" Michael demanded urgently.

"I don't know!" Richard yelled. He looked around

the room frantically. Then he looked back at Michael. "I just got an idea that might work."

"Good," Michael said. "Where?"

"First help me pick him up," Richard said. He stepped over the body, rolled it over, and then got his hands under Sart's arms.

Michael got Sart's feet, and together they hoisted the boy off the floor.

CHAPTER TWELVE

The new day arrived gradually just as it would on the earth's surface. The light slowly increased in intensity, causing the darkened, vaulted ceiling to lose its stars. Its color went in stages from deep indigo to a rosy pink and finally to a pure sky blue. Saranta began to stir.

Suzanne was the first of the earth surface visitors to awaken with the arrival of the artificial dawn. As she scanned her room, taking in the white marble, the mirrors, and the pool, she realized with a start that the surreal Interterran experience had not been a dream.

Slowly she turned her head to the side and gazed at Garona's sleeping form. He was on his side, facing her. She was amazed at herself for having allowed the man to stay the night. This was not her norm. The only way she'd shown some restraint had been by staunchly refusing to remove her silken tunic and shorts. She had spent the night with her clothes on, such as they were.

Suzanne wasn't sure she could blame her decision to allow him to stay on the small amount of crystal she'd drunk or whether it was simply Garona's handsome looks and winning flattery. As much as she hated to admit it, when it came to men, physical attractiveness was important to her. In fact, it had been part of the reason she'd remained mired in a volatile relationship with an actor back in L.A. long after it had ceased to be healthy.

As if sensing her gaze, Garona opened his dark, liquid eyes and smiled dreamily. It was difficult for Suzanne to feel much regret.

"I'm sorry if I woke you," Suzanne managed. He was as handsome in the first light of day as he'd been the night before.

"Please, don't be sorry," Garona said. "I appreciate being awakened to see that I am still with you."

"How is it you always say the right thing?" Suzanne said. She was being sincere, not sarcastic.

"I say what I would like to be told," Garona said.

Suzanne nodded. It was a sensible variation of the Golden Rule.

Garona rolled toward her and tried to envelop Suzanne in an embrace. Suzanne ducked under his arm and slid off the bed.

"Please, Garona," Suzanne said. "Let's not replay last night. Not now."

Garona flopped back onto the bed and stared up at Suzanne.

"I don't understand your reluctance," he said. "Could it be that you don't care for me?"

Suzanne groaned audibly. "Oh, Garona, for all your sophistication and sensitivity, I can't imagine why this is so hard for you to grasp. As I told you last night, it takes me a little time to get to know someone."

"What do you need to know?" Garona questioned. "You can ask me any personal question you like."

"Look," Suzanne said. "I certainly care for you. Just letting you stay here is a testament to that. It's not usual for me when I've known someone for such a short time. But I did let you stay, and I'm glad I did. But you can't expect too much from me. Think of everything I'm trying to take in."

"But it's unnatural," Garona said. "Your emotions should not be so contingent."

"I disagree!" Suzanne remarked. "It's called self-protection. I can't go around allowing spur-of-the-moment desires to dictate my behavior. And it should be the same for you. After all, you don't know anything about me. Maybe I have a husband or a lover."

"I assume you do," Garona said. "In fact, I would be surprised if you didn't. Anyway, it doesn't matter."

"That's nice." Suzanne put her hands defiantly on her hips. "It doesn't matter to you, but what about me?" Suzanne stopped herself. She reached up and rubbed her sleep-filled eyes. She was getting herself all worked up, and she'd only been awake for a few minutes.

"Let's not discuss any of this right now," Suzanne said. "This day is going to be challenging enough. Arak has promised to answer our questions, and believe me, I have a lot." She walked over to one of the many mirrors and cautiously moved into the line of sight of her image. She grimaced at the reflection. Her mind might have been in a turmoil, but there was one thing she knew for certain: she did not look her best in inch-long hair.

Putting his legs over the edge of the bed, Garona sat up and stretched. "You second-generation humans are so serious."

"I don't know what you mean by 'second generation'," Suzanne said. "But I think I have reason to be serious. After all, I didn't come here on my own accord.

As Donald said, we've been abducted. And I don't have to remind you that means being carried off by force."

As he had promised, Arak showed up just after the group had eaten breakfast and asked if everyone was ready for the didactic session. Perry and Suzanne were demonstrably eager, Donald less so, and Richard and Michael completely uninterested. In fact, they acted tense and subdued, hardly their normal brazen selves. Perry assumed they were suffering from hangovers and suggested as much to Suzanne.

"I wouldn't doubt it," Suzanne responded. "As drunk as they were it stands to reason. How do you feel?"

"Great," Perry said. "All things considered. It was an interesting evening. How about your friend, Garona. Did he stay long?"

"For a while," Suzanne said evasively. "How about Luna?"

"The same," Perry said. Neither one looked the other in the eye.

As soon as the group was ready, Arak led them across the lawn toward a hemispherical structure similar to the pavilion although on a much smaller scale. Perry and Suzanne kept up with Arak. Donald lagged a few steps behind and Richard and Michael even more so.

"I still think you should tell Donald," Michael insisted in a whisper. "He might have an idea about what to do."

"What the hell is that bastard going to do?" Richard responded. "The kid's dead. Fuller's not going to bring him back to life."

"Maybe he'll have a better idea where to put the body," Michael said. "I'm worried about the kid being found. I mean, I don't want you to find out what they do down here to murderers."

Richard stopped short. "What do you mean, me?"

"Hey, you killed him," Michael said.

"You hit him, too," Richard said.

"But I didn't kill him," Michael said. "And the whole thing was your idea."

Richard glowered at his friend. "We're in this together, dirtbag. It's your room. Whatever happens to me is going to happen to you. Plain as day."

"Come on, you two," Arak called. He was holding open a door to the small hemispherical, windowless structure. The other members of the group were standing to the side and looking back in the divers' direction.

"Regardless," Michael whispered nervously, "the point is that the body is hardly hidden. You got to ask Donald if he can think of a better place for it. He might be an ex–officer asshole, but he's smart."

"Okay," Richard said reluctantly.

The two divers quickened their pace and caught up to the others. Arak smiled congenially and then entered the building followed by Suzanne and Perry. As Donald crossed the threshold Richard gave his sleeve a tug. Donald snatched his arm away and glared back at Richard, but kept walking.

"Hey, Commander Fuller!" Richard whispered. "Hold up a second."

Donald glanced briefly over his shoulder, treated Richard to a contemptuous look, and continued walking. Arak was leading them along a curved, windowless corridor.

"I wanted to apologize about last night," Richard said, catching up to Donald so that he was walking right behind him.

"For what?" Donald asked scornfully. "Being stupid, being drunk, or allowing yourself to be duped by these people?"

Richard bit his lower lip before responding. "Maybe all three. We were bombed out of our gourds. But that's not the reason I want to talk to you."

Donald stopped short. Richard all but collided with him. Michael did bump into Richard.

"What is it, sailor?" Donald demanded in a no-nonsense voice. "Make it on the double. We've got an interesting talk ahead of us that I don't want to miss."

"Well, it's just that . . ." Richard began, but then he stumbled over his words, unsure of how to begin. Contrary to his early braggadocio, he was intimidated by Donald.

"Come on, sailor," Donald snapped. "Out with it."

"Michael and I think we better get the hell out of Interterra," Richard said.

"Oh, that's very intelligent of you boneheads," Donald said. "I suppose this sudden epiphany just occurred to you this morning. Well, perhaps I should remind you that we don't know where the hell we are until Arak decides to tell us. So once we've learned that, maybe we can talk again." Donald made a motion to leave. Richard grabbed his arm out of desperation. Donald glared down at Richard's hand. "Let go of me before I lose complete control."

"But—" Richard said.

"Can it, sailor!" Donald snapped, cutting off the conversation and yanking his arm away from Richard. He walked briskly ahead and ducked through a door at the end of the corridor in pursuit of the others.

"Why the hell didn't you tell him?" Michael demanded in an irritated whisper.

"You didn't tell him either," Richard pointed out.

"Yeah, because you said you'd do the talking," Michael said. He threw up his hands in frustration. "Some talking! My grandmother could have done a better job. Now we're back where we started. And you've got to admit, that body's not in the world's best hiding place. What if they find it?"

Richard shuddered. "I hate to think. But it was the best we could do under the circumstances."

"Maybe we should just stay in the room," Michael suggested.

"That's not going to solve anything," Richard said. "Come on! Let's at least find out where we are so we can figure out how to get the hell out."

The two men followed Donald and found themselves in a futuristic, circular room thirty feet in diameter with a domed ceiling. There were no windows. A single row of a dozen molded seats surrounded a dark, slightly convex central area.

Arak and Sufa were sitting directly opposite the entrance, in seats with consoles built into their arms. To Arak and Sufa's immediate right were two people the divers had never seen before. Although this couple was dressed in the usual white, they were not as attractive as the other Interterrans. Suzanne and Perry were seated to Arak and Sufa's left. Donald was to the far right, sitting by himself with lots of empty seats between him and the others.

"Please, Richard, Michael," Arak called out. "Take your seats. Anyplace you'd like. And then we'll begin."

Richard made it a point to pass several empty seats to take one next to Donald. Richard nodded to him, but Donald responded by shifting his weight away from the diver. Michael took the seat next to Richard.

"Welcome again to Interterra," Arak said. "Today we are going to challenge your intellects in a very positive way. And in the process you will soon learn how very lucky you all are."

"How about starting by telling us when we'll be heading home?" Richard said.

"Shut the hell up!" Donald growled.

Arak laughed. "Richard, I do appreciate your spontaneity and impulsiveness, but be patient."

"First we'd like to introduce everyone to two of our distinguished citizens," Sufa said. "I'm certain you will find talking with them extremely helpful since they, like yourselves, have come from the surface world. May I present Ismael and Mary Black."

The couple stood for a moment and bowed. Michael clapped from habit but immediately stopped when he realized he was the only one doing so. Suzanne and Perry regarded the couple with wide-eyed curiosity.

"Mary and I would like to extend our welcome as well," Ismael said. He was a rather tall man with gaunt, hatchetlike features and deeply set eyes. "We are here because we have experienced what you are about to experience, and because of that we may be able to help. As for a general suggestion, I would encourage you at this point not to try to absorb too much too quickly."

Michael leaned over to Richard and whispered, "Do you think he's referring to that fabulous hand cream stuff we used last night?"

"Shut up!" Donald snapped, emphasizing each word. "If you men keep interrupting, I want you to move away from me."

"All right already," Michael said.

"Thank you, Ismael," Arak said. Then looking at each of the visitors in turn he added, "I hope you will all take advantage of the Blacks' offer. We feel that a division of labor will be helpful. Sufa and I will be available for informational issues whereas adjustment issues will be best handled by Ismael and Mary."

Suzanne leaned over to Perry. There was a new look of concern on her face. "What does he mean, 'adjustment issues'? How long do you think they intend to keep us here?"

"I don't know," Perry whispered back. He'd been struck by the same implication.

"Before we begin I would like to present each of you with a telecommunicator and an eyepiece," Sufa said. She opened a box that she'd brought to the meeting and lifted out five small parcels, each with a name printed in bold letters across the top. Carrying them in her arms she walked around the room and handed them out to the designated recipients. Richard and Michael tore theirs open like kids attacking Christmas presents. Suzanne and Perry opened theirs with care. Donald let his sit unopened on his lap.

"It's like a pair of glasses and a wristwatch without a face," Michael said. He was disappointed. He tried on the glasses. They were aerodynamically shaped with clear lenses.

"It's a telecommunicator system," Sufa said. "They are voice activated, and each is mated to your individual voices, so they are not interchangeable. We'll be showing you how to use them later."

"What do they do?" Richard asked. He tried the glasses on as well.

"Just about everything," Sufa said. "They connect with central sources whose information will be displayed virtually through the glasses. They also provide communication with anyone else in Interterra by sight and sound. They even do such mundane things as call air taxis, but more about them later."

"Let's get started," Arak said. He touched the pad on the console in front of him and the darkened convex area turned a phosphorescent blue.

"The first thing we must talk about is the concept of time," Arak said. "This is perhaps the most difficult subject for people like yourselves to grasp because here in Interterra time is not the immutable construct it appears to be on the earth's surface. Your scientist, Mr. Einstein, recognized the relativity of time in the sense that it depends on one's position of observation. Here in Interterra you will confront many examples of such relativity. The simplest, for example, is the age of our civilization. From the perspective of earth surface references, our civilization is incredibly ancient, whereas from our reference point and those of the rest of the solar system, it is not. Your civilization is measured in terms of millennia, ours in millions, and the solar system in billions."

"Oh, for chrissake," Richard complained. "Do we have to sit through all this? I thought you were going to tell us where the hell we are."

"Unless you comprehend the basics," Arak said, "what I'm going to be telling you will be unbelievable, even meaningless."

"Why not work backwards," Richard said. "Tell us where we are and then the other stuff."

"Richard!" Suzanne snapped. "Be still!"

Richard rolled his eyes for Michael's benefit. Michael showed his impatience by uncrossing and recrossing his legs.

"Time is not a constant," Arak continued. "As I said, your clever scientist Mr. Einstein recognized this, but where he made his mistake was thinking that the speed of light was the upper boundary of motion. It is not the case, although it takes a huge quanta of focused energy to break the boundary. A good analogy from everyday life is the extra amount of energy necessary for a phase change that takes a solid to a liquid or a liquid to a gas. Pushing an object beyond the speed of light is like a phase change into a dimension where time is plastic and related only to space."

"Good grief," Richard blurted. "Is this a joke?"

Donald stood up and took a seat far from the two divers.

"Try to be patient," Arak said. "And concentrate on time not being a constant. Think about it! If time is truly relative then it can be controlled, manipulated, and changed. Which brings us to the concept of death. Listen carefully! On the earth's surface death has been a necessary adjunct of evolution, and evolution the only justification of death. But once evolution has evolved to create a sensate, cognitive being, death is not only not needed, it is a waste."

At the mention of death Richard and Michael sank lower into their seats. Perry raised his hand. Arak immediately acknowledged him.

"Are we permitted to ask questions?" Perry asked.

"Absolutely," Arak said agreeably. "This is to be more of a seminar than a lecture. But I ask you only to question what I have already said and not question what you believe I am about to say."

"You talked about measuring time," Perry said. "Did you mean to imply that your civilization, as you put it, predates our civilization on the earth's surface?"

"Indeed," Arak said. "And by a quantum of time almost incomprehensible to your experience. Our Interterran recorded history goes back almost six hundred million years."

"Get out of here!" Richard scoffed. "That's impossible. This is all a bunch of bull crap. That's older than the dinosaurs."

"Much older than your dinosaurs," Arak agreed. "And your disbelief is entirely understandable. That is why we go slowly with this introduction to Interterra. I don't mean to belabor the point, but it is far easier to adapt to your present reality in stages."

"That's all well and good," Richard announced. "But how about some proof for all this baloney. I'm starting to think this whole setup is an elaborate put-on, and frankly, I'm not interested in sitting here wasting time."

Neither Donald nor Suzanne complained about Richard's current interruption. Both were harboring similar thoughts although Suzanne certainly would not have worded her skepticism so rudely. Arak, however, was unfazed.

"All right," Arak said patiently. "We will provide some proof that you can relate to your civilization's history. Our civilization has been observing and recording the progress of your second-generation human civilization since the time of your evolution."

"What do you mean exactly by second-generation human?" Suzanne asked.

"That will be apparent shortly," Arak said. "First, let's show you some interesting images. As I said, we have been observing your civilization's progress, and until about fifty years ago we could do so at will. Since then your increasing technological sophistication has limited our surveillance to avoid detection. In fact, we have stopped using most of our old-fashioned exit ports, like the one used to admit you to Interterra or the one at Barsama, our sister city to the west. Both were ordered to be sealed with magma, but worker clone bureaucratic ineptitude has stalled the execution of the decree."

"My god, you're one long-winded dude," Richard said. "Where's the proof?"

"The cavern our submersible ended up in?" Suzanne questioned. "Was that what you call an exit port?"

"Exactly," Arak said.

"Is it normally filled with seawater?" Suzanne asked.

"Correct again," Arak said.

Suzanne turned to Perry. "No wonder Sea Mount Olympus was never picked up by Geosat. The seamount doesn't have the mass to be sensed on a gravimeter."

"Come on!" Richard complained. "Enough stalling. Let's see the proof!"

"Okay, Richard," Arak said patiently. "Why don't you suggest some period in your history that you would care to observe from our reference files. The more ancient the better in order to make my point."

Richard looked at Michael for help.

"How about gladiators," Michael said. "Let's see some Roman gladiators."

"Gladiatorial combat could be seen," Arak said reluctantly. "But such violent recordings are under strict censorship. To view them would require special dispensation by the Council of Elders. Perhaps another era would be more suitable."

"This is goddamn ridiculous!" Richard voiced.

"Try to control yourself, sailor," Donald snapped.

"Let me understand what you mean," Suzanne said. "Are you suggesting that you have recordings of all of human history, and you want us to suggest some historical time so we can see some images of it?"

"Precisely," Arak answered.

"How about the Middle Ages?" Suzanne said.

"That's a rather large era," Arak said. "Can you be more specific?"

"Okay," Suzanne said. "How about fourteenth-century France."

"That's during the Hundred Years' War," Arak said without enthusiasm. "It's curious even you, Dr. Newell, request images from such a violent time. But then again, you second-generation humans have had a violent record."

"Show people at play, not war," Suzanne said.

Arak touched the keypad on his console and then leaned forward to speak into a small microphone at its center. Almost immediately the room's illumination dimmed, and the floor screen came alive with blurred images flashing by at an incredible speed. Captivated, everyone leaned over the low wall and watched.

Presently the images slowed, then stopped. The projected scene was crystal clear with natural coloring and perfect holographic three dimensions. It was of a small wheat field in the late summer from an altitude of about four or five hundred feet. A group of people had paused in their harvest activities. Their scythes were haphazardly strewn around several blankets on which a modest meal was spread. The audio was of summer cicadas buzzing intermittently.

"This is not interesting," Arak said after a quick glance. "It's not going to be proof of anything. Other than the peoples' crude garments, there is no indication of the time frame. Let's let the search recommence."

Before anyone could respond the screen again blurred as thousands of images flashed by. It was dizzying to watch the rapid flickering, but soon it again slowed and then stopped.

"Ah, this is much better," Arak exclaimed. Now the view was of a castle erected on a rocky prominence that was hosting a tournament of some kind. The vantage point was significantly higher than the previous scene.

The coloration of the vegetation around the castle walls suggested midautumn. The courtyard was packed with boisterous people whose voices formed a muted murmur. Everyone was dressed in colorful medieval attire. Heraldic pennants snapped in the breeze. At either end of a long, low log fence running down the center of the courtyard, two knights were in the final preparations for a joust. Their colorfully caparisoned horses were facing each other, pawing with excitement.

"How are these pictures taken?" Perry asked. He was transfixed by the image.

"It's a standard recording device," Arak said.

"I mean from what vantage point?" Perry asked. "Some kind of helicopter?"

Arak and Sufa laughed. "Excuse our giggles," Arak said. "A helicopter is your technology. Not ours. Besides, such a vehicle would be too intrusive. These images were taken by a small, silent, unmanned antigravity ship hovering at about twenty thousand feet."

"Hey, Hollywood does this stuff all the time," Richard said. "Big deal! This is not proof."

"If this is a set it's the most realistic one I've ever seen," Suzanne said. She leaned closer. As far as she was concerned the detail was far more than Hollywood was capable of.

As they watched, the attendant pages of the armored knights stepped back, and the men-at-arms lowered their lances. With a crisp fanfare sounding, the two horses charged forward on opposites sides of the log fence. As they bore down on each other the cheering of the crowd mushroomed. Then, just before the horsemen made contact, the screen went blank. A moment later it reverted back to its initial phosphorescent blue. A message window popped up and said: "Scene censored. Apply to Council of Elders."

"Damn!" Michael voiced. "I was getting into it. Who the hell won: the guy in green or the guy in red?"

"Richard's right," Donald said suddenly, ignoring Michael. "These scenes can be staged too easily."

"Perhaps," Arak said without taking the slightest offense. "But I can show you whatever you want. We wouldn't be able to stage the full complement of first-generation history subject to your on-the-spot whim."

"How about something more ancient?" Perry suggested. "How about Neolithic times in the same location where the castle was."

"Clever idea!" Arak said. "I'll plug in the coordinates without a specific time other than, say, prior to ten thousand years ago, and let the search engine see if there is an image in storage."

The screen again came to life. Once again images flashed by. This time the flashing continued much longer.

Suzanne touched Perry's arm. She leaned toward him when he turned to her. "I think we're looking at real images," she said.

"I do, too," Perry said. "Can you imagine the technology involved!"

"I'm thinking less about the technology than the fact that this place is real," Suzanne whispered. "We're not dreaming all this."

"Ah!" Arak commented. "I can tell the search has found something. And the time frame will be in the twenty-five-thousand-year range." As he spoke, the images slowed and again stopped.

The scene was the same rocky prominence although there was no castle. Instead the crown of the hill was dominated by a short escarpment undercut in the center to form a shallow cave. Grouped around the entrance to the cave was an assemblage of Neanderthals clothed in fur and working on crude implements.

"It does look like the same place," Perry commented.

As everyone watched, the image telescoped in on the domestic scene.

"And the pictures are clearer," Perry added.

"At that time we didn't worry about our ships being seen," Arak explained, "so we felt comfortable dropping down to a mere hundred feet or so to study behavior."

As they watched, one of the Neanderthal men straightened up from scraping a hide. In the process of stretching he happened to look straight up. When he did, his brutish face suddenly went blank, and his mouth dropped open in a mixture of surprise and terror. The image on the screen was close enough and clear enough to reveal his large square teeth.

"Well," Arak commented, "here's an example of our antigravity drone being seen. The poor devil probably thinks he's being visited by the gods."

"My gosh," Suzanne said. "He's trying to get the others to look up!"

"Their language was very limited," Arak said. "But I know that there was another subspecies in this same time frame and in the same general area that you called the Cro-Magnon. Their language skills were far better."

The Neanderthal grunted and leaped up and down while pointing toward the camera. Soon the entire group was looking skyward. Several of the women with young children immediately scooped their babies into their arms and disappeared into the cave while others dashed out.

One enterprising man bent down, picked up an egg-sized stone, and hurled it skyward. The missile approached, then went out of sight to the side.

"Not a bad arm," Michael said. "The Red Sox could use him out in center field."

Arak touched his console and the image faded. At the same time the lights went up in the room. Everyone moved back in their seats. Arak and Sufa looked around the room. The visitors were all quiet for the moment, even Richard.

"What was the supposed date of that recording?" Perry asked finally.

Arak consulted his console. "In your calendar it would have been July fourteenth, twenty-three three forty-two B.C."

"Didn't it bother you people that your camera platform was seen?" Suzanne asked. The image of the Neanderthal's face was haunting her.

"We were starting to be concerned about detection," Arak agreed. "There was even some talk among our conservative wing at the time to eliminate cognitive beings from the surface of the earth."

"Why would you be concerned about such primitive people?" Perry asked.

"Purely to avoid detection," Arak said. "Obviously twenty-five thousand years ago, due to the primitivism of your civilization, it didn't matter. But we knew it would, eventually. We know that our ships have been sighted occasionally even in your modern times, and it does concern us. Thankfully the sightings have mostly been greeted with disbelief, or if not with disbelief then with the idea that our interplanetary ships have come from someplace else in the universe, not from within the earth itself."

"Wait a second," Donald said suddenly. "I don't like to rain on anyone's parade, but I don't think this little show you're putting on here proves anything at all. It would be too easy to pull this off with computer-generated images. Why don't you cut all this gibberish, and just tell us who you represent and what you want from us."

For a moment no one spoke. Arak and Sufa leaned over and consulted with one another sotto voce. Then they conferred with Ismael and Mary. After a short, hushed conference, the hosts repositioned themselves back in their chairs. Arak looked directly at Donald.

"Mr. Fuller, your skepticism is fully understandable," Arak said. "We're not sure everyone else shares your suspicions. Perhaps later they can influence your opinion. Of course there will be more proof as your introduction proceeds, and I'm confident that you will be won over. Meanwhile, we'd like to beg for your patience for a while longer."

Donald did not respond. He merely glared back at Arak.

"Let's move on," Arak said. "And allow me to give you a capsule history of Interterra. To do that we must begin in your domain, the earth's surface. Life there began about five hundred million years after the earth formed and took several billion years to evolve. Your earth scientists are well aware of this. What they are not aware of is that we, the first-generation humans, evolved about five hundred and fifty million years ago during evolution's first phase. The reason your scientists are unaware of this first phase is because almost the entire fossilized record of it disappeared during a time we call the Dark Period. More about that later. First we have some images of these early times of our civilization, but the quality is not good."

The light dimmed progressively. In the gathering darkness Suzanne and Perry exchanged glances, but didn't speak. Their attention was soon directed at the floor screen. After another flickering interval a scene appeared taken at eye level, depicting an environment similar to the one the visitors had seen in Interterra. The main difference was that the buildings were white instead of black although the shapes were similar. And the people appeared like normal human beings—they weren't all gorgeous and they were engaged in a variety of everyday tasks.

"Watching these scenes makes us smile at our own primitiveness," Sufa said.

"Indeed," Arak agreed. "We didn't have worker clones at that ancient time."

Suzanne cleared her throat. She was trying to sort through everything Arak was saying. As an earth scientist, his lecture collided with everything she knew about evolution in general and human evolution in particular. "Are you suggesting that these images we're seeing are from five hundred and fifty million years ago?"

"That's correct," Arak answered. He suppressed a laugh. He and Sufa were apparently amused by the antics of an individual trying to lift a block of stone. "Excuse us from finding this so funny," he said. "We haven't seen any of these sequences for a very long time. It was back when we had something akin to your nationalities, although they disappeared after the first fifty thousand years of our history. Wars disappeared at the same time, as you might imagine. As you can see, the surface of the earth was very different from the way it is now, and it is that appearance that we have re-created here in Interterra. Back then there was just one supercontinent and one superocean."

"What happened?" Suzanne asked. "Why did your civilization choose to go underground?"

"Because of the Dark Period," Arak said. "Our civilization had almost a million years of peaceful progress until we became aware of ominous developments in a galaxy close to ours. Within a relatively short time a series of cataclysmic supernova explosions occurred, effectively showering earth with enough radiation to dissipate the ozone layer. We could have dealt with that, but our scientists also recognized that these galactic events also upset the delicate balance of the solar system's asteroid population. It became evident the earth was to be showered with planetesimal collisions, just as had happened when it was in its primordial state."

"For crying out loud!" Richard moaned. "I can't take much more of this."

"Quiet, Richard!" Suzanne snapped without taking her eyes off Arak. "So Interterra was driven underground."

"Exactly," Arak said. "We knew the surface of the earth would become uninhabitable. It was a desperate time. We searched the solar system for a new home without success, and had not yet developed the time technology to search other galaxies. Then it was suggested that our only chance for survival was to move underground, or actually under the ocean. We had the technology so we did it in a miraculously short time. And very soon after we moved, the world as we knew it was consumed in deadly radiation, asteroidal bombardment, and geological upheaval. It was a close call even under the protective layer of the ocean, because at one point the ocean came close to boiling away from the intense heat. All life forms on earth were destroyed except for some primitive bacteria, some viruses, and a bit of blue-green algae."

Suddenly the screen went blank and the illumination in the room returned.

Everyone was quiet.

"Well, there you have it," Arak said. "A concentrated capsule of Interterran history and scientific fact. Now, I'm sure you'll have questions."

"How long did the Dark Period last?" Suzanne asked.

"A little more than twenty-five thousand years," Arak answered.

Suzanne shook her head in amazement and disbelief, yet it all made a certain amount of scientific sense. And most important, it explained the reality she presently found herself in.

"But you stayed under the ocean," Perry said. "Why didn't your people return to the earth's surface?"

"For two main reasons," Arak said. "First, we had everything we needed and we'd become accustomed to our environment. And second, when surface life evolved anew, the bacteria and viruses that developed were organisms to which we had never been exposed. In other words, by the time the climate would have permitted our reemergence, the biosphere was antigenically inimical to us. Perhaps deadly is a better word, unless we were willing to go through a strenuous adaptation. And so here we remain, very happy and content especially since here under the ocean we are not at the whim of nature. Of all the universe we have visited thus far, this small planet is the best suited to the human organism."

"Now I understand why we had to go through such a strenuous decontamination," Suzanne said. "We had to be microorganism-free."

"Exactly," Arak said. "And at the same time you had to be adapted to our organisms."

"In other words," Suzanne continued, "evolution occurred twice on earth with essentially the same outcome."

"Almost the same outcome," Arak said. "There were some differences in certain species. At first we were surprised about this, but then it made sense in that the original DNA is the same. Multicellular life evolved from the same blue-green algae in both instances and with approximately the same climatic conditions."

"Which is why you refer to yourselves as first-generation humans," Suzanne said, "and to us as second-generation humans."

Arak smiled with satisfaction. "We counted on your understanding all this as rapidly as you have, Dr. Newell," he said.

Suzanne turned to Perry and Donald. "Scientific studies confirm some of this," she said. "Both geological and oceanographic evidence suggest there was an ancient single continent on earth, called Pangaea."

"Excuse me," Arak said. "I don't mean to interrupt, but that's not the same as our original continent. Pangaea formed de novo during the latter part of the Dark Period geological upheavals. Our continent suffered complete subduction into the asthenosphere prior to that."

Suzanne nodded. "Very interesting," she said. "And that must be the reason the fossil record of the first evolution is not available."

Arak smiled contentedly again. "Your grasp of these basic fundamentals is heartening indeed, Dr. Newell. But we had anticipated as much even before your arrival."

"Before I arrived?" Suzanne questioned. "What is that supposed to mean?"

"Nothing," Arak added quickly. "Nothing at all. Perhaps we should remind your colleagues that it was the breakup of Pangaea that formed the present continental configuration."

"That's true," Suzanne agreed while she eyed Arak searchingly. She had the uncomfortable sense that there was something Arak was not telling her. She looked over at Donald and Perry and wondered how much even they were taking in. Arak's presentation was clearly beyond Richard and Michael. They looked like bored schoolkids.

"Well, then," Arak said, marshaling some enthusiasm by rubbing his hands together. "I can only imagine how all this information affects you people. Having one's preconceived and accepted notions dashed is a daunting experience. That's why we have been insisting on going slowly with your introduction to our world. I'd venture to guess that you've already had enough talk, too much perhaps. At this point I think it would be better to show you some of the ways we live, firsthand."

"You mean go out into the city?" Richard asked.

"If that will be agreeable to everyone?" Arak said.

"Count me in," Richard said eagerly.

"Me, too," Michael echoed.

"What about the rest of you?" Arak asked.

"I'll go," Suzanne said.

"Of course I'll go," Perry said when Arak looked at him.

When it was Donald's turn he merely nodded.

"Wonderful," Arak said. He stood. "Now if you'll give Sufa and me a few minutes by remaining in your seats, we'll make the arrangements." He extended a hand toward Sufa, and she rose as well. Together they exited the small conference room.

Perry shook his head. "I feel shell-shocked. This whole situation keeps getting more and more unbelievable."

"I'm not sure I believe anything," Donald said.

"Ironically enough, it seems to me to be too fantastic not to be true," Suzanne said. "And it all makes a certain amount of scientific sense." She looked over at

Ismael and Mary Black, who had been sitting patiently. "Please, folks, tell us your story. Is it true you are from the surface world?"

"Yes, it is," Ismael said.

"From where?" Perry asked.

"From Gloucester, Massachusetts," Mary said.

"No kidding," Michael said. He sat up. "Hey, I'm from Massachusetts, too: Chelsea. Ever been there?"

"I've heard of it," Ismael said. "But I've never been there."

"Everybody from the North Shore has been to Chelsea," Michael said with a snicker. "Because one end of the Tobin Bridge sits on it."

"I've never heard of the Tobin Bridge," Ismael said. Michael's eyes narrowed in disbelief.

"How'd you two end up down here in Interterra?" Richard questioned.

"We were very lucky," Mary said. "Very lucky indeed. Just like you people."

"Were you diving?" Perry asked.

"No," Ismael said. "We ran into a terrible storm en route from the Azores to America. We should have drowned like the others on our ship. But, as Mary said, we were lucky, and we were inadvertently rescued by an Interterran interplanetary vehicle. We literally got sucked into the same exit port you people did and were then revived by the Interterrans."

"What was the name of your ship?" Donald asked.

"It was called the *Tempest*," Ismael said, "which turned out to be rather appropriate considering the fate. It was a schooner out of Gloucester."

"A schooner?" Donald questioned suspiciously. "What year did this happen?"

"Let's see," Mary said, "I was sixteen. That makes it eighteen hundred and one."

"Oh, for chrissake," Donald muttered. He closed his eyes and ran a hand over his bald head. He'd shaved it that morning. "And you people wonder why I'm skeptical?"

"Mary, that's about two hundred years ago," Suzanne said.

"I know," Mary said. "It's hard to believe, but isn't it wonderful? Look how young we look."

"You expect us to believe that you are over two hundred years old?" Perry questioned.

"It's going to take time for you to comprehend the world that you are now in," Mary said. "All I can say is that you should try to avoid making any hardened opinions until you've seen and heard more. We can remember how we felt when we were being subjected to the same information. And remember, for us it was even more astounding since your technology has come a long way in the last two hundred years."

"I second Mary's advice," Ismael said. "Try to keep in mind what Arak said at the beginning of the session. Time has a different meaning here in Interterra. In fact, Interterrans don't die the way they do on the surface."

"My ass they don't die," Michael whispered.

"Shut up," Richard whispered back through clenched teeth.

CHAPTER THIRTEEN

To Perry and the others the air taxi looked the same as the one they'd been in the day before, but Arak said it was a newer model and far superior. Regardless, it whisked the group in a similarly effortless and silent fashion from the visitors' palace grounds into the bustling city.

"Immigrants usually spend an entire week in the conference room before venturing out like this," Sufa said. "It can be taxing to the intellect as well as the emotions. We hope we're not pushing you too fast."

"Do you have any thoughts about this?" Arak asked. "We're certainly open to suggestions."

The group eyed each other, each hoping another would respond. As Sufa intimated, the situation was stupefying, especially with the cloud of other air taxis zipping by in every conceivable direction. The fact that there were no collisions was astounding in and of itself.

"Doesn't anybody have an opinion?" Arak persisted.

"Everything is overwhelming," Perry admitted. "So

it's hard to have an opinion. But I believe from my perspective, the more I see, the better. Merely experiencing your technology like this air taxi makes everything you've said more credible."

"What are you going to show us?" Suzanne asked.

"That was a difficult decision," Arak said. "It's why Sufa and I took so long arranging things. It was hard to decide where to start."

Before Arak could finish, the hovercraft came to a sudden stop then rapidly descended. A moment later the exit port appeared where previously there had not even been a seam.

"How does the door open like that?" Perry asked.

"It's a molecular transformation in the composite material," Arak said. He gestured for everyone to disembark.

Perry leaned over to Suzanne as he got up. "As if that's an explanation," he complained.

The air taxi had deposited the group in front of a relatively low, windowless structure sheathed in the same black basalt as all the other buildings. Its sides were about a hundred feet long and twenty feet high, and they slanted in at sixty degrees to create a squat, truncated pyramid. There was little pedestrian traffic. Even so, the moment the secondary humans appeared, a crowd began to form.

"I hope you people don't mind being celebrities," Arak said. "As I'm sure you realized from last night, all of Saranta is thrilled about your arrival."

The gathering crowd was boisterous but polite. Those closest to the visitors eagerly put out their hands in an effort to press palms with them. Richard and Michael were happy to oblige, especially with the women. Arak had to act like a border collie to get the group through the door, particularly the two divers. The crowd respectfully stayed outside.

"I'm liking this place more and more," Richard said.

"I'm glad," Arak said.

"Everyone is remarkably friendly," Suzanne said.

"Of course," Sufa said. "It is our nature. Besides, you people are extraordinarily entertaining."

Suzanne glanced at Donald to see his reaction. All he did was give an almost imperceptible nod, as if his suspicions were confirmed.

Inside, the group found themselves in a large square room with a black interior instead of the usual white. It was quite plain, with no decoration, furniture, or even doors save for the entrance. A number of Interterrans were standing in the room facing blank walls. When they saw who had arrived, they became animated.

Arak hustled the five through the well-wishers to an empty section of wall and murmured into his wrist communicator. To the group's astonishment, the wall before them opened the same way the air taxis had. Arak shepherded them into a small cubicle beyond.

"Sometime you've got to explain to me how this opening and closing works," Perry said to Arak. Perry put his hand on the wall once he'd stepped into the smaller but equally blank room. The material's texture and heat conductivity suggested to him something akin to fiberglass.

"Certainly," Arak said, but he was distracted by talking into his communicator. A moment later the wall sealed over and the room plunged.

Everyone instinctively grabbed onto whomever was next to them as they became practically weightless.

"My god!" Michael blurted. "The room is falling."

"It's only an elevator," Arak said.

All the second-generation humans laughed self-consciously.

"Hey, how was I supposed to know?" Michael complained. He thought people were laughing at him.

"Getting back to the decision of what to show you first," Arak said. "Sufa and I decided to do the opposite of what you might do on the surface. Instead of showing you life from the cradle to the grave, we thought we'd show you life from the grave to the cradle." Arak smirked at this apparent illogical inversion and Sufa joined in.

"We must be going rather deep," Suzanne said. She was too preoccupied by the surroundings to respond to Arak's comment. Although there was no noise or perceived movement, the comparative weightlessness gave a clue as to the speed of the descent.

"We are going deep indeed," Arak said. "As a consequence, it will be a bit warm down here."

Eventually the descent slowed, and everyone braced themselves instinctively. Perry put his hand back on the wall and felt a pulse of heat prior to its opening up. Arak and Sufa led the way out.

Brightly illuminated corridors stretched out in three directions: straight ahead and to either side. Each was a study in perspective. Multiple other corridors could be seen oriented at right angles.

Waiting at the elevator was a small, open vehicle. It suggested the same technology as the air taxi since it was silently suspended several feet off the floor. Arak motioned for everyone to board. Perry and Suzanne climbed on along with Sufa, but Donald hesitated, effectively blocking Richard and Michael. He looked up and down the apparently endless hallways. As Arak had warned, the air was warm. The top of Donald's head glistened with sweat.

"Please," Arak said, gesturing again toward a seat on the small antigravity bus.

"This looks like some kind of prison," Donald said suspiciously.

"It is not a prison," Arak assured him. "There are no prisons in Interterra."

Michael glanced at Richard and gave a thumbs-up sign.

"If it's not a prison, what is it?" Donald asked.

"It's a catacomb," Arak said. "There's no need to be concerned. It is entirely safe, and we'll only be here for a short, instructive visit."

Reluctantly, Donald stepped up into the bus. It was apparent he wasn't much more thrilled about being in a burial vault as he had been about being in a prison. Richard and Michael followed. Once Arak was seated, he spoke into the microphone on the console. Within seconds they were shooting along the corridor like a silent express train save for the sound of the wind.

The reason for the vehicle was apparent after they had been underway for a few minutes. Traveling as quickly as they were at a speed magnified by the proximity of the walls, they covered a great distance in what turned out to be an enormous, subterranean labyrinthine grid. After a quarter hour and a half dozen dizzying right-angle turns, the vehicle slowed and stopped.

Small rooms budded off each corridor, and into one of these Arak directed the group. Donald made it plain he was not happy to be so isolated and stayed by the entrance.

The walls of the small room were filled with niches. Arak went to a particular niche chest-high and pulled out a box and a book. "I haven't been here for a long time," he said. He brushed off dust from both objects. "This box is my tomb." He held it up. It was black and about the size of a shoebox. "And this book contains a list of the dates of all my previous deaths."

"Bull!" Richard blurted. "Now you want us to believe you've risen from the dead! And not once but rather a bunch of times. Come on, man!"

Suzanne found herself nodding as Richard put words to her own reaction. Just when she was beginning to believe everything she'd been told, Arak had to come out with a statement that totally defied credulity. She glanced at Perry to see if he had the same response. But Perry was transfixed by the book, which Arak had placed in his hands.

Arak carefully opened the lid of the box, looked in, and then passed it around for the others to examine. Suzanne glanced in reluctantly, unsure of what she was going to see. It turned out to be only a mat of hair.

Arak and Sufa both smiled. It was as if they were deriving enjoyment out of their guests' confusion.

"Let me explain," Arak said. "In the box is a lock of hair from each of my former bodies. The bodies themselves have been returned to the molten asthenosphere, which is not far from where we are standing. As you might expect, everything is recycled in Interterra."

"I don't understand this book," Perry said. He flipped through some of the pages, glancing at the columns of handwritten figures, which made no sense as dates in the Gregorian calendar. As an added complication there were hundreds of them.

"You're not supposed to," Arak said with a playful smile. "Not yet. Or at least not until we go up to the main processing hall." He took the book from Perry and replaced it along with the box in the niche.

Confused, the group followed Arak out of the small room and reboarded the antigravity vehicle. The inbound trip seemed to take less time than the outbound and soon they were back to the elevator.

"If we're supposed to get something out of this little visit, it didn't work," Suzanne said as they entered the lift.

"It will," Arak assured her. "Have a little patience."

They exited the elevator onto a busy floor thronged with primary humans and a few worker clones. It was so crowded it was difficult for the group to stay together, especially when a number of individuals recognized the secondary humans from the gala the night before and mobbed them in hopes of pressing palms. Richard and Michael were particularly sought after.

Despite this congestion, Arak and Sufa were eventually able to herd their charges over to a large screen. On the screen were hundreds of names of individuals followed by room numbers and times. Arak scanned it for a few moments before finding a name he recognized.

"Well, well," Arak said to Sufa. He pointed to one of the names. "Reesta has decided to pass on. How wonderfully convenient. And he has reserved room thirty-seven. That couldn't be better. It's one of the newer rooms with the download apparatus in full view."

"It's about time he passed on," Sufa commented. "He's been full of complaints with that body for years."

"It will be perfect for our purposes," Arak said.

"Perhaps, with that decided, I'll run over to the spawning center," Sufa said. "It will give me a chance to prepare things and let the clones know the group will be over shortly."

"Wonderful idea," Arak said. "We should be there within the hour. See if you can manage to have an emergence about that time."

"I'll try," Sufa said. "And what about taking the group to our quarters afterward?"

"That was the idea," Arak said. "I just hope we have time."

"See you shortly," Sufa said as she touched palms lightly with Arak. Then she was gone.

"All right, everybody," Arak called to the group. "Let's try to stick together. If anybody gets separated, just ask for room thirty-seven." Arak set out by easing himself through the cluster of people viewing the screen.

Suzanne made it a point to stay abreast of him as best she could. "Is 'passed on' the same euphemism it is in our world?" Suzanne asked.

"Similar is a better word," Arak said. He was distracted by the divers who were busy pressing every female palm they encountered. "Richard and Michael," he called. "Please keep up! There will be plenty of time for palm pressing this evening. You'll be at your leisure."

"Are we going to witness some kind of euthanasia?" Suzanne asked with misgiving.

"Heavens, no!" Arak said.

"Ismael and Mary said that you people don't die the way we do," Suzanne said.

"That's for certain," Arak said. Then he had to stop and walk back to where Richard and Michael had been surrounded. As he was busy freeing the two divers Suzanne leaned toward Perry.

"I'm not prepared to witness any morbid scene," she said.

"Me neither," Perry agreed.

"Maybe we should have opted for more seminar time

before this field trip," Suzanne said, trying to indulge in a little humor.

Perry laughed hollowly.

Arak got Richard and Michael moving and stayed with them to ward off enthusiastic fans. Suzanne and Perry followed in their wake with Donald close behind. In that configuration they managed to arrive outside room thirty-seven.

Perry looked at the relief on the large bronze door. He recognized it as the three-headed dog, Cerberus, who guarded the underworld in Greek mythology. Surprised, he mentioned it to Arak.

"We didn't get it from your Greeks," Arak said with a smile. "No, it was the other way around."

"You mean the Greeks got it from Interterra?" Perry asked.

"Exactly," Arak said.

"How?" Perry asked.

"From a failed experiment," Arak said. "A number of thousands of years ago, a contingent of liberal-minded individuals from Atlantis endured the surface adaptation with grandiose plans of modifying earth surface socio-logical development. Unfortunately it turned out to be a bust. After several hundred years of fruitless endeavor, it became painfully apparent there was no way to alter the second-generation humans' penchant for violence. So the whole experiment was abandoned. Yet a number of Interterran legacies remained after the island they'd raised was sunk, like our architectural forms, the concept of democracy, and a smattering of our own primitive mythology including Cerberus."

"So there was a factual basis for the Atlantis legend," Suzanne interjected.

"Absolutely," Arak said. "Atlantis pushed up one of

its seamount exit ports to form an island just outside the entrance to the Mediterranean Sea."

"Hey, come on!" Richard complained. "Let's cut the jawboning! Either we're going in here or Mike and I are going back to the main hall where all the action is."

"All right, I'm sorry," Arak replied. Then to Suzanne he added, "We can talk more about the Atlantean experiment at another time if you'd like."

"I'd very much like to do that," Suzanne said. Then as Arak was opening the door she leaned toward Perry. "Plato did put the island of Atlantis outside the Strait of Gibraltar in his dialogues."

"Really?" Perry questioned. But he was distracted by the sights and sounds of the scene beyond the bronze door. It was hardly morbid as Suzanne had feared. Instead it was a joyous gala reminiscent of the one the group had attended the evening before, although on a smaller scale. The room was only the size of a large living room. The hundred or so people assembled were dressed in the usual garb save for one individual who stood out sharply. He was dressed in red instead of white. In the back of the room built into the wall opposite the door was a large donut-shaped apparatus that reminded Perry of an MRI machine. Next to it was a table with a box and a book similar to the ones Arak had shown the group in the vault below.

"Arak!" the man in red called out as he caught sight of the new visitors. "What a pleasant surprise!" He immediately excused himself from the people he was chatting with and headed over toward the door. "And you have brought your wards! Welcome!"

"My gosh," Suzanne whispered to Perry as the man in red neared. "I met him last night." Suzanne distinctly remembered him as one of the two men who'd joined her and Garona. "He hardly looks like he is about to pass on." To her he appeared to be the picture of health and the archetype of masculine attractiveness with thick dark hair, flawless skin, and sparkling eyes. She guessed he was in his late thirties.

"This is hardly a mournful wake," Perry commented.

"Thank you, Reesta," Arak said. "I didn't think you would mind if our visitors looked in on your party. Did you meet them at the celebration last night?"

"I had the honor of meeting Dr. Newell," Reesta said. He bowed to Suzanne and then extended his upright palm.

Self-consciously, Suzanne touched her own palm with his. He beamed.

"Let me present Perry, Donald, Richard, and Michael," Arak said. He pointed toward the men as he spoke. Reesta responded by bowing to each in turn. Richard and Michael were not paying much attention. They were more interested in the female guests, several of whom they'd seen the previous night.

"Sufa and I have decided to show our visitors some of our culture," Arak continued. "We're doing it before much explanation. We thought it might reduce the disbelief usually encountered in orientation."

"A wonderful plan," Reesta commented. "Come in! Please." He stepped out of the way and graciously gestured for them to enter.

"So they have no idea what this celebration is for?" Reesta asked as the second-generation humans filed into the room.

"Not really," Arak said.

"Ah, such wonderful innocence," Reesta commented. "It's so refreshing."

"But we did just come from a visit to my niche,"

Arak added. "Yet I purposefully did not give them a full explanation."

"A masterful approach," Reesta commented while winking and giving Arak a nudge with his elbow. Then he looked at the group, before locking eyes with Suzanne. "Today is an important day for me. Today this body of mine dies."

Suzanne could not help but recoil at this news. Not only did the man appear perfectly hale, but he acted it as well. The announcement even got Richard and Michael's attention.

"Ah, but do not despair," Reesta said, smiling at Suzanne's unease. "Here in Interterra it is a reasonably happy time, more in the realm of an inconvenience or nuisance. And for me it is none too soon. This body was somewhat of a lemon from the beginning. I've had to replace many of the organs and the knees twice. Every day it seems that there is another problem. It's been an endless struggle. And I've just heard this morning that the downtime has dropped to only four years due to lack of current demand. For some reason, no one is dying these days."

"Only four years!" Arak exclaimed. "That's wonderful! I was wondering why you decided so abruptly. Only last week you'd said you were thinking about doing something over the next couple of years."

"It's one of those things that never seems to be convenient," Reesta said. "I had been putting it off, I have to admit. But now I can't pass up this current, short downtime offer."

"Excuse me," Perry said. "I'm confused, but how long do you people generally live in Interterra?"

"It depends on what you're talking about," Reesta

said with a twinkle in his eye. "There's a big difference between the body and the essence in terms of life span."

"Each body generally lasts two to three hundred years," Arak said. "But there can be exceptions."

"As I've had to learn the hard way," Reesta added. "I've only gotten one hundred and eighty out of this one. It's been the worst one I've had."

"Are you suggesting that mind-body dualism is a fact in Interterra?" Suzanne said.

"We are indeed," Arak said. He smiled like a proud parent. Then to Reesta he added: "Dr. Newell is a quick study."

"That's apparent," Reesta said.

"What the hell are you people talking about?" Richard asked.

"If you'd listen instead of gawk you might have a better idea," Suzanne said.

"Pardon me!" Richard said, faking an English accent.

"What do you mean by essence?" Perry questioned.

"I mean your mind, your personality, the full complement of your spiritual and mental being," Arak said. "Everything that makes you you. And here in Interterra essences live forever. They are transferred intact from an old body to a new one."

Both Suzanne and Perry erupted with a slew of questions, then Perry tried to defer to Suzanne. But Arak raised his hands to quiet them both.

"Remember we are intruders here," he said. "I'm sure you have many questions. That's the purpose of this visit. But it is rude to interrupt this private time, and I will explain more of the details later." Then he turned to Reesta. "Thank you, my friend. We won't bother you any longer. Congratulations, and have a good rest."

"There is no need to thank me," Reesta said. "It is

an honor for me that you have brought these guests. Their presence makes this occasion that much more special."

"We'll communicate later," Arak said. "When are you going to die?" He began to herd the group back through the door.

"Sometime later," Reesta said casually. "We have the room for several more hours. But wait!"

Arak stopped and turned back to his friend.

"I just got an idea," Reesta said with excitement. "Perhaps our second-generation guests would like to see me die."

"That's a very generous offer," Arak said. "We certainly do not want to impose, but it would be instructive."

"It's no imposition," Reesta said, warming to the idea. "I've had enough of this party, and they can surely keep going without my physical presence."

"Then we accept," Arak said. He waved for Richard and Michael to come back since the bored divers had moved out into the hall.

"I hope this isn't gruesome," Suzanne whispered to Arak.

"Certainly not in comparison to what you people watch for entertainment in your surface world," Arak said.

Reesta used his wrist communicator before making a circuit around the room to press palms with everyone present. This caused a building sense of excitement. Then he approached the table with the box and the book. As he did so the crowd began to cheer. First he cut a lock of his hair and put it inside the box. Next he entered a date in the book and the cheering reached a crescendo.

A door appeared next to the MRI-like machine and

two worker clones stepped into the room. Both carried golden goblets which they gave to Reesta. Reesta held the goblets aloft and the crowd went silent. Then Reesta drained both vessels, one after the other.

Applause followed the drinking. Reesta bowed to his guests and even to the secondary humans. Then the two clones helped him climb into the three-foot wide opening of the MRI-like machine. He entered feet first and slid in until his head was well within the lip. At that point a mirror dropped down so that Reesta could look back at his guests and his guests could see his face. After a final wave, Reesta closed his eyes and appeared to settle down as if in sleep.

One of the worker clones stepped to the side of the apparatus and placed his hand palm down on a white square. Almost immediately a hum could be heard followed by a reddish glow that filled the apparatus's aperture. A moment later Reesta's body went rigid and his eyes flew open. This tetanic state was maintained for several minutes, after which Reesta's body went flaccid, his eyes sank in their sockets, and his mouth sagged in death.

The murmuring crowd fell silent. The red glow within the opening of the machine faded and the hum dissipated. Next, a powerful sucking sound could be heard, followed by the thump of a large valve closing, and Reesta's body disappeared from sight. One minute it was in plain view, the next minute it was gone.

The crowd remained still and mute. Seconds ticked away. Suzanne was confused emotionally as well as intellectually. Death in any form disturbed her. She hazarded a glance at Perry. He shrugged his shoulders in equivalent bewilderment.

"So, is that it?" Richard queried.

Arak gestured for him to be silent and to wait.

Michael shifted his weight and yawned.

All at once there was a simultaneous activation of everyone's wrist communicators, including those of the secondary humans. Although Ismael and Mary Black had given them the simple instructions to use the units—which involved merely speaking into them in an exclamatory fashion—no one had actually tried them yet. So when Reesta's voice issued forth, the five were taken aback.

"Hello, my friends," Reesta's voice said. "All is well. Death was successful and without complication. See you all in four years, but don't forget to communicate."

A general cheer arose from the primary humans, and they enthusiastically touched palms with each other in obvious celebration.

"Death's no big deal down here," Michael whispered to Richard.

"Yeah, but I think it's got to be done in this special way," Richard whispered back.

"This is a good time for us to leave," Arak said. As unobtrusively as possible, he shepherded the secondary humans out into the hallway and then directed them back toward the elevators. Suzanne and Perry were full of questions, but Arak put them off. He was too busy keeping Richard and Michael moving. Donald was his usual stony self.

It wasn't until they were back in an air taxi that conversation was possible. Even before the craft's entrance sealed over Perry said, "I'm afraid this visit has posed more questions than it has answered."

Arak nodded. "Then it was successful," he said. He put his palm onto the central, circular black table and said, "Spawning center, please!" Almost immediately the saucer sealed, rose, then shot off horizontally.

"What actually did we witness back there?" Suzanne asked.

"The death of Reesta's current body," Arak said. He sat back and began to relax. He was unaccustomed to the stress of being out in public with such a large, uninitiated group of secondary humans.

"Where did the body go?" Richard asked.

"Back into the molten asthenosphere," Arak said.

"And what about his essence?" Perry asked.

Arak paused as if he were searching for words. "It's difficult to explain these things, but I suppose you'll get the idea if I say his memory and personality imprint was downloaded into our integrated informational center."

"Holy shit," Michael exclaimed. "Look down there in front of that building! It's a goddamned 'Vette!"

Despite everyone's intense interest in Arak's explanation, they couldn't help but respond to Michael's outburst and follow his pointing finger. What they saw was a barnacle-encrusted vintage Chevrolet Corvette on a basalt dais in front of a building that appeared like a haphazard pile of children's blocks.

"What's a 'Vette doing down here?" Michael asked as they zipped past. "It's a sixty-two," he continued. "I had one just like it but in green."

"That building is our Earth Surface Museum," Arak explained. "The automobile is the one object that we feel currently symbolizes your culture."

"It's in sorry shape," Michael said. He sat back down.

"Obviously," Arak said. "It had spent a good deal of time underwater before we salvaged it. But getting back to Perry's question. When the worker clone started the death sequence, Reesta's entire mind in terms of memory, personality, emotions, self-awareness, and even his unique way of thinking was extracted and stored en masse available for total recall."

The secondary humans stared at Arak in stunned silence.

"Not only can Reesta's essence be recalled," Arak continued. "He can be consulted and even chatted with through your wrist communicator prior to his recall. Or better yet, he can be not only communicated with but viewed in his last body configuration via the media center in each of your quarters. Central Information creates a virtual image in conjunction with whatever conversation you are having."

"What if someone dies before they get to that download machine?" Richard asked.

"It doesn't happen," Arak said. "Death is a planned exercise in Interterra."

"This is all too much," Perry said. "What you are telling us is so far from believability that for the moment I don't even know what to ask."

"I'm not surprised," Arak said. "That's exactly why Sufa and I decided to start showing you things rather than just telling you about them."

"I have a hard time believing the mind can be downloaded," Suzanne said. "Intelligence, memory, and personality are associated with dendritic connections in the human brain. The number is staggering. We're talking about billions of neurons with up to a thousand connections each."

"It's a lot of information," Arak agreed. "But hardly overpowering by cosmic standards. And you are right that dendritic arrays are important. What our central information does is reproduce the dendritic arrays on a molecular level using isomeric, double-bonded carbon atoms. It's like a fingerprint, we call it a mindprint."

"I'm lost," Perry said.

"Don't despair," Arak encouraged. "Remember, this is just the beginning. There will be time for you to put all of this into context. Besides, our upcoming visit to the spawning center will show you what we do with the mindprint."

"What's in that Earth Surface Museum we passed?" Donald asked.

Arak hesitated. Donald's question had interrupted his train of thought.

"I mean, what's specifically on display?" Donald said. "Other than the water-soaked Corvette."

"Many different objects," Arak said vaguely. "A cross-section of things representing secondary human history and culture."

"Where have they come from?" Donald asked.

"Mostly from the ocean floor," Arak said. "Besides maritime tragedies and war, you people have been progressively and foolishly using the ocean as your garbage dump. You'd be surprised what refuse says about a culture."

"I'd like to visit there," Donald said.

Arak shrugged. "As you wish," he said. "You're the first visitor to voice such a request. Considering the wonders of Interterra that are now available to you, I'm surprised you are interested. Certainly there's nothing in there that you are not already entirely familiar with."

"Everybody's different," Donald said laconically.

A few minutes later the air taxi deposited the group at the front steps of the spawning center. It was housed in a building that resembled the Parthenon, only it was black. When Perry mentioned the resemblance, Arak told him it was again the other way around, similar to the Greek adaptation of Cerberus, since the Interterran spawning center was many millions of years old.

Like the death center, the structure was sited in a less congested section of the city. Regardless, once the secondary humans appeared, they again attracted a crowd, forcing Arak to be put to the task of maneuvering Richard and Michael inside the door and out of reach of the primary humans' eagerly outstretched hands.

This interior was the antithesis of the death center's. It was bright and white like the buildings at the visitors' palace. The other difference was that many more worker clones were in evidence here, busily scurrying from place to place.

Arak hustled the group into a side room with a vast number of small stainless steel tanks that looked like miniature bioreactors to Suzanne. They were attached to each other by a complicated tangle of piping in what looked like a high-tech assembly line. The air was warm and moist. A number of worker clones were monitoring various gauges and dials.

"This is not the most interesting part," Arak said. "But we might as well start at the beginning. These tanks hold our ovarian and testicular tissue cultures. Eggs and sperms are randomly selected and their chromosomes are scanned for molecular imperfections and then microsomally shuffled. The re-formed germ cells are then checked before allowing them to fertilize. If anyone would care to take a peek, there's a view port available." Arak pointed toward a binocular eyepiece along the assembly line apparatus.

Suzanne was the only one who took him up on the offer. She bent over and peered within. Inside a tiny chamber below the microscope objective she could see an oocyte being penetrated by an active sperm. The process happened rapidly. A moment later the zygote was gone, and two new gametes were injected into the chamber.

"Anybody else?" Arak asked after Suzanne straightened up.

No one moved.

"Okay," Arak said. "Let's move along to the gestation room and a more interesting phase." He led the way down the length of the gamete room to a room the size of several football fields placed end to end. Within the room were numerous rows of shelves supporting countless numbers of clear spheres. Between the rows walked hundreds of worker clones checking each sphere in turn.

"My word!" Suzanne murmured as it dawned on her what she was seeing.

"The replicating zygotes coming from the fertilization process are checked again for chromosomal molecular abnormalities," Arak explained. "Once they are determined to be free of any imperfection whatsoever, and they have reached the requisite number of cells, they are implanted into a sphere and allowed to develop."

"Can we walk along the spheres?" Suzanne asked.

"Of course," Arak said. "That's why we are here, so you can see for yourselves."

Slowly the group walked down an aisle several hundred yards long with lines of spheres on either side. Suzanne was fascinated and appalled at the same time. Each sphere contained a floating embryo of varying size and age. Plastered to the base of each sphere was an amorphous, dark purple placenta.

"This is all so artificial," Suzanne said.

"Indeed," Arak said.

"Is all reproduction in Interterra done by ectogenesis?" Suzanne asked.

"Absolutely," Arak said. "Something as important as reproduction we're not about to leave to chance."

Suzanne stopped and looked in at an embryo no more than six inches in length. She shook her head. Its tiny arms and legs were moving as if swimming.

"Does the process trouble you?" Arak asked.

Suzanne nodded. "It's mechanizing a process I think that's best left to nature."

"Nature is uncaring," Arak said. "We can do so much better, and we care."

Suzanne shrugged. She wasn't about to get into an argument. She started walking again.

"These are like the spheres you guys were in," Perry said to Richard and Michael.

"No shit!" Richard said.

"Please!" Suzanne barked irritably at Richard. "I'm getting tired of the language you fellows seem compelled to use."

"Sorry to offend your majesty," Richard shot back.

"These containers are similar but not the same," Arak said quickly. The last thing he wanted was any kind of an altercation in the spawning center.

Suzanne stopped abruptly and peered into one of the spheres. She was aghast at what she saw. Inside was a child who looked at least two years old. "Why is this child still in the sphere?" she questioned.

"It's perfectly normal," Arak assured her.

"Normal?" Suzanne questioned. "At what age are they . . ." she struggled for the right word, "decanted?"

"We still say born," Arak said. "Or, as a more technical term, we say emerge."

"Whatever," Suzanne said. Seeing the child imprisoned in the fluid-filled sphere made her shiver with nausea. It seemed so cold, calculating, and cruel. "At what age are the children freed?"

"Preferably not until four," Arak said. "We wait until the brain is mature enough to receive the mindprint. We also don't want the brain cluttered with unorganized natural input any more than necessary."

Suzanne exchanged a look with Perry.

"Come!" Sufa called out. She beckoned them over. "There's an emergence imminent. I've tried to delay it as much as possible; you'll have to hurry." Sufa turned and darted back in the direction she'd come.

Arak urged the group to follow with the intent of passing quickly through a room he called the imprinting room in order to get to the emergence room beyond. But Suzanne faltered on the imprinting room threshold taken aback by the spectacle.

The room was a quarter the size of the gestation room. Instead of sealed spheres with embryos the space was filled with transparent tanks containing angelic-looking four-year-olds. Each child was suspended in fluid but in a fixed position. Umbilical cords and placentas were still present despite the children's relatively advanced ages.

"I'm not sure I want to see this," Suzanne said as Arak gently prodded her.

The others silently gathered around the first tank with mouths agape. The child's head was immobilized as if prepared for stereo tactic brain surgery. His eyes were held open with lid retractors, and the eyes themselves were fixated with limbal sutures. From a gunlike apparatus, beams of light were directed through the side of the transparent tank and into each of the child's pupils. The beams flickered with a rapid, alternating frequency.

"What's happening here?" Perry asked. It looked like torture.

"It's perfectly safe and painless," Arak said. He joined the group and motioned for Suzanne to do likewise.

"The kid looks like he's being shot with an arcade gun," Michael said.

"From your violent culture I can understand why that would be your assumption," Arak said. "But it couldn't be further from the truth. To extend the previous analogy about downloading that I used at the death center, this child is merely receiving the download of a mindprint from an individual whose essence had been stored in Central Information. What you are seeing here is the recall procedure."

Suzanne advanced slowly with a hand over her mouth. She felt like a child at a scary movie: afraid to watch but unable to take her eyes away. Gazing at the immobilized toddler she shuddered. For her, the image was the embodiment of biotechnology gone amuck.

"As you saw at the death center," Arak continued, "it only takes seconds to extract the mindprint. But implanting it is another matter. We have to rely on a primitive technique using low-energy laser since no one has ever come up with a better access route than the retina. Of course, the retinal route makes sense since the retina is embryonically an out-pocketing of the brain. The process works, but it's not fast. In fact, it can take up to thirty days."

"Jeez!" Richard commented. "The poor kid has to be strung up like that for a month?"

"Believe me, there is no suffering involved," Arak said.

"What about the child's own essence?" Suzanne asked.

"We're giving him his essence as we speak," Arak said, "along with an extraordinary fund of knowledge and experience." He smiled proudly.

Suzanne nodded, but not in agreement. She saw the process as pure exploitation. For her it was a kind of parasitism, attaching an old soul to an innocent newborn. The mindprint was abducting the infant's body.

"Arak! Hurry!" Sufa called insistently from a doorway at the opposite end of the room. "You're missing the event!"

"Come on!" Arak urged to the group. "This is important for you to see. It's the finished product."

Suzanne was happy to break off from the disquieting image of the fixated child. She hurried after Arak, purposefully avoiding looking into any of the other tanks. Donald, Richard, and Michael lingered, mesmerized by the sight. Michael lifted his finger and reached out with the intention of interrupting the laser beam. Donald batted his hand away.

"Don't screw around, sailor!" Donald growled.

"Yeah," Richard said, "the kid might miss his piano lessons." He laughed.

"This is freakin' weird," Michael said. He walked around the tank to see if he could see into the barrel of the laser gun.

"Well, look on the bright side," Richard said. "It's a lot easier than going to school. If it doesn't hurt nothing, like Arak says, I would have gone for it. Hell, I hated school."

Donald looked at Richard scornfully. "As if I couldn't have guessed."

"Come on!" Arak called back to the three men from the distant doorway. "You need to see this."

The three men hurried after their hosts. In the next

room they found Arak, Sufa, Suzanne, and Perry standing around a satin-upholstered area at the base of a stainless steel slide. The slide came out of the wall; its upper end was closed off by double swinging doors. Sitting in the center of the cushioned depression was a darling four-year-old girl already dressed in the typical Interterran manner. It was apparent she'd recently arrived by sliding down the slide. A number of worker clones were in attendance.

"Welcome, gentlemen," Arak said to Donald and the divers. He pointed to the little girl. "Meet Barlot."

"Hey, sugarplum," Richard said in squeaky, babylike voice. He reached out to pinch the girl's cheek.

"Please," Barlot said as she ducked Richard's hand. "It's better not to touch me for fifteen or twenty minutes since I've just come out of the dryer. The nerves in my integument need a chance to adapt to the gaseous environment."

Richard recoiled.

"These three men are also newly arrived earth surface visitors," Arak said as he gestured toward Donald, Richard, and Michael.

"My word," Barlot said. "Isn't this an occasion! Five surface visitors at the same time. I'm happy to be so honored on my emergence day."

"We were just welcoming Barlot back to the physical world," Arak explained.

Barlot nodded. "And it's wonderful to be back." She examined her tiny hands, turning them over and then stretching them out. She then glanced at her legs and her feet. She wiggled her toes. "Looks like a good body," she added. "At least so far." She giggled.

"I think it looks like a superb body," Sufa said. "And

such beautiful blue eyes. Did you have blue eyes last body?"

"No, but I did the body before that," Barlot said. "I like variation. Sometimes I allow the eye color to be selected randomly."

"How do you feel?" Suzanne asked. She knew it was a stupid question, but under the circumstances she couldn't think of anything else to ask. She was distracted by the marked contrast between the puerile voice and the adult syntax.

"Mainly, I'm hungry," Barlot said. "And impatient. I'm looking forward to getting home."

"How long have you been in storage?" Perry asked. "If that's the right word."

"We call it being in memory," Barlot said. "And I'm assuming it was about six years. That was the advertised waiting time when I was extracted. But to me, it seems like it was overnight. When we're in memory our essences are not programmed to record time."

"Do your eyes hurt?" Suzanne asked.

"Not in the slightest," Barlot said. "I suppose you're referring to the flamelike scleral hemorrhages I undoubtedly have."

"I am," Suzanne admitted. The whites of both Barlot's eyes were fire engine red.

"That's from the limbal fixation sutures," Barlot said. "They were probably just removed."

"Do you remember being in the fish tank?" Michael asked.

Barlot laughed. "I've never heard the implant tank referred to as a fish tank. But to answer your question, no! My first conscious memory in this body, and in all previous bodies for that matter, was waking up on the conveyer belt in the dryer."

"Is the experience of extraction, memory, and recall at all stressful?" Suzanne asked.

Barlot thought for a moment before responding. "No," she said finally. "The only stressful part is that now I have to wait until puberty to have any real fun." She laughed, as did Arak, Sufa, Richard, and Michael.

"This is our home," Sufa said from a hovering air taxi as the exit door materialized. She pointed to a structure similar to the cottages at the visitors' palace minus the large lawns. It was clustered Levittown-style with hundreds of others just like it. "Arak and I thought it would be instructive for you to experience how we live and perhaps have a bite to eat. Are you all too tired or would you like to come inside for a visit?"

"I could eat," Richard said eagerly.

"I would love to see your home," Suzanne said. "It's very hospitable of you."

"I'm honored," Perry said.

Donald merely nodded.

"I'm starved," Michael said.

"Then it's decided," Sufa said. She and Arak climbed from the hovercraft and motioned for the others to follow.

Similar to the quarters at the visitors' center, the interior was uniformly white—white marble with white fabric and lots of mirrors. Also the main room opened to the outdoors with a pool extending from the inside to the outside. The place was sparsely furnished. Several large holographic displays like those the group had seen in the decon quarters were the only decoration.

"Please come in," Sufa said.

The group filed in, taking in the surroundings.

"It looks like my apartment in Ocean Beach," Michael said.

"Get outta here!" Richard scoffed while he playfully cuffed him on the top of his head.

"Are all Interterran homes open to the exterior?" Perry questioned.

"Indeed," Arak said. "As ironic as it may seem we who dwell inside the earth prefer to be outdoors."

"Makes it kind of hard to lock up," Richard said.

"Nothing is locked in Interterra," Sufa said.

"Nobody steals anything?" Michael questioned.

Both Arak and Sufa giggled. They then self-consciously excused themselves.

"We don't mean to laugh," Arak said. "But you people are so entertaining. We can never anticipate what you are going to say. It's very endearing."

"I suppose it's our charming primitiveness," Donald said.

"Exactly," Arak agreed.

"There's no thievery in Interterra," Sufa said. "There is no need because there is plenty for everyone. Besides, no one owns anything. Private ownership disappeared early in our history. We Interterrans merely use what we need."

The group sat down. Sufa called for worker clones, who appeared instantly. Along with them came one of the pets the secondary humans had seen from the air taxis. Up close it was even more bizarre looking, with its curious mixture of dog, cat, and monkey traits. The animal loped into the room and made a beeline for the visitors.

"Sark!" Arak bellowed. "Behave!"

The animal obediently stopped in its tracks and, using catlike eyes, it regarded the secondary humans with great curiosity. When it stood up on its hind feet, which were monkeylike with five distinct toes, it was about three feet tall. Its doglike nose twitched as it sniffed.

"This is one weird-looking animal," Richard said.

"It's a homid," Sufa said. "A particularly fine homid, actually. Isn't he adorable?"

"Get over here, Sark!" Arak cried. "I don't want you bothering our guests."

Sark immediately darted behind Arak and, standing on its hind legs, began scratching Arak's head.

"Good boy," Arak said contentedly.

"Food for the guests," Sufa commanded the worker clones, who quickly disappeared.

"Sark looks like a bunch of animals rolled into one," Michael said.

"That's one way to put it," Arak said. "Sark is a chimera developed eons ago and cloned ever since. He's a remarkable pet. Would anyone care to see one of his best tricks?"

"Sure," Richard said. To him the animal looked like a biology experiment that went haywire.

"Me, too," Michael echoed.

Arak stood and motioned for Sark to head outside. As he followed the animal he asked Richard and Michael to join him out in the yard. The divers dutifully got up and trooped into the garden, where they found Arak busily searching for something in the depths of a fern thicket.

"Okay, here's one," Arak said. He straightened up, clutching a short, rubberized stick in his hand. He stepped out onto the grass. "Now you men are not going to believe this. It's very entertaining."

"Try us!" Richard said dubiously.

Arak bent down and extended the stick to Sark. Sark took the stick with great excitement, chattering like a monkey. Then after a windup he threw the stick to the far corner of the yard.

Arak watched the piece of wood until it came to a complete halt. Then he turned back to the divers. "Quite a throw, wouldn't you say?"

"Not bad," Michael agreed. "At least for a homid."

The corners of Richard's mouth curled into a wry smile.

"Wait until you see the rest," Arak said. "Just a second." Arak ran out to where the stick had fallen, picked it up, and carried it back. He then returned it to Sark. The animal wound up and threw the stick back to approximately the same spot. Dutifully Arak trotted out and retrieved it for the second time. When he returned he was slightly out of breath. "Can you believe it?" he asked. "This cute little devil will keep this up all day. As long as I get the stick, he'll throw it."

The two divers looked at each other. Michael rolled his eyes while Richard swallowed a laugh.

"The food is here!" Sufa called from inside.

Arak extended the stick toward Richard. "Would you like to give it a try?"

"I think I'll pass," Richard said. "Besides, I'm starved."

"Then let's eat," Arak said agreeably. He tossed the stick back into the fern thicket and headed back inside. Sark followed.

"This place is getting weirder by the minute," Richard mumbled to Michael as they skirted the pool.

"You can say that again," Michael said. "No wonder they didn't care when I took the gold goblets last night. Nothing belongs to nobody. I'm telling you, we could make a fortune down here, and they wouldn't care."

Along with food, the worker clones had brought a

folding table, which they'd placed in the center of a ring of seven contour chairs. Arak and the divers joined the others. Sark climbed the back of Arak's chair and began scratching behind his ears. Everyone helped themselves to the food and started eating.

"Well, here's where we spend most of our time," Arak said after a short awkward silence. He sensed the secondary humans were a bit confounded by the day's events. "Does anyone have any questions for us?"

"What do you do here?" Suzanne asked to make conversation. She was happier to stick to small talk rather than tackle the larger issues swimming in her head.

"We enjoy our bodies and our minds," Arak explained. "We read a lot and watch a lot of holographic entertainment."

"Don't people work in Interterra?" Perry asked.

"Some people do," Arak said. "But it is not necessary, and those who do, only do what they want to do. All menial work, which most work is, is done by worker clones. All monitory and regulatory work is done by Central Information. Thus, people are free to pursue their own interests."

"Don't the worker clones mind?" Donald asked. "Don't they ever strike or revolt?"

"Heavens, no," Arak said with a smile. "Clones are like . . . well, like your domestic pets. They were made to look like humans for esthetic reasons, but their brains are much smaller. They have limited forebrain function so their needs and interests are different. They love to work and serve."

"Sounds like exploitation," Perry said.

"I suppose," Arak said. "But that is what machines are for, like automobiles in your culture, which I don't believe you feel you exploit. The analogy would be bet-

ter if your automobiles had living parts as well as machine parts. I'm sure you have to use your cars or they'd
deteriorate. Same with worker clones, only it's leisure
they cannot tolerate. They become despondent and
regress without work and direction."

"It is uncomfortable for us," Suzanne said. "Since
they appear so human."

"You have to remind yourself that they are not," Sufa
said.

"Are there different types of clones?" Perry asked.

"They all look essentially the same," Arak said. "But
there are servant, worker, and entertainment clones, male
and female. It's in the programming."

"With your technology, why not use robots?" Donald
asked.

"A good question," Arak said. "We had androids ages
ago; a whole line of them, in fact. But pure machines
tend to break down and have to be fixed. We had to
have androids to fix androids ad infinitum. It was in-
convenient, even ridiculous. It wasn't until we learned
to wed the biological with the mechanical that we solved
the problem. The ultimate result of this research and development was worker clones, and they are far superior
to any android. They take care of themselves completely,
even to the point of repairing themselves and repro-
ducing to keep their population in a steady state."

"Amazing," Perry said simply. Suzanne nodded.

The group fell silent. When they were through with
their food Sufa said, "I think perhaps it's time to take
you all back to your quarters at the visitors' palace. You
need some time to process what you've seen and heard.
Also, we don't want to overburden you on your first
day. There is always tomorrow." She smiled benignly as
she stood up.

"You're right about needing some time," Suzanne said, getting to her feet as well. "I think I've been a bit overburdened already. Without an ounce of doubt, this has been the most startling, staggering, and stunning day of my life."

Michael hesitated at the door to his cottage. Richard was standing directly behind him. They just had been dropped off by Arak and Sufa.

"What do you think we're going to find?" Michael asked.

"For chrissake!" Richard complained. "How am I supposed to know until you open the goddamn door?"

Michael grasped the handle and pulled. The two divers stepped over the threshold and glanced around the room.

"Do you think anybody was here?" Michael questioned nervously.

Richard rolled his eyes. "What do think, birdbrain?" he said. "The bed's made and the place has been picked up. Look, somebody even stacked all the dishes and the goblets you lugged back from the gala and the dining hall."

"Maybe it was just the clones," Michael said.

"It's possible," Richard said.

"Do you think the body is still there where we put it?"

"Well, we sure as shootin' ain't going to know until we look," Richard said.

"All right, I'll see."

"Hold on!" Richard said, grabbing Michael's arm. "Let me make sure the coast is clear."

Richard looked around beyond the pool and was quickly satisfied. No one was near, and he rejoined his buddy. "Okay, check the body."

Michael hastily positioned himself in front of the cabinets opposite the bed. "Drinks, please!" he commanded. The refrigerator door swung open. It was crammed full of various containers of beverage and food.

"It looks like the way we left it," Michael said.

"That's encouraging," Richard said.

Michael bent down and removed several containers exposing Sart's pale face. The lifeless eyes stared back at Michael accusingly. Michael quickly jammed the containers back to hide the horrid image. Sart's was the first dead body Michael had seen other than his grandfather's corpse. But his grandfather had been laid out in a casket in a tuxedo. Besides, the old man had been ninety-four.

"Well, that's a relief," Richard said.

"For now," Michael said. "But it doesn't mean they might not find him tonight or tomorrow. Maybe we should take him out and bury him in one of those clumps of fern."

"What are we going to dig with, teaspoons?" Richard asked.

"Then maybe we should carry him over to your cottage and put him in your refrigerator. It gives me the creeps having him here."

"We're not going to take the chance carrying him around," Richard said. "He stays where he is."

"Then let's swap rooms," Michael suggested. "Remember, you killed him, not me."

Richard's eyes narrowed threateningly. "We already had this conversation," he said slowly. "And it was decided: we're in this together. Now shut the hell up about the body."

"What about telling Fuller?" Michael said.

"Nah," Richard said. "I changed my mind about that."

"How come?"

"Because that straight arrow nerd's not going to have any better idea of what to do with the body. And I don't think we have to be so worried. Hell, nobody has even asked about the twerp all day today. Besides, Arak said they don't have any prisons."

"That's because they don't have any thievery," Michael snapped. "Arak didn't say anything about murder, and with all that stuff they showed us about mind extraction, I have a bad feeling they'll be pretty upset about it. We might get ourselves recycled, like Reesta."

"Hey, calm down!" Richard said.

"How can I calm down with a dead body in my refrigerator?" Michael yelled.

"Shut the hell up," Richard yelled back. Then in a lower voice he added, "Jeez, everybody in the neighborhood is going to hear you. Get control of yourself. The main thing is to get our asses out of here ASAP. Meanwhile Sart's in the cooler, which is going to keep him from stinking up the joint. We'll think about moving him if someone starts nosing around and asking about him. Okay?"

"I suppose," Michael said but without much enthusiasm.

CHAPTER FOURTEEN

The ceiling of the subterranean cavern darkened gradually, mimicking a normal evening just as it had the previous night. Suzanne and Perry, marveling how much the vaulted roof looked like sky, watched in awe as the pseudo stars began to blink on in the purple twilight. The ever glum Donald in contrast was staring morosely at the darkening shadows beneath the fern thickets. All three were standing on the lawn about forty feet away from the open end of the dining room. Inside, worker clones were busily laying out the dinner. Richard and Michael were already in their chairs eager for food.

"This is absolutely amazing," Suzanne said. She was craning her neck to look straight up.

"The bioluminescent stars?" Perry questioned.

"Everything," Suzanne said. "Including the stars." She'd just joined the others from her quarters, where she'd taken a swim, bathed, and had even tried to take a nap. But sleep had been impossible. She had too much on her mind.

"There are some astounding aspects," Donald admitted.

"I can't think of anything that's not," Suzanne said. She looked across the lawn at the dark hall of the pavilion where the gala had been held the previous evening. "Starting with the fact that this spacious paradise is buried in the earth under the ocean. How strange that I mentioned Jules Vernes's *Voyage to the Center of the Earth* back when we were starting our dive, since now we're actually here."

Perry chuckled. "Pretty apropos."

"Apropos and mind-boggling," Suzanne added. "Especially now that it appears everything Arak and Sufa have been telling us is true, no matter how fantastic it all seems."

"It is hard to deny the technology we're seeing," Perry said animatedly. "I can hardly wait to learn more of the details—like the biomechanics of the worker clones or the secrets of the air taxis. Patents on any of this could make us all billionaires. And what about tourism? Can you imagine what the demand for coming down here will be? It's going to be off the charts." Perry chuckled again. "One way or the other, Benthic Marine is going to become the Microsoft of the new century."

"Arak's revelations are extraordinary," Donald agreed grudgingly. "But there are a couple of important gaps that you bedazzled people seem to be forgetting."

"What are you talking about?" Perry questioned.

"Take off the rose-colored glasses," Donald said. "As far as I'm concerned, the overarching question hasn't even come up: What are we doing here? We weren't saved from drowning from a wrecked schooner like the Blacks. We were purposefully and deliberately sucked into their so-called exit port, and I'd like to know why."

"Donald's right," Suzanne said, suddenly thoughtful. "In the excitement, I keep forgetting we are, after all, victims of an abduction. That certainly does beg the question of what we are doing here."

"They are certainly treating us well," Perry said.

"For the moment," Donald said. "But as I said before it could change in the blink of an eye. I don't think you people realize how vulnerable we are."

"I know how vulnerable we are," Perry said with a touch of irritation. "Hell, as advanced as these people are, they could snuff us out in an instant. Arak talked about interplanetary travel, even galactic travel and time technology. But they like us. It's apparent to me even if it isn't to you. I think we should be more appreciative and not so paranoid."

"Like us, my foot," Donald spat. "We're entertaining to them. How many times have they told us that? They find our primitiveness funny or cute, sort of like a house pet. Well, I'm tired of being laughed at."

"They wouldn't be treating us this well unless they liked us," Perry persisted.

"You are so naive," Donald said. "You refuse to remember that we're prisoners, for all intents and purposes, who have been forcibly kidnapped and manipulated in that decon center. We were brought here for a reason that has yet to be revealed."

Suzanne nodded. Donald's remarks reminded her of an offhand comment of Arak's that had given her the impression he'd been anticipating her arrival. She'd found the comment unsettling at the time, but then it had gotten buried by other more astonishing disclosures.

"Maybe they're recruiting us," Perry said suddenly.

"For what?" Donald asked dubiously.

"Maybe they're making such an effort to show us

everything to prepare us to be their representatives," Perry said, warming to the idea as he spoke. "Maybe they have finally decided it's time to relate to our world, and they want us to be ambassadors. Frankly, I think we could do a damn good job, especially if we handled it through Benthic Marine."

"Ambassadors!" Suzanne repeated. "That's an interesting idea! They are not fond of going through the adaptation to our atmosphere because of their lack of immunity to our bacteria and viruses, and they don't like the decon process necessary to return to Interterra either."

"Exactly," Perry said. "If we were their representatives they wouldn't have to do any of that."

"Ambassadors? Good god!" Donald mumbled. He threw up his hands and shook his head in frustration.

"What's the matter now?" Perry asked, his irritation returning. Donald was beginning to get on his nerves.

"I knew you two were optimists," Donald grunted, "but this ambassador idea takes the cake."

"I think it is a perfectly reasonable possibility," Perry said.

"Listen, Mr. President of Benthic Marine!" Donald spat as if the appellation were derogatory. "These Interterrans don't plan to let us go. If you weren't such a hopeless optimist you'd understand that."

Suzanne and Perry were silent as they mulled over Donald's comment. The issue was something neither had wanted to think about much less discuss.

"You feel that they plan to keep us here forever?" Suzanne asked finally. She had to admit that nothing either Arak or Sufa had said had indicated a plan to return them to their ship back upon the ocean's surface.

"I believe that's what it means if they never let us go," Donald said sarcastically.

"But why?" Perry pleaded. The anger had gone out of his voice.

"It stands to reason," Donald said. "These people have been avoiding detection of Interterra for thousands of years. How could they feel good about letting us return to the surface knowing what we know?"

"Oh dear!" Suzanne whispered.

"Do you think Donald's right?" Perry asked.

"I'm afraid he has a point," Suzanne said. "There's no reason they would be less worried about contamination now than in the past. And with our advancing technology there's reason they should be more worried. They might be entertained by our primitiveness but I'd suspect they're terrified of our culture's violence."

"But they keep referring to us as visitors," Perry interjected. "This place we're staying is called the visitors' palace. Visitors don't stay forever." Then, irrationally, he added, "Besides, I can't stay here forever. I've got a family. I mean, I'm already worried that I haven't been able to let them know I'm okay."

"That's another point," Donald said. "They know a lot about us. They know about our families. With all their technology they could have offered to us an opportunity to let our loved ones know we're not dead. The fact that they haven't, I believe, is more proof they intend to keep us here."

"Good point," Suzanne said. She sighed. "Just a half hour ago in my room I was wishing there was an old-fashioned phone so I could call my brother. He's the only relative I have who'll miss me."

"No family?" Donald asked.

"I'm afraid not," Suzanne said. "That part of my life

just hasn't come together, and I lost both parents years ago."

"I've got a wife and three kids," Donald said. "Of course, that doesn't mean much to the Interterrans. To them the whole concept of parenthood seems quaintly out of date."

"My god!" Perry said. "What are we going to do? We have to get out of here. There has to be a way."

"Hey, everybody!" Michael called out from the dining room. "Soup's on. Come and get it!"

"Unfortunately they're holding all the cards," Donald said, ignoring Michael who disappeared back into the dining room. "There's nothing we can do at this point except keep our eyes open."

"Which means taking advantage of their hospitality," Suzanne said.

"To a point," Donald said. "I'm never one to condone fraternizing with the enemy."

"That's the confusing part," Suzanne said. "They don't act like enemies. They're so gracious and peaceful. It's hard to imagine them doing anything unkind to anybody."

"Keeping me away from my family is about as mean as I can imagine," Perry said.

"Not from their perspective," Donald said. "With reproduction carried out mechanically and four-year-old newborns imbued with the mind and personality of adults, there are no families in Interterra. It's possible they cannot understand the bond."

"What the hell are you people doing out there in the dark?" Michael shouted. He'd returned to the juncture between the dining room and the lawn. "The worker clones are waiting for you. Aren't you going to eat?"

"I guess we might as well," Suzanne said. "I am hungry."

"I'm not sure I am, after this discussion," Perry said.

They started walking toward the light spilling out onto the dark grass.

"There has to be something we can do," Perry said.

"We can avoid offending them," Donald said. "That could be critical."

"What could we do to offend them?" Perry asked.

"It's not us that I'm worried about," Donald said. "It's the numbskull divers."

"What about being direct about all this?" Perry suggested. "Why not ask Arak when we meet him tomorrow whether we're going to be able to leave? Then we'd know for sure."

"That might be risky," Donald said. "I don't think we should emphasize our interest in leaving. If we do, they might curtail our freedoms. As it is now, theoretically we can call air taxis with our wrist communicators and can come and go as we please. I don't want to lose that privilege. We may need it if there's any chance of our breaking out of here."

"That's another good point," Suzanne agreed. "But I don't see any reason we couldn't ask why we are here. Maybe the answer to that question will tell us whether they expect us to stay forever."

"Not a bad idea," Donald said. "I could go for that provided we don't make a big deal asking. In fact, why don't I ask tomorrow morning at the session Arak mentioned we'd be having."

"Sounds good to me," Suzanne said. "What do you think, Perry?"

"I don't know what to think at this point," Perry said.

"Come on, hurry up!" Michael said as the others entered the room. "This asshole worker clone won't let us touch the serving dishes until everybody's here, and he's stronger than an ox."

A worker clone was standing next to the center table with his hands resting on the covers of the chafing dishes.

"How did you know he was waiting for us?" Suzanne asked as she took one of the chairs.

"Well, we didn't know for sure, since the bozo doesn't talk," Michael admitted. "But we're hoping it's the case. We're starved."

Perry and Donald sat down. Almost immediately the worker clone lifted the covers from the food.

"Bingo!" Richard said.

Within minutes the food was served. For a time, there was no conversation. Richard and Michael were too busy eating; the others were absorbed in thoughts of their recent conversation on the lawn.

"What were you people doing out there in the dark?" Richard asked, then burped loudly. "Talking about a funeral? You're all so gloomy."

No one responded.

"Lively group," Richard muttered.

"At least we have table manners," Donald snapped.

"Screw you," Richard answered.

"You know, I suddenly find this strangely ironic," Suzanne said.

"What, Richard's table manners?" Michael questioned with a loud guffaw.

"No, our response to Interterra," Suzanne said.

"What do you mean?" Perry asked.

"Think about what we have here," Suzanne said. "It's like heaven even though it's not up in the sky like our traditional image. Nonetheless, it has everything that we consciously and unconsciously yearn for: youth, beauty, immortality, and plenty. It's a true paradise."

"We can attest to the beauty, eh, Mikey?" Richard said.

"Why do you find it ironic?" Perry asked, ignoring Richard.

"Because we're worried about being forced to stay," Suzanne said. "Everyone else dreams about getting to heaven, and we're worried we're not going to be able to leave."

"What do you mean, forced to stay?" Richard demanded.

"I don't find it ironic," Donald said. "If my family were here with me, maybe I would. But not now. Besides, I don't like to be forced to do anything. It may sound corny, but I value my freedom."

"We're getting out of here, aren't we?" Richard asked insistently.

"Not according to Donald," Perry said.

"But we have to," Richard blurted.

"And why is that, sailor?" Donald asked. "What makes you so eager to get out of Suzanne's heaven?"

"I was speaking in general terms, not personal," Suzanne interjected. "Frankly, finding out how they manage their immortality made me a little sick today."

"I don't know what you people are talking about," Richard said. "But I want to get out of here ASAP."

"Me, too," Michael seconded.

A soft chime sounded that no one had heard before. Everyone looked at each other quizzically, but before anyone could speak, the door opened and in walked Mura, Meeta, Palenque, and Karena. The bevy of beautiful women were in high spirits. Mura went directly to Michael and extended her palm in the usual Interterran greeting. After a quick palm press, she sat down on the edge of Michael's chair. Meeta, Palenque, and Karena approached Richard, who leaped to his feet.

"Oh, babies, you came back!" Richard cried. He touch palms with all three and then hugged them enthusiastically. They briefly acknowledged Suzanne, Perry, and Donald but lavished their attention on Richard, who swooned with utter delight. As he tried to collapse back onto his chaise, they restrained him. They told him they were eager to get him back to his room to go for a swim.

"Well, yeah, sure," Richard stammered. He saluted Donald before exiting with his miniharem.

"Come on!" Mura urged Michael. "Let us go as well. I've brought you a present."

"What is it?" Michael asked. He allowed himself to be pulled toward the door.

"A jar of caldorphin!" Mura said. "I heard you liked it."

"Loved it is more accurate," Michael cried. With that, the two of them skipped out of the room.

Before the remaining diners could comment, the soft chime sounded again. This time it heralded the arrival of Luna and Garona. The Interterrans seemed to be rounding up their previous evening's partners.

"Oh, Suzanne!" Garona cooed as he pressed palms with her. "I have been longing for the night so that I could come and once again spend it with you."

"Perry, my love," Luna gushed. "It's been too long a day. I hope it was not too stressful for you."

Neither Suzanne nor Perry could decide if they were mortified or delighted, especially being greeted with such mushily amorous protestations. Both stammered unintelligible responses while allowing themselves to be lifted to their feet.

"I guess we're leaving," Suzanne said to Donald as Garona playfully towed her toward the open end of the room.

"And we must be going to the same place they are," Perry said to him as Luna dragged him.

Donald gave a halfhearted wave but didn't say anything. The next instant, he found himself alone with the two mute worker clones.

Michael could not remember ever being so excited. Never had a woman this gorgeous and desirable seemed so interested in him. At her insistence they began to spin around as they cavorted across the dark lawn toward his room. With her long hair floating in the wind, the image was intoxicating for Michael, and he would have gone on for hours had his inner ear not intervened.

Feeling dizzy, Michael stopped revolving but his surroundings didn't. He staggered to his right, vainly trying to maintain his balance. Unable to keep his legs under him, he collapsed in a heap. Mura collapsed with him. Together they laughed uncontrollably. They got to their feet unsteadily, then ran on to his cottage. Once they got inside, they were both out of breath.

"Well," Michael said. He took a couple of deep breaths but still felt light-headed. Just looking at Mura in the slinky outfit made him quiver with desire. "What would you like to do first? Take a swim?"

Mura gazed at Michael provocatively. She shook her head. "No, I don't want to swim now," she said, her voice husky. "Last night you were too tired for intimacy. You sent me away before I could make you happy."

"But that's not true," Michael protested. "I was happy."

"You mean, Sart made you happy?"

"Hell, no!" Michael barked, taking immediate offense. "What the hell kind of question is that?"

"Don't get upset," Mura said, taken aback by Michael's response. "I'm not suggesting anything. Besides, it's perfectly all right to have pleasure from either sex."

"Hey, it's not okay with me," Michael snapped. "No way!"

"Michael, please calm yourself," Mura pleaded. "What's making you so agitated?"

"I'm not agitated!" Michael shot back.

"Did Sart do something to make you angry?"

"No, he was fine," Michael said nervously.

"Something made you angry," Mura said. "Did Sart stay all night? I didn't see him all day."

"No! No!" Michael stammered. "He left right after you did. Richard just apologized for getting mad at him and that was it. He was out of here. Nice kid, though."

"Why did Richard get mad at him?"

"I don't know," Michael said irritably. "Do we have to talk about Sart all night? I thought you came here to see me."

"I did indeed," Mura said. She sidled up to Michael and stroked his chest. Beneath her fingers she could feel that his heart was racing. "I think you must have had a difficult day. We should get you to calm down, and I know just the thing."

"What's that?"

"You lie down on the bed," Mura instructed. "I will rub your body and massage your muscles."

"Now you're talking."

"And once you are serene we will press palms with the caldorphin."

"Sounds great, baby," Michael said, recovering his composure. "Let's do it."

"All right, I'll be there in a moment," Mura said. She gave Michael a gentle nudge toward the bed. Dutifully Michael sauntered over and lay down on the soft coverlet.

Mura went to the refrigerator to get something cold to drink. She gave the command directly to the receptor so she could do it as softly as possible so as to avoid disturbing Michael. After his minor outburst, she sensed he was tense and needful of every consideration. She knew from experience how easily agitated secondary humans could become over the strangest things.

Mura was surprised to discover the compartment so full. "My word," she said. "What all do you have in here?"

In response to Mura's nagging about Sart, Michael's ardor had significantly waned. Instead of fantasizing as he lay facedown on the bed waiting for her ministrations, he found himself fretting over the dinner table discussion that their group was stuck in Interterra. Consequently her comment about his refrigerator being full didn't even penetrate his consciousness until he heard beverage and food containers crash to the floor followed by a gasp. It was only then that he remembered Sart's body, and by then it was too late. . . .

"Oh shit!" Michael whispered as he leaped off the bed. Just as he'd feared, Mura was standing in front of the open refrigerator with a hand clasped over her mouth. Her expression was one of pure horror.

Inside the refrigerator, Sart's frozen, pale face was framed haphazardly by stacked containers.

Michael rushed to Mura's side and enveloped her

with his arms. She sagged against him and would have collapsed had he not been supporting her.

"Listen! Listen!" Michael urged in a forced whisper. "I can explain."

Mura regained her balance and pulled herself from Michael's embrace. With a trembling hand she reached into the refrigerator and felt Sart's cheek. It was as firm as wood and as cold as ice. "Oh, no!" she moaned. Cradling her own drained cheeks with her hands, she shivered as if a cold wind had suddenly wafted through the room. When Michael tried again to put his arms around her, she shoved him to the side to keep Sart's face in view. As frightful as the image was, she could not turn away.

Frantically Michael bent down, retrieved the fallen objects, and crammed them back into the refrigerator to block her view of the dead boy. "You have to calm down," he said nervously.

"What happened to his essence?" Mura demanded. Blood surged back into her face turning her cheeks crimson. Shock and dismay were turning to anger.

"It was an accident," Michael said. "He fell and hit his head." Michael reached for her again, but she backed up to keep him at arm's length.

"But his essence?" Mura questioned again, although deep down she already knew the horrid truth.

"Look, he's dead, for chrissake," Michael snapped.

"His essence is lost!" Mura managed. Her fleeting anger was already giving way to grief. Tears welled up in her emerald green eyes.

"Look, baby," Michael said in a tone halfway between solicitude and irritation. "Regrettably, the kid is dead. It was an accident. You have to pull yourself together."

Tears turned to sobs as the reality of the tragedy struck the core of Mura's own essence. "I must go and tell the elders," she said. She turned and started toward the door.

"No, wait!" Michael said. He was frantic. He rushed around to head her off. "Listen to me!" He grabbed her with both hands.

"Let me go!" Mura cried. She tried to break from his grasp. "I must announce the calamity."

"No, we must talk," Michael insisted. He grappled with her as she tried to free herself.

"Let go!" Mura yelled, her voice rising through her sobs. She got one arm free.

"Shut up!" Michael shouted back. He slapped her across the face with an open palm, hoping to snap her out of her hysteria. Instead, she opened her mouth and let loose an earsplitting scream. Fearful of the consequences, Michael clapped a hand over her mouth. But it was not enough. Mura was a tall, strong woman, and she twisted from his grasp, letting out another cry.

With some difficulty Michael got his hand over her mouth again, but no matter what he tried, he could not keep her quiet. Impulsively he dragged her over to the deep end of the pool and launched them both into the water. But even the sudden dunking did not contain her screams until he forced her head beneath the water's surface.

Still she struggled, and when he brought her up for a breath, she let out a cry as loud as any previous. Again Michael pushed her under the water, and this time he held her until her violent flailing slowed, then ceased.

Slowly he eased up on the grip he had around her head, afraid she'd suddenly rear up and yell once more.

Instead her limp body slowly bobbed to the surface, her face submerged.

He pulled her body to the edge and lifted her onto the pool's marble lip. A foamy mixture of mucus and saliva issued from her nose and slack mouth. As he looked at her and realized she was dead, a shudder passed down his spine. His teeth began to chatter uncontrollably. He had killed someone—someone he cared for.

For a moment he stood perfectly still. He wondered if anyone could have heard Mura's screeches. Thankfully, the night was still. In a panic, he dragged her over to the bed, laid her alongside, and pulled the coverlet over her. Then he ran past the pool and out into the night.

Richard's cottage was no more than fifty yards away, and Michael covered the distance in seconds. He pounded on the door.

"Whoever it is, go away!" Richard's voice commanded from within.

"Richard, it's me!" Michael shouted.

"I don't care who it is!" Richard yelled back. "We're busy in here."

"It can't wait, Richie," Michael insisted. "I got to see you."

A string of expletives preceded a short silence. Finally the door was pulled open. "This better be good," Richard growled. He was buck naked.

"We got a problem," Michael announced.

"You're about to have another one," Richard warned. Then he noticed that Michael was sopping wet. "Why'd you go swimming with your clothes on?" he asked.

"You gotta come with me back to my cottage," Michael stammered.

Richard noted the degree of his friend's anxiety. Richard glanced over his shoulder to make sure none of the women were close enough to hear. "Does this have something to do with Sart's body?" he asked in a whisper.

"Yeah, unfortunately," Michael said.

"Where's Mura?"

"She's the problem," Michael said. "She saw the body."

"Oh, Christ!" Richard moaned. "Is she upset?"

"She went ballistic on me," Michael said. "You gotta come!"

"All right! Calm down. So she really got psycho?"

"I'm telling you, she went completely crazy. You gotta get your ass over there."

"Okay already," Richard soothed. "Don't shout! I'll be over in a few minutes. I'll have to get rid of my friends."

Michael nodded as Richard closed the door in his face. Turning around, he sprinted back to his quarters. After checking to make sure Mura's body was where he'd left it, he changed into a dry set of clothes. Then he paced up and down the room, waiting for Richard.

True to his word, Richard arrived in less than five minutes. He scanned the room the moment he stepped over the threshold. Everything looked peaceful enough. He half expected to see Mura sobbing uncontrollably on the bed, but she was nowhere to be seen. "Well, where is she?" he demanded. "In the bathroom?"

Michael didn't answer. He motioned for Richard to follow him and walked around the end of the bed. Reaching down with a shaky hand, he grasped the corner of the coverlet and whipped it aside to expose the corpse. Mura's previously translucent alabaster skin had become a mottled blue and the foam oozing from her mouth and nose was tinged with red.

"What the hell?" Richard gasped. He knelt down and felt for a carotid pulse. He stood back up. His face was slack with shock. "She's dead!"

"She opened the refrigerator," Michael explained. "She saw Sart's body."

"All right, I understood that," Richard said. He stared at his friend. "But why did you kill her?"

"I told you, she went crazy," Michael said. "She was screaming bloody murder. I was afraid she was going to wake up the entire goddamn city."

"Why the hell did you let her open the refrigerator?" Richard demanded angrily.

"I wasn't watching for two seconds," Michael said.

"Yeah, well, you should have been more careful," Richard complained.

"That's easy for you to say," Michael snapped. "I told you I didn't want the body over here. He should have been in your refrigerator, not mine."

"Okay, calm down," Richard said. "We got to think what to do."

"There's no more room in my refrigerator," Michael said. "She's got to go in yours."

Richard wasn't wild about dragging the body over to his place, but he couldn't come up with an alternate idea, and he knew they had to do something quickly. If Mura was found, then Sart would be, too. One way or the other he'd be involved.

"All right," Richard said reluctantly. "Let's get it over with."

With dispatch they rolled Mura up inside the coverlet. Then with Richard at the head and Michael at the foot, they carried her across the lawn to Richard's cottage. They had a little trouble navigating her in through the door since it was relatively narrow.

"Jeez," Michael complained. "Carrying a body is a little like carrying a mattress. It's harder than you'd think."

"That's because it's so much dead weight," Richard said, smirking at the double meaning.

They dumped the body in the middle of the floor. While Michael unraveled the blanket, Richard went to the refrigerator and emptied it. Since this was his second time through the body-in-the-refrigerator routine, he knew exactly what to do, meaning to get Mura inside required a complete rearrangement of the contents.

"All right," Richard said. "Give me a hand."

Together they got Mura wedged into place. She was taller and heavier than Sart, so she was a tighter fit. In the end, they had to leave a few containers out.

Richard straightened up after finally managing to get the door to shut. "This has got to stop," he said.

"What?" Michael asked.

"Knocking off these Interterrans," Richard said. "We're out of refrigerators."

"Very funny," Michael said. "How come I'm not laughing?"

"Don't make me answer that, birdbrain," Richard said.

"I'll tell you what it really means," Michael said. "We gotta get our asses out of Interterra! With two bodies, the chances of someone stumbling across one has just doubled."

"You should have thought of that before you knocked her off," Richard said.

"I'm telling you, I didn't have any choice!" Michael yelled. "I didn't want to ice her, but she wouldn't shut up."

"Don't shout!" Richard said. "You're right. We got to get the hell out of here. The only good news is that it seems the straightlaced admiral is thinking the same way we are."

Suzanne couldn't remember the last time she'd swum in the nude, and she was pleasantly shocked by the sensation as she struck out across the pool. And although she was mildly self-conscious about being naked, especially given Garona's perfect form, she wasn't as uptight as she had imagined she'd be. It was probably because Garona made her feel so accepted the way she was despite her physical imperfections.

Reaching the far end of the pool, Suzanne flipped over and, with a burst of speed, swam back to where Garona was contentedly sitting at the edge with just his feet in the water. She grasped one of his ankles and succeeded in pulling him into the water. They ducked under the water and embraced.

Eventually tiring of their underwater play, they swam to the side, and hauled themselves out of the water. With the slight breeze wafting in from the open end of the room, Suzanne felt gooseflesh pop out along the backs of her arms and the sides of her thighs. "I'm glad you came back tonight," she said. She was genuinely glad to see him.

"I'm glad, too," Garona said. "I was anticipating it all day."

"I wasn't sure if you would come back," Suzanne said. "To be honest, I was worried you wouldn't. I'm afraid I acted immaturely last night."

"What do you mean?"

"I should have made a clearer choice," Suzanne said. "Either I should not have allowed you to stay or, having done so, I should have acted more appropriately. What I did was somewhere in between."

"I enjoyed every minute," Garona said. "Our interaction was not goal-oriented. The idea was just to spend time together, which we did."

Suzanne gazed at Garona appreciatively, silently lamenting that it required a trip to a surreal, mythic world to find such a sensitive, giving, and handsome man. As her mind naturally drifted to the idea of taking him back with her, the thought yanked her back to the reality of whether she was ever going to be able to go back herself. It also brought up the other, major unanswered question. "Garona, can you tell me why we've been brought to Interterra?" Suzanne asked suddenly.

Garona sighed. "I am sorry," he said. "I cannot interfere with Arak. You and your group are his charges."

"Just telling me why we're here would be interfering?"

"Yes," Garona said without hesitation. "Please don't put me in that position. I want so much to be open and honest with you, but in that sphere I cannot, and it distresses me to have to deny you anything."

Suzanne stared into her new friend's face and could see his sincerity. "I'm sorry for asking," she said. She lifted her hand and he lifted his. They slowly pressed palms. Suzanne smiled with contentment; she was becoming pleasantly acclimated to the Interterran embrace.

"Perhaps I should ask how Arak is doing with his orientation?" Garona said.

"I'd say very well," Suzanne commented. "He and Sufa are such gracious hosts."

"But of course," Garona said. "They were lucky to get such an interesting group. I heard that they have already taken you out into the city. Did you enjoy that?"

"It was fascinating," Suzanne said. "We visited the death center and the spawning center as well as Arak and Sufa's home."

"Such rapid progress," Garona commented. "I'm impressed indeed. I've never heard of second-generation humans progressing so quickly. What is your reaction to what you have seen and heard? I can hardly imagine how extraordinary it must be for you."

"The expression *beyond belief* has never been so appropriate."

"Have you found anything disturbing?"

Suzanne tried to figure out if Garona wanted the truth or platitudes.

"There was one thing that bothered me," Suzanne began, deciding to give Garona honesty. She went on to explain her negative reaction to the implant process.

Garona nodded. "I can appreciate your point of view," he said. "It is a natural consequence of your Judeo-Christian roots, which puts such high value on the individual. But I assure you we do as well. The child's essence is not ignored but rather added to the implanted essence. It is a mutually beneficial process, a true symbiosis."

"But how can an unborn's essence compete with that of a learned adult?"

"It is not a competition," Garona said. "Both benefit, although obviously the child benefits the most. I can tell you, as someone who has gone through the process countless times, I have been strongly influenced by each essence from each body. It is definitely an additive process."

"It seems like a rationalization," Suzanne said. "But I'll try to keep an open mind."

"I hope you do," Garona said. "I'm sure Arak plans to return to this issue in the didactic sessions. Remember, today's outing was not to explain things thoroughly but rather to help overcome the usual disbelief with which our visitors initially struggle."

"I'm aware of that," Suzanne said. "But it is true I tend to forget. So thank you for reminding me."

"My pleasure," Garona said.

"You're a sensitive, beautiful man, Garona," Suzanne said with all sincerity. "It is a delight to be with you." She found herself wondering what it would be like to walk with him on the beach at Malibu or to drive on Route 1 around Big Sur. One thing that Interterra lacked was an ocean, and as an oceanographer, the ocean was central to Suzanne's universe.

"You are a beautiful woman. You're extraordinarily entertaining."

"Thanks to my alluring primitiveness," Suzanne said. She guessed Garona imagined he was complimenting her, but she would have preferred a word other than *entertaining*, especially after Donald's complaint.

"Your primitiveness is endearing," Garona agreed.

Briefly Suzanne entertained the idea of letting Garona know her response to being called primitive, but she resisted. At this stage of their relationship she wanted to be positive. Instead she said, "Garona, there's something I want you to know about me."

Garona pricked his ears.

"I want you to know I don't have another lover. I did, but that ended."

"It doesn't matter," Garona said. "The only thing that matters is that you are here this moment."

"It matters to me," Suzanne said mildly hurt. "It matters to me a lot."

CHAPTER FIFTEEN

The morning of the secondary humans' second full day in Interterra began similarly to the first day. Suzanne and Perry were offhand with each other about their previous evening's experiences and eager for what the day was to bring. Donald was less enthusiastic and a touch morose. Richard and Michael were tense and silent, and when they did talk, it was only about leaving. Donald had to shut them up when Arak made his entrance.

After bringing the group back to the same conference room they used the day before, Arak and Sufa launched into an educational session that dragged on for hours. This was mainly a scientific discussion that included the way Interterra tapped the earth's geothermal energy; how the Interterran climate was maintained, including the mechanism used to generate the nightly rain; how bioluminescent technology was used to provide even lighting both indoors and out; how water, oxygen, and carbon dioxide were handled; and how photosynthetic and chemosynthetic food plants were grown hydroponically.

As the image on the floor screen faded and the general illumination began to return, the only two secondary humans paying attention were Suzanne and Perry. Donald was staring off, obviously absorbed in his own thoughts. Richard and Michael were fast asleep. As the lighting reached its apogee both divers revived, and they and Donald tried to make it appear as if they had been listening all along.

"In conclusion for this morning's session," Arak said, seemingly mindless of certain parties' inattention, "I'm sure you have a clearer idea of why we have remained here in our subterranean world, that is, in addition to the microbial issue. In contrast to what transpires on the earth's surface, we have been able to construct a perfectly stable environment with no climatic fluctuations such as ice ages or other weather-related disasters; essentially limitless, pollution-free energy; and a completely adequate and replenishable food source."

"Is plankton your exclusive source of protein?" Suzanne asked. She and Perry remained fascinated by all the scientific revelations.

"The major source," Arak said. "The other source is vegetable protein. We used to use some fish species, but we stopped when we became concerned about the ability of larger sea animals to be able to replenish themselves. Unfortunately, this is a lesson secondary humans seem unwilling to accept."

"Particularly with whales and cod," Suzanne said.

"Exactly," Arak said. He looked around the room at the others. "Any more questions before we go back out into the field?"

"Arak, I have a question," Donald said.

"Of course," Arak said. He was pleased. Donald had thus far shown very little interest in participating.

"I'd like to know why we were brought here," Donald said.

"I was hoping you had a question about what we have been discussing," Arak said.

"It's hard for me to concentrate on technical matters when I don't know why I'm here."

"I see," Arak said. He bent over and conferred in a hushed whisper with Sufa and the Blacks. Then, leaning back, he added, "Unfortunately, I cannot answer your question completely since we have been specifically proscribed from telling you the main reason why you are here. But I can say this: one of the reasons was to stop the attempted drilling into the Saranta exit port, which I can happily say was accomplished. I can also assure you that today you will learn the main reason. Will that suffice for the moment?"

"I suppose," Donald said. "But if we're going to learn, I don't see why you can't tell us now."

"Because of protocol," Arak said.

Donald nodded reluctantly. "As a career naval officer, I suppose I can accept that."

"Any other questions about today's presentation?" Arak asked.

"I'm a bit overwhelmed at the moment," Perry admitted. "But I'm sure I'll have questions as the day progresses."

"Well, then," Arak said. "Let's begin our excursion. With what you have heard this morning, where would you like to visit first?"

"How about the Earth Surface Museum?" Donald suggested before anyone else could respond.

"Yeah!" Michael blurted enthusiastically. "The place with the 'Vette out front."

"You'd like to see the Earth Surface Museum?" Arak

questioned with obvious bewilderment. He glanced at
Sufa. Her reaction was the same.

"I think it would be interesting," Donald said.

"Me, too," Michael said.

"But why?" Arak questioned. "Pardon our surprise,
but with all the things we have been telling you, we're
mystified that you would rather look back than forward."

Donald shrugged. "Maybe it's just a touch of nos-
talgia."

"Seeing what you have chosen to display might give
us a feeling for your response to our world," Suzanne
offered. She wasn't as interested in seeing the museum
as the other sites Arak had been describing, but was
happy to support Donald's request.

"Very well," Arak said agreeably. "The Earth Surface
Museum shall be our first stop of the day."

Everyone got to their feet. For the first time Donald
acted eager, especially when they got outside. He asked
Arak to show them how to call an air taxi, and Arak
was happy to oblige. Arak went a step further and had
Donald place his palm on the taxi's center black table
and give the destination command.

"That was easy," Donald said as the craft silently and
effortlessly rose, then shot off in the corresponding direction.

"Of course," Arak said. "It's meant to be easy."

All of the visitors found the air taxi rides mesmeriz-
ing. They never tired of the vista of the city and the
surrounding area. With craning necks they tried to take
in everything, but it was difficult; there was so much to
see and the vehicle was moving at an astounding speed.
Within a few minutes they found themselves hovering
at the entrance to the museum, a half dozen yards from
the barnacle-encrusted Chevrolet Corvette.

"God, I loved that car," Michael said with a wistful sigh as he climbed from the air taxi. He paused and gazed longingly at the monument. "I was dating Dorothy Drexler at the time. I don't know which had the better body."

"Did they both need an ignition key to get them started?" Richard asked with a smirk.

Michael took a swipe at his buddy with an open palm, but Richard evaded it with ease. Then he danced briefly on his toes like a professional boxer before taking a swing of his own.

"No fighting," Donald snapped, insinuating himself between the two divers.

"Your Corvette might have been fine for you and Dorothy," Suzanne said, "but I feel rather embarrassed the Interterrans feel that this symbolizes our culture."

"It does suggest we're rather superficial," Perry agreed. "Besides being rusty and in sorry shape."

"Superficial and materialistic," Suzanne said, "which, I suppose, is probably the case when you think about it."

"You're reading too much into the symbolism," Arak said. "The reason we have put it here at the front of the museum is much simpler. Since we are now relegated to observing you from afar to keep from being detected by your advancing technology, the automobile is what we notice most. From a great distance it almost appears that the cars are the dominant life form on the surface of the earth, with secondary humans acting like robots to take care of them."

Suzanne had trouble suppressing a laugh at such an absurd suggestion, but when she thought about it, she could understand how it might seem from a distance.

"What is more symbolic is the design of the museum itself," Arak said.

All eyes turned to the building. Up close, the structure possessed an overpowering sepulchral aura. Four and five stories tall, it was composed of rectilinear segments either stacked or at right angles to create a complicated, sharply geometric form. Most segments were covered with square fenestrations.

"The building symbolizes secondary human urban architecture," Arak commented.

"It's rather ugly in its boxiness," Suzanne said.

"It isn't pleasing to the eye," Arak admitted. "Nor are most of your cities, which are essentially so many boxlike skyscrapers built on grids."

"There are some exceptions," Suzanne said.

"A few," Arak agreed. "But unfortunately, most of the architectural lessons the Atlanteans bestowed on your ancient forebears have been lost or disregarded."

"It's an enormous building," Perry commented. It covered the equivalent of a modern city block.

"It needs to be," Arak said. "We have an extensive earth surface collection. Remember, we're talking about a time span of millions upon millions of years."

"So the museum is not just of secondary human culture?" Suzanne asked.

"Not at all," Arak said. "It is also the whole panoply of current earth surface evolution. Of course, we have been mostly interested in the last ten thousand years or so for obvious reasons. Although that segment of time represents a mere eyeblink in comparison to the period as a whole, we have concentrated our collections on it."

"What about dinosaurs?" Perry questioned.

"We have a small but representative exhibit of preserved specimens," Arak said. Then he added as an aside:

"Such frightfully violent creatures!" He shook his head as if experiencing a passing wave of nausea.

"I want to see that exhibit," Perry said eagerly. "I've been dying to know what color dinosaurs were."

"For the most part they were a rather nondescript gray-green," Arak said. "Rather ugly if you must know."

"Let's go inside," Sufa suggested.

The group trooped into the entrance hall. It was an enormous room sheathed in the same black basalt as the exterior. Shafts of bright light came from apertures in the high ceiling. They crisscrossed in the general dimness like miniature searchlights to illuminate displayed objects in a dramatic fashion. Multiple corridors emanated from this central hub.

"Why are there no people?" Suzanne asked. In every direction she looked, all she saw was empty, marbled hallways. Her voice echoed repeatedly in the sepulchral silence.

"It's always like this," Arak explained. "As important as this museum is, it is not particularly popular. Most people would rather not be reminded of the threat your world poses for us."

"You mean threat of detection," Suzanne added.

"Precisely," Sufa said.

"This looks like a place where it would be easy to get lost," Perry said. He peered down some of the lengthy, dimly lit, and silent corridors.

"Not really," Arak said. He pointed to the left. "Starting here, with blue-green algae, the evolutionary exhibits are chronological." Then he pointed to the right. "And on this side we have secondary human culture starting with the earliest African hominids and extending up to the present. At any given location in the museum one could determine how to find the way back here to the entrance hall by following the direction of progressively older specimens."

"I'd like to see the exhibits depicting our modern times," Donald said.

"Certainly," Arak said. "Follow me. We'll take a shortcut through the first five or six million years."

The group followed Arak and Sufa like schoolchildren on a day trip to the museum. Suzanne and Perry found it difficult not to stop and view every display, especially when they reached the halls devoted to Egyptian, Greek, and Roman artifacts. Neither Suzanne or Perry had seen anything quite like them. It was as if someone had stepped back in time with free rein to pick the choicest objects. Suzanne was particularly enthralled with the period clothing tastefully displayed on life-sized mannequins.

"You'll notice there is a marked quantity difference in our collections," Arak explained. He had remained with Suzanne and Perry as the others wandered on. "We have comparatively little modern material. The farther back in your history, the more extensive the exhibits are. A very long time ago we used to make actual trips in isolation suits to collect for the museum. Of course, we eventually had to stop that practice for fear of exposure once your forebears developed writing."

"Arak!" Sufa called from several galleries ahead. "Donald, Richard, and Michael are moving quickly, so I'll go ahead with them!"

"That's fine," Arak called back. "We'll all meet up in the entrance hall in about one hour."

Sufa nodded and waved good-bye.

"Why were you worried about exposure to ancient peoples?" Suzanne asked. "They certainly did not have the technology to cause you any trouble."

"Very true," Arak admitted. "But we knew you second-generation humans would have it someday, and we didn't want any record of our visits. It was enough to worry about the failed Atlantean experiment, although that was less of a concern since the primary humans involved had been posing as second-generation humans."

Suzanne nodded, but her attention had drifted to an elaborate, ancient Minoan dress which would leave the breasts completely exposed.

"There is one period in your modern history that we have a lot of artifacts from," Arak said. "Would you care to see?"

Suzanne looked at Perry, who shrugged. "Certainly," Suzanne said.

Arak turned left and strode off through a side gallery filled with exquisite Greek pottery. With Suzanne and Perry at his heels he turned another corner and climbed a nondescript flight of stairs. On the floor above they emerged into a huge gallery filled with World War II materiel. The artifacts ranged from items as small as dog tags and uniform insignia to those as large as a Sherman tank, a B-24 Liberator aircraft, and an intact U-boat, with all sorts of objects in between. It was apparent that everything in the gallery was at one time submerged in the ocean.

"My word," Perry commented as he strolled between the displays. "This is more like a junkyard than a museum exhibit."

"It appears that our last world war contributed substantially to your museum's collection," Suzanne said. She and Arak remained at the head of the stairs. This was not an exhibit Suzanne was at all interested in.

"A big contribution," Arak agreed. "Objects such as you see here rained down to the ocean floor for over five years. For the last few hundred years of your history, scavenging the ocean floor has been our only source of curios."

Suzanne glanced at the U-boat. "Did the explosive growth of submarine technology and operations concern you?"

"Only in regard to sonar capability," Arak said. "Especially when the sonar technology was combined with making bathypelagic contour maps. Such technology was one of the reasons we'd elected to close the entrance ports like the one you came through."

While Suzanne and Arak continued to discuss sonar and its threat to Interterran security, Perry wandered the full width of the World War II gallery. Some of the paraphernalia seemed in pristine condition, other objects were barnacle-encrusted like the Corvette outside the museum. At the end of the aisle, he poked his head out a window facing east and caught a glimpse of the immense spires that served as supports for the Azores.

Perry glanced down at the courtyard below and did a double take. The *Oceanus,* the Benthic Marine submersible, was sitting on what appeared to be a flatbed attached to a large air taxi.

"Hey, Suzanne!" Perry cried out. "Come look!"

Suzanne hurried over to join him. Arak followed. Both leaned out the window and followed Perry's pointing finger.

"My gosh!" Suzanne said. "It's our submersible! What is it doing here?"

"Oh, yes," Arak said. "I forgot to mention how much interest your ship has generated with the curators of the museum. I believe, with your permission, they intend to make it one of the exhibits."

"Was it damaged?" Perry asked.

"Only minimally," Arak said. "Skilled worker clones have repaired the outside lights and manipulator arm. It's also been decontaminated, but is otherwise intact. Are you familiar with the boat's components?"

"Somewhat," Perry said. "But not from an operational perspective. Suzanne knows more than I. I've only been in it twice."

"Donald is the real expert," Suzanne said. "He knows the craft like the back of his hand."

"Excellent," Arak said. "We do have some questions about the sonar, which we have found to be even more sophisticated than we'd imagined."

"He's the one to ask," Suzanne said.

"What's the submersible sitting on?" Perry asked.

"That's an air taxi freighter," Arak said.

Michael made it a point to keep up with Donald, who was cruising through the museum as if he were out for exercise rather than studying the exhibits. Every few steps Michael had to run a couple of strides. Donald had long since left Sufa and Richard far behind.

"Why the hell are you going so fast?" Michael panted. "What is this, a race?"

"You don't have to stay with me," Donald shot back. He turned another corner and continued on. They were moving through a gallery containing Renaissance sculptures and paintings.

"Richard and I think we should get out of Interterra ASAP," Michael managed. He was short of breath.

"You both made that clear over breakfast," Donald said jeeringly. He turned another corner and entered a room hung with carpets.

"We're getting a little worried," Michael continued,

trying to stay alongside the fast-moving ex–naval officer.

"About what, sailor?" Donald asked.

"Because . . . well . . . we have a problem," Michael said hesitantly. "It involves a couple of these Interterrans."

"I'm not interested in your personal problems," Donald snapped.

"But there was an accident," Michael said. "Or actually, two accidents."

Donald stopped short and Michael did the same. Donald stabbed the air in front of Michael's face. Donald's lips were pulled back in a sneer. "Listen, bonehead! You two decided to fraternize with these Interterrans. I don't want to hear about your difficulties getting along with them. Understand?"

"But—"

"No buts, sailor!" Donald spat. "I'm trying to get us out of here, and I don't want to be distracted by either you or your half-wit buddy."

"Okay, okay," Michael said, raising his hand defensively. "I'm glad you're working on it. Getting out of here as soon as we can is all I'm concerned about. I mean, I'll help any way I can."

"I'll keep that in mind," Donald said scornfully.

"Do you have any ideas about how we're going to be able to do it?"

"It'll be difficult," Donald admitted. "We're going to have to find someone besides Arak to get some real answers. Information is the key. The best thing, of course, would be to find someone who's not happy here, yet who's been around long enough to be knowledgeable about how to get out."

"Nobody seems unhappy," Michael commented. "It's like they're living one big party."

"I'm not talking about Interterrans," Donald said. "Arak has implied that a number of people from our world have ended up down here. Some of them must be homesick and not quite as chummy with the Interterrans as Ismael and Mary Black seem to be. It's human nature, or at least secondary-human nature, to resist constraint. That's the kind of person I'd like to find."

"How do you propose to do it?"

"I don't know," Donald admitted. "We've got to keep our eyes open for when opportunity knocks. I can tell you I like being out in the city. We're surely not going to find such a person while we're sitting in that damn conference room."

"But this place is deserted," Michael complained. His eyes took a momentary detour up and down the empty corridors.

"I didn't come here to meet anyone," Donald said. "I came to this damned museum with the hope of coming across some weapons. I thought there'd be some, but I haven't seen a single one. Having a museum about human history without weapons is ridiculous. The pacifism of these Interterrans is driving me up the wall."

"Weapons!" Michael commented. He nodded. The idea hadn't dawned on him, but he immediately was intrigued. "Cool idea! To tell you the truth, I was wondering why you wanted to come here."

"Well, now you know, sailor," Donald said. "And maybe you can even help, since this place is so enormous. If we spread out we can cover a lot more ground."

No sooner had Donald uttered this suggestion than his eye caught something he'd not seen in any other exhibition hall: a closed door with the words RESTRICTED ENTRY written over its upper panel. Curious as to what it might conceal, he approached it, with Michael at his heels. As Donald got closer he could see that there were several other words in smaller letters: FOR ENTRY, APPLY TO COUNCIL OF ELDERS.

"What the hell is the Council of Elders?" Michael asked over Donald's shoulder.

"Some sort of governing body, I imagine," Donald said. He put his hand on the door and pushed. It was unlocked, like all doors in Interterra.

"Eureka!" Donald said as he caught a glimpse of some of the objects displayed in the room beyond. He pushed the door all the way open and stepped over the threshold. Michael entered behind him and whistled.

"No wonder we haven't seen any weapons," Donald said. "It looks like they got their own hidden gallery." The room was comparatively narrow but extremely long. On both sides were display shelves cluttered with arms.

The two men had entered the gallery approximately halfway along its length. On the shelf directly opposite the entrance was a medieval crossbow with a quiver of needle-sharp quarrels. Michael leaned over and lifted the crossbow from its resting place. He whistled again. He'd never handled such a weapon. "Jeez!" he commented. "What a fierce-looking contraption." He knocked the stock with his knuckle. The sound was a solid thunk. He twanged the bowstring. It was still sound. He held it up in the air and sighted along its shaft. "I bet this thing still works."

Donald had started off to the right, but soon recognized he was going in the wrong chronological direction. The weapons were becoming older. Ahead he could see a collection of Greek and Roman short swords, bows, and spears. He turned and passed Michael, who was busy trying to bend the crossbow with a hand crank to slip the string into its locking device.

"There's still a lot of strength in the bow," Michael said as he succeeded finally. He placed one of the bolts into the guide and held the loaded weapon up for Donald to see. "What do you think?"

"It's got possibilities," Donald said vaguely while heading down the other way. He was encouraged when he saw the first examples of early harquebuses. "But I was hoping for something a bit more definitive than an arbalest."

"I thought this thing was called a crossbow," Michael said.

"Same thing," Donald said without turning back.

Michael put his finger on the release lever and, without meaning to, discharged the weapon. The bolt hissed from its position in the guide, ricocheted off the basalt wall with a high-pitched scraping sound, shot past Donald's right ear, and buried itself into one of the wooden shelves. Donald had felt the wind from the missile as it sailed by.

"Jesus H. Christ!" Donald roared. "You almost nailed me with that goddamn thing!"

"Sorry," Michael said. "I hardly touched the trigger."

"Put it down before one of us gets hurt," Donald yelled.

"At least we know it works," Michael said.

Donald shook his head with disgust while he reached up with his hand to check his ear. Thankfully there was no blood. The bolt had come that close. Mumbling expletives about the clowns he'd gotten stranded with, he continued down the gallery. Soon he was looking at a collection of World War II rifles and handguns. To his chagrin, they were in sorry shape, having suffered the ill effects of salt water. He became progressively discouraged until he came across a German Luger near the room's end. At first sight it appeared to be in excellent condition.

Unaware he was holding his breath, Donald reached for the pistol and hefted it. To his delight, the gun appeared pristine even under close scrutiny. With great anticipation he released the magazine. A smile spread across his face. The clip was full!

"Did you find something good?" Michael asked. He'd come up behind Donald.

Donald pushed the magazine home in the pistol's hand grip. It made a definitive, reassuringly solid mechanical sound. He held the gun aloft. "This is what I've been looking for."

"Cool!" Michael said.

Lovingly Donald put the Luger back where he'd found it.

"What are you doing?" Michael questioned. "Aren't you going to take it?"

"Not now," Donald said. "Not until I know what I'm going to do with it."

Richard stopped dead in his tracks. He could not believe what he was seeing. It was a room chock full of treasure, mostly from ancient times. There were innumerable cups, bowls, and even whole statues made of solid gold, all dramatically lit with concentrated beams of light. In one corner was a series of chests filled with doubloons. The display was dazzling.

What made the sight even more astounding for Richard was that the entire collection of inestimable value was all within easy grasp since the objects were out in the open and not behind protective glass barriers like he was accustomed to in all the museums he'd ever visited. And this was on top of the fact that the museum's front door had no guards.

"This is unbelievable," Richard managed. "God, this is fantastic. What I would do for a wheelbarrow of this stuff!"

"You like these objects?" Sufa questioned.

"Like them? I love them," Richard stammered. "I've never seen anything like this. I doubt there's this much gold in Fort Knox."

"We have storerooms filled with these things," Sufa said. "Ships have been sinking with gold for years. I can arrange to have a quantity of similar objects sent to your room for your own enjoyment if you'd like."

"You mean stuff like we're seeing here?"

"Certainly," Sufa said. "Do you prefer the large statues or the smaller objects?"

"I'm not picky," Richard said. "But what about jewels? Does the museum have jewels, too?"

"Certainly," Sufa said. "But most of it comes from your ancient times. Would you care to view it?"

"Why not?" Richard answered.

On the way to the gallery of ancient jewelry, Richard caught sight of an artifact in a display of twentieth-century curios that brought a smile to his face. On a chest-high pedestal a Frisbee was carefully illuminated with a pencil of light, as if it, too, were as priceless as gold.

"Well, I'll be!" Richard mumbled to himself as he stopped in front of the chartreuse disk. He noticed a few canine indentations along the Frisbee's edge. "What on earth is this here for?" he called ahead to Sufa.

Sufa came back to where Richard was standing to see what he was referring to. "We don't know exactly what that is," she admitted. "But some have suggested it might be a model of one of our antigravity vehicles like our air taxis or our interplanetary cruisers. We were afraid for a time that there had been a direct sighting."

Richard threw his head back and laughed. "You got to be kidding," he said.

"No, I'm not joking," Sufa said. "Its shape is very suggestive, and it can be spun to capture a cushion of air that mimics an antigravity ship."

"It's not a model of anything," Richard said. "It's nothing but a Frisbee."

"What is it used for?" Sufa asked.

"It's to play with," Richard said. "You spin it like you said and then someone else catches it. Let me show you." Richard picked up the Frisbee and gently flipped it up into the air on an angle. The toy reached an apogee then returned. He caught it in his palm between his thumb and fingers. "That's all there is to it," he said. "It's easy, don't you think?"

"I suppose," Sufa said.

"Let me throw it to you and you catch it just like I did," Richard said. He trotted down the gallery about fifty feet. He turned and tossed the Frisbee toward Sufa. She went through the motions as if she were going to catch it, but she was too clumsy. Although it grazed her hand, she failed to grab it; it clattered to the floor. After rolling his eyes at her ineptness, Richard trotted back and showed her again how to do it. But his efforts were in vain. On the next toss she was even more awkward than on the first.

"You people aren't into physical activity, are you?" Richard said scornfully. "I've never met anyone who couldn't catch a Frisbee."

"What's the purpose?"

"There's no purpose," Richard snapped. "It's just fun.

It's a sport. Tossing this thing back and forth gives you a chance to run around."

"It seems pointless to me," Sufa said.

"Don't you people get any exercise down here in Interterra?"

"Certainly," Sufa said. "We enjoy swimming particularly but also walking and playing with our homids. Of course there's always sex, as I'm sure Meeta, Palenque, and Karena have shown you."

"I'm talking about a sport!" Richard complained. "Sex is not a sport."

"It is for us," Sufa said. "And it's certainly a lot of exercise."

"What about a sport in which you try to win?" Richard asked.

"Win?" Sufa questioned.

"You know, competition!" Richard said with annoyance. "Don't you have any competitive games?"

"Heavens, no!" Sufa said. "We stopped that kind of nonsense eons ago when we eliminated wars and violence."

"Oh, for chrissake," Richard blurted. "No sports! That means no ice hockey, no football, not even golf! Jeez! And to think Suzanne thinks this place is heaven!"

"Please calm down," Sufa urged. "Why are you so agitated?"

"Do I seem agitated?" Richard questioned innocently.

"Indeed you do," Sufa said.

"I guess I need some exercise," Richard offered. With the Frisbee under his arm, he nervously cracked his knuckles. He knew he was strung out, and he knew why: in his mind's eye he kept picturing a worker clone stumbling onto Mura's corpse scrunched up inside his refrigerator.

"Why don't you take the Frisbee?" Sufa suggested. "Perhaps Michael or one of the others will participate with you."

"Why not," Richard said, but without much enthusiasm.

"All right, everybody!" Arak called out. The group had reunited out on the terrace in front of the museum after spending more than an hour inside. They were all discussing what they had seen during the visit, except for Richard, who remained on the periphery, repeatedly tossing the Frisbee into the air and catching it. At the base of the steps three air taxis were waiting.

"Let's talk about the arrangements for the rest of the morning," Arak said. "Sufa will accompany Perry to the air taxi construction and repair facility. Perry, I believe that is what you had wanted to see."

"Very much so," Perry agreed.

"Ismael and Mary will accompany Donald and Michael to Central Information," Arak continued.

Donald nodded.

"What about you, Richard?" Arak asked. "Which of those two destinations appeals to you?"

"I don't really care," Richard said, continuing to flip the Frisbee into the air.

"You have to choose one or the other," Arak said.

"Okay, then, the air taxi factory," Richard said impassively.

"What about Suzanne?" Perry questioned.

"Dr. Newell will go with me for a meeting with the Council of Elders," Arak said.

"By herself?" Feeling protective, Perry glanced at Suzanne.

"It's okay," Suzanne said reassuringly. "While you

climbed into the U-boat in the World War Two hall, Arak explained the elders wanted to talk with me professionally, as an oceanographer."

"But why alone?" Perry asked. "And why not me? After all, I run an oceanographic company."

"I don't think it's the business side they're interested in," Suzanne said. "Don't worry."

"Are you sure?" Perry persisted.

"Quite sure," Suzanne said. She patted Perry's shoulder.

"Then let us go," Arak called out. "We'll all meet back at the visitors' palace later in the day." Beckoning for the others to follow, he skirted the old Corvette's dais and started down the wide steps toward the hovering air taxis.

It did seem strange to Suzanne to be alone with Arak as the air taxi swept them off to their destination. It was the first time Suzanne had been away from the others except to sleep in her cottage. She looked over at Arak, and he smiled back at her. Being in such quiet proximity made her again aware of how handsome he was.

"Are you enjoying your orientation?" Arak questioned. "Or are you finding it frustratingly fast or slow?"

"Overwhelming is the best way to describe how I'm finding it," Suzanne said. "Speed is not the issue, and I certainly don't feel frustrated in the slightest."

"Your group is quite a challenge for designing and tailoring the best orientation protocol. You are all so different, a fact that we Interterrans find fascinating but also daunting. You see, because of selection and adaptation, we are all very much alike, which I'm sure is something you've recognized."

"You are all very nice," Suzanne said with a nod,

wincing at voicing such a platitude. She realized that until Arak's comment, she hadn't given the issue much thought. Now that she had, she realized it was true. Not only were they all similarly attractive in a classical sense, but they all were equally gracious, intelligent, and easygoing. There was little if any variation in their temperaments.

"*Nice* is a rather sanitized word to choose," Arak said. "I hope you are not bored with us."

Suzanne gave a little, self-conscious laugh. "It's hard to be bored when you are overwhelmed," she said. "I can assure you, I am not bored." Her eyes wandered to the incredible vista out over the city with the swarms of air taxis whizzing by. Being bored was the furthest thing from her mind, yet she suddenly understood what Arak was alluding to. After a while, Interterra might become tiresome because of its homogeneity. Some of the very aspects that made it such a paradise also rendered it bland.

Suzanne focused on a striking structure that loomed out of the tapestry of the city and pulled her from her musing as the air taxi quickly approached. It was an enormous black pyramid with a bright gold top. As the air taxi stopped and then descended to a causeway that led up to the pyramid's entrance, she was struck by its resemblance to the Great Pyramid of Egypt at Giza. Having been to Giza, she could tell that the Interterran version was even approximately the same size. When she mentioned this similarity to Arak, he smiled patronizingly.

"The design was one of our gifts to that culture," Arak said. "We had great hopes for them since they were, initially, a rather peaceful civilization. We sent a delegation to live among them early in their history with the idea of promoting them over the other extremely warlike peoples who had evolved. The experiment was not as big an undertaking as the Atlantean movement, and we did try, but it all came to naught."

"Did you show them how to build it as well as provide the design?" Suzanne asked. For her the riddle of the Great Pyramid was one of the most fascinating of the ancient world.

"Of course," Arak said. "We had to. We also showed them the concept of the arch, but they steadfastly refused to believe it would work and never tried it on a single structure."

The air taxi came to a stop and the side opened.

"After you," Arak said graciously.

Once they gained entry, Suzanne realized that any similarity between the two structures vanished. The Interterran pyramid interior was gleaming white marble, and the interior spaces were grand instead of claustrophobic.

As Suzanne and Arak walked down a corridor heading toward the center of the building, Suzanne was met by another surprise. Garona stepped out of a side passageway directly in front of her and enveloped her in a warm embrace.

"Garona!" Suzanne murmured with obvious delight. She hugged him back. "What a nice surprise! I didn't expect to see you until tonight. Or at least I was hoping I'd see you tonight."

"Of course you would have seen me tonight," Garona said. "But I could not wait." He looked into her eyes. "I knew you were coming to the Council of Elders today so I came over to wait for you."

"I'm pleased," Suzanne said.

"We'd better move," Arak said. "The council is waiting."

"Certainly," Garona said. He took his arms from Suzanne and grasped her hand instead. The three began walking.

"How was your morning?" Garona inquired.

"Enlightening," Suzanne said. "Your technology is astounding."

"We had a scientific session," Arak explained.

"Any site visits?" Garona asked.

"We went to the Earth Surface Museum," Suzanne said.

"Really?" Garona seemed surprised.

"It was a specific request of Mr. Donald Fuller," Arak explained.

"Did you find it instructive?" Garona asked.

"It was interesting," Suzanne said. "But it wouldn't have been my choice, not with what we had learned during the didactic session."

They approached an impressive set of bronze doors. Within each panel was an embossed figure Suzanne recognized as an ankh, or ancient Egyptian symbol of life. It was another reminder for her of the apparent exchange of information from the Interterrans to ancient secondary human civilization. It made her wonder what else had come from this advanced culture.

The moment they arrived at them, the doors swung inward on silent hinges. Beyond was a circular room with a domed ceiling supported by a colonnade. Like the rest of the pyramid's interior it was constructed of white marble, although the capitals of the columns were gold.

At Arak's urging, Suzanne stepped over the marble threshold. She took a few hesitant steps before stopping.

She scanned the stately chamber. Twelve imperial-looking chairs ringed the periphery. Each was situated between a pair of columns. All the chairs were occupied—presumably by council members—who ranged in age from about five to twenty-five. The unexpectedness of such a mixed age group had Suzanne mildly flustered. Some of the people were so young, their feet didn't reach the ground when they sat.

"Come in, Dr. Suzanne Newell," one of the elders said in a clear preadolescent voice. To Suzanne she looked like a ten-year-old girl. "My name is Ala, and it is my rotation as speaker of the council. So, please, don't be afraid! I know these surroundings are imposing and intimidating, but we only desire to speak with you, and if you will come to the center of the room we will all be able to hear you clearly."

"I'm more surprised than fearful," Suzanne said as she advanced to a point directly beneath the high point of the dome. "I was told I was coming to the Council of Elders."

"And indeed you have," Ala said. "The determining factor for sitting on the council is the number of body lives you've passed, not the age of the current body."

"I see," Suzanne said, although she still found it unsettling to be standing before a governmental body partially composed of children.

"The Council of Elders formally welcomes you," Ala said.

"Thank you," Suzanne replied, not knowing what else to say.

"You were brought to Interterra with the hope that you could provide us with information we have not been able to glean from monitoring your earth surface communications."

"What kind of information?" Suzanne asked. She felt her guard go up. In the back of her mind she heard Donald's voice saying that the Interterrans wanted something from them, and once they got it, they might treat them very differently.

"Don't be alarmed," Ala said soothingly.

"It is hard not to be," Suzanne said. "Especially when you help remind me that I and my colleagues have been abducted into your world which, I have to say, was a terrifying experience."

"For that we extend our apologies," Ala said. "And you should understand that we intend to reward your sacrifice. But it is we who are alarmed. You see, the integrity and safety of Interterra are our responsibility. We know that you are a learned oceanographer in your world."

"That's being overly generous," Suzanne said. "The reality is that I am a relative newcomer to the field."

"Excuse me," one of the other elders said. He was a teenager at the very beginning of his growth spurt. "My name is Ponu, and I am currently the vice-speaker. Dr. Newell, we are aware of the esteem in which you are held by your professional colleagues. It is our belief that such respect is a reliable testament to an individual's abilities."

"As you will," Suzanne said. It wasn't a point she wanted to argue under the circumstances. "What is it you want to ask me?"

"First," Ala said, "I'd like to make sure you have been informed that our environment is devoid of your common bacteria and viruses."

"Arak has made that clear," Suzanne said.

"And I assume you understand that detection of our

civilization by a civilization like yours would be disastrous."

"I can understand the worry about contamination," Suzanne said. "But I'm not convinced it would necessarily be disastrous, especially if the proper safeguards were put in place."

"Dr. Newell, this is not meant to be a debate," Ala said. "But surely you must be cognizant of the fact that your civilization is still in a very early stage of social development. Naked self-interest is the prime motivational force, and violence is an everyday occurrence. In fact your particular country is so primitive that it allows anyone and everyone to own a gun."

"Let me paraphrase," Ponu offered. "What my esteemed fellow elder is saying is that your world's hunger and greed for our technology would be so great that our special needs would be forgotten."

"Exactly," Ala said. "And we cannot accept such a risk. Not for at least another fifty thousand years or so, to give secondary humans a chance to become more civilized. Provided, of course, they don't destroy themselves in the process."

"Okay," Suzanne said. "As you say, this is not a debate, and you have convinced me that you believe my culture is a risk to yours. Assuming that as a given, what do you want from me?"

There was a pause. Suzanne looked from Ala to Ponu. When neither responded she glanced at the other faces. No one spoke. No one moved. Suzanne looked back at Arak and Garona. Garona smiled reassuringly. Suzanne turned back to Ala. "Well . . . ?" she asked.

Ala sighed. "I would like to ask you a direct question," she said. "A question whose answer we are afraid to hear. You see, your world has started several deep-ocean drilling operations over the last few years, on a seemingly random basis. We have watched these episodes with growing concern since we are uncertain what the goals are. We know the drilling is not for petroleum or natural gas since there is none in the areas where this drilling is being undertaken. We've been monitoring communications as we have always done, but without success of learning why this drilling is occurring."

"Are you interested in knowing why the *Benthic Explorer* has been drilling into the seamount?" Suzanne asked.

"I am very interested," Ala said. "You were drilling directly over one of our old-style exit ports. The probability of that occurring purely by chance is extremely small."

"It wasn't by chance," Suzanne admitted. As soon as she spoke these words a general murmur erupted among the elders. "Let me finish," Suzanne called out. "We were drilling into the seamount to see if we could tap directly into the asthenosphere. Our echo sounder suggested the seamount was a quiescent volcano with a magma chamber filled with low-density lava."

"Was any part of the decision to drill at that particular site motivated by a suspicion of the existence of Interterra?" Ala asked.

"No!" Suzanne said. "Absolutely not!"

"There was no thought of an undersea civilization in the decision-making process?" Ala questioned.

"As I said, we were drilling purely for geological reasons," Suzanne said.

The elders again conferred loudly with one another. Suzanne turned and glanced back at Arak and Garona. Both smiled encouragement.

"Dr. Newell," Ala said to redirect Suzanne's attention

to herself, "have you, in your professional capacity, ever heard of anything from any source that would suggest someone suspected the existence of Interterra?"

"No, not in any scientific circles," Suzanne said. "But there have been a few novels written about a world within the earth."

"We are aware of the work of Mr. Verne and Mr. Doyle," Ala said. "But that was purely entertainment fiction."

"That's correct," Suzanne said. "It was pure fantasy. No one thought their story lines were based in any way on fact, although they probably got the theme from a man by the name of John Cleves Symmes, who did believe the center of the earth was hollow."

The elders erupted in another loud, anxious murmuring.

"Did Mr. Symmes's beliefs influence scientific opinion?" Ala asked.

"To some degree," Suzanne said. "But I wouldn't give it much concern since we're talking about the early part of the nineteenth century. In eighteen thirty-eight his theory did launch one of the first United States scientific expeditions. It was under the command of Lt. Charles Wilkes, and its initial purpose was to find the entrance to the earth's hollow interior, which Symmes believed to be beneath the South Pole."

Additional excited murmuring echoed throughout the room.

"And the result of this expedition?" Ala questioned.

"Nothing that would concern Interterra," Suzanne said. "In fact, the goal of the expedition changed even before it began. Instead of looking for the entrance to the interior of the earth, by the time they got underway they were tasked to find new sealing and whaling grounds."

"So Mr. Symmes's theory was ignored?" Ala questioned.

"Completely," Suzanne said. "And the idea has never resurfaced."

"We are indeed thankful," Ala said, "especially considering Mr. Symmes was correct in some respects. The South Pole was and still is our major interplanetary and intergalactic port."

"Isn't that curious," Suzanne said. "Unfortunately it's a bit late for Mr. Symmes to be vindicated. Be that as it may, I gather from your questions that you are asking me if your secret is safe, and I have to say it is, as far as I know. But while we're on the subject, perhaps I should mention that although no one currently believes in a hollow earth, there have always been fringe groups who talk about aliens from advanced cultures that have visited us or are among us. There has even been a hit TV show with that as its theme. But these ideas of alien visitations refer to aliens coming from outer space, not from within the earth."

"We are aware of what you are describing," Ala said. "And we have been pleased with that association. It has been particularly useful on the few occasions that one of our interplanetary craft have been observed by secondary humans."

"The only other thing I should mention," Suzanne said, "is that our culture has had enduring myths about Atlantis that have come down to us from the ancient Greeks. But I assure you the scientific community considers them to be pure myths or possibly the result of the destruction of an ancient secondary human culture by a violent volcanic eruption. There has never been a theory that a primary human culture lives beneath the ocean."

The elders noisily conferred again. Suzanne shifted uncomfortably as they deliberated.

Ala concluded the private discourse with a nod to her colleagues and then redirected her attention to Suzanne. "We would like to inquire about the episodes of random deep-ocean drilling that have been occurring over the last number of years in the general area of Saranta. None of these have been on the crest of a seamount."

"I imagine you are referring to the drilling that has been done to confirm the latest theories of sea-floor spreading," Suzanne said. "It's been done merely to provide rock cores for dating purposes."

The elders again erupted in a short burst of excited chatter. At its conclusion Ala asked, "Was there ever any suggestion the supposed magma chamber into which you were drilling was filled with air instead of low-density lava?"

"Not that I was aware of," Suzanne said. "And I was the senior scientist on the project."

"Those exit ports should have been sealed ages ago," one of the other elders said with some vehemence.

"This is not a time for recrimination," Ala advised diplomatically. "We are dealing with the present." Then, looking back at Suzanne, she said, "To summarize, in your professional life you have never heard any suggestion that a civilization exists under the ocean or any theories to that effect?"

"Only as myths, as I've mentioned," Suzanne said.

"And now for the last question we would like to direct to you," Ala said. "We have become increasingly apprehensive about your civilization's progressive lack of respect for the ocean environment. Although we have heard some mention of this problem in your media, the rate of pollution and overfishing has increased. Since we are dependent to some degree on the integrity of the ocean, we wonder if your civilization's talk of this issue is mere lip service or a real concern?"

Suzanne sighed. This issue was close to her heart. She knew all too well that the truth was discouraging at best.

"Some people are trying to change the situation," Suzanne said.

"That response suggests it is not considered an important issue by the majority," Ala said.

"Perhaps not, but those who do care, care passionately."

"But perhaps the general public is not aware of the crucial role the ocean plays in the grand scheme of earth surface environment, for example, the fact that plankton modulates both oxygen and carbon dioxide on the earth's surface."

Suzanne felt her face flush, as if somehow she were to blame for the way secondary humans treated the world's oceans. "I'm afraid that most people and most countries view the ocean as an inexhaustible food supply and a bottomless pit for refuse and waste."

"That is sad indeed," Ala said. "And worrisome."

"It is self-interested shortsightedness," Ponu said.

"I have to agree," Suzanne admitted. "It's something I and my colleagues are working on. It's a battle."

"Well, then," Ala said. She pushed herself off her chair. Once she got her feet on the ground she walked directly over to Suzanne with her hand outstretched, palm forward.

Suzanne raised her own hand and pressed palms with Ala. Ala's head only came to Suzanne's chin.

"Thank you for your helpful counsel," Ala said with sincerity. "At least in relation to the security of Interterra, you have allayed our fears. As a reward we offer to you the full panoply of the fruits of our civilization. You have much to see and experience. With your background you are uniquely qualified, far better than any of our other earth surface visitors. Go and enjoy!"

Sudden applause by the other elders left Suzanne momentarily flustered. She self-consciously acknowledged the acclaim by nodding before speaking above the persisting applause. "Thank you all for providing me this opportunity to visit Interterra. I'm honored."

"It is we who are honored," Ala said. She gestured toward Arak and Garona, directing Suzanne to follow.

Later as the three exited the great pyramid, Suzanne paused to glance back at the imposing structure. She wondered if she should have posed the question to the Council whether she and the others were temporary visitors to Interterra or permanent, captive residents. Part of the reason she hadn't was her fear of what the answer would be. But now she found herself wishing she had.

"Are you okay?" Garona asked, interrupting her thoughts.

"I'm fine," Suzanne replied. She resumed walking, still engrossed in her thoughts. The one thing the visit did clear up was the reason she and the others had been brought to Interterra. The elders had wanted to quiz a professional oceanographer about suspicions of Interterra's existence. She didn't think that the treatment she and her crewmates would receive was about to change now that the Interterrans had achieved their goal. On the other hand she now felt solely responsible for their plight. If it hadn't been for her, they would not have been abducted.

"Are you sure you are all right?" Garona asked. "You seem so pensive."

Suzanne forced herself to smile. "It's hard not to be," she said. "There's so much to take in."

"You have provided a great service to Interterra," Arak remarked. "As Ala said, we all are grateful."

"I'm glad," Suzanne said as she tried to maintain her grin. But it was difficult. Sensing that Donald was right and that they were in Interterra to stay, her intuition was telling her that a confrontation was inevitable, and given the personalities of some of her colleagues, the situation could soon turn violent and ugly.

CHAPTER SIXTEEN

"This place gives me the creeps," Michael said.

"It is weird that it is so deserted," Donald said. "It's also weird that they let us roam around in here by ourselves."

"They are trusting," Michael said. "You got to give them that."

"I'd call it foolish," Donald said.

The two second-generation humans were wandering around inside Central Information. Ismael and Mary Black had accompanied them to the entrance of the vast building but had chosen to remain outside while Donald and Michael paid their visit. Inside, the two men found themselves in an enormous labyrinth of intersecting corridors and passageways. The place was a hive of rooms filled floor to ceiling with what appeared to be the hard drives of a colossal computer array. Except for two worker clones they'd come across in one room near the entrance, they had not seen another living thing.

"You don't think we're going to get lost in here, do

you?" Michael asked uneasily. He looked back the way they'd come. Every corridor looked the same.

"I've been keeping track of our movements," Donald said.

"Are you sure?" Michael said. "We've made a lot of turns."

Donald stopped. "Listen, bonehead," he said. "If you're worried why don't you just go the hell back to the entrance and wait?"

"That's okay," Michael said. "I'm cool."

"Cool, my ass," Donald said. He started walking again.

"What did you want to come here for anyway?" Michael asked a few minutes later.

"Let's just say I was curious," Donald replied.

"It's like a nightmare," Michael said. "Or like a horror movie about technology gone wild." He shuddered.

"For once, I agree with you, sailor," Donald said. "It's like technology has taken over."

"What do you think all this equipment does?"

"Arak suggested it runs the place," Donald said. "Apparently it monitors everything. And it stores peoples' essences. God knows how many people are locked up inside this thing right now."

Michael shuddered again. "Do you think they know we're here?"

"You got me there, sailor," Donald said.

They walked for a few minutes in silence.

"Haven't you seen enough?" Michael questioned.

"I suppose," Donald said. "But I'm going to press on for a while yet."

"I wonder if this thing repairs itself."

"If it does," Donald said, "then we'd have to question who was more alive, this machine or these people who seem to have so little to do."

Suddenly Donald put out a hand, stopping Michael in his tracks.

"What is it?" Michael cried.

Donald pressed a finger to his lips for Michael to be quiet. "Don't you hear that?" Donald whispered.

Michael cocked his head and listened intently. He did hear faint sounds in the far distance: soft bursts piercing the otherwise heavy silence.

"Do you hear it?" Donald asked.

Michael nodded. "It sounds like laughter."

Donald nodded as well. "A curious kind of laughter," he said. "It comes at such regular intervals."

"If I didn't know better I'd say it was canned laughter, like what you hear on a TV sitcom."

Donald snapped his fingers. "You're right! I knew it sounded familiar."

"But that's crazy," Michael said.

"Let's check it out!" Donald said. "Let's follow our ears!"

With mounting curiosity the two men proceeded, hoping to find the source. At the junctures of each corridor they had to stop and listen to choose a direction. Gradually the sounds became louder, and with it, their choices became clear. As they rounded a final bend, they could tell the noise was coming from a room on the left. At that point they were convinced they really were hearing a TV sitcom; they could even hear the dialogue.

"It sounds like a *Seinfeld* rerun," Michael whispered.

"Shut up!" Donald mouthed. He flattened himself against the wall to the side of the room's entrance and motioned for Michael to move beside him. Slowly Donald eased himself forward. To his surprise, it looked like the screening room of a TV station. The far wall was covered with more than a hundred monitors. All were turned on, most tuned to various programs although a few aired only test patterns.

Leaning forward a bit more Donald noticed a man sitting in a white contour chair in the center of the room facing the monitors. The guy was a far cry from the typical Interterran; he was balding with scruffy gray hair. Sure enough, on the screen directly in front of him were Elaine, George, Kramer, and Jerry.

Donald flattened himself back against the corridor wall, away from the open door. He looked at Michael and whispered, "You were right! It's an old episode of *Seinfeld*."

"I'd recognize those voices anyplace," Michael said.

Donald raised his finger to his lips again. "There's a geezer in there watching it," he whispered. "And he surely doesn't look like an Interterran."

"No shit?" Michael questioned in a whisper.

"This is unexpected," Donald said. He rolled his lower lip into his mouth while he gave the situation some thought.

"That's for sure," Michael said. "What should we do?"

"We're going to walk in and meet this guy," Donald said. "We might have lucked out here. But listen! Let me do the talking, okay?"

"Be my guest," Michael said.

"All right, let's go," Donald said. He pushed off the wall and stepped into the room. Michael followed. They moved quietly although the TV was so loud, the man could never have heard their approach.

Unsure of how to avoid startling the man and yet get his attention, Donald merely stepped into what he thought was the man's field of vision but off to the side. The ploy didn't work. The man was mesmerized by the show; his face was frozen into a slack, comatose expression with lidded, unblinking eyes glued to the screen.

"Excuse me," Donald said, but his voice was lost in another burst of canned laughter.

Gently Donald reached out and nudged the man's arm. The man leaped from his seat. Seeing the two intruders in the process, he shrank back. But his recovery was almost as rapid.

"Wait a minute! I recognize you two!" he said. "You are two of the surface people who've just joined us."

"*Join* is not the right word," Donald said. "We had no choice in the matter. We were abducted." He eyed the man, who was no more than five-two with a stooped, bony frame. He had deeply set, rheumy eyes, course features, and a heavily lined face. He was the oldest-looking man Donald had seen in Interterra.

"You weren't shipwrecked?" the man asked.

"Hardly," Donald said. He introduced himself and Michael.

"Glad to meet you," the man said cheerfully. "I was hoping I would." He came forward to shake their hands. "And that's the way people should greet each other," he added. "I've had it with that foolish palm-pressing nonsense."

"What's your name?" Donald asked.

"Harvey Goldfarb! But you can call me Harv."

"Are you here by yourself?"

"Sure as shootin'. I'm always here by myself."

"What are you doing?"

"Not much," Harvey said. He glanced briefly at the bank of monitors. "Watching TV shows, particularly the ones that take place in New York."

"Is this a job?"

"Sorta, I suppose, but it's more like I'm a volunteer. It's mostly that I like to see bits and pieces of New York. I like *All in the Family* quite a bit but it's hard to catch reruns nowadays. It's too bad. *Seinfeld*'s all right but I don't get much of the humor."

"What is this room for?" Donald asked. "Just entertainment?"

Harvey laughed derisively while shaking his head. "The Interterrans are not interested in TV, and they don't watch it much. It's Central Information that's interested. Saranta Central Information is one of the main media reception sites for Interterra. It monitors the surface media to make certain there is no reference to Interterra's existence." Harvey made a sweep toward the monitors with his hands. "This stuff plays twenty-four hours a day, seven days a week.

"Hey, that reminds me. You guys got a lot of coverage up there on CNN and the networks. You're all in the news for having gotten consumed in an undersea volcano."

"So there were no suspicions about anything abnormal?" Donald asked.

"Not a peep," Harvey said. "Just a lot of geological jabber. Anyway, to get back to me, I volunteered to come down here and monitor TV shows for the files and to censor out any violence."

"That doesn't leave much TV," Donald said with a cynical laugh. "Why bother?"

"I know, it doesn't make much sense," Harvey agreed. "But if they do watch it, it can't have any violence. I don't know if you know it or not, but these people, the real Interterrans, cannot stand violence. It makes them sick. Literally!"

"So you're not a real Interterran."

Harvey gave another short laugh. "Me? Harvey Gold-farb an Interterran? Do I look like an Interterran? With this face?"

"You do look a bit older than everyone else."

"Older and uglier," Harvey snorted. "But that's me. They've been trying to get me to agree to let them do all sorts of stuff to me, even grow me hair, but I've re-fused. Yet, I have to say they have kept me healthy. No question about that. Their hospitals are like taking your car to a garage. They just put in a new part and out you go. Anyway, I'm not an Interterran. I'm a New Yorker. I have a wonderful house in the best section of Harlem."

"Harlem has gone through some changes," Donald said. "How long has it been since you've been home?"

"It was nineteen twelve when I came to Interterra."

"How'd you get here?"

"A bit of luck and the intervention of the Interter-rans. I was saved from drowning along with a few hun-dred others after our ship ran into an iceberg."

"The *Titanic*?" Donald questioned.

"None other," Harvey said. "I was on my way home to New York."

"So there are quite a few *Titanic* passengers in Inter-terra?" Donald asked.

"Several hundred at least," Harvey said. "But they're not all in Saranta. A lot of them moved over to Atlantis and on to other cities. They were in demand. You see, the Interterrans find us entertaining."

"I've gotten that impression," Donald said.

"Take advantage of it while you can," Harvey ad-vised. "Once you become acclimated here, you won't be considered so entertaining anymore. Trust me."

"You must have had a horrible experience," Donald
said.

"No, I've been pretty happy here," Harvey said defensively. "It's got its ups and downs."

"I meant the night of the *Titanic* sinking."

"Oh, yeah! It's true. That night was awful. Awful!"

"Do you miss New York?"

"In a way," Harvey said. He got a faraway look in
his eye. "Actually, it's funny what I really miss, and
that's the stock exchange. I know it sounds strange, but
I was a self-made man . . . a broker actually, and I loved
trading. I worked hard, but how I thrived in the excitement." Harvey took a deep breath and then let it out all
at once with a sigh. He refocused on Donald. "Well, so
much for my story. What about you? Were you people
really abducted to Interterra? If you were, you're the
first in my experience. I was under the impression you'd
been saved from the undersea volcano CNN reported."

"There was some sort of an eruption at the time,"
Donald said. "But I think it was a cover for our being
sucked into one of the Interterran exit ports. One way
or the other, our arrival in Interterra wasn't an act of
nature. We were hijacked here for a purpose, which
we've not yet been told."

Harvey looked from Donald to Michael and then back
to Donald. "You sound less than enchanted with Interterra."

"I'm impressed," Donald said. "It would be hard not
to be, but I'm not enchanted."

"Hmmm," Harvey said. "That puts you in a unique
category. Everybody else who's been brought here becomes an overnight advocate. What about your friend
here?"

"Michael feels the way I do," Donald said. Michael

nodded. "You see," Donald continued, "we don't like to be forced into anything, no matter how good it may seem. But what about you, Harv?"

Harvey studied Donald's face and even took another quick glance at Michael, who at the moment was laughing in sync with the sitcom laughter. "You're serious, you're not enthralled with this place even with all the beautiful people and their parties?"

"I'm telling you, we don't appreciate being coerced."

"And you're actually interested in my opinion?"

Donald nodded.

"Okay," Harvey said. He leaned closer and lowered his voice. "Let me put it to you this way: if I could leave for New York City tonight it wouldn't be soon enough. It's so damn peaceful and perfect here it's enough to drive a normal person crazy."

Donald couldn't help but smile. The old codger was a man after his own heart.

"I'm telling you, nothing ever happens down here," Harvey continued. "Everything's the same day in and day out. Nothing goes wrong. I can't tell you what I'd do for one day on the New York exchange. I mean, I need a little stress to make me feel alive, or at the very least, some bad news or trouble once in a blue moon to make me appreciate how good life is."

Michael flashed Donald a thumbs-up. But Donald ignored him. Instead he asked Harvey if anyone had ever left Interterra.

"Are you kidding? We're under the goddamn ocean! I mean, really. What do you think, you can just walk out of here? If that were the case you wouldn't see Harvey Goldfarb sitting in here trying to catch a glimpse of the Big Apple. I'd be there, kicking up my heels."

"But the Interterrans go out," Donald said.

"Sure they go out. But the exits and entrances are all controlled by Central Information. And when the Interterrans go out, they're sealed in their spacecraft. Besides, they usually just send their worker clones. You see, the Interterrans are very careful about any connection between this world and ours. Remember, one wayward streptococcus would cause havoc down here."

"It sounds like you've given this some thought."

"Absolutely," Harvey said. "But only in my dreams."

Donald directed his attention to the bank of TV monitors. "At least you can feel connected to the surface world in this room."

"That's why I'm here," Harvey said proprietarily. "It's a fantastic setup. I hang out here all the time. I can watch just about every major TV channel from the surface world."

"Can you transmit as well as receive?" Donald asked.

"No, it's a passive system," Harvey said. "I mean, there's unlimited power and antennae in just about every mountain range on the surface of the globe, but there's no camera. Interterra's own telecommunication is totally different and a lot more sophisticated, as I'm sure you've gathered."

"If we gave you a standard TV analog camcorder, do you think you could connect it with the equipment you've got here without anybody knowing about it and be able to transmit?"

Harvey stroked his chin as he pondered Donald's question. "Maybe if I got one of the electronic worker clones to help, it could be done," he said. "But where are you going to get a TV camera?"

"I know what you're thinking," Michael said as a conspiratorial smile spread across his face. "You're thinking about the cameras on the submersible." When the group had gathered out in front of the museum after their visit, Perry and Suzanne told them about spotting the *Oceanus* in the museum's courtyard.

Donald treated Michael to another glare. Michael took the hint and closed his mouth.

"But I don't understand," Harvey said. "Why would you want to do that?"

"Look, Harv," Donald said, regaining his composure. "My colleagues and I are not enthused about being compelled to stay here to serve as entertainment for these Interterrans. We'd like to go home."

"Wait a minute," Harvey said. "I must be missing something. You think setting up a TV camera can get you out of Interterra?"

"It's possible," Donald said. "At this stage it's just an idea: one piece of a puzzle I haven't figured out yet, but whatever it might be, we won't be able to do it alone. We'd need your help since you've been here long enough to know the ropes. The question is: Would you be willing?"

"Sorry," Harvey said with a shake of his head. "You have to understand that the Interterrans would not take kindly to this at all. If I were to help, I'd be one of the most unpopular guys in town. They'd turn me over to the worker clones. The Interterrans don't like to do anything nasty, but the clones don't mind. They just do what they're told."

"But why would you care what the Interterrans thought?" Donald asked. "You'd be with us. In return for your help, we'd give you New York."

"Really?" Harvey asked. His eyes lit up. "Are you serious? You'd get me to New York?"

"It would be the least we could do," Donald said.

• • •

The fluorescent Frisbee sailed across the lawn. Richard had made an excellent toss, and the Frisbee slowed and began to settle just within the grasp of the worker clone that Richard had ordered to play with him. But instead of grabbing the Frisbee, the worker clone allowed it to float past his outstretched hand. It hit him in the forehead with a resounding thud. Richard slapped a hand to his own forehead in total frustration. He swore like the sailor he'd been.

"Nice toss, Richard," Perry called out, suppressing a giggle. Perry was sitting by the dining room pool with Luna, Meeta, Palenque, and Karena. Sufa had ferried the two men back to the visitors' palace after their stopover at the air taxi works before any of the others had returned from their respective excursions. Initially Richard had been cheered by the near simultaneous arrival of his three girlfriends and Luna, but that euphoria had worn off when none of them could master the Frisbee.

"This is freakin' ridiculous," Richard complained as he walked over to retrieve the Frisbee from the worker clone's feet. "Nobody down here can catch a goddamned Frisbee, much less throw one."

"Richard seems so high-strung again today," Luna said.

Perry agreed. "He's been this way all day as near as I can tell."

"He was strange last night, too," Meeta said. "He sent us away early."

"Now *that,* I'd have to guess, is really out of character," Perry said.

"Can't you do anything?" Luna asked.

"I doubt it," Perry said. "Unless I go out there and toss that stupid piece of plastic around some more."

"I wish he'd calm down," Luna said.

Perry cupped his hands around his mouth. "Richard!" he called. "Why don't you just come over here and relax. You're working yourself up for no reason."

Richard flipped Perry the finger.

Perry shrugged at Luna. "Obviously he's not in a very amenable mood."

"Why don't you at least walk out there and talk to him?" Luna suggested.

With a groan Perry heaved himself to his feet.

"We have a surprise for him when we get him back to his cottage," Meeta said. "Try to convince him to go."

"Did you ask him yourselves?" Perry questioned.

"We did, but he said he wanted to play Frisbee."

"Cripes!" Perry said, shaking his head. "Well, I'll give it a whirl."

"Don't mention the surprise," Meeta said. "Otherwise it won't be as much fun. We don't want him guessing what it might be."

"Yeah, sure," Perry grumbled. Irritated to be pulled away from Luna, he strode out to Richard, who was impatiently instructing the worker clone.

"You're wasting your time," Perry said. "They don't play our games here, Richard. They don't have the mindset. Physical prowess is not something they're interested in."

Richard straightened up. "That's pretty damn obvious." He sighed and cursed anew. "It's frustrating because they've got great bodies. The trouble is, they have zero sense of competition, and I need it. Hell, even the girls are too easy. There's no chase or hot pursuit. The whole freakin' place seems dead to me. What I'd give for a good hard game of hoops or in-line hockey."

"I tell you what," Perry said. "I'll race you across the big pool over at the pavilion. What do you say?"

Richard eyed Perry for a moment before giving the Frisbee a good toss off into the distance. Then he told the worker clone to go and get it. Dutifully the worker clone took off at a jog. Richard watched him for a moment before turning back to Perry.

"Thanks but no thanks," Richard said. "Beating you at swimming is not going to make my day. In fact, what would make my day is getting the hell out of here. I'm a nervous wreck."

"I think we are all concerned about the *leaving* issue," Perry said, lowering his voice. "So we're all a little nervous."

"Well, I'm more than a little nervous," Richard said. "What do you think they do down here to people who commit a major crime?"

"I haven't the faintest idea," Perry said. "I don't think they have major crime. Arak said they have no prisons. Why do you ask?"

Richard fidgeted with his toe against the grass and then looked off into the distance. He started to speak and then stopped.

"Are you worried what they'll do if we try to leave and they catch us?"

"Yeah, that's it," Richard said, jumping on the suggestion.

"Well, that's something we'll have to consider," Perry said. "But until then, worrying about it isn't going to accomplish anything."

"I guess you're right," Richard said.

"Why don't you just enjoy yourself with those three gorgeous ladies?" Perry said. He indicated Meeta, Palenque, and Karena with a nod of his head. "Why not channel some of that wild energy of yours by taking them back to your cottage. I can't quite understand it, but they seem crazy about you."

"I'm not sure I ought to take them back to my room," Richard said.

"And why not?" Perry asked. "Isn't it a dream come true? I mean, look at those three girls. They're like lingerie models."

"It's too complicated to explain," Richard said.

"Whatever it is, I can't imagine it being more important than satisfying three eager sirens."

"Yeah, well, maybe you're right," Richard said without much enthusiasm. He snatched the Frisbee away from the worker clone, who had dutifully retrieved it. He returned to the dining room with Perry. Meeta, Palenque, and Karena got to their feet and greeted him with outstretched palms. Richard reacted perfunctorily.

"Are you ready to retire to your cottage?" Meeta asked.

"Let's go," Richard said. "But there's one condition. There's going to be no eating or drinking the stuff from my refrigerator. Agreed?"

"Sure," Meeta said. "We won't even be tempted. We've got something in mind other than food." She and the other girls giggled conspiratorially as they draped themselves over Richard's shoulders.

The group started off across the lawn. "I'm serious," Richard said.

"So are we," Meeta answered.

Perry watched them for a beat before turning back to Luna.

"Is Richard so aggressive because of his young age?" she inquired.

Perry sat down next to her. "No. That's just the way he is. He'll be the same in ten years, even twenty years."

"And that's because of the dysfunctional family that you surmise he had," Luna said.

"I suppose," Perry said vaguely. He didn't want to encourage another sociological discussion. He felt ill equipped in such an arena as evidenced by their last discussion.

"It's hard for me to understand since we don't have families," Luna said. "But what about his friends, acquaintances, and the schooling secondary human's attend? Can't they overcome negative familial influence?"

Perry stared off into the distance and tried to organize his thoughts. "Schooling and friends can help," he said, "but friends can be a negative influence as well. Within some communities social pressure keeps kids from taking much advantage of the education that is afforded them, and often it's the lack of education that breeds bigoted narrow-mindedness."

"So, for someone as young as Richard there is a chance he'll improve."

"I already told you, Richard's not going to change!" Perry said with a tone that bordered on irritation. "Look, I'm no sociologist so maybe we should talk about something else. Besides, he's not that young. He's almost thirty."

"Well, that's young," Luna contended.

"You should talk," Perry snapped.

Luna laughed and battered her pale blue eyes. "Perry, my dear, how old do you think I am?"

"You said you were over twenty," Perry said nervously. "What are you? Twenty-one?"

Luna smiled and shook her head. "No, I'm ninety-four and that's just this body."

Perry's mouth slowly fell open as he made one of his characteristic high-pitched squeaks.

• • •

After issuing several more admonitions against going in his refrigerator, Richard allowed the three women to lie him out on his bed with his arms outstretched. As soon as they had positioned him, they began massaging him with an oil that made his skin tingle and his tense muscles relax.

"Wow!" Richard closed his eyes and purred with delight. "You girls are good! I feel like a piece of wet spaghetti."

"And this is just the beginning," Meeta cooed. The three women looked at each other over Richard's reclining body and tried to suppress their laughter. If Richard had been more aware he would have known they were up to something.

After a quarter hour of intense massaging, Palenque detached herself from the group, unbeknownst to Richard, and silently made her way around the pool to the edge of the lawn. There she waved silently for others to join them.

Within minutes two men appeared and, suppressing their own laughter, they tiptoed over to the bed. Smoothly they took over massaging Richard from Karena, so that it was now Meeta and the two men who were providing the ministrations to Richard's body. Palenque and Karena directed their attention to the bodies of the two men. The goal was an orgy on an ancient Roman scale.

"You know," Richard mumbled, his voice muffled from the coverlet, "if it weren't for you girls this place would drive me certifiably crazy. And to think, I've never even had a massage before. I never knew what I was missing!"

The men and women exchanged fervid glances. They were building each other up to a fever pitch.

"I just can't help being an active person," Richard continued, totally unaware of what was happening around him. "I need competition. It's that simple."

One of the men allowed his bulky, masculine hands to run down Richard's forearms to massage the diver's palms. Sensing a discrepancy in the sensation versus what he expected, Richard's eyes blinked open. To his consternation the hands massaging his were as large as his own.

"What the hell?" Richard snapped. With a suddenness that took everyone by surprise, Richard flipped over and found himself looking up into five flushed faces instead of three, and worst of all, two of them were male.

"What the hell is this?" Richard bellowed. He leaped from the bed, inadvertently knocking Palenque to the floor. The others quickly stood up from their kneeling positions.

"It's all right, Richard," Meeta said urgently, seeing the sudden rage reflected in Richard's face. "It is a surprise orgy for your pleasure."

"Pleasure?" Richard shouted. "Who the hell are these men? How'd they get here?"

"They are our friends," Meeta said. "Cuseh and Uruh. We invited them."

"What the hell do you think I am?" Richard bellowed.

"We've come to make you happy," the man closest to Richard said. He stepped forward and extended his palm.

Richard reacted with a vicious blow to the man's jaw, sending him hurling back against the wall. Everyone gasped at the unexpected violence.

"Get out of here!" Richard shouted. To make his point he swept the night table clear of the golden goblets he'd been collecting. They clattered to the floor with a tremendous racket. As his guests fled out the open end of the room, he looked around the room in a frenzy for something to smash to smithereens.

Suzanne let out a whoop of joy as she and Garona ran hand in hand down a frond-canopied path through a fern forest. Reaching the edge of a crystal clear lake, they came to a sudden stop. Mesmerized by the sublime vista, and out of breath from their run, Suzanne gazed out at the scene.

"This is gorgeous!" she managed.

Garona, who was even more out of breath than Suzanne, had to rest before he could speak. "It's my favorite spot," he gasped. "I come here often. I've always thought it to be very romantic."

"I should say," Suzanne commented. Several other lakes could be seen in the middle distance, nestled among the luxuriant vegetation. In the far distance, jagged mountains rose and merged with the vaulted ceiling. "Which direction are we facing?"

"West," Garona said between breaths. "Those mountains are the bases of what you people call the Mid-Atlantic Ridge."

Suzanne shook her head in amazement. "It is so beautiful. Thank you for sharing it with me."

"It is my pleasure," Garona said. "It is nice to see you more relaxed."

"I suppose I am," Suzanne said. "At least now I know why we were brought to Interterra."

"You have been a great help to us."

"I really didn't do much."

"But you did! You have relieved our anxieties about deep-sea drilling."

"But there's been drilling for many years," Suzanne said. "Why the anxiety now?"

"That was drilling for oil," Garona said. "We don't mind that. In fact, it helps us because oil is a bother. It can seep into our deepest buildings and cause havoc. It was the random drilling that had us concerned."

"Well, I am glad to have been of assistance."

"It calls for a celebration," Garona said. "How about coming to my home for a few hours? We are very close. We'll absorb caldorphin for our mutual pleasure, and then we'll dine."

"In the middle of the day?" Suzanne questioned. As a motivated, hard worker, who as a student had had little time for personal pleasure, the idea of an afternoon tryst seemed unusually decadent. Yet enticingly erotic.

"Why not?" Garona questioned seductively. "Your essence will ring with ecstasy."

"You make it sound so deliciously sensual," Suzanne joked.

"And it will be," Garona said. "Come." He grabbed her hand and led her back the way they'd come.

Garona's home was a mere five-minute air taxi ride away. As they disembarked Suzanne mentioned his home was similar to Arak and Sufa's although the neighborhood seemed slightly less congested.

"The structure is exactly the same," Garona said. "But we have more space since we are farther away from the town center." He again took her hand, and the two ran up the causeway and into the cottage together.

Once inside, the pair acted like impatient adolescents in their haste to shed their satin robes and slip into the pool. Suzanne exuberantly struck out for the opposite end. She swam with strong strokes, excited to have Garona right behind her. They came face-to-face after

Suzanne executed a racing turn against the pool's far end. They embraced in the water. Garona touched his palm with hers and beamed with pleasure. Suzanne laughed with joy.

"This is paradise," Suzanne proclaimed. She dipped her head beneath the water to smooth her short hair back. "It goes beyond my wildest imagination."

"I have so much to show you," Garona told her. "Millions of years of progress. I shall take you to the stars . . . to other galaxies."

"You have already," Suzanne said playfully.

"Come," Garona said. "Let us share some caldorphin."

They swam back across the pool. Garona helped her out of the water. She was again taken by how comfortable she felt in his presence despite her nakedness.

"Please!" Garona said, gesturing toward a satin divan.

"I'm soaked," Suzanne said.

"It doesn't matter," Garona said. He bent down and picked up a small jar and removed the top.

"Are you sure?" Suzanne questioned. The upholstered couch was immaculate.

"Absolutely," Garona said. He held the jar out for Suzanne to put some onto her palm. He did the same, and as they both reclined they pushed their hands together.

Suzanne swooned with pleasure to the very core of her being. Over the next half hour she and Garona made love in a sensitive, giving way that reached a crescendo of passion before melding into sublime, intimate relaxation.

Suzanne had never felt so close to another person. Never in her life had she acted with such abandon, and yet she did not feel guilty. In this utopian netherworld, the usual constraints just didn't apply.

Time seemed to stand still as Suzanne luxuriated in the afterglow of an intimacy the likes of which she'd never experienced. But then, suddenly, it all changed. A soft feminine voice coming from close range shattered her mental and physical repose: "If you two have finished your beautifully tender lovemaking, which I have to say I've enjoyed vicariously, I've arranged a lovely lunch."

Suzanne opened her eyes. To her shock, she found herself looking into the smiling face of an exquisitely attractive woman with stunning features, ice blue eyes, and flaxen hair. The woman's expression was like a proud parent gazing down at her adorable children.

Suzanne sat bolt upright and pulled the coverlet up. Her sudden movement disturbed Garona, who rolled over and opened his eyes. "What did you say, Alita?" he asked.

"Time for you two to eat," she said. She pointed to a table by the pool, which was being set by a worker clone.

"Thank you, my dear," Garona said. He sat up. "I think we're both quite hungry."

"The food will be out momentarily," Alita said. She turned and walked back to the worker clone to help with the preparations by arranging three chaiselike chairs around the table.

Garona stretched, yawned, and then reached for his clothing.

Suzanne made a beeline for her own clothes. Although she hadn't been self-conscious earlier, she was now. She put on the tunic and pulled on the shorts.

"Who is this woman?" she whispered.

"Alita," Garona said. "Come, let us eat."

Still confused, Suzanne let herself be led over to the table. She took the chair Garona indicated and allowed the worker clone to serve her some food. While Garona and Alita attacked theirs with relish, Suzanne toyed with hers. Having been caught flagrante delicto she felt acutely embarrassed and emotionally fragile.

"Suzanne met with the Council of Elders today," Garona said to Alita between mouthfuls of food. "She was every helpful and gave us good news."

"Wonderful," Alita said.

Garona leaned over and gave Suzanne's shoulder an affectionate squeeze. "She's assured us that the secret of Interterra is still secure."

"What a relief," Alita said sincerely. "We sorely needed the reassurance."

Suzanne could only nod.

Garona and Alita launched into a discussion of Interterra's security needs vis-à-vis the surface world. Suzanne didn't listen; instead she watched Alita, who was directing her full attention to Garona. Suzanne was amazed at how calm the woman seemed. Suzanne was still feeling too awkward to eat or speak.

Gradually Suzanne's emotions calmed and she began to collect her thoughts. What began to bother her was the apparently familiarity with which Garona and Alita treated each other. Eventually, Suzanne's curiosity got the better of her. "Excuse me, Alita," she said during a break in her fellow diners' conversation. "Have you and Garona known each other for long?"

Both Garona and Alita laughed heartily.

"I'm sorry," Alita said, struggling to contain herself. "It's a perfectly reasonable question, but so very unexpected here in Interterra. You see, Garona and I have known each other for a long, long time."

"Years then," Suzanne suggested curtly. Despite Alita's apology, she found the laughter rude.

Garona burst out laughing again. He had to cover his face with his hand.

"Certainly years," Alita said. "Years and years."

"Alita and I have spent many lives together," Garona explained as he wiped tears from his eyes.

"Oh, I see," Suzanne said, struggling to keep calm. "Isn't that wonderful."

"It is indeed," Garona said. "Alita is . . . well, I guess you'd call her my permanent woman."

"Or we can say Garona is my permanent man," Alita said.

"Either way," Garona agreed.

"It's nice that it is mutual," Suzanne commented sarcastically. "Now, perhaps you can tell me what 'permanent' means socially in Interterra."

"It's something like your institution of marriage," Alita said. "Only it transcends one body life to another."

Suzanne rolled her lower lip into her mouth and bit down on to it to keep from allowing her rekindled emotions to bubble over into tears. After her unconditional surrender to her feelings toward Garona in response to his persistence and flattery, she felt violated now that she knew he was already in a type of long-term commitment that she could not even fathom. She also felt stupid and appalled that her intuition had let her down so dramatically and that she hadn't even asked about his social status.

"Well, that's all very interesting," Suzanne managed. She put down her flatware and napkin and stood up.

"Thank you for the meal and a most enlightening afternoon. I think it's time I get back to the visitors' palace."

Garona got to his feet. "Are you sure you want to leave so quickly?"

"Quite sure," Suzanne said. Then to Alita she added. "It's been a pleasure."

"For me as well," Alita said. "Garona has spoken so highly of you."

"Has he now?" Suzanne said. "That's very nice."

"I trust we'll be seeing a lot of you," Alita said.

"Perhaps," Suzanne said vaguely. She nodded goodbye to Garona and started for the door. Garona was immediately at her side.

"I'll see you to an air taxi," Garona said. "Unless you'd prefer that I accompany you back to the visitors' palace."

"That's quite all right," Suzanne said as she passed out of the house. "I'm sure you and Alita have things you need to discuss."

"Suzanne, you are acting strangely," Garona said. He took a few running steps to keep up with her while he used his wrist communicator to summon an air taxi.

"You think?" Suzanne asked. "How sensitive of you to notice."

"What is the matter, Suzanne?" Garona reached for her arm, but she pulled away from his grasp and kept walking.

"It's just a minor cultural thing," she said over her shoulder.

"Come now," Garona said. Catching up with her, he grabbed her arm again and this time succeeded in bringing her to a stop. "Be open with me. Don't make me guess."

"It would be interesting to have you guess. But from my perspective it wouldn't be much of a challenge."

"I suppose this has something to do with Alita."

"Very clever," Suzanne said. "Now, if you let go of me, I'm going back to the visitors' palace."

"Suzanne, you are in Interterra. We have different customs. You must adjust."

Suzanne stared into Garona's dark eyes. One part of her wanted him to leave her alone; the other side of her wanted to give him the benefit of the doubt. After all, this was Interterra, not L.A. "My background is so different . . ." she said.

"I know," Garona insisted. "But I ask you not to judge by your earth surface standards. Try not to be selfish. You don't have to feel you own things to enjoy them. We share ourselves with those we love, and love is an endless font."

"I'm happy for you," Suzanne said. "I'm glad you have all this love. Unfortunately, I'm used to sharing love with only one person."

"Can't you look at it from the Interterran perspective?"

"At this point, I doubt it."

"Remember, a lot of your earth surface morality tends to be self-indulgent, selfish, and ultimately destructive."

"From your perspective," Suzanne said. "From ours it's good for raising children."

"Perhaps," Garona said. "But that's not important here."

"Garona, look," Suzanne said. She put a hand on his shoulder. "You're probably a wonderful Interterran man. Since we are in Interterra, I admit this is my problem not yours. I'll try to deal with it."

The air taxi suddenly loomed out of nowhere, and its side opened up.

"Do you need me to command the air taxi?" Garona asked.

"I prefer to do it myself," Suzanne said.

"Then I will come over tonight," Garona said. "Is that all right?"

"As we secondary humans say, I believe I need a little space," Suzanne said. "Let's just let things slide for a day or so." She climbed in and took a seat.

"I will come anyway," Garona insisted.

"It's up to you," Suzanne said. She was too emotional to get into any kind of argument. Instead, she put her palm onto the center table and said, "Visitors' palace." She waved to Garona as the craft's skin sealed over.

CHAPTER SEVENTEEN

"I'm sure you are all a bit overwhelmed," Arak said. "I can see it in your faces."

Arak and Sufa had brought the group back to the circular conference room for a debriefing late in the afternoon. The Interterrans were standing in the central area, looking up at their charges whose moods differed drastically and not from what Arak assumed.

Perry was irritated with Richard. Just when he had gotten cozy with Luna, Meeta and the others had appeared in a panic, saying that Richard had gone berserk. Worried that Richard's violent behavior might ruin it for all of them, Perry had run back and spent an hour trying to calm the diver down—with little success.

Richard sat sullen and silent. He glowered at Arak and Sufa as if his problems were their personal fault.

Suzanne was sitting next to Perry, reviewing her own emotional wounds. She was also feeling responsible for their predicament. As soon as she'd gotten back, she'd explained how she was the reason behind their abduction. She'd apologized, and everyone had assured her that they didn't hold her responsible, but still she felt bad.

Only Donald and Michael seemed unphased. Arak interpreted this as a reflection of their particularly successful visit to Central Information. Engaging Donald with eye contact, Arak addressed him directly: "Before we close for the day, are there any questions or comments about what you have seen during your excursions? Perhaps it might be helpful for each to share with the others your experiences."

"I have a question that I'm sure all of us are interested in," Donald said.

"Then by all means ask it," Arak said.

"Are we prisoners here for life?"

Everyone was taken aback, especially Suzanne and Perry who were jolted from their inward preoccupation. The question surprised them because it was just the previous night that Donald had urged the issue not be broached for fear of having their freedoms curtailed.

Arak was more disappointed than shocked. It took a moment for him to gather his thoughts. "*Prisoners* is not the right word," he said finally. "We'd rather emphasize that you will not be forced to leave Interterra. Instead, we welcome you to our world with full rights to enjoy the panoply of advances to which you have just begun to be exposed."

"But we weren't asked—" Perry began.

"Hold up!" Donald ordered, interrupting Perry. "Let me finish! Arak, just to make this crystal clear, you're saying that we will not be able to leave Interterra, even if we want to."

Arak squirmed uncomfortably.

Sufa interceded. "Generally, we eschew discussing

such an emotional subject so early in your introduction to Interterra. It's our experience that visitors are better equipped to deal with this topic after they have been acclimated to the benefits of life here."

"Please, just answer the question," Donald said bluntly.

"A simple yes or no will do," Michael added.

Arak and Sufa conferred in whispered tones. Donald leaned back and haughtily crossed his arms while the other visitors watched in stunned, nervous silence. Their fate hung in the balance.

Finally Arak nodded. He and Sufa had come to an agreement. He looked up at the group and eventually fixed his gaze on Donald. "All right" he said. "We shall be honest. The answer to your question is, no. You will not be able to leave Interterra."

"Never?" Perry gasped.

"What about communicating with our families?" Suzanne asked. "We need to let them know we are alive."

"To what end?" Arak questioned. "Such a message would be cruel to people destined never to see you again and who are already adapting to your loss."

"But we have children," Perry cried. "How do you expect us not to contact them?"

"It's out of the question," Arak said firmly. "I'm sorry, but the security of Interterra supersedes personal interests."

"But we didn't ask to come here," Perry exclaimed, close to tears. "You brought us here to help you, and Suzanne did. I've got a family!"

"We can't stay here," Richard sputtered.

"No way," Michael seconded.

"We all have emotional ties to our world," Suzanne

added. "As sensitive fellow humans you can't think that we can just forget them."

"We understand it is difficult," Arak said. "We empathize with you, but remember the rewards are infinite. Frankly I'm surprised none of you is tempted at this early juncture. But it will change. It always does. Remember we have had thousands of years of experience with earth surface visitors."

"Temptation is not the point," Donald said haughtily. "In our ethical value system, ends do not justify means. The problem is, we're being forced, and particularly because of our heritage as Americans, we find that a difficult cross to bear."

"Oh please!" Perry shouted angrily at Donald. "Cut the patriot nonsense. This is not about being American. This is about being human."

"Calm down!" Arak ordered. He took a breath then added: "It is true you are in a sense being forced due to the security needs of Interterra, but a better term would be *directed* because in this instance the analogy of parent to child is apropos. Due to your primitive innocence you are confusing short term interests with long term benefit. We who have lived for lifetime after lifetime know better and are more capable of making a more rational decision. Try to keep in mind what we are directing you to: namely the goal of all your religions. You have been brought into a very real heaven."

"Heaven or no heaven," Richard sputtered. "We ain't staying here."

"I'm sorry," Arak said quite sincerely. "You are here and here you will stay."

Suzanne, Perry, Richard, and Michael looked at each other with varying mixtures of agitation, dismay, and resentment. Donald, on the other hand still had his arms folded in an attitude of priggish self-satisfaction.

"Well," Arak said with a sigh, "this has not gone as planned. I regret that you have insisted on talking about this so early in your orientation. But please trust me; you will all change your minds as time goes on."

"What is the general plan for us?" Suzanne asked.

"The orientation period usually lasts one month," Arak said, "depending on each visitor's individual needs. During that time you will have the opportunity to travel to other cities. After the completion of orientation, you will be relocated to a city of your choice."

"Can you tell us where these cities are located?" Donald asked.

"Of course," Arak said. He was glad to move the conversation away from the emotional issue of their custody. Swinging up into his seat with the console, Arak dimmed the lights and turned on the floor screen. A moment later an enormous map of the Atlantic portion of Interterra appeared, including overlying oceans and continental margins. The cities were either orange, blue, or green. Sufa stepped to the side to avoid blocking anyone's view.

"I'm sure you all recognize Saranta," Arak said. He touched his console and its name blinked in orange. Then the entire image switched to the Pacific part of Interterra. "Here you see the older cities beneath the Pacific Ocean. You'll be visiting many of them. All have their own, individual characters, and you will be able to live in any one you choose."

"Does the orange type signify anything?" Donald asked.

"They are cities with the interplanetary exit ports," Arak said. "Like the port you entered through. But most of these have become obsolete and are not used. Here you see Calistral in the southern Indian Ocean. That's probably the only one still in operation, although it's used rarely. Nowadays we rely almost exclusively on the intergalactic ports under the South Pole."

"Could we see the other map again?" Donald asked. He leaned forward.

"Certainly," Arak said. The image of the Atlantic portion of Interterra reappeared.

"So the city of Barsama due east of Boston has an interplanetary port?" Donald said.

"It does," Arak said. "But it has not been used for hundreds of years. The city of Barsama is very pleasant, however, although it is quite small."

"When you say unused," Donald continued, "does that mean it has been sealed like the port here in Saranta?"

"Not yet," Arak said. "But it will be soon. The shafts of those outmoded ports were all supposed to have been sealed ages ago, as I said yesterday. Just today the Council of Elders issued a new decree to speed up the process."

Donald nodded. He eased back in his chair and re-crossed his arms.

"Any other questions?" Arak asked.

No one moved.

"I think we are too stunned for more questions," Perry said.

"You need to spend time together to help each other adapt," Sufa said. "And we encourage you to seek the counsel of Ismael and Mary. I'm sure you can benefit from their wisdom and experience."

No one responded.

"Well then," Arak said. "We'll resume your orientation in the morning after you've had a deserved rest.

Remember, in addition to everything else, you are all still recovering from the decon process. We know that the stress of that ordeal heightens emotional volatility."

A quarter hour later the group found themselves walking back toward the dining hall after Arak and Sufa's departure. Evening was beginning to fall. Trudging through the thick grass no one spoke. Each was absorbed in his own thoughts.

"We have to talk," Donald said, suddenly breaking the silence.

"I agree," Perry said. "Where?"

"I think it best if we do it outside," Donald said. "But let's wait until we get to the dining hall so we can leave our wrist communicators inside. I wouldn't be surprised if they serve as a surveillance device along with their other functions."

"Good idea," Perry said. He had recovered enough to be angry.

"I want to apologize again to everyone," Suzanne said. "I just feel terrible that I'm responsible for everyone being here."

"You're not responsible," Perry said irritably.

"We don't blame you," Michael said. "It's these goddamn Interterrans."

"Let's keep the talk to a minimum until we get rid of our communicators," Donald suggested.

The group walked the rest of the way in silence. Inside the dining hall they stripped off the wrist units, then filed back outside.

"How far do you think we should go?" Perry asked. He glanced over his shoulder. They were already about a hundred feet from the tip of the dining room pool. Light from the interior spilled out into a puddle on the lawn.

"This is fine," Donald said. He stopped and the others huddled around him. "So now we know," he said. "I don't like to say that I told you so."

"Then don't say it," Perry grumbled.

"At least we know where we stand," Donald said.

"That's a lot of comfort," Perry said sarcastically.

"I was surprised you posed the question," Suzanne said. "Why did you change your mind about not being direct?"

"Because we needed to know sooner rather than later," Donald said. "If we've got to break out of here, which we now know is the case, then we've got to do it soon."

"Do you think there is a way?" Suzanne asked.

"I think it is possible," Donald said. "The most promising piece of news is your having seen the *Oceanus* and it being intact. If we could get it to that exit port in Barsama and figure out how to flood the chamber and open the shaft, we'd have enough power and life support to get us to Boston."

"That's not going to work," Suzanne said. "As paranoid as the Interterrans are, the exit ports have to be heavily guarded and monitored. Even if we knew how it worked, we wouldn't be able to get away with it."

"Suzanne's right," Richard said. "They'd have a bunch of those worker clones hanging around for sure."

"I agree," Donald said. "We can't sneak out or even break out. We have to be let out."

"Cripes!" Perry complained. "They're not going to let us out. Arak made that perfectly clear."

"Not willingly," Donald said. "We have to force them."

"And how do you propose to do that?" Suzanne asked. "We're talking about an extremely advanced civilization here, with powers and technology that we can't even anticipate."

"Blackmail," Donald said. "We have to convince them it would be safer to let us out than detain us."

"Keep talking," Perry said dubiously.

"They are terrified of exposure," Donald said. "My idea is to threaten to transmit to surface TV and expose this place."

"Do you think people on the surface would believe it?" Suzanne asked.

"All that matters is that the Interterrans believe it," Donald said.

"Do they have facilities to transmit TV signals?" Perry asked.

"No, but they receive. Michael and I found a man who will help us."

"It's true," Michael said. "He's an old bird from New York City named Harvey Goldfarb. He's been here for years but spends his days hidden in Central Information watching TV reruns. He wants out, too, big time."

"The important thing is that he's familiar with their TV equipment," Donald said. "We've got two camcorders on the *Oceanus* that could be jury-rigged to transmit. Goldfarb says there's plenty of power."

"Hmmm. You know," Perry said, "it sounds promising."

"Not to me," Suzanne said with a shake of her head. "I don't see how it is going to work. I get the threat idea, but how do we use it to pressure the Interterrans into doing something they obviously do not want to do?"

"I don't know exactly," Donald admitted. "We've got to put our heads together and work it out. I envisioned having Goldfarb with his finger on the switch ready to transmit."

"Is that all?" Perry questioned with dismay. "If that's all you've got, then Suzanne's right. It wouldn't work. I mean, they could just send a worker clone in to clobber Goldfarb or, simpler still, they could just shut the power off. If blackmail is going to work, it's got to be more involved to be a credible threat."

"It's a start," Donald said. "Like I said, we've got to brainstorm on this."

Suzanne looked at Perry. "What do you mean, 'more involved'?" she asked.

"Something like having two coexisting threats," Perry said. "That way if they block one, the other does the job. You know what I mean? In order to neutralize the threat they'd have to address both flanks."

"That's not a bad idea," Donald said. "Can anybody think of another threat?"

No one volunteered anything.

"I can't think of anything on the spur of the moment," Perry said.

"Nor can I," Suzanne said.

"We'll start off with the camcorder idea," Donald said. "While we're getting that set up, something else will occur to us."

"What about the weapons in the museum?" Michael asked.

"You found some weapons?" Perry asked.

"A whole room full," Donald said. "But unfortunately they're mostly old, outdated, damaged ordnance scavenged off the ocean floor from ancient Grecian times to World War Two. The most promising piece we saw was a German Luger."

"Do you think it would fire?" Perry asked.

"It might," Donald said. "The clip is full. Mechanically it seemed clean."

"Well, that's something," Perry said. "Especially if it works."

"One thing we know for sure," Donald said, "we're not going to be able to pull this off once we get separated into different cities."

"That's right," Perry said. "So we've got less than a month."

"We might have a lot less time than a month," Richard said.

"Why do you say that?" Suzanne asked.

"Michael and I had a little problem," Richard said. "And I imagine all hell is going to break loose around here one of these days when it's discovered."

"Richard, no, don't say anything!" Michael cried.

"What is it?" Perry questioned. "What have you done now?"

"There was an accident," Richard said.

"What kind of accident?" Donald demanded.

"Maybe it would be better if I showed you," Richard said. "You might have an idea of what to do in the interim."

"Where?" Donald barked.

"My room or Mikey's room," Richard said. "It's the same difference."

"Lead the way, sailor," Donald growled.

No one spoke as the group hiked across the expanse of lawn to the open end of Richard's cottage. They filed in around the edge of the pool. Richard went to the cabinet containing the refrigerator and commanded it to open. Once it had, he bent down and yanked on several of the tightly packed containers, which then tumbled out onto the marble floor. Framed by the remaining haphazardly stacked containers was the frozen, pallid face of Mura. Her hair was matted against her forehead, and the bloody froth had collapsed onto her cheek in a brownish smudge.

Suzanne immediately covered her eyes.

"Now, you got to understand, it was an accident," Richard explained. "Michael didn't really mean to kill her. He was just trying to get her to shut up from screaming by holding her head under water."

"She went crazy," Michael blurted. "She saw the body of the guy Richard killed."

"What guy?" Perry demanded.

"It was a little squirt from the gala," Michael said. "The one who hung around Mura."

"Where's his body?" Donald demanded.

"He's jammed into my refrigerator," Michael said.

"You idiots!" Perry snapped. "How did the boy die?"

"It doesn't matter," Donald muttered. "What's done is done, and Richard is right: the moment these bodies are discovered all hell could break loose."

"Of course it matters," Suzanne snapped as she took her hands away from her face to glare at the divers. "I cannot believe this! You men killed two of these peace-loving, gentle people and for what?"

"He made a pass at me," Richard explained. "I punched him and he fell and hit his head. I was stoned. I didn't mean to kill him."

"You narrow-minded, bigoted bastards," Suzanne sneered.

"Okay, okay," Perry intoned. "Let's ratchet it down a notch. We've still got to work together if there's any hope of getting out of here."

"Perry's right," Donald said. "If we're going to make a break it has to be soon. In fact, we'd better start tonight."

"I'm with you," Richard said as he squatted down to

jam the packages back into the refrigerator to re-cover Mura's lifeless face.

"What can we do tonight?" Perry asked.

"A lot, I'd suspect," Donald said.

"Well, you're the military man," Perry said. "Why don't you take command?"

"How does that set with everyone else?" Donald asked.

Richard stood up and managed to get the refrigerator door closed with the help of his hip. "Fine by me," he said. "The sooner we're out of here the better."

"Me, too," Michael said.

"What about you, Suzanne?" Donald asked.

"I can't believe this has happened," Suzanne muttered. She was staring into the middle distance. "They spent a month decontaminating us but we managed to bring disease in anyway."

"What the hell are you mumbling about?" Perry asked.

Suzanne sighed sadly. "It's like we're Satan's minions invading heaven."

"Suzanne, are you all right?" Perry asked. He grasped her shoulders and looked into her eyes. They were brimming with tears.

"I'm just sick at heart," she said.

"I'll take three out of four to be a reasonable mandate," Donald said, ignoring Suzanne. "Here's what I propose. We'll get our wrist communicators, call an air taxi, and get ourselves over to the Earth Surface Museum. Richard and I will visit the submersible to check it out. He'll help me salvage one of the TV cameras. Perry, you and Michael will go into the museum and get weapons. Michael can show you where they are. Take anything you think might be appropriate but be sure you get the Luger."

"Sounds good," Perry said. "What about you, Suzanne? Do you want to come along?"

Suzanne didn't answer. Instead, she lifted her hands back to her face and massaged her watery eyes. She could not get over the fact that they were responsible for the death of two Interterrans. She wondered what kind of grief such a crime was likely to evoke in Saranta. Two essences who'd survived for eons had been lost forever.

"Okay," Perry said soothingly. "You stay here. We shouldn't be long."

Suzanne nodded but didn't even watch as the group filed out of the room through the open end of the cottage. Instead, she looked at the cabinetry that hid the refrigerator and allowed herself to cry. The violent and ugly confrontation she feared was already coming to pass.

CHAPTER EIGHTEEN

Donald treated the operation like a military exercise, as did Richard and Michael, who'd had even more covert operational experience than he. Getting into the spirit of the affair, the two divers blackened their faces and garments with soil. Perry wasn't as gung ho, but he was relieved to be taking his fate in his own hands.

"Is that necessary?" Perry asked when he saw what Richard and Michael had done with the mud.

"It's what we did for any night operation in the Navy," Richard replied.

The ride in the air taxi was in some respects even more exhilarating at night than it had been during the day. There was significantly less traffic but what traffic there was lurched unexpectedly out of the shadows.

"This is like a goddamned amusement park ride," Richard said after a particularly close pass.

"I wish I could find out how these things work," Perry commented. "There were only worker clones at the factory Richard and I visited this morning."

"That was one colossal waste of time," Richard said.

"What do you think about Suzanne?" Donald asked Perry.

"What do you mean?" Perry responded.

"Do you think we have to worry about her?" Donald asked. "She could mess up this whole operation."

"You mean alert the Interterrans?" Perry asked.

"Something like that," Donald said. "She seemed pretty upset back there about the two casualties."

"She was upset, but it wasn't just about the deaths," Perry said. "She confided to me that Garona disappointed her somehow. And she feels responsible about us being here, as she said. Anyway, I don't think we have to worry about her. She'll be okay."

"I hope so," Donald said.

The craft decelerated, hovered for a moment, then rapidly descended.

"Stand by, troops," Donald said.

As Donald had directed, the air taxi was settling down in the museum's courtyard. Over the edge of the craft the dim outline of the *Oceanus* could be seen, silhouetted against the black basalt of the museum.

"There's the target," Donald said. "Once the side of the taxi opens I want everyone flat against the museum wall. Understood?"

"That's affirmative," Richard said.

The moment the exit appeared the group piled out, ran to the wall, and flattened themselves against it. All eyes swept the immediate area. It was dark, particularly in the shadows, and perfectly still without any signs of life. Behind them the sharply geometric form of the museum soared up into the blackness. The only light on the scene came from the thousands of faux, bioluminescent stars above and a low-level, glow emanating from the museum's windows. The dark hulk of the submersible was about fifty feet away, sitting on chocks on the flatbed of an antigravity freighter.

The air taxi's side seamlessly sealed over and the craft silently rose before disappearing in the darkness.

"I don't see a soul," Richard whispered.

"I guess the museum's not much of a night spot," Michael whispered back.

"Keep the conversation to a minimum," Donald ordered.

"The place is deserted," Perry said. He let himself relax. "That's going to make this a whole lot easier."

"Let's hope it stays that way," Donald said. He pointed to a window to their left. "Perry, you and Michael climb through and come back out through the same one. We'll either be working on the *Oceanus* or we'll be waiting here in the shadows."

"Do you think there's an alarm system in the museum?" Perry questioned.

"Nah!" Richard said. "There's no locks or alarms or any of that kind of stuff. Apparently nobody ever steals anything down here."

"All right," Perry said. "We're off."

"Good hunting," Donald said. He waved as Perry and Michael ran hunched over to just below the window. Grunting and groaning, Perry boosted Michael up so he could get a grip on the sill. Once he was inside, he leaned back out and pulled Perry up. A moment later the two disappeared inside the building.

Donald redirected his attention to the submersible.

"Well, are we going over there or not?" Richard questioned.

"Let's do it!" Donald said.

They kept low to the ground as they sprinted over to

the minisubmarine. Donald lovingly patted its HY-140 steel hull. In the darkness its scarlet color was a dull gray although the white lettering on the sail stood out sharply. Donald made a slow inspection of the craft with Richard close on his heels. He was impressed with the Interterran repairs; the outside lights and the manipulator arm that had been destroyed in the plunge down the vent shaft looked completely normal.

"It looks perfect," Donald said. "All we have to do is get it into the ocean and we're home free."

"None too soon for me," Richard said.

Donald went to an outside toolbox, opened it, and took out several wrenches. He handed them to Richard.

"Start with the starboard side camcorder," he said. "Just detach it from its housing. I'm going below to check out the battery level. If we don't have power, we're not going anywhere."

"Roger," Richard said.

Donald climbed the familiar rungs, rapidly ascending to the ship's hatch. He was mildly surprised to find it undogged and slightly ajar. Grabbing it with two hands he raised it all the way. After one last visual sweep around the area, he lowered himself into the opening and clambered down into absolute darkness.

Once Donald had reached the deck, he moved forward by feel. He was so familiar with the craft, he could literally move around inside with his eyes closed, or so he thought until he tripped over the two books Suzanne had brought along to impress Perry. Donald cursed less for the tripping than for striking his hand against the back of one of the passenger seats while trying to maintain his balance. At least he didn't fall which could have been lethal in the tight quarters.

After rubbing his hand to dispel the pain, he inched

forward. As he neared the dive station a bit of light filtered in through the four view ports, making his progress easier. Careful not to hit his head on any of the protruding instrumentation, Donald lowered himself into the pilot seat. Outside he could hear Richard clanking against the hull with the wrench.

The first thing Donald did was switch on the instrument lights. Then, with trepidation, he allowed his eyes to move over to the battery level indicator. He sighed with relief. There was plenty of power. Then, as he was about to check gas pressures, he froze. A noise coming from behind him told him that he was not alone. Someone besides himself was inside the submersible.

At first Donald held his breath, straining to listen. Cold sweat appeared along his hairline. Seconds passed, though it seemed like hours, but the noise did not repeat itself. Just when Donald began to wonder if his imagination had misinterpreted the sounds of Richard removing the camcorder, a voice came out of the darkness. "Is that you, Mr. Fuller?"

Donald swung around. His eyes vainly tried to penetrate the darkness. "Yes," he said with a voice that cracked. "Who's here?"

"Harv Goldfarb. Remember me from Central Information?"

Donald relaxed and took a breath. "Of course," he said irritably. "What the devil are you doing in here?"

Harvey inched forward. The lights from the instruments illuminated his deeply creased face. "You got me thinking today," Harvey said. "You're the first hope I've ever had for getting back. I was afraid you might forget me, so I thought I'd sleep in here."

"Mr. Goldfarb, we can't forget you," Donald said.

"We need you. Did you check out the TV cameras on the outside?"

"I did," Harvey said. "I don't think they'll be a problem. What is it you are planning on transmitting?"

"We're not sure at this stage," Donald said. "Maybe you or us or even all of us."

"Me?" Harvey questioned.

"Actually we only want the capability to transmit," Donald said. "It's the threat that's important."

"I'm getting the picture," Harvey said. "They let you out because they're afraid that I'll expose Interterra over the airwaves."

"Something like that," Donald said.

"It won't work," Harvey said flatly.

"Why not?"

"Two reasons," Harvey said. "First, they'd cut my power before they'd let you out. And second, I won't do it."

"But you said you'd help."

"Yeah, and you said you'd take me to New York."

"That's true," Donald admitted. "Actually we haven't worked out any of the details."

"Details, ha!" Harvey scoffed. "But listen. I live here. I can tell you how to get out. Many a night I've dreamed about escaping the monotony of all these interminably pleasant days."

"We're open to suggestions," Donald said.

"I gotta be sure you'll take me along," Harvey said.

"We'll be happy to include you," Donald said. "What's your idea?"

"Will this submarine work?" Harvey asked.

"That's what I'm checking," Donald said. "We've got plenty of power, so if we can get it out into the water, it will work."

"Okay, now listen," Harvey said. "Has your orientation gotten around to telling you that the Interterrans live forever? Not in the same body but in multiple bodies?"

"Yes," Donald said. "We've already visited the death center and witnessed an extraction."

"I'm impressed," Harvey said. "They are moving you right along. So you understand that the process works only if they are extracted before death. In other words, it all has to be planned. You get what I'm saying?"

"I'm not sure," Donald admitted.

"They have to be alive when the memory is extracted," Harvey said. "Or more properly, their brains have to be functioning normally. If they die by violent means, the story's over. That's why they are so terrified of violence, and that's why there hasn't been any violence in Interterra for millions upon millions of years. They are incapable of it except by proxy."

"So we threaten violence," Donald said. "We already thought of that."

"I'm talking about something more specific than just violence," Harvey said. "You threaten death specifically. Death without any of their extraction nonsense unless they do what you want."

"Aha!" Donald exclaimed. "Now I get you. You're talking about taking hostages."

"Correct!" Harvey said. "Two, four, as many as you can get, and not clones, because they don't count. And a word of caution: the clones don't mind violence. They do whatever they are told."

"Slick!" Donald commented. "It's a multiple threat built into one."

"Correct," Harvey said proudly. "And you don't have to monkey around with this TV camera nonsense."

"I like it," Donald said. "How about you going out and telling Richard to hold up on removing the camcorder. I just want to check the gas pressures, and I'll be right out."

"You promise you'll be taking me," Harvey said.

"You're going," Donald said. "Stop worrying."

"All right, hold up!" Perry ordered. "Either you know where you are going or you don't. We've been wandering around in here like a couple of dopes for twenty minutes. Where are the goddamn weapons?"

Michael shook his head. "I'm sorry, but I get lost in museums even in the daytime."

"Try to remember something about the gallery," Perry said.

"I remember it was long and narrow," Michael said.

"What was it near? Can you remember anything like that?"

"Wait a second," Michael said. "Now I remember. It was behind a door that said we were supposed to get permission from the Council of Elders to enter."

"I haven't seen many doors," Perry said as his eyes scanned the immediate area. "And there are none here so obviously we're not in the right place."

"I also remember we'd stopped in a gallery filled with Persian carpets," Michael said. "It's coming back to me now. The carpets were beyond the room with all the Renaissance stuff."

"That's a start," Perry said. "I know where that gallery is. Come on! Follow me for a change!"

A few minutes later the two men were standing outside the door with the restricted entry admonition. It was located near the window they'd climbed in.

"Is this it?" Perry asked. "If it is, we've come full circle."

"I think so." He reached around Perry, pushed the door open, and glanced inside. "Pay dirt!" he exclaimed.

"It's about time," Perry grumbled as he entered. "The others are going to start thinking we got lost, so we'd better make this snappy."

"What should we take?" Michael asked.

The two men stopped just inside the door while Perry looked up and down the dimly lit room. He was impressed with the room's length and the subsequent square footage the shelving afforded. "This is more than I expected!" he commented. "We've got quite a selection in here."

"The older stuff is to the right, newer to the left," Michael said.

"I guess it doesn't matter what we take as long as it functions," Perry said, "and as long as I find the Luger."

"I know one thing I want," Michael said. He reached over and picked up the crossbow and its quiver. As he did so he nicked his finger. "Jeez, these arrow points are razor sharp."

"Those are quarrels, or bolts, not arrows," Perry said.

"Whatever," Michael said. "They're damn sharp."

"Do you remember which way the Luger was?"

"To the left, Bozo," Michael said.

"Don't call me Bozo," Perry warned.

"Well, I just got finished telling you the modern stuff was to the left."

Perry set out without responding to Michael's last comment. It irritated him that he had to put up with the divers. He had never been forced to spend time with two more juvenile idiots in his life.

Michael turned and went the other way. As long as

everything was water-damaged and barnacle-encrusted, he thought the ancient armaments would be better since, in their simplicity, there were fewer working parts for the salt water to foul up. Soon he was in an area with a superb collection of ancient Greek weapons. He gathered an armful of short swords, daggers, and shields along with several helmets, greaves, and a brace of breastplates. What impressed him was the worked gold and the encrusted jewels he could see despite the darkness. Thus encumbered he clanked his way back to the door they'd entered.

"Any luck yet?" Michael called out to Perry.

"Not yet," Perry called back. "Just a bunch of rusted rifles."

"I'm going to take this stuff I got back to the window."

"All right, I'll be there as soon as I find the pistol."

Michael added the crossbow to his burden and then struggled with the door. No sooner had he taken a step into the hall than he collided with Richard.

Michael whimpered and dropped everything he was carrying. The heavy gold and bronze implements made a tremendous clatter against the marble floor.

"Shut up, you ass!" Richard hissed. The racket exploding in the silence of the dark, deserted museum had scared him as much as the unexpected encounter had scared Michael.

"What do you mean sneaking in here and scaring me shitless?" Michael spat.

"What the hell's been taking you so long?" Richard demanded.

"We couldn't find the room, okay?"

Perry appeared in the doorway. "Good God, what on

earth are you guys doing? Trying to wake up the entire city?"

"It wasn't my fault," Michael said as he bent down to retrieve his booty.

"Did you guys find the Luger?" Richard asked.

"Not yet," Perry said. "Where's Donald?"

"He's already on his way back to the visitors' palace," Richard said. "There's been a change in plans. The old fart Harvey Goldfarb was hiding in the submersible, and he's come up with a new and better escape plan for us."

"Really?" Perry questioned. "What is it?"

"We're going to take hostages," Richard said. "He says the Interterrans are so afraid of violent death that they'd do anything, including letting us out into the ocean with the submersible, if we got a couple of their people and threaten to do them in."

"I like it," Perry said. "But why did Donald go back before us?"

"He's worried about Suzanne, especially now that things look so promising. But he told me to tell you to get a move on it; as soon as you're ready I'll call an air taxi to get us back."

"All right," Perry said. "Both of you come on in here. With all of us looking for the damn pistol we should be able to find it a lot faster."

The air taxi came to a halt and opened. It was hovering directly in front of the visitors' palace dining room. Richard and Michael disembarked with some difficulty, both weighed down with an array of ancient armament. All Perry was carrying was the Luger, which he'd finally found.

The three made their way up the ramp to the door. Both divers had donned the breastplates, helmets, and greaves rather than carry them in their arms. It was enough to be holding the shields, swords, daggers, and crossbow. Perry had tried to talk them out of taking the armor, but they were determined, and he gave up trying to reason with them. Michael and Richard were convinced in their words that the stuff was going to be worth a fortune topside.

To their surprise the dining room was empty.

"That's odd," Richard said. "He told me to meet him here."

"You don't suppose he's planning on bugging out of here without us, do you?" Michael questioned.

"I don't know," Richard responded. "The idea never occurred to me."

"He's not going without us," Perry assured the two divers. "We just saw the *Oceanus* still parked where it's always been, and he's not going anyplace without that."

"How about Suzanne's room?" Michael suggested.

"I'd say that's a good possibility," Perry said.

The long walk across the lawn was significantly noisy thanks to the continual clatter of the ancient armor.

"You guys sound ridiculous," Perry commented.

"We didn't ask for your opinion," Richard said.

As they rounded the open end of Suzanne's cottage they saw Donald, Suzanne, and Harvey sitting in contour chairs near the pool's edge. It was obvious the atmosphere was tense.

"What's wrong?" Perry questioned.

"We've got a problem," Donald said. "Suzanne's not sure we're doing the right thing."

"Why not, Suzanne?" Perry asked.

"Because murder is wrong," Suzanne said. "If we take hostages to the surface world without adaptation, they will die, plain and simple. We brought violence and death here and now we want to escape by it. I say it's ethically despicable."

"Yeah, but I didn't ask to come here," Perry said hotly. "I don't like to sound like a broken record, but we're being held against our will. I think that justifies violence."

"But that's confusing ends with means," Suzanne said. "That's exactly what we're supposed to be against."

"All I know is that I have a family that I miss," Perry said. "I'm going to see them again come hell or high water!"

"I empathize with you," Suzanne said. "Truly! And I feel responsible about the whole situation. And it is true we were abducted. But I don't want to see any more deaths, nor do I want to see Interterra unwittingly destroyed. We're ethically obligated to negotiate. These people are so peaceful."

"Peaceful?" Richard questioned. "I'd say boring!"

"I can vouch for that," Harvey said.

"Perry, this is Harvey Goldfarb," Donald said.

Perry and Harvey shook hands.

"I don't know what we're supposed to negotiate," Donald said. "Arak made it clear we're here for good, no buts, ifs, or maybes. A statement like that precludes negotiation."

"I think we should let a little more time pass," Suzanne said. "What's wrong with that? Maybe we will change our minds, or maybe we'll be able to convince them to alter theirs. We've got to remember that we've all brought down here our personalities and psychological baggage geared to the world above, plus we're so accustomed to seeing ourselves as the 'good guys' that it's difficult to realize when we are the monsters."

"I don't feel like a monster," Perry said. "I don't belong here."

"Me neither," Michael said.

"Let me make another point," Suzanne said. "For the sake of argument, let's say we manage to get out of here. What happens then? Do we reveal Interterra's existence?"

"It will be hard not to," Donald said. "Where would we say we've been for the last month or however long it's been?"

"And what about me?" Harvey said. "I've been here for almost ninety years."

"That's even harder to explain," Donald agreed.

"We'd also have to have some explanation where we got all the gold and armor," Richard said. "'Cause this stuff's going with me."

"And what about the economic possibilities of our serving as intermediaries?" Perry said. "We could help both sides and end up millionaires many times over. Just the wrist communicators alone will cause a technological sensation."

"I rest my case," Suzanne said. "One way or the other we'd be exposing Interterra. Stop and think about our civilization and its exploitive greed. We don't like to think of ourselves in that light, but it's true. We are selfish, both as individuals and as nations. There'd be a confrontation without doubt, and as advanced as the Interterran civilization is, with power and weapons we cannot even imagine, it will be a disaster, maybe even the end of the world as far as secondary humans are concerned."

For several minutes no one spoke.

"I don't care about all that crap," Richard said suddenly, breaking the silence. "I want out of here."

"No question," Michael chimed in.

"Me, too," Perry said.

"Ditto," Donald said. "Once we're out, we can negotiate with these Interterrans. At least at that point it will be a real negotiation without them dictating to us."

"What about you, Harvey?" Perry asked.

"I've been dreaming about getting out for years," Harvey said.

"It's decided, then," Donald said. "We're going!"

"Not me," Suzanne said. "I don't want any more deaths on my conscience. Maybe it's because I don't have any immediate family, but I'm willing to give Interterra a chance. I know I've got a lot of adjusting to do, but I like paradise. It's worth a bit of self-examination."

"I'm sorry, Suzanne," Donald said, staring her in the eye. "If we go, you go. Your high moral standards are not going to screw up our plan."

"What are you going to do, force me to go?" Suzanne demanded irritably.

"Absolutely," Donald said. "Let me remind you, field commanders have been known to shoot their own men if the men's behavior threatens to compromise an operation."

Suzanne didn't respond. Instead she slowly looked around at the others in the room. Her expression was blank. No one made a motion in her defense.

"Let's get back to business," Donald said finally. "Did you get the Luger?"

"We did," Perry reported. "It was hard to find, but we managed."

"Let me see it," Donald said.

As Perry took the pistol out of his tunic pocket, Suzanne bolted from the room. Richard was the first to respond. Dropping what he had in his hands, and disregarding the armor he was wearing, he raced out into the night after her. Thanks to his superb physical shape he was able to close the gap quickly and managed to get hold of Suzanne's wrist. He pulled her to a stop. Both were panting.

"You're playing into Donald's hands," Richard managed to say between breaths.

"As if I care," Suzanne replied. "Let me go!"

"He'll shoot you," Richard said. "He loves playing this military crap. I'm warning you."

Suzanne struggled for a moment in an attempt to free herself, but it was soon clear that Richard was not about to let her go. The others arrived and gathered round. Donald was holding the Luger.

"You're forcing me to act," Donald said menacingly. "I hope you realize that."

"Who is forcing whom?" Suzanne asked scornfully.

"Bring her back inside!" Donald said. "We have to resolve this once and for all." He started back toward the cottage. The others followed with Richard maintaining an iron grip on Suzanne's wrist. She tried briefly to struggle but quickly became resigned to be dragged back toward her room.

"Bring her in and sit her down," Donald called over his shoulder as the group rounded the pool.

Coming into the light Richard noticed how blue Suzanne's hand had become. Concerned about her circulation, he loosened his hold. The instant he did, she yanked herself free and straight-armed him with a resounding thump in the center of his chest. Caught off guard, Richard toppled into the deep end of the pool. Suzanne bolted back out into the night.

With the heavy armor dragging him under the surface, Richard floundered despite his being a powerful and accomplished swimmer. Donald tossed the pistol onto one of the contour chairs and dove into the water. Perry and Michael did what they could from the pool's edge until they realized that Suzanne had escaped yet again.

"Get her!" Perry cried. "I'll help here."

Michael took off and the effort expended gave him unqualified respect for the famed hoplites of old, and he wondered how those ancient warriors had managed considering the weight of their armor. He found the breastplate particularly difficult to run in although the heavy helmet and greaves did not help either. Once clear of the cone of light emanating from the interior, he clanked to a halt. Without being dark adapted he was blinded by the darkness. Suzanne was nowhere to be seen although she'd had only a minute or so head start.

As the minutes ticked by and his eyes adjusted, details of the scene emerged from the gloom but still no Suzanne. Then, sudden movement and a startling patch of bright light off to his right got his attention. When he looked his heart leaped. It was an air taxi that had arrived and opened some fifty yards away in the vicinity of the dining hall.

Michael took off running again with his strong legs pumping. As he rapidly closed on the craft, he knew it was going to be close. Ahead he could see Suzanne clamber aboard and throw herself onto the banquette with her right hand palm down on the central table.

"No!" Michael yelled as he launched himself at the taxi's port. But he was too late. What had been an opening only moments earlier was now the seamless cowling of the air taxi. Michael collided against it and ricocheted off with the clang of metal against metal. The collision knocked him to the ground and the helmet from his head. In the next instant the air taxi ascended with a whoosh, leaving Michael momentarily weightless in its wake. Like a helium balloon he floated free from the ground for almost a foot before falling back like a dead weight.

The second collision knocked the wind out of him. He writhed on the ground. When he managed to catch his breath, he scrambled to his feet and made his way back to the cottage. By then, the others had gotten the sodden Richard into one of the contour chairs, where he was coughing deeply.

Donald looked up as Michael charged in. "Where the hell is she?"

"She got away in an air taxi!" Michael gasped.

"You let her get away?" Donald cried. He stood up from where he was squatting next to Richard. He was incensed.

"I couldn't stop her," Michael said. "She must have called the damn taxi the second she left here."

"Christ!" Donald said. He put a hand to his forehead and shook his head. "Such incompetence! I can't believe it!"

"Hey, I did what I could," Michael complained.

"Let's not argue," Perry chimed in.

"Shit!" Donald shouted as he stormed around in a circle.

"I should have decked her," Richard choked.

Donald stopped his angry pacing. "We've hardly started this operation, and we've already got a crisis. There's no telling what she'll do. We've got to move and move fast! Michael, you get your ass back to the *Oceanus* and don't let anyone near it!"

"Roger!" Michael said. He grabbed his crossbow and quiver and darted back out into the night.

"We need hostages and we need them fast," Donald said.

"What about Arak and Sufa?" Perry said.

"They'd be perfect," Donald said. "Let's call them over here and hope Suzanne hasn't talked to them first. We'll have them come to the dining hall."

"What about Ismael and Mary Black?" Perry suggested.

"The more the better," Harvey said.

"Fine," Donald said. "We'll call them, too. But that's all the room we have in the *Oceanus*."

Suzanne's pulse was racing. She'd never felt such anxiety. She knew she was lucky to have gotten away from the group and couldn't help wondering what would have happened had she not been able to. She shuddered. They seemed to have become strangers, even enemies in their single-mindedness to escape and their concomitant willingness to murder.

Despite what she'd said on the spur of the moment back in her cottage, she wasn't sure how she felt about anything other than her abhorrence at the idea of being a party to more death. Yet despite her confusion, in order to flee by air taxi she'd had to come up with a destination quickly to get the craft to seal. The first place that had come to her mind was the black pyramid and the Council of Elders.

By the time the air taxi deposited Suzanne at her destination, she was more composed. The transit time had given her an opportunity to think more rationally. She reasoned that the Council of Elders more than anyone should know how to handle the crisis quickly and without injury to anyone.

As she mounted the causeway leading to the pyramid

she noticed the entire area was deserted. As a major Interterran governmental center, she'd assumed there would be people available twenty-four hours a day. But this hardly seemed to be the case even after she'd entered the gigantic structure.

Suzanne walked down the gleaming white marble corridor. She saw no one. Approaching the huge, paneled bronze doors, she began to wonder what she should do. Knocking seemed ridiculous given the scale of the surroundings. But she need not have been concerned. The doors opened automatically just as they had that morning.

Walking into the circular colonnaded room beyond, Suzanne advanced to the center and stopped in the same place she'd stood that morning. She looked around at the empty chamber, wondering what to do next.

The silence was complete.

"Hello!" Suzanne called. When there was no answer she called again, louder. Then she called out again, this time at the top of her lungs. Thanks to the dome, she heard her voice echo clearly.

"Can I be of assistance?" a young girl's voice asked calmly.

Suzanne turned. Behind her, framed in the huge portal, was Ala. Her fine blond hair was in disarray, as if she'd just been pulled from her bed.

"I'm sorry to bother you," Suzanne said. "I've come because of an emergency. You must stop my fellow secondary humans. They are about to attempt an escape, and if they do, the secret of Interterra will be lost."

"Escape is difficult from Interterra," Ala said. She rubbed her eyes with the back of her hand. It was a gesture so childlike that Suzanne had to remind herself she was dealing with an individual of extraordinary intelligence and experience.

"They plan to use the submersible we arrived in," Suzanne said. "It is at the Earth Surface Museum."

"I see," Ala said. "It would still be difficult, but perhaps it would be best if I send some worker clones to incapacitate the vessel. I will also call the Council for an emergency session. I trust you will be willing to stay and confer with us."

"Of course," Suzanne said. "I want very much to help." She thought about bringing up the tragic deaths that had already occurred but decided there would be time for that later.

"This is an unexpected and disturbing development," Ala said. "Why have your friends decided to try to escape?"

"They say because of their families and because they have not been given a choice. But they are a very varied group, and there are other issues as well."

"It sounds as if they don't yet realize how very lucky they are."

"I think that's fair to say," Suzanne agreed.

An air taxi settled down and opened in the dark and deeply shadowed museum courtyard. Two heavily muscled worker clones disembarked. Both carried sledgehammers, but only one set out for the Benthic Marine submersible. The other kept the air taxi from leaving by maintaining a grip on the edge of the taxi's opening port.

The first worker clone wasted no time. Reaching the submersible he went directly to the housing for the main battery pack. With practiced hands he opened the fiberglass access panel to expose the main power connector.

Then, stepping back, he raised the sledge over his head in preparation of rendering the unit inoperable.

But the heavy hammer did not come down in its normal arc. Instead it slipped from the clone's hands and fell to the ground with a thud the moment a crossbow bolt pierced the clone's throat. With a gasping sound he staggered back, clawing at the imbedded missile. A mixture of blood and a clear fluid like mineral oil gushed forth, drenching his black coveralls. After a few awkward steps, the clone toppled over onto his back. Several twitches later, he was still.

Michael cranked the crossbow drawstring back and positioned another bolt. Thus armed he stood up from his hiding place alongside the museum wall and cautiously approached the downed clone. Michael had neither seem nor heard the air taxi: it had landed just out of sight. He felt lucky he'd looked back at the submersible the moment he did, for he had been dozing on and off despite his efforts to stay alert.

Keeping the crossbow trained on the clone, Michael reached out with his right foot and gave the body a kick. The clone didn't respond although there was another small surge of blood and fluid from the through-and-through neck wound.

Taking one hand away from the crossbow to give himself better balance, Michael gave the body one last, good kick to make sure there was no question about its status. To his shock, the crossbow was ripped out of his hand.

Startled, Michael whirled around to find himself facing a second clone, who'd tossed the crossbow aside and was raising a sledgehammer over his head. Michael instinctively put his hands up although he knew it would be no defense against the coming blow. Back peddling he tripped over the fallen clone and fell across the downed worker, losing his helmet in the process.

Michael desperately rolled to the side as the hammer came down with jarring force, crunching the already incapacitated clone. As the second clone regained his balance and retracted his weapon for another blow, Michael pushed himself up on one knee and drew his Greek short sword. As the clone again lifted the sledge over his head, exposing his abdomen, Michael lunged forward. With Michael's full weight behind the thrust the sword buried itself to its hilt. A mixture of blood and clear oil gushed onto Michael's chest.

The startled clone dropped the sledge and grabbed Michael's head with his two hands. Michael felt himself being lifted off the ground. But it didn't last. The inordinate strength of the clone ebbed, and he toppled over, dragging Michael with him.

It took almost five minutes for the worker clone's grip around Michael's head to relax enough for Michael to extract himself. As he got to his feet he shuddered through a wave of nausea at the smell of the fluid leaking out of the two downed clones. It was like a combination of a slaughter house and an auto repair shop.

Michael retrieved the crossbow. He had new respect for the danger the clones represented. He'd been surprised the second clone had attacked him, and he reasoned that they must have been given some blanket order. The episode also underlined the fact that the clones had no trouble with violence, just as Harv had warned.

CHAPTER NINETEEN

"Maybe we should have pulled this off after dinner," Richard said. "I'm starved."

"This is no time for humor," Perry said.

"Who's making a joke?" Richard said.

"This must be them," Harvey called from the door, where Donald had ordered him to stay as a lookout. "An air taxi has just dropped down outside."

The group was in the dining room waiting for Arak, Sufa, and the Blacks.

"All right, troops," Donald said. "This is it. Let's be prepared."

Richard picked up one of the Greek swords. After his dunk in the pool he'd dispensed with the armor. Donald removed the clip from the Luger for the twentieth time, checked it, and replaced it. He made sure a cartridge was in the firing chamber.

Arak, Sufa, the Blacks, and four large worker clones swept into the room.

"Okay," Arak said, slightly out of breath. "Everything is going to be fine, so please just relax."

According to plan, Harvey pushed the door closed with a resounding thud. Arak ignored the noise. Harvey walked around the periphery of the room. Along with Perry and Richard he stood behind Donald.

"First," Arak said, "you must understand that you cannot escape. We cannot permit it."

"Word travels fast," Donald said. "So Suzanne has already gotten to you."

"We were informed by the Council of Elders," Arak said. "We heard from them just after you requested our presence. Now that we are here, we'd like to request that you return to your individual cottages. I repeat: you cannot escape."

"We shall see," Donald said. "For the time being, *we* are going to be giving the orders."

"That is out of the question," Arak remarked. Then, turning to the clones, he said, "Restrain them without hurting them, please!"

Obediently the clones surged forward.

Donald brandished the pistol and took several steps back. His coconspirators did the same.

"Don't come any closer!" Donald commanded.

"I don't think they know what a gun is," Perry said nervously.

"They are going to learn quickly," Donald said. While continuing to back up he raised the gun and aimed at the face of the clone coming directly at him.

"Arak!" Ismael cried. "He's got a gun. Arak—"

"Stop, please!" Donald ordered the clones.

Having been commanded by an Interterran, the clones ignored Donald and continued closing in on the retreating secondary humans. Donald pulled the Luger's trigger and it fired with a roar. The slug hit the lead clone in the forehead. He wobbled and then collapsed backward to the floor. A clear viscous fluid flowed out of the wound onto the marble. Curiously his legs continued to move as if he were still advancing.

Arak and Sufa gasped.

Undaunted, the other clones continued to approach. Donald swung the gun around to the one closing on Perry and fired again. The bullet struck the second clone in the temple. He collapsed as well, though his legs, too, continued moving.

"Halt, please," Arak shouted with a quavering voice to the two remaining clones. The clones obeyed instantly. Arak's face had gone pale and he was shaking. Meanwhile, the scissoring motion of the legs of the two on the ground slowed, then stopped.

Donald was now holding the pistol with two hands. He swung it around and pointed it at Arak. "That's better," he told the terrified Interterran. "Just so we understand one another, you are next."

"Please," Sufa cried. "No more violence. Please!"

"We're happy to oblige," Donald said without lowering the gun. "Just do as we say, and everything will be cool. Arak, I want you to make a few contacts with your wrist unit, then we'll be leaving here."

Suzanne was impressed with the equanimity the elders displayed despite the grave crisis. She, on the other hand, was growing progressively more anxious; the dispatches coming back to the council suggested that her former colleagues were succeeding.

While the council had convened, Suzanne had been offered food and then returned to the colonnaded hall. Like that morning she was again asked to be in the center although on this occasion she'd been supplied with a chair similar in style though smaller than those occupied by the elders. She was facing Ala with the bronze doors at her back.

"The problem seems to be getting worse," Ala said after listening for a moment to her wrist communicator. Her clear, high-pitched voice was not hurried or harried. "The wayward group along with four human hostages are now approaching Barsama with their intact submersible. Arak is awaiting our orders."

"I've never dealt with such a situation as this in all my lifetimes," Ponu said. "Four worker clones have been prematurely dispatched. That is disturbing, indeed."

"You can stop them, can't you?" Suzanne blurted. She was beginning to find the calmness of the council unnerving. "And you can do it without injuring them, can't you?"

Ala leaned forward toward Suzanne, ignoring her questions. "There is one issue we must be absolutely sure of," she said calmly. "We have witnessed that your colleagues have surprisingly little compunction about damaging worker clones. What about humans? Would they really be capable of hurting a human?"

"Yes, I'm afraid so," Suzanne said. "They are desperate."

"It is hard to believe they would do such a thing after they have had an opportunity to experience our culture," Ponu said. "All our other visitors have unerringly adapted to our peaceful ways."

"Perhaps they would, too, given more of a chance," Suzanne said. "But at this point they are dangerous to anyone who would thwart them."

"I'm not sure I believe that," another elder said. "It's contrary to our experience, as Ponu mentioned."

Suzanne felt frustrated to the point of anger. "I can prove the iniquity they are capable of," she snapped. "They've left ample evidence in two of the cottages."

"And what might that be?" Ala asked as serenely as if she were discussing gardening.

"They have already caused the deaths of two primary humans."

Suzanne's words clearly stunned the council. They sat dumbfounded. "Are you sure of this?" Ala asked. For the first time her voice reflected distress.

"I saw the bodies a few hours ago," Suzanne said. "One was bludgeoned and the other drowned."

"I'm afraid this tragic news puts the current situation on a different plane," Ala said.

I should hope so, Suzanne thought to herself.

"I recommend we seal the Barsama vent immediately," Ponu said.

A murmur of assent filled the chamber.

Ala raised her wrist communicator and spoke briefly then lowered her arm. "It will be done," she said.

"How long will it take to connect the vent to the earth's core?" Ponu asked.

"A few hours," Ala said.

The doors were enormous, about two stories high and nine feet thick. They began to open inward on silent hinges. Arak was directing the activity with his wrist unit. He was in direct contact with Central Information. Donald was standing behind him with the pistol pressed into his back.

Perry, Richard, and Michael were off to the side, keeping Sufa, Ismael, and Mary under close guard. Michael was still in his Greek armor, refusing steadfastly to give it up. Harvey was in the passenger portion of the antigravity freighter, which was carrying the *Oceanus* as its payload. He was ready to direct the craft into the decon chamber behind the great doors.

"That looks familiar," Donald said as he caught sight of the stainless steel interior. "It reminds me of the room where we had our unsolicited bath on our way into Interterra."

A sudden rumble shook the ground, causing everyone to struggle with their balance. It lasted four or five seconds.

"What the hell was that?" Perry demanded.

Harvey poked his head out of the freighter. "We'd better hurry," he called. "They must be opening a geothermal shaft."

"What would that do?" Donald yelled back.

"Seal the exit vent," Harvey shouted.

"Come on, Arak!" Donald growled. "Speed this process up."

"I can't do any more than I'm doing," Arak said. "Besides, Harvey is right, there won't be enough time. The port is going to be disabled."

"We're not giving up after coming this far," Donald warned. "In fifteen minutes Sufa's going to be shot if we're not out of here."

Another short vibration rumbled through the ground, signifying that the monstrous pressure doors were fully open.

"Now it's up to you," Arak said. He waved to Harvey to bring in the freighter. "When the inner door opens, power into the launch and retrieval chamber. When that floods and the launch doors are open you're free to ascend the vent."

"That's not the way it is going to happen," Donald said. "You're going all the way, Arak. You and Sufa."

"No!" Arak cried. "No, please! We can't. I've done what you've asked, and we cannot be exposed to the atmosphere without adaptation. We'll die."

"I'm not asking," Donald said. "I'm ordering."

Arak started to protest. Donald responded by pistol-whipping him across the face. Arak screamed and slapped his hands to his face. Blood oozed out between his fingers. Donald pushed him into the stainless steel room.

The freighter responded to Harvey's commands, effortlessly gliding into the decon chamber.

"Come on, you guys," Donald called to Perry and Richard. "Bring Sufa but leave the others."

As soon as everyone was inside, Donald pulled Arak away from Sufa, who was trying to comfort him. The man's right eye was deeply purple and swollen.

"Get this outer door closed and the inner one open, Arak," Donald ordered.

Arak mumbled into his wrist communicator and the big doors began to close. Another rumble, signaling a second earthquake, echoed through the room; it lasted slightly longer than the first.

"Come on, Arak," Donald warned. "Speed this up!"

"I told you I can't," Arak cried.

"Richard," Donald called. "Get over here with one of your knives and cut off one of Sufa's fingers."

"No, wait!" Arak sobbed. "I'll do what I can."

Arak spoke into his wrist unit and the swing of the great doors quickened.

"That's much better," Donald said. "Much better indeed."

The whole room shook for a moment with the concussion of the doors sealing. Almost simultaneously, inner doors of equal size began to swing open. Beyond was a huge black cavern similar to the one in which the secondary humans had found themselves on their way into Interterra. It had the same briny odor, no doubt from having been filled with salt water long ago.

As soon as the inner door was fully open, Harvey directed the freighter to carry the submersible within. The others ran after it but were impeded by the mud.

"Damn," Perry said. "I forgot about this part."

"Get those inner doors closed!" Donald yelled to Arak as they caught up to the freighter. His voice echoed. He handed the gun to Perry. "We need lights. I'm going inside the submersible."

"Okay," Perry said. He slipped his index finger around the trigger. It gave him a strange feeling. He'd never held a handgun, much less shot one.

As Donald ascended the submersible's rungs another earthquake hit. He had to hold on to keep from being flung off. In the distance a sputtering sound heralded a geyser of lava.

"Shit!" Richard exclaimed. "We're in a goddamn volcano."

As soon as the latest tremor stopped, Donald scampered the rest of the way up the ladder and disappeared inside the *Oceanus*. A moment later the exterior lights came on. It was none too soon; the inner doors were nearing their jambs. Once they were shut the only light sources would be the submersible and the fountain of lava in the distance. It was growing by the second.

Donald's head popped out of the submersible. "Let's go, everybody," he said. "Power's up and life support's on. We're ready to button up."

Arak and Sufa were ordered to climb into the submersible followed by Harvey, Perry, and Michael. Michael finally had to take off the breastplate in order to get down the hatch. Richard was the last in. As he closed the hatch, he saw a surge of water begin to fill the cavern. He also heard popping noises as the water collided with lava to form steam.

When Richard climbed down the ladder into the submersible, Donald told him to take a seat: he didn't have any idea how much buffeting they would experience as the cavern filled. A few minutes later the *Oceanus* was bouncing around like a cork. Everyone held on for dear life.

"What are we supposed to do at this point?" Donald yelled to Arak.

"Nothing," Arak said. "The water will carry the ship up the vent."

"So does this mean that we've made it?" Donald asked.

"I guess you made it," Arak responded sullenly. He reached over and gripped Sufa's hand.

Ala slowly lowered her arm. She'd had an ear to her wrist communicator. Although she'd been visibly upset at the word of Sart and Mura's murders, her expression was again tranquil. In a calm voice she announced, "The Barsama vent was not sealed in time. The submersible has left the lock and is now in open ocean heading due west."

"And the hostages?" Ponu queried.

"Only two are on board," Ala said. "Arak and Sufa are still with the secondary humans. Ismael and Mary were left behind and are safe."

"Excuse me," Suzanne said, trying to get her attention. What she was hearing seemed impossible. With all the powers and technology she'd imagined the Interterrans to have at their disposal, her erstwhile colleagues had apparently gotten away!

"I believe we must now deal directly with these people," Ala said, continuing to ignore Suzanne. "Too much is at stake."

"I think we should send them back and be over with this problem," one of the elders to Suzanne's left said. Suzanne swung around to face the woman. In contrast to the speaker of the council, this elder appeared to be in her midtwenties.

"What do you mean send them back?" Suzanne asked incredulously. She felt that, with such a simple solution possible, it was no wonder none of the elders appeared particularly distraught by the developments.

"I agree we must send them back," an elder on the opposite side of the room said, disregarding Suzanne. Suzanne turned to look at the speaker, a boy of five or six.

"Do we have general agreement?" Ala asked.

A murmur of assent rose up from all the elders.

"So be it," Ala said. "We'll send out a clone in a small intergalactic ship."

"Tell them to use the lowest power possible on the grid," Ponu said as Ala spoke briefly into her wrist communicator.

"Such an unfortunate episode," one of the other elders said. "It is a tragedy, indeed."

"They aren't going to be hurt, are they?" Suzanne asked. She refused to give up and, to her surprise, Ala finally responded to this question.

"Are you asking about your friends?" Ala asked.

"Yes!" Suzanne said with vexation.

"No, they will not be hurt," Ala said. "Just very surprised."

"I think Arak and Sufa's sacrifice should be publicly acknowledged," Ponu said.

"With full honors," the boy child said. There was another general murmur of assent.

"Won't Arak and Sufa be sent back, too?" Suzanne questioned.

"Of course," Ala said. "They will all be sent back."

Suzanne looked from one elder to another. She was totally confused.

"I see light out the view port!" Perry said excitedly. They had been running for several hours with no conversation and with the instrument lights providing the only illumination. Everyone was exhausted.

"Me, too," Richard said from the opposite side of the *Oceanus*.

"There better be light," Donald said. "According to the gauge we're at a depth of a hundred feet, and it's dawn up there on the surface."

"Sounds reassuring," Perry said. "How much longer do you think?"

Donald glanced down at his sonar display. "I've been watching the bottom contours. I'd say in a couple of hours at most we'll be within sight of the harbor islands off Boston."

"All right!" Richard and Michael cried simultaneously. They high-fived across the narrow aisle.

"How much battery time do we have left?" Perry asked.

"That's the only problem," Donald said. "It's going to be close. We may have to swim the last hundred yards."

"That's fine by me," Harvey said. "I'd swim all the way to New York if I had to."

"What about my armor?" Michael said, suddenly concerned about his booty.

"That's your problem, sailor," Donald said. "You're the one who insisted on bringing it all."

"I'll give you a hand if you share it with me," Richard offered.

"Screw you," Michael said.

"No arguments!" Perry said emphatically.

They traveled in silence for several minutes until Arak spoke up. "You have your freedom from Interterra. Why did you take us, knowing what would happen to us?"

"Insurance," Donald said. "I wanted to be certain there would be no interference by your Council of Elders once we'd left Barsama port."

"You guys will also come in handy if anyone is foolish enough to doubt our story," Richard said.

Michael let out a guffaw.

"But we shall perish," Arak said.

"We'll take you to Massachusetts General Hospital," Donald said. He smiled wryly. "I happen to know they like challenges."

"It would be to no avail," Arak said glumly. "Your medicine is too primitive to help."

"Well, it's the best we can do," Donald said. He started to say something else, but then stopped. His smile faded.

"What's the matter?" Perry demanded. As tense as Perry was he was particularly sensitive to Donald's expression.

"We've got something weird here," Donald said. He reached out to adjust the sonar display.

"What is it?" Perry demanded.

"Check the sonar," Donald said. "It looks as if something is pursuing us, and it is coming very rapidly."

"How rapidly?" Perry asked.

"This can't be true," Donald said with growing urgency. "The instruments are telling me it's going over a hundred knots underwater!" He whirled about to face Arak. "Is this thing for real, and if so, what the hell is it?"

"Probably an Interterran interplanetary ship," Arak said, leaning forward to see the display.

"They still know you are aboard, don't they?" Donald demanded.

"Certainly," Arak said.

Donald swung back around to the controls. "I don't like this," he snapped. "I'm going to surface."

"I don't think we can," Perry said. "It just got dark outside. It must be hovering directly over us."

The submersible began to shake with a low-frequency vibration.

"Arak, what the hell are they doing?"

"I don't know," Arak said. "Maybe they are about to draw us up into their air lock."

"Harvey, do you have any idea what's going on?" Donald demanded.

"Not the slightest idea," Harvey said. Like the others he was holding on to the sides of his seat to keep from being thrown out of it. The vibration was increasing.

Donald snatched the Luger and pointed it at Arak. "Contact these bastards and get them to stop whatever they are doing! If not, you are history."

"Look," Perry called out, pointing to the side-scan sonar display. "You can see an image of the craft. It looks like a double-layered saucer."

"Oh, no!" Arak exclaimed when he saw the new image. "It's not an interplanetary ship! It's an intergalactic cruiser!"

"What difference does that make?" Donald yelled. The vibration had increased to the point that it was truly difficult to stay in their seats. The heavy steel hull of the submersible creaked and groaned under the stress.

"They are going to take us back!" Arak cried. "Sufa, they are going to take us back!"

"It is all they could do," Sufa sobbed. "It's all they could do."

The vibration stopped with a jarring suddenness, but before anyone could respond, there was a tremendous upward acceleration. All the occupants were pressed into their seats with such force that, for the moment, they could not move or even breathe, and they were rapidly brought to the brink of unconsciousness. The inertial force was accompanied by a strange light that enveloped the submersible's interior. In the next instant, everything reverted to normal except for a yaw, suggesting a wave action that wasn't present earlier.

"My God!" Donald groaned. "What the hell happened?" He moved, but his limbs felt heavy and sluggish, as if the air had become viscous. But the effect lasted only until he'd flexed his joints several times. Then he felt normal. Instinctively, his eyes scanned the instruments. He was surprised to see they were reading normally. But then he glanced at the battery level. To his dismay, the gauge showed the batteries had been drained of what charge they had had, indicating the submersible was on the brink of losing power. Then he saw something else astonishing: they were in only fifty feet of water! No wonder they were being buffeted by waves.

Donald's eyes shot over to the sonar display. The Interterran vessel, or whatever it was, had disappeared. Instead Donald could see that the ocean floor sloped upward. It appeared that dry land was a mere hundred fifty feet ahead.

The other occupants of the submersible were reviving themselves after the bizarre ordeal.

"I wonder if that's what astronauts feel when they blast off into space?" Perry moaned.

"If it is, I'm not interested in going," Richard said.

"It's similar," Arak said. "But not the same. Of course, you are too unsophisticated to recognize the difference."

"Shut up, Arak," Donald said. "I've had enough of you."

"Indeed you have," Arak said. "And you deserve your fate."

"Prepare to surface," Donald said. "We're running out of power."

"Oh, no!" Perry cried.

"It's going to be okay," Donald assured everyone as he used compressed gas to blow ballast. "We've got dry land dead ahead."

The surge of the submersible increased dramatically as they came up and broached. While there was still a bit of power left, Donald frantically tried to get a LORAN fix. When that didn't work he tried the Geosat. That didn't work either. "I can't understand this," he said. He scratched his head. It didn't make sense. "Somebody go up into the sail, crack the hatch, and see if they recognize where we are. We should be somewhere in Boston Harbor."

"I'll go," Michael said. "This area's my old stomping ground."

"Be careful with this wave action," Donald warned.

"As if I haven't been in boats much," Michael scoffed.

While Michael climbed the ladder up into the hatchway, Donald rapidly took everything nonessential off-line to conserve what little power remained in the batteries. But it was no use. The batteries were drained, and a moment later the lights went out, and they lost all headway.

Up in the sail they heard Michael crack the hatch. Pale morning light shined down into the darkened submersible. They could feel the humid sea air and hear the harsh but welcome cry of seagulls.

"That's music to my ears," Richard said.

"We're just off one of the harbor islands," Michael called out from above. "I don't know which one."

At that moment the submersible struck the sandy bottom with a jolt and began to turn sideways in the surf.

"We've got to get out of here!" Donald cried. "This thing is going to founder."

As the secondary humans scrambled out of their seats, Arak and Sufa raised their hands and pressed palms lovingly. "For Interterra," Arak said.

"For Interterra," Sufa repeated.

"Come on, you two," Donald yelled to the two primary humans. "This sub's about to tip over, and when it does it's going to flood."

Arak and Sufa ignored him but instead continued to press palms dreamily.

"Suit yourselves," Donald said.

"Someone bring up my armor," Michael yelled down the hatch.

There was a mad scramble up the ladder, especially after the sub careened and a slosh of water came crashing down the hatchway. Topside everyone except Michael jumped into the surf and struck out for nearby shore. Michael tried to go back down the ladder but changed his mind when the boat heeled over completely.

It was with some difficulty that he managed to swim free.

Harvey had to be helped in the wild surf, but everyone except the Interterrans made it to the steeply pitched beach, where they flopped down in the warm sand. Michael was the last to pull himself from the undertow. Richard teased him mercilessly about his sunken Greek armor.

The weather was superb. It was a mild, hazy summer morning. Warm sunlight sparkled across the water, giving an inkling of what its midday power would be. After the effort in the surf, the group was content to rest, suck in the fresh air, watch the gulls soar, and allow the sun to dry the flimsy satin garments clinging to their bodies.

"Now I feel sad about Arak and Sufa," Perry said wistfully. The *Oceanus* had tipped over on its side and was filled with water. It was already farther off the shore than when they'd disembarked. The wave action was dragging it back out to sea.

"Not me," Richard said. "Good riddance as far as I'm concerned."

"It's too bad about the submersible, though," Donald said. "It's not going to last long out there. It will probably end up on the bottom off the continental shelf. Damn! I was hoping to power it right into Boston Harbor."

Just after Donald spoke a particularly big set of waves reared up. After they broke and the foam receded, the submersible was gone from sight.

"Well, there it goes," Perry said.

"After our story is told I'm sure there will be a lot of pressure to salvage it," Michael said. "It'll probably end up in the Smithsonian."

"Where are we?" Harvey asked. He pushed himself up on one elbow and looked back at the low, windswept island. It seemed to be only sand, seashells, and saw grass.

"We told you," Donald said. "It's one of the many Boston Harbor islands."

"How are we going to get to town?" Perry asked.

"A couple hours from now there'll be pleasure boats all around here," Michael said. "Once people hear our story they're going to be fighting over the honor of giving us a ride."

"I'm looking forward to a nice dinner where I know what I'm eating," Perry said. "And a telephone! I want to call my wife and daughters. Then I want to sleep for about forty-eight hours."

"I'll second that," Donald said. "Come on! Let's walk around to the windward side. Even from a distance a gander at old Beantown will do my heart good."

"I'm with you," Perry said.

The group got to their feet, stretched, and started hiking along the beach in the hard-packed sand at the water's edge. Despite their exhaustion, they began to sing. Even Donald was drawn into the merriment.

Rounding a point forming the side of a small inlet, the group stopped in their tracks and fell silent. Not more than a couple of hundred feet upwind from them was an old gray-haired man clamming in the shadows. He had beached a moderate-sized skiff. Its lateen sail was luffing in the steady breeze.

"Isn't this a happy coincidence?" Perry said.

"I can taste the coffee and feel those clean sheets already," Michael said. "Come on, let's make this old guy a hero. They'll probably put him on CNN."

With a whoop, the group broke into a run. The fisherman panicked at the sight of the pack of bellowing men charging toward him across the dunes. Dashing to his boat, he tossed in his pail and net and tried to flee.

Richard was the first on the scene, and he raced out into waist-deep water to grasp the boat's transom and slow its progress.

"Hey, old man, what's the rush?" Richard questioned.

The fisherman responded by releasing his sail. With an oar he tried to fend Richard off. Richard grabbed the oar, yanked it out of the man's grip, and tossed it aside. The others ran out into the water and latched onto the boat.

"Not a very friendly chap," Richard remarked. The fisherman was standing amidships, glaring at the group.

Harvey retrieved the oar and brought it back.

"No wonder," Perry said. He looked down at himself and then at the others. "Look at us! What would *you* think if four guys dressed in lingerie came running out of the morning mist?"

The entire group broke down into giddy laughter fueled by exhaustion and stress. It took them several minutes to regain a semblance of control.

"Sorry, old man," Perry said between chokes of laughter. "Pardon our appearance and our behavior. But we've had one hell of a night."

"Too much grog, I suspect," the fisherman said.

The fisherman's response sent them off on another laughing jag. But eventually they recovered enough to convince the man that they were not dangerous and that he would be generously compensated if he gave them a ride into Boston proper. With that decided, the men climbed into the boat.

It was a pleasant ride especially in comparison with the tense hours in the tight, claustrophobic submersible.

Between the warm sun, the soft whisper of the wind in the sail, and the gentle roll of the boat, all but the fisherman were fast asleep before the skiff rounded the island.

With a steady breeze the fisherman expertly brought the boat into the harbor in good time. Unsure of where his passengers wanted to be dropped off, he gave the nearest person's shoulder a shake. Perry responded groggily to the prodding and for a moment had trouble opening his eyes. When he did, the fisherman posed his question.

"I guess it doesn't matter where," Perry said. With supreme effort he sat up. His mouth was dry and cottony. Blinking in the bright sunlight, he glanced around the harbor. Then he rubbed his eyes, blinked again, and stared at the surroundings.

"Where the hell are we?" he demanded. He was confused. "I thought we were supposed to be in Boston."

"'Tis Boston," the fisherman said. He pointed to the right. "Them there is Long Wharf."

Perry rubbed his eyes again. For a moment he wondered if he were hallucinating. He was looking at a harbor scene of square-rigged sailing ships, schooners, and horse drays along a granite quay. The tallest buildings were wood frame and a mere four or five stories.

Fighting off a wave of disbelief that bordered on terror, Perry shook Donald awake in a panic, crying that something was terribly wrong. The commotion awoke the others as well. When they took in the scene, they were equally dumbfounded.

Perry turned back to the fisherman, who was lowering the sail. "What year is this?" he asked hesitantly.

"Year of our Lord seventeen hundred ninety-one," the fisherman said.

Perry's mouth dropped open. He looked back at the square-rigged sailing ships. "Good God! They put us back in time."

"Come on!" Richard complained. "This has got to be some kind of joke."

"Maybe they're making a movie," Michael suggested.

"I don't think so," Donald said slowly. "That's what Arak meant when he said they were going to take us back. He meant back in time not back to Interterra."

"The intergalactic ships must involve time technology," Perry said. "I guess that's the only way travel to another galaxy is possible."

"My god," Donald muttered. "We're marooned. Nobody is going to believe our story about Interterra, and the technology doesn't exist to prove it or for us to get back there."

Perry nodded as he stared ahead with unseeing eyes. "People are going to think we're mad."

"What about the submersible?" Richard cried. "Let's go back!"

"And do what?" Donald asked. "We'd never find it, much less salvage it."

"I'm not going to see my family after all," Perry cried. "We gave up paradise for colonial America? I don't believe it."

"You know, I've finally figured out where you lubbers are from," the fisherman said as he readied the oars.

"Really," Perry said, without interest.

"There's not a doubt in my mind," the fisherman continued. "You've got to be from that college up the Charles River. You Harvard fellows are always making fools of yourselves."

GLOSSARY

asthenosphere A zone within the earth ranging in depth from 50 to 200 km; it is the upper part of the *mantle* (see below), situated directly below the *lithosphere* (see below). This area is theorized to be molten and yielding to plastic flow.

basalt A dark, almost black rock formed from the cooling and solidification of molten silicate minerals. It forms a large part of the oceanic crust.

bathypelagic An adjective relating to moderately deep ocean depths (2,000–12,000 ft).

caldera A crater formed by the collapse of a volcano's summit.

circadian An adjective relating to a twenty-four-hour cycle.

dike A tabular rock formation arising from molten rock forced up a cleft or fissure and then solidifying.

dinoflagellates A type of *plankton* (see below) that includes many bioluminescent varieties. Dinoflagellates also cause red tide.

ectogenesis Embryonic development outside the womb.

epipelagic An adjective relating to the part of the surface ocean in which enough light penetrates to support photosynthesis.

foraminifera Tiny marine protozoans whose calcerous shells form chalk and the most widely distributed limestone.

gabbro A dark, sometimes green rock that makes up a significant part of the lowest part of the oceanic crust.

gamete A male or female germ cell.

globigerina ooze A cream-colored muck that covers a good portion of the deep ocean floor and is composed mainly of the minute skeletons of *foraminifera* (see above).

graben A fault block that has dropped below the height of the surrounding rock.

guyot A *seamount* (see below) with a flat top.

lithosphere The rigid crust of the earth; it includes the sea floor as well as the continents.

mantle An inner layer of the earth, between the *lithosphere* (see above) and the central core.

microsome Any of the various minute subcellular structures.

Mohorovičić discontinuity An area within the earth where there is a large change in the transmission of seismic waves. It is between 5 and 10 km below the ocean floor and about 35 km below the continents.

Pangaea A single continent that began breaking up in the Mesozoic era by the action of plate tectonics to form the present-day continents.

peridotite A dark rock deep within the mantle.

plankton Microscopic plants (phytoplankton) and animals (zooplankton) that exist in such prodigious numbers that they form the base of the oceanic food chain.

Richter scale A method of expressing the magnitude of earthquakes.

seamount An underwater mountain usually formed by volcanic activity.

thermocline A relatively stable, abrupt temperature change in a body of water.

zygote A cell formed by the union of two *gametes* (see above) which has the potential to form a new individual.

SELECTED BIBLIOGRAPHY

Ballard, Robert, *Explorations: A Life of Underwater Adventure*. New York: Hyperion, 1995.

Ellis, Richard, *Deep Atlantic: Life, Death, and Exploration in the Abyss*. New York: Knopf, 1996. The illustrations alone make this a joy!

Ellis, Richard, *Imaging Atlantis*. New York: Knopf, 1998.

Kunzig, Robert, *The Restless Sea*. New York: Norton, 1999. An extremely well-written, enjoyable book that gives one a sense of the importance and breadth of oceanography.

Verne, Jules, *Voyage au Centre de la Terre*. Paris: 1864. (English translation: *Voyage to the Center of the Earth*. New York: Kensington, 1999.)

Verne, Jules, *Vingt Mille Lieues Sous les Mers*. Paris: 1870. (English translation: *Twenty Thousand Leagues Under the Sea*. Annapolis, Md.: United States Naval Institute, 1993.)